bandbox

BOOKS BY THOMAS MALLON

FICTION

Arts and Sciences
Aurora 7
Henry and Clara
Dewey Defeats Truman
Two Moons
Bandbox

NONFICTION

Edmund Blunden
A Book of One's Own
Stolen Words
Rockets and Rodeos
In Fact
Mrs. Paine's Garage

THOMAS MALLON

bandbox

PANTHEON BOOKS, NEW YORK

Copyright © 2004 by Thomas Mallon

All rights reserved under International and Pan-American Copyright
Conventions. Published in the United States by Pantheon Books,
a division of Random House, Inc., New York, and simultaneously
in Canada by Random House of Canada Limited, Toronto.

Pantheon Books and colophon are registered trademarks
of Random House, Inc.

Library of Congress Cataloging-in-Publication Data

Mallon, Thomas, 1951–
Bandbox / Thomas Mallon.
p. cm.
ISBN 0-375-42116-5
1. Periodicals—Publishing—Fiction.   2. Nineteen twenties—Fiction.
I. Title.
PS3563.A43157B36 2004   813'.54—dc21   2003054861

www.pantheonbooks.com

Book design by M. Kristen Bearse

Printed in the United States of America
First Edition
2 4 6 8 9 7 5 3 1

for Lucy Kaylin,

s.w.a.k.

"For twenty years [he] raced and gambled, philandered with the prettiest girls, danced, ate in the most expensive restaurants, and dressed beautifully. He always looked as if he had just stepped out of a bandbox."

—W. Somerset Maugham,
"The Ant and the Grasshopper"

band'·box' (bănd'bŏks'), *n.* A neat box of pasteboard or thin wood, usually cylindrical, for holding light articles of attire, orig. for the *bands* [clerical collars] of the 17th century. Also, attrib., flimsy; unsubstantial; as, a *bandbox* reputation.

—*Webster's New International Dictionary,*
2nd ed.

Acknowledgments

A generous fellowship from the John Simon Guggenheim Memorial Foundation helped me to write this novel.

I owe special thanks to the General Society of Mechanics and Tradesmen's Library on West Forty-fourth Street in Manhattan— already long established in 1928, and still going strong. Among many dozens of books treating 1920s New York, I am particularly grateful to: Will Irwin, *Highlights of Manhattan* (1927); Joe Laurie, Jr., *Vaudeville: From the Honky-Tonks to the Palace* (1953); Caroline Seebohm, *The Man Who Was* Vogue: *The Life and Times of Condé Nast* (1982); and *The Encyclopedia of New York City,* ed. Kenneth T. Jackson (1995). As always, I hasten to note that I am writing fiction, not history, and that I've availed myself of many small liberties, from the architectural to the zoological.

I could not have done without the crazy rhythms of Roger Wolfe Kahn, whose incomparably evocative music has filled my study for the past three years.

Over the past decade it's been my great good fortune to have Dan Frank as an editor. Andrea Barrett is a near-daily source of advice and inspiration in my life. Frances Kiernan, Richard Bausch, André Bernard, Michael Collier, and Sloan Harris are other indispensable presences.

But, above all, thanks to Bill Bodenschatz.

Westport, Connecticut
July 12, 2003

bandbox

I

Cuddles Houlihan got clipped by the vodka bottle as it exited the pneumatic tube.

"Goddammit!"

The cry of pain that filled the office came not from Cuddles, whose head still lay asleep on his desk, but from the tube. Its ultimate source was the office of Joe Harris, the editor-in-chief. At this late, sozzled hour, Harris had mistakenly fed the interoffice mail chute not the translucent canister containing his angry communication to Cuddles, but the still-half-full, six-dollar quart of hooch he was regularly supplied with by the countess in the fact-checking department.

Harris glowered for several seconds at the undispatched canister, before giving in to the impulse to open it up and look once more at what had enraged him in the first place: a photograph of Leopold and Loeb, smiling, each with an arm around the other, perched on the edge of an upper bunk in the Joliet State Prison, both of them avidly regarding the latest issue of *Bandbox*. The thrill killers held it open with their free hands, like a box of candy they were sharing on a back-porch swing.

Would make a great ad, said the inked message on the back of the photograph, whose bold penmanship Harris recognized as belonging to Jimmy Gordon, up until eight months ago his best senior editor here at *Bandbox*. "I think of you as a bastard son," he'd once told

Jimmy in a burst of bibulous sentiment. Now, as editor-in-chief of *Cutaway,* the younger man was his head-to-head, hand-to-throat, competition. If Harris didn't think of something, this picture of those two murderous fairies reading *Bandbox*—the magazine that had *made* goddamn Jimmy Gordon, and remade Jehoshaphat Harris—would be plastered to the side of every double-decker bus crawling up Fifth Avenue.

Rummaging his bottom drawer for another quart of vodka, Harris—a great curator of his own life story—managed to consider, yet again, with prideful amazement, how only five years had passed since Hiram Oldcastle, the publisher, had said, "You want it? It's yours," giving him the *Bandbox* job as if it were the keys to a jalopy. "An overpriced rag for overaged pansies," Oldcastle had called the dying men's fashion book, which had somehow never evolved out of the tintyped, stiff-collared days of McKinley. Harris would be the magazine's last chance before Oldcastle killed the sclerotic monthly and concentrated on his more robust publications, like *Pinafore,* for the "young miss"—edited by Harris's girlfriend, Betty Divine—and the shelter book, *Manse.*

"Give me six months," Harris had said.

"Take a year," Oldcastle had replied, sounding almost guilty about the eagerness with which the new editor wanted to take charge.

It took Harris one business quarter to bring *Bandbox* to life, to hit upon a formula that lured young men and advertisers back to a magazine no one had paid attention to for years. He kept the fashion—even made it fashionable—then butched up the rest of the production, adding a slew of stylish articles about all the sports, politics, crime, money, and movies that went into the current age's cocktail. Newsstand buyers and subscribers were now deciding they craved the camel-hair coat on page 46 just as much as they needed to sleep with the screen siren or buy the radio stock described a few pages away. The table of contents might sometimes seem a tasteless whipsaw—

"New Hope for the Shell-Shocked" sitting right above "Look Terrific for Under Two Hundred"—but the magazine's turnaround had been so successful that by the spring of last year, Condé Nast decided he could not leave a whole new field to his usually more downmarket competitor, Oldcastle. Last March he had announced the start-up of *Cutaway,* exactly the sort of clothes-and-journalism book Harris had concocted; and on April 30, he had named Jimmy Gordon its editor.

Jimmy Gordon: who had brought in most of Harris's expensive new writers; who had three bad story ideas for every good one, but so many of each that, with Harris as a filter, every issue of *Bandbox* still abounded with first-rate stuff. Jimmy Gordon, who was now stealing not only Harris's formula but every keister not nailed down to the swivel chairs here on the fourteenth floor of the Graybar Building. He'd pried away three of his old writers, a photographer, and two production assistants, and had even made a run at Mrs. Zimmerman, the receptionist. But the real prize for Jimmy was Harris's readers and advertisers, whom he would surely keep wooing away if he managed, with stunts like this Leopold and Loeb picture, to undo the makeover of *Bandbox.* Things could turn around so quickly—hadn't Harris himself proved it?—that the older editor would be left with a shrunken subscriber base consisting chiefly of the perfumed boys you saw gazing at each other across the tables of the Jewel cafeteria.

Hazel Snow buzzed Harris from the outer office.

"It's a bad time!" he shouted.

Hazel ignored him. "Mr. Lord and Miss O'Grady here to see you," she said, indifferent to anything but her desire to go home. Through the intercom Harris could hear the squeaky sound of Hazel putting on her galoshes.

"You picked the worst possible moment!" he shouted to Richard Lord and Nan O'Grady once Hazel had ushered them in.

The English art and fashion director looked at his expensive shoes, still unscuffed at this late hour, and whispered, "It's about Lindstrom, I'm afraid."

"What about him?" Harris asked, in a voice that made plain, for all its volume, that he would rather know nothing new concerning Waldo Lindstrom, the handsomest young man in New York, and *Bandbox*'s most frequent cover model now that photographs were replacing illustrations. Harris would be more receptive to tidings of this Adonis were Lindstrom not also an omnisexual cocaine addict who had escaped from the Kansas State Penitentiary a few years ago at the age of twenty, and whose work for Oldcastle Publications depended on frequent payments from Harris to the NYPD's vice squad.

"He never showed up," murmured Lord, while he adjusted the two points of his breast-pocket handkerchief.

"Find his pusher!" bellowed Harris. "Call the morgue! Why are you bothering *me*? And why are *you* bothering me?" he continued, turning his eyes and anger to Nan O'Grady, the copy chief, whose lower lip had begun to tremble. A tear wobbled in the lower reaches of her left eye, ready to drip down her powdered cheek and cut a line that would run parallel to her straight red hair.

"It's Mr. Stanwick's piece on Arnold Rothstein."

Max Stanwick, a successful writer of hard-boiled mystery novels, now also wrote features for *Bandbox* on the nation's ever-burgeoning crime wave. The fact-checkers sometimes muttered that he had made no discernible shift from the methods of his old genre to those of nonfiction, but Stanwick's pieces were immensely popular and the occasion for some of Harris's more memorable cover lines: LEND ME YOUR EARS had announced Max's recent report on a spate of loan-sharking mutilations in Detroit. Harris trembled at the thought of losing him to Jimmy Gordon, who had brought him to *Bandbox* in the first place.

"And what's the problem with Stanwick, Miss O'Grady? Some

people in his piece saying 'who' instead of 'whom'? They're *gangsters,* Irish."

Nan, who until two years ago had edited lady novelists at Scribner's, and who had taken this better-paying job to help support the mother she lived with out in Woodside, forced her lower lip to stiffen. The tear in her left eye sank backwards without spilling. She glared at her boss. "It's not a question of subject versus object, Mr. Harris. It's a question of . . . *schvantz.*" She pronounced it with the lilting precision of a lieder singer.

"Whose schvantz?" Harris wanted to know.

"Mr. Rothstein's, apparently."

Harris hesitated for only a second. "Well, keep it in!"

Nan, her lower lip now fully retracted, held her ground. "I assure you that it's in no known style book, and I *guarantee* you that within a week of publication, a half-dozen of your precious advertisers will have protested its use in—"

"More *schvantzes* all around!" cried Harris, suddenly on his feet. "And the balls to go with them! This is a *men's* magazine! Out! And close the door behind you!"

After Harris watched a trio of departing forms—Hazel's among them—through the frosted glass of his door, he allowed himself to sit back down and light a cigar. He looked out the fourteenth-floor windows of his corner office to the vertical world aborning all around him. The Bowery Savings Bank loomed in the southeast, and a few streets over, close to the river, he could see the absurd new towers of Tudor City, in whose tiny apartments his aging pals had taken to stashing their chorines and tootsies. Directly across Lexington Avenue, and also one block south, squares of earth were roped off for the great excavations now sprouting the Chrysler and Chanin buildings.

It all made Harris dizzy. From his long-ago days on the *Newburgh*

Messenger until this past fall, when Oldcastle had moved the company a few blocks up from its old quarters and into the gleaming new Graybar, Harris had always climbed a single flight of stairs to reach his job. Now every morning and evening his stomach endured the fast jumps and drops of the Graybar's elevator, the trip made worse if he happened to be sharing the car with Jimmy Gordon, who'd be on his way to and from the Graybar's fanciest floor— reserved by Condé Nast even before the building went up, thus exciting Oldcastle's competitive relocation.

Harris took a gulp of the countess's hooch and opened up the *Evening Graphic* to a cartoon panel above the "Aviation News" column, a few square inches he liked to settle into for a moment or two each evening as the clouds began turning pink outside his skyscraping aerie. Tonight—January 13, 1928—"New York's Gas Lit Life" featured the sketch of a buxom "stagestruck damsel," a young Lillian Russell type, auditioning for a well-fed theatrical manager. Little more than her parasol and bloomers shielded her ample virtues.

Harris sighed, recalling the days of his youth, the long-ago eighties and nineties, an era before big trenchermen had ever heard of exercise and before bosoms had deflated to the pitiful boyish protuberances on modern girls like Hazel Snow. He closed his eyes and, for a few seconds, took himself back to summer nights alive with the tootlings of oompah bands instead of the discordant, mystifying notes of jazz; to the orating politician's thrilling cry for free silver instead of Everyman's current pursuit of ubiquitous easy money.

Harris was sixty years old and, in truth, as much a throwback to the age of McKinley as the old *Bandbox* had been. But in order to sustain his reanimating magic, he had to keep current with all the flat chests and blues singers and tennis champions driving this frantic new age into which he'd outlived himself. If only he could bring himself to leave the game, gracefully conclude his career by editing *Knife and Fork,* Oldcastle's food magazine, for a couple of years. All he'd have to do for each month's cover was find a good-looking pork chop or strawberry cake, neither of which, unlike Waldo Lindstrom, would have a cocaine habit.

But the setting sun chose this moment to catch a silver cigarette case near the edge of Harris's desk. The case's inscription—JEHOSHAPHAT HARRIS, EDITOR OF THE YEAR, 1927—glinted upwards into his still-clear, still-avid eyes, reminding him of his greatest moment. It had come only last year, from the Gotham Magazine Editors Association, whose GME Awards—the Gimmes, to those in the trade—still stirred Harris's competitive juices to an almost indecent degree for a man of his age and at-last-recognized achievements.

No, this was not going to be Jimmy Gordon's year. In fact, so long as there was anything he could do about it, Jimmy Gordon's year would forever fall somewhere on the calendar between yesterday and never. Harris threw the *Graphic* into his leather wastebasket and grabbed the photograph of Leopold and Loeb. Beneath Jimmy's taunt he underlined his own inscription, the brief directive he had scrawled before dispatching the wrong cylinder through the pneumatic tube to Houlihan: *Take care of this.*

He at last succeeded in sending the picture on its way. Once he heard the cylinder's distant thunk, he rose from his chair and put on his hat.

2

Loyalty was Becky Walter's strong suit. No longer secretary to Cuddles Houlihan, she nonetheless darted into his office once she heard him coming to with a low moan. Taking note of his already-rising shiner, Becky opened the window and scooped up a handful of snow from the fourteenth-floor ledge. "Here," she said, gently pressing it against Cuddles' eye. The city was in the sixth day of a terrible cold snap, and a rush of air through the open window furthered his revival.

Becky noted how, with his remaining open eye, Cuddles had begun giving her "the look," that moony, lovesick one, which, even at half-strength, bothered her. For her first four years out of Wells College—until six months ago, when Joe Harris gave her a staff writer's slot, covering movie stars, and even a few on Broadway— Becky had been Cuddles' Girl Friday and the object of his gentlemanly but still quite evident affections. It was proving as difficult to graduate from this latter role as it had been to climb two notches up the masthead. So, seeing the Cyclops version of the look, she turned her head away, a small movement that brought her gaze to the vodka bottle lying on Cuddles' blotter. She frowned.

"I don't know where it came from," he said. "Honest injun."

Becky had heard this song before, but Cuddles, in his usual near-murmur, persisted through a complicated alibi. "I was at the Palace all afternoon, talking to Doc Cook and Morris, seeing if we could work up some new angle—'Elevator Boys Tell of Vaude Stars' Ups and Downs'—something like that, anyway. But I only came away with a sick feeling. Do you know they've put an electric piano in the lobby? The *Palace*—having to lure people in off the streets! They've started keeping the doors open so the passing parade will hear the music and come in from the sidewalk. Jesus, Becky, they're going to be booking radio acts before the year is out."

After a dozen fat blots on his copybook, Cuddles' turf had been reduced by Harris to little more than the ever-shrinking vaudeville beat. But as she lifted the snow from his eye and repacked it into a linen handkerchief, Becky doubted her old boss's alibi. She could hear him fleshing out this tale of his afternoon with just enough specifics to make it seem real. She wondered if Cuddles hadn't really been to Manking, their old Times Square Chinese restaurant, a place so inauthentically awful it couldn't even transliterate the name of the city whose cuisine it claimed to be serving. Two of the waiters were actually Japanese and kept a bottle of sake around for Mista Hoorihan and his young lady friend when they arrived for those dozens of three-hour lunches during which Cuddles gave her the lowdown on the magazine business and life, and, as their first year together turned into the second, gave her, more and more intently, the look.

"Ouch," cried Cuddles, upon Becky's reapplication of the snowpack. His small protest raised in her the same tender feelings she used to experience when, past three o'clock, she would try to get up from the booth at Manking, and he'd say, "Don't go," lest he have to return to the office and Jehoshaphat Harris's increasingly baleful stare.

After two years turned into three and then four, Cuddles finally arranged her promotion as the best thing for them both. Since then, Becky had felt like a creature released into the wild, sometimes wondering whether it wouldn't be easier to continue suffering Cuddles' overage calf love than to hunt down stories to feed the bulldog— namely, Harris.

"Do you know that *Oh, Kay!* closes this weekend?" asked Cuddles, who knew he was going to steal Becky's linen handkerchief once its anti-inflammatory work was done. "You call yourself our Broadway correspondent, and I'll bet you've never seen it. Why don't you let me get two comps for tomorrow night?"

Becky, now mopping up the inside of the windowsill, didn't answer.

"I suppose you've got plans with the monk," said Cuddles.

Becky turned and frowned, and started to say "medievalist," the proper title of her boyfriend, a Columbia Ph.D. candidate with a job at the Cloisters. But she had corrected Cuddles on this matter a dozen times before and had recently pledged herself to the avoidance of any further banter about Daniel.

"Why don't you concentrate on not getting canned?" she replied.

"I suppose I'd better look at this," he said, nodding at the pneumatic canister that had arrived on his desk sometime after the vodka bottle. He opened it up, looked at the photograph, and groaned at the message in Jimmy Gordon's big handwriting. He handed the picture to Becky.

"Oh my God," she said. "Why you? Why doesn't he make Spilkes handle this?"

Norman Spilkes, the managing editor who used to work for AT&T, had brought a certain smooth efficiency to the month-by-month running of Harris's great makeover.

" 'Phat's deepest reflexes are twitching," said Cuddles, who now comprehended the origin of the vodka bottle. "During yesteryear's crises I was his right-hand man. Comrade Stoli was always on the left."

Becky noticed that, despite the snowpack, Cuddles' shiner was turning into a deep purple bull's-eye against his small, boyish features and still prematurely gray hair. The strategy of his little mustache, grown long ago in an effort to look older, now seemed telltale and obvious; it made the forty-six-year-old Aloysius Houlihan a living spectre of his endearing, quenched youth. The slight limp, which had kept him out of the war, now also seemed a faded adolescent charm, like a stammer; fewer and fewer people knew that this by-now-consummate New Yorker had acquired it when a wheel on his parents' wagon had accidentally rolled over him during a pilgrimage between Salt Lake City and some Utah holy site. Cuddles had been raised a strict Mormon in the 1890s, grandson of an upstate Irishman who'd joined the westward trek of Brigham Young.

"I'm going to get some actual ice," said Becky, who on her way out of the room inserted the thrill killers' photo back into the canister: better to take it with her, lest Cuddles attend to it in ill-considered haste. She made her way through the fourteenth floor's warren of offices, most of which had their doors open, toward the distant icebox. The little chains on the overhead lights had been pulled on during the past half-hour, but their illumination couldn't really bleach the dark blue twilight that was pouring through the windows and giving the floor a peaceful, almost eternal feeling, so at odds with the nerve-wracked perishability of the product produced on it.

When Becky passed the open office of darkly handsome Stuart Newman, author of "The Bachelor's Life" column, she gave a thin smile and picked up her pace. Melancholy and priapic, Newman had dated almost every girl at *Bandbox* and nearly half the ones at *Pinafore*. He was the sort of man women liked to think they could change—could make, in his case, less brooding and less of a sex hound. Newman liked Becky—everyone did—though his most deeply buried, unrealized affection was probably for the crisply mannered Nan O'Grady, whose paper cuffs seemed to ward him off the way a surgeon's gloves guarded against germs. A girl who might, deep down, dislike him as much as he disliked himself didn't come along every day, and if Newman gave himself half a chance, he might yet get almost serious about her.

But Newman's biggest problem lay in his already *being* reformed, in one respect. A once-serious drinker, prone to blackouts and brawls that threatened to leave his Olympian face looking like a palooka's, he had two years ago gone off the sauce. Newman was now the only entirely sober man at the magazine, and abstinence of any kind made Harris nervous. Newman gave his boss the creeps whenever he went in to get next month's column idea approved and asked for ginger ale once Harris invited him to pull up a chair. The editor-in-chief's discomfort would soon kill the conversation, and the two of them would just sit there, listening to the fizz in Newman's Canada Dry until Harris threw him out.

Newman's dark side gave him a certain good sense when it came to office politics, but Becky, passing his door, decided that she couldn't let this tempest out of its pneumatic teapot without putting Cuddles at risk. For all she knew, solving this sordid little problem was his last chance to save his job. So she continued down the corridor, past the Copy Department, wherein Nan and Allen Case were beavering over Max Stanwick's galleys.

"In graf six," Allen inquired in his soft stutter. "Rothstein's sh-shoe size has been changed?"

"The countess adjusted it upwards from eleven to thirteen." Nan rolled her eyes.

"S-source?" asked Case.

"Personal knowledge," answered Nan. No one would think of questioning Daisy DiDonna on such a matter; if she said Rothstein trod the earth in thirteens, it was because she had, on at least one night, unlaced them herself. Stanwick's piece made no direct reference to the size of the gangster's now-sanctioned *schvantz,* but the astute reader had only to travel up Rothstein's socks and garters to make an inference from his footwear.

Now beyond Copy's door, Becky didn't see Allen Case, who had just made the shoe-*schvantz* connection, blush to the top of his already receding hairline. Painfully shy, painfully thin, and astronomically farsighted, Allen was even more a fish out of water here than his supervisor, Nan. The formative influence upon his life had been a photograph he'd seen at twelve years old of a horse lying dead on the Somme battlefield. Since then he had been a passionate vegetarian and reader of Shavian pamphlets. Each morning, after saying goodbye to his pet bunny rabbit, Sugar, Allen left his room on Cornelia Street, shutting his eyes until he got past the pork butcher that lay between his apartment house and the subway. He carried with him a lunch of dried fruit and zwieback toast, in addition to his flawless grammar.

Nan wouldn't allow the office hearties to tease him about his lack of a girlfriend or his thinning, unbrilliantined hair. She protected him, not just out of kindness, but because he wrote like a dream. Allen could not only activate a writer's verbs and resolder his infinitives; he could also, when a piece came in a few lines under, create sentences in the voice and style of whichever scribe's prose had just crossed his desk. It amazed Nan to see him perform these ventriloquial feats, to *become* Stuart Newman or Max Stanwick or David Fine, just as completely as he entered the souls of horses on the street and cats in the pet-shop windows. In the course of a lunchtime walk with him, Allen would endow the poor creatures with anthropomorphic names and life stories that seemed less charming than eerily real.

Finally at the icebox, Becky chipped off what remained of the morning block, while she eyed the countess in the Research Department's bull pen. Its lack of privacy hardly bothered Daisy DiDonna, herself a *rite de passage* for the boys at the magazine just as surely as Newman was for the girls. Becky put Daisy's age at forty-five, though you'd never guess it from her still-nifty figure and too-tight dresses. Born Daisy Glazer, she'd been a young divorcée at the start of the war; by its end she was the Countess DiDonna, having gone off to Italy and married the seventeen-year-old Count Antonio Di-Donna, a delicate asthmatic half her age. When he died in 1920, Daisy got the title; the count's mother got the villa, as well as several injunctions against Daisy, who made a little splash, upon her return stateside, with *My Antonio*, a steamily lyrical memoir excerpted in *Vanity Fair* back in '24.

She had met Harris in an elevator that year, not long after he'd taken over *Bandbox*. She handed him one of her vellum calling cards,

put her face the four inches she always deemed the appropriate distance to be kept from any male visage, and said hello with the sweet
suggestive breathiness that could de-ice a windshield on even a
night like this. He had hired her on the spot, though she couldn't
write (*My Antonio* had been ghosted by one of Nan O'Grady's lady
novelists at Scribner's) and had appalling gaps in the common
knowledge required by anyone in the Research Department, which
is where Harris put her. Only two months ago, when checking a
story about how Governor Smith could be expected to try for the
presidential "brass ring" in '28, Daisy had called the White House to
make sure each new chief executive was indeed given this piece of
commemorative jewelry. But on matters like which tomato belonged
to which Tammany sachem, which Black Sox ballplayer still had his
money, and what size shoes were under the bed in Arnold Rothstein's apartment at 912 Fifth Avenue, Daisy was unbeatable.

"What have you got there?" asked Chip Brzezinski.

"Jeepers!" cried Becky, wheeling around so fast she sprayed some
flakes of ice onto his shirt. "You scared me." When she saw him looking through the clear tube with something like recognition, she
quickly added, "Nothing," and walked away, chilled with the realization that Chip Brzezinski, another of the magazine's fact-checkers,
knew about this photo. She double-timed it back to Cuddles' office,
worrying all the way about Brzezinski, who was known as the Wood
Chipper, because of his smart mouth and reputed sexual prowess. A
tough Chicago kid who'd hauled papers and ice and been knocked
around by his old man way past what was normal, the already-balding
Chip lived over on Ninth Avenue and mostly dated dance-hall host-
esses and cashiers instead of the nice girls here and at *Pinafore*. No
woman thought she could reform Chip, though his initiation period
with Daisy had lasted longer than was customary, at Daisy's request.

Since Jimmy left, Chip had been moaning about his general underappreciation and blocked ascent. For a while he'd been given lit-

tle fashion squibs to report and write, but now he was back to full-time fact-checking. He made no secret of how he would love to leave this place for *Cutaway*. *So what's stopping you?* was the retort everyone from Hazel Snow up to Spilkes made when he started whining. Becky, darting past Nan's door and then Stuart's, now felt pretty sure *she* knew what was stopping him, at least for the moment: Jimmy Gordon was keeping Brzezinski here as a spy. When he delivered, he would get his reward: a job halfway up the *Cutaway* masthead.

"Here," she said, allowing her hand with the cup of ice to precede the rest of her into Cuddles' office. But he didn't hear her; he was gone again—not out cold, just fast asleep. Putting down the ice, but holding on to the canister, Becky shook her head in silent sorrow over this man who knew more about music and books and politics than anyone else on the floor; who had given *Puck* and *Judge* most of their sparkle during the ten years he'd worked at each; who'd been Harris's first hire; and who these days, having lost all clout and ambition, lay snoozing with his head atop a pile of the form rejection letters he had recently managed to stencil. Cuddles now affixed a combination of Bartleby and Coolidge to whatever submissions he received each day and returned unread: "I do not choose to run your piece in 1928."

At a loss, thinking about how Cuddles was now up against both Harris's wrath and the horrid little wiles of the Wood Chipper, Becky looked out the window and considered just tossing Leopold and Loeb the fourteen floors down to Lexington Avenue. It was no more than they'd deserved in the first place.

3

"And you're letting *Houlihan* take care of this?" asked David Fine. He took a sip of grappa, his and Harris's after-dinner usual here at Malocchio.

"Could it really wind up on a bus?" asked the editor-in-chief.

"Are you kidding?" answered his food columnist and confidant. "Are you the only guy in New York who hasn't seen *this*?" He reached under the table for the *Daily News,* whose front page roared with the image of Ruth Snyder at the instant of her electrocution in Sing Sing. Late last night the paper's photographer had strapped a camera under his pants leg, raising it at just the moment the screws pulled the switch. "You think the guy who took this picture is going to get a summons? Forget about it—he's going to get a prize."

Harris cringed at this sight of the blindfolded, husband-killing cutie, who'd been the subject of two *Bandbox* pieces by Max Stanwick: if the kiddies could buy a picture of Ruth's sizzling flesh on their way to school, Leopold and Loeb ought to be riding the side of a private bus any morning now. Noticing for the first time that it was Friday the thirteenth, Harris realized he was jumping one more watershed in the age of You Ain't Heard Nothin' Yet. He'd only managed to get Jolson himself onto the pages of *Bandbox*—in blackface and white tie—a month after *The Jazz Singer* opened last fall, which was really a month too late. Talking pictures were one more thing he now had to understand and keep track of. To Harris, it seemed more like the age of You've Heard Too Much Already.

Fine lacked anything more to say. The two men put the newspaper aside and returned to their grappa as the restaurant violinist launched into "Sometimes I'm Happy." Had David Fine composed the lyrics for this new tune, he would have made its next line "But more often I'm not." It was Fine, chronically certain of his underappreciation by others, who usually got *his* reassurance and perspective from Joe Harris.

He had grown up in Philadelphia and come to New York in 1898 to cover baseball and the horses for the *Brooklyn Eagle*. Two decades later, fleeing a misguided engagement to a jockey's daughter, the thirty-seven-year-old bachelor enlisted in the army and wound up winning a Bronze Star at Belleau Wood. Overseas, Fine had cultivated a taste for wine and food, subjects the *Eagle* had no desire to see him write about once he returned to America. So he went to work as the sommelier for Giovanni Roma at the then-brand-new Malocchio.

It was here that he'd met Joe Harris in '23, when the editor was just assuming control of both *Bandbox* and his regular corner table. Fine had, in more or less the same breath, said something to Joe about Christy Mathewson's fastball and a 1912 cabernet, and the editor had decided he was a man of parts. Within a month, Fine was writing "The Groaning Board"—his column about food and drink and anything else on his disappointment-prone mind. *Bandbox* staffers called the column "Fine Whines," but Fine's cranky, suspicious voice became immediately popular with readers, who liked the humor, intentional and otherwise, in almost everything he wrote. Harris felt sure Fine would eventually bring in a GME; he'd already attracted enough new subscribers that the editor was happy to put up with his constant complaints about being poorly paid; cheated by a cabdriver; snubbed by his landlady; stood up by a date. Now forty-eight, Fine lived alone in Brooklyn and occasionally went out with one of the secretaries at the magazine, but his real romance was with his expense account, upon which Harris instructed the book-keeper to put no significant limits, even when Fine failed to write a single word about some foreign clime he'd just spent two weeks eating his way through.

"So you haven't told me," he now implored Harris, who was sneaking another look at Ruth Snyder. " 'Williamsburg versus Williamsburg'?"

"Yeah," said Harris. "Do it. It's good." The editor knew that it would be more than good, that a Fine column comparing the Brooklyn neighborhood and the Virginia home of William and Mary— popovers versus blintzes; college titles beside Yiddish nicknames; burgesses competing with rabbis—would be a hit with readers and maybe even the GME committee. "Spend whatever it takes," said Harris. "And take as long as you have to."

He began the slow process of lighting his cigar. Looking through the flame as it bobbed up and down a half-dozen times, he noticed some RCA executives and then Mayor Walker and then Horace Liveright, the party-giving publisher, all at tables less prominent than his own. His berth was reimbursement for the business *Bandbox* had been bringing Malocchio these past five years. Harris might have stolen Giovanni Roma's sommelier, but he'd made 50,000 New York readers eager to get into this place the magazine kept pronouncing the essence of dining in style.

"Is a nice night, no?" said Roma, tapping Harris's shoulder from behind. "So nice it make me stupid. I got the mayor here, and I come to sit with you, you fat *cetriolo*."

Harris's countenance lightened for the first time all evening. He turned around with his now properly lit cigar. "You'd better pay attention, *goombah*. Walker's been as dry as my guy Newman since about September. Watch and see he doesn't put your Italian behind in jail for serving what passes for booze here."

"Nah," said Roma. "He ain't got religion on the subject. He just take the pledge to please his lady friend. Is a, how you say, 'personal' thing."

Giovanni Roma had been born and brought up in Saugatuck, Connecticut, but from an occupational affectation he now spoke English with less facility and a thicker accent than his immigrant parents. He'd come to New York fifteen years ago, at the age of twenty-seven, when local scandal forced him off the family fishing boat. Gianni liked to chase the *ragazzi,* but after a year of waiting tables in the city, he had allowed a well-known older actor to chase and catch him. The price of temporary surrender was the stake he used to start Malocchio. For six years the restaurant had only just stayed afloat on the stream of newspaper guys and ballplayers that David Fine coaxed through the door, but things started to bubble once Harris designated the restaurant as his home with a mention in *Bandbox* every month.

"So when you go to London?" he asked Harris.

"End of the month." With Jimmy Gordon on his tail, the editor wondered how he'd even find the breathing space to sail over for his annual tour of the men's shops along Savile Row. A report on them always accompanied *Bandbox*'s piece on whatever sartorial rule had just been repealed by the Prince of Wales, but Harris made the trip mostly to enjoy evenings with Fine and Spilkes in the woody hotel bars that satisfied his longings for the antique.

"Before that we've got the editorial retreat up in Dutchess," he said to Roma. "You're going to do the food for me, remember?"

The restaurateur made a put-upon face and nodded, while David Fine complained: "I always catch cold up there. Why can't we avoid all those Herkimer Jerkimers and do it down here? Rent a big hotel suite."

"I like it there," said Harris, thinking of his big weekend house, the woods latticed with snow. "Nobody pays attention if we stay in town."

"You got to give me plenty notice," said Gianni.

Harris and Roma and Fine made a tiptop male trio, combining

more comfortably than most much closer friends might have. Their libidinal variety helped: Roma remained as devoted to young men as Harris did to Betty Divine and the lost ideal of full-bosomed woman-hood; Fine, at bottom, was more indifferent to sex than any man the other two knew. Together, the three sailed along in insult-hurling harmony, their self-display and jockeyings for a small measure of re-pute undisturbed by the slightest undercurrent of sexual competition.

The restaurant owner and the editor-in-chief also had the un-spoken fellow feeling that arises between two men each aware that the other is keeping secrets. Roma had a whole thrilling store of them, legally perilous and never far from his mind. Harris's skeletons, older and less dangerous, were still potentially unsettling: he did not, for instance, wish Jimmy Gordon or the GME board to know all the details of how, for a brief period a half-dozen years ago while he was between jobs, his editorial skills had been applied to the pro-duction of a line of postcards in decidedly questionable taste.

"So, *brutto,*" said Roma, trying to stoke the guttering conversa-tion, "whatsa matter you? You don' look too good."

Harris would have liked being able to tell Gianni about Jimmy Gordon's photographic salvo, but the restaurant owner didn't dis-courage Jimmy from eating here, and no doubt nurtured the hope of a gossip-column item about the wayward protégé crossing paths, and swords, with his old boss at Malocchio. So Harris just shrugged and said, "It's nothing. I'm only wondering when this lunatic Lind-strom is going to show up and do his hour of 'work.' Standing still for a camera."

Gianni regarded his fingernails and affected a lack of interest in the cocaine-crazed cover model. When the need arose, he could be discreet. A few months ago he'd removed a Maxfield Parrish paint-ing of Ganymede from a stretch of wall near the kitchen, lest the place start looking too much like the Jewel. Now he eyed Walker, and decided that Harris was right: he had more than one reason to stay in the mayor's good graces. " *'Scusi,*" he said, getting up from the table to pay Hizzoner a little attention.

"So," said Harris to Fine. "Have you got any advice at all?"

The food columnist, impatient to be recognized by one of the RCA big shots—maybe even asked for an autograph, or offered a stock tip—managed only to look at Harris and say, "Sleep on it?"

"Sleep on it?" cried his boss, pushing away the grappa. "It's *Friday*. I can't sleep on this for three nights. Even Houlihan would know better than to tell me that. *Sleep* on it, for Christ's sake."

"You're assuming Houlihan knows the day of the week," said Fine.

Disgusted, the editor got up—there was never a check to settle here—and walked outside to wait on the hack line. The handsome doorman's umbrella only half-protected Harris and another customer from the ice-cold drizzle. The editor wished he'd brought along that copy of the *Daily News* to hold over his head.

Death, he thought, recalling the electrified Ruth Snyder. It was today's essential thrill, the way every drama now had to end. The music played so fast you couldn't follow it, but every listener wanted it to play faster still, until the phonograph exploded.

Before Harris could proceed too far with his gloomy reflections, Giovanni Roma came out the front door with two *cannoli* in a small cardboard box. "Here, *bambino,*" he said, handing them to the editor. "Take them to La Divina. Go. *Walk.* It do you good."

Harris gave him a quizzical look.

"Let a smile be your umbrella," said Gianni, pushing his best customer off into the freezing night.

At that moment, up in the Warwick Hotel, Betty Divine was finishing the evening papers, a form of literature she still secretly preferred to magazines, though she'd started working in the latter twenty years ago, in the ad department at *Collier's* for Condé Nast himself, just before he'd begun to buy and run his own publications. Betty had been one of the few girls ever to say no to Nast, who always kept up a professorial look and manner until he pounced upon the latest little secretary in the back of a taxicab. Two decades ago, Betty, in just such a circumstance, had unmanned him by saying, quite calmly, as his tongue darted into her ear, "I'm sorry, but I can't hear you."

She'd come east from St. Louis at eighteen, in 1902, and taken some little parts in musicals. She'd never been stagestruck, just realistic about what lay available to a girl as quick and cute as herself. What she'd never be, however, was tall, so she'd soon left the stage and gone to work in magazines. When Nast bought *Vogue,* sometime after being thwarted in the taxicab, he had brought her over and switched her from business to editorial. And she'd been happy there for a long time, until seven years ago, when Hi Oldcastle, pretty sure she could understand this new class of career girl now in the city, lured her away with an offer to edit *Pinafore.*

Not long after that she'd met Joe. He'd been crazy about her from the start. Immediately, and continually, he'd asked her to marry him. She always said no, having tried that years ago with a dull, bullying lawyer who'd put her off both matrimony and excessively good looks. The arrangement she'd imposed on Joe was much nicer: weekends up in Dutchess County, and two or three nights of togetherness here during the week, listening to the radio or eating a late supper, trying to figure out their mutual boss's latest whim. Joe spent the other nights out of her hair, either late at Malocchio or over at his own place in Murray Hill.

That had been her own neighborhood until just a few months ago, when, determined to keep a bit of control, she'd taken this more glamorous set of rooms at the Warwick. She let Joe help out with the rent—not because she needed him to, but as a signal that she expected to be treated right. That Hearst kept an apartment for Marion Davies on these same premises was a fact lost on neither of them.

"Hearst *can't* marry Davies," Joe would say from time to time, never quite giving up the hope of something more for himself and Betty. "He's *already* married."

"So was I," Betty would reply.

And so had Harris been, years ago, to a schoolteacher who'd made him so miserable he took tremendous care not to press his luck with Betty, who at forty-four remained as cute as Mabel Normand and more sensible than Andrew Mellon. Joe might be shrewd, but he was also excitable, and he depended on Betty to rip up the letters he shouldn't mail or turn off the motor he was in no condition to have started on the way home.

Earlier tonight, when he'd telephoned, she'd said fine, don't worry about dinner—go off to Malocchio if there's something you need to discuss with David. She'd ordered up from the hotel kitchen, and now, awaiting Joe's late arrival, she listened to the Chicago Civic Opera on WJZ and finished making her way through a stack of take-home work: the latest photos of Marie of Roumania; the results of a *Pinafore* poll asking: "Is it ever proper to visit your fiancé's mother *sans chapeau?*"

Betty had the radio up so loud that her white Eskimo puppy, Mukluk, was cowering by the door. His mistress's one real vanity involved her hardness of hearing. Only the moment's emergency had permitted her confession of it to Condé Nast, years ago in that taxicab. When she and Joe went to see Ina Claire's comeback performance next month, she would allow herself, once the houselights went down, the use of her little silver ear trumpet. But amidst the glare and noise of a party, she always covered up her difficulty by nodding yes or no, even as she misheard a name, misunderstood a story, or missed somebody's point. And yet, Betty again and again realized—perhaps the greatest truth she had grasped about life—that all these misapprehensions, in the end, never made the slightest difference.

She knew a serenity that Joe would never attain. When he came through the door tonight, worries as thick upon him as his cologne, Mukluk would give him a wide berth, and she would massage his shoulders, imparting the same wise counsel she did during the dozen or so phone calls he made to her, from one floor of the Graybar Building to another, every day that they worked there. She was glad she'd been out this afternoon, having her light brown bob attended to by Sydney over at the Saks salon, when Joe's latest crisis broke. She'd gotten back to the office in time for only that last call, when he'd announced his need to take David Fine to Giovanni Roma's awful restaurant.

"It's all right, baby," she said, soothing Mukluk, who had raced under the couch upon Mary Garden's ejaculation of an E-sharp seven hundred miles away in Chicago. "You'll see."

4

At this same hour, despite Betty's belief in the essential rightness of things, three of Joe Harris's staffers found themselves coming to their own nervous crossroads:

Down on Cornelia Street, Allen Case already lay in bed under his blanket. As the wind slid in over the warped windowsill, he gave unspoken thanks to whatever lamb had provided the wool now keeping him warm. A young man with so little self-love he had difficulty masturbating, Allen lay with his eyes open, distracted from his woe only by the munchings of Sugar, his rabbit, and Freddy, his Siamese.

Keeping him awake were thoughts about the last piece of copy Nan O'Grady had put on his desk before the office closed, after they'd finished with Max Stanwick's piece on Arnold Rothstein.

The spots on this ocelot's coat are no match for the polka-dot vitality of our "Bandbox" gentleman's tie. . . .

The caption as yet lacked a picture, but Allen knew the words were intended to run beneath whatever photo Waldo Lindstrom had failed to pose for this afternoon. Richard Lord and the fashion editors wanted Copy to be ready for an image they still hoped to jam in before the March issue closed. The photographer who'd been stood up, Gardiner Arinopoulos, had already, before Thanksgiving, shot a model wrapped in a python that matched his snakeskin tie. This illo of 1928's so-far-most-gruesome fashion craze had not, Allen could tell, been taken at the Bronx Zoo, and when Nan informed him that Arinopoulos had shot it at a garage somewhere in Queens, his stomach had dropped. Who was keeping these exotic animals, and how were they living?

Allen feared he would soon reach the point he always reached wherever he worked, the one beyond which he could not go. At the *American,* for instance, he had accepted having to surround with inverted commas the cruel phrase "no pets," when editing real estate ads. But there had come the week when he had to work on a two-part article celebrating the role of cowhide in the making of baseballs. The pieces were so happy and triumphal—one had to imagine *The Jungle* as produced by George M. Cohan—that Allen's conscience and abdomen had been forced to give notice.

Up until now, he'd been managing pretty well at *Bandbox,* even if it wasn't easy having to blue-pencil, say, a piece of David Fine's on the chateaubriand at Durgin Park. But there was something truly ominous about these animal shoots Arinopoulos was doing. Would they prove the by-now-familiar last straw? Tonight, while cutting up the *Daily News* for Sugar's cage, the only electrocution Allen could think of was Topsy the Elephant's, at Coney Island all those years ago. They'd put her down for quite reasonably trampling to death some humans. Drifting off to sleep at last, Allen thought, rather hopelessly, that if these poor things being abused by Arinopoulos could only acquire language—something *he* used effortlessly but to such little purpose—they'd almost certainly rise up and organize and break free.

Daisy DiDonna rose from the couch to close the window. She was never cold, not even on a night like this, but she had to do something about the smell making its way ten blocks up the East River, all the way to her little patch of Beekman Place. The slaughterhouse was even worse for Daisy's friend Gladys, who had a little place practically on top of it, in the first-opened building of Tudor City. There the architect, despite the river view, had put in windows the size of a medicine cabinet, because of the aromas. But at least Gladys had somebody paying for her place, even if her fancy man had gone home to his wife in Douglaston tonight, leaving Gladys to have supper with Daisy in a chop-suey dance joint.

Daisy needed to find someone steady—at least as steady as Mr. Douglaston. Since her long-ago divorce, she had never been with anyone for more than the six months she'd spent with Antonio Di-Donna, whom Joe Harris now sometimes referred to as The Long Count. Daisy's standard and motto—"Always be faithful, but always be looking"—by now made for a pretty worn-out coat of arms, and she wondered if she shouldn't put more effort into the long-term cultivation of whomever she was with, perhaps even forgoing the initiations she loved to provide for the greenhorn boys just hired by Oldcastle Publications.

She sighed, remembering her own first job, typing away inside the Flatiron Building in 1903, the year it opened. Outside at lunch-time, on the sidewalks, men would come from blocks around to gawk at the girls, when the downdrafts created by the building's peculiar shape blew their long skirts up over their thighs. Every gust brought another show, and another half-dozen men.

It had been Daisy's misfortune to waste her own legs' best days in the era of ankle-length dresses. Now, when her stems lacked the supreme tautness they'd once had, skirts had risen right to the knees. She needed the next gust of wind to send her somebody truly well-heeled—and to blow her eyes shut against whatever farm-fresh boy she could see over his shoulder.

She might be forty-four, but she still deserved an ardent, permanence-minded suitor. The way she saw things, she had earned one, by the serious attention she paid to every advertisement for combating corns, halitosis, bad pronunciation, superfluous hair, and wrinkles. Except for a few of the latter, Daisy had none of the above. She had always been her own mechanic, keeping herself in top-notch form, and she was beginning to think she merited a bit more from those who got to drive her well-tended chassis—however much she enjoyed having it taken for a spin.

Right now she was dismayed to find herself still in her leopard-print slip. She liked to sleep in the nude, and not yet being down to that meant some part of her secretly wished the phone would ring and that it would be the Wood Chipper, calling from some Automat, as he still sometimes did when he'd struck out with everyone else. Was this all she had to look forward to?

These days you could live above your means even on Beekman Place. The block, slaughterhouse smells and all, was getting fancier by the month, as yet another wave of stockbrokers displaced the unsuccessful sculptors and out-of-work actresses. Daisy herself was down to the last of her *My Antonio* money and knew she couldn't make it on what Joe Harris paid her. Where would the rest come from?

She glanced at the kitchen calendar. Friday the thirteenth didn't faze her in the least—Daisy was too lucky to be superstitious—but the number did set her to thinking. She remembered how it had come up this afternoon relative to Mr. Rothstein's shoes. She had seen him unshod only once, the single evening she had been up to 912 Fifth Avenue. She couldn't remember exactly which recent unpromising escort had brought her there, but those feet weren't something you forgot. She'd massaged them—and nothing more—for a solid half-hour, until the man became more occupied with business than with her. No matter; Eddie Diamond had driven her home and been a perfect gent. Daisy looked back on the evening, which had taken place only weeks ago, with a certain wistfulness. And she allowed herself, for just a minute, to consider how nice it would be if her whole long future might somehow be found in that tiny piece of her past.

The singer's Ruth Etting imitation might be pretty second-rate, but Stuart Newman, falling asleep on a banquette at Mirador, was taking the song's title to heart. *After you've gone,* Miss . . . what was the name of this girl who was half-on, half-off his lap? . . . *after you've gone,* Miss Brattle—that was it—maybe I can go home and go to bed.

Stuart and Miss Brattle had already been to the Deauville, and her appetite for nightlife appeared to be such that he feared seeing the dawn break at some rent party up in Harlem.

"I want to meet Texas Guinan!" she burbled, while tickling Stuart's nose.

He managed a smile. "That's for tourists, honey."

Now that he could remember Miss Brattle's name, he tried to remember how he'd met her. She was a Bryn Mawr girl, no? A member of the Art Students League? Which would indicate, perhaps, that he'd been introduced to her by Millicent, the artists' model, whom he was quite sure he'd met through Miss Cronin, who worked in that little gallery. Stuart's last dates were always recommending his next ones, because he knew how to stop short of breaking any of their hearts. Handsome and worldly as he was, he had an odd, almost little-boy's voice, and he understood how to inspire maternal concern. Before he was through with them, his girls almost always came to regard Stuart as a species of social work. His evenings were like referrals: "Here, see what *you* can do with him," each girl would say to the next. If no one so far had accomplished his emotional animation, the author of "The Bachelor's Life" was never short on material. Miss Brattle would end up in a column on "Artistic Girls," along with Millicent and Miss Cronin, so long as—he'd have to check—he hadn't already used either of those two in "Greenwich Village Girls."

So entranced was Miss Brattle by his still-Greek profile that Stuart knew he could use it, should he so desire, to point her homeward to his lair in Gramercy Park. But instead of jutting his jaw in that southerly direction, Stuart surprised his date by saying, "How about me getting you a taxi, honey?"

Miss Brattle made a little pout. It went unnoticed by Stuart, thinking now of Nan O'Grady, who would soon be complaining, in that precise little voice, about his overdue column. Shot through with longing and anxiety, Stuart could feel an old enemy suddenly banging on a door somewhere inside him. He allowed his profile to sink deep into Miss Brattle's marcel wave.

"Now, *that's* better," she said, falsely encouraged by the gesture.

Stuart said nothing. His full concentration was on breathing in the smell of alcohol from Miss Brattle's setting lotion.

5

And, finally tonight, several hundred miles to the west, in the small town of Greencastle, Indiana, where the temperature was several degrees higher, and the pace of life several knots slower, nineteen-year-old John Shepard turned a page of his magazine and pondered the necktie being worn by the man with the python.

He wasn't altogether sure that such a tie was "him," John Chilton Shepard, but he *was* sure that nobody would ever find this bold piece of neckwear in any shop in Greencastle—not even two years from now, when, as a *Bandbox* subscriber, John knew it would certainly be out of fashion.

The magazine's January issue had arrived only today, and as John fingered the Addressographed subscription label, he felt *connected* to the whole glamorous production; he felt part of the scene just by knowing that in some print shop in New York City a machine had chattered out the characters of his name.

What to read first? The short story by Stark Young? Stuart Newman's piece on "The Girls Who Can't Stop Loving Sacco and Vanzetti"? Or just the latest page of wisecracks collected from Malocchio? With allowance made for rereading, the issue would last John nearly a week, after which he would have to return to O. O. McIntyre's syndicated newspaper column for vicarious glimpses of New York life. But McIntyre's *own* glimpses had come to seem vicarious to John; he was tired of hearing about the columnist's apartment way up in the Hotel Majestic. *Bandbox,* by contrast, made a fellow feel he was truly down there in the thick of things, that he didn't just have to use his imagination. John had been applying that quality to New York life ever since he'd been ten years old and the sound of the 8:30 chime from the dining-room clock had come to mean that the curtains were going up—*at that very moment!*—in every theatre on Broadway.

"John!"

At this cry from his mother, he turned down Cass Hagan and His Park Central Orchestra, who were on the radio playing songs from *Manhattan Mary.*

"Yes, Mother! I've lowered it!"

Mrs. Shepard treated him like Penrod, whereas John's self-image was catching up to the idea he had of Waldo Lindstrom, a young man who even in that snakeskin tie, one could tell, never lost his effortless command of a yacht or a wine list or a woman.

"John!" Mrs. Shepard's voice came once more up the stairs. "Never mind the noise—mind the time! You've got errands to run all day tomorrow!"

"Yes, Mother," he replied, so wearily his words never carried all the way down to the parlor.

He looked at the trunk, already sealed and labeled with the address of his fraternity house at IU. The new term was about to begin, and he would soon be there instead of—*there,* he thought, closing his eyes to imagine the clarinets in Hagan's orchestra, pointed upwards, spouting their music like a row of singing skyscrapers.

Turning the radio back up, John, seized with inspiration, rushed to get a blank card, a pen, and some shears, in order to fashion a new label for the trunk, one that would ensure its GENERAL DELIVERY, about a week from now, in NEW YORK CITY.

6

"Raus!" cried Mrs. von Erhard, who with her much milder husband ran the newsstand in the Graybar's lobby. The hapless accountant she'd caught browsing a magazine replaced it on the rack and beat his retreat to the elevator. Each day at least a dozen patrons vowed to tell Mrs. von Erhard off, but so far none had ever done anything more than cast a wounded look at her silent, cowed spouse.

Hannelore and Siegfried had come to the U.S. from Hamburg just after the outbreak of war in 1914, and throughout America's year and a half Over There had kept their sidewalk newsstand at Forty-second and Lex so festooned with Old Glory that out-of-towners catching sight of it would sometimes mistake the little shed for a parade float. The couple had gotten the Graybar concession by keeping a shrewd eye on the construction site, ingratiating themselves with everyone who showed up at it wearing a suit.

Becky Walter loathed Mrs. von Erhard, but she didn't risk a glance at *Photoplay* while reaching for a copy of this morning's *Times*.

"Trading up?" said a voice behind her.

It belonged to Paul Montgomery, *Bandbox*'s Harvard man, regarded as the magazine's true stylist, rangy and lyrical, not a Johnny One-Note like David Fine or Max Stanwick. You might not want him to cover Arnold Rothstein, but Paul could bring a touch of the poet to everything from the boxing ring to the assembly line to some Iowa kid building a soapbox racer. Becky found his simile-saturated copy to be as insincere as Paul Montgomery himself, who pretended to be collegial instead of ambitious and claimed to see the wisdom in every word anybody spoke to him. For all his self-deprecation, he so believed in the importance of his own success that he had no room left to believe in anything else. His politics were however you were voting; his drink was whatever you were having; and his take on any assigned subject was whatever he determined, from guesswork or direct instruction, Joe Harris's to be. "You're a horse's ass, Montgomery," Cuddles had once, in a moment of alcoholic candor, declared to his face. "I couldn't agree more," Paulie had responded.

"Huh?" asked Becky, turning around.

"Trading up?" he repeated, pointing at her *Times*. He'd all but said "Atta-girl." Becky knew the real meaning of this supposedly encouraging remark to be that someone like herself should stick to the *News* or the *American* and leave the *Times* and *World* to men of consequence like himself. But she decided to say, simply, "That's right, Paul," since he would only wind up harmonizing any disagreement into unanimity. She handed him the paper and took another copy for herself.

"Dot vill be two cents, sir," said Hannelore von Erhard, nodding gravely. This cranial bow was part of the hushed deference she and Siegfried always paid Montgomery, whose industrialist father had gone down with the *Lusitania* in 1915.

"Where were you last week?" Becky asked Paulie on their way to the elevator. "You look like an unmade bed."

"I do, don't I?" he said, taking off his hat to pat down his hair. "Just got off the sleeper from Atlanta. Long interview with Ty Cobb. Spent a few days with him back home. His last season's coming up. So sad. But I think the Big Guy will be pleased."

"I'm sure he will be," said Becky. So, no doubt, would Ty Cobb. Montgomery never departed from a subject without clasping the person's hands as if *he*, or the interviewee, were about to board the *Lusitania*. Surely, Becky had thought more than once, all the little ruts and sinkholes in Paulie's mind had been drilled by his father's catastrophe.

"So what've I missed?" he asked.

"Nothing special," said Becky. She knew better than to tell him about Friday's greeting from Leopold and Loeb, especially with the Wood Chipper, wrapped into a ridiculous raccoon coat, now following them into the elevator.

"Joe College?" asked Montgomery. He meant to sound, once more, encouraging, as if it were nice to see the lower orders of the masthead taking a turn at self-improvement.

"I borrowed it from Fashion," said Chip Brzezinski, without further explanation.

"Trading up?" Becky asked him, trying to insult Chip and Paul simultaneously. She was still wondering how much involvement the Wood Chipper had had in the photo's arrival on Friday, and, more important, whether what she now had in mind as a way out for Cuddles had a prayer of working.

"You changed the part of your hair," said the endlessly pleasant Mrs. Zimmerman as Paul and Becky and Chip stepped off the elevator into *Bandbox*'s reception area. "It looks *nice*."

"Thanks, Mrs. Z," said Montgomery. "One doesn't make these decisions lightly."

He walked with Becky and Chip to the coffee wagon at the other end of the floor. Passing by each open office, he shouted hello as if its occupant were the person he'd missed more than anybody else during his week in Georgia.

"Allen Case!" he shouted into the Copy Department. "The best blue pencil *and* the best fellow in New York!"

Allen made no response, only because his eyes had just dilated in revulsion over the sight of Chip Brzezinski in that coat. The manufacturer might as well have left the raccoons' heads attached to the pelts, so vividly could Allen imagine all their little faces with those bandit kerchiefs nature had fashioned for them.

"How about some tea?" suggested Nan. "I'm going to get a danish."

The two of them joined a small crowd at the coffee cart run by

Mrs. Washington, a fine, churchgoing Negro lady who couldn't wait to get through with this bunch and bring her wagon up to the much more respectable underwriters on fifteen. She made no effort to conceal her contempt for these filthy-tongued fashion plates who—except for nice Mr. Newman—would be pouring an inch of booze into their cups as soon as they got the coffee back to their desks.

Daisy thought she might need a little more than that this morning. Her gloomy Friday-night reflections had continued through the weekend, and the sight of Chip's coat made her realize why, perhaps, there had been no late call the other evening: he'd been dating against type, she supposed; making a successful play in this borrowed costume for some college girl half her age.

Becky looked down the corridor to Cuddles' office and saw no sign of him. What's more, ten minutes past what should have been the start of Monday's 9:30 lineup meeting, Harris's door was still closed.

"He's on the phone with Betty," Hazel explained to the lengthening line of editors and writers outside it; they now included Stuart Newman, who looked so strained that the others were staring at him.

"Probably the clap," whispered Max Stanwick to Montgomery.

"I'm sure you're right," responded Paulie.

"The third call he's already made to her today," said Hazel, pointing to Harris's door, as the clock moved closer to 9:45.

"His mood's bad," said David Fine to Spilkes. "I can feel it."

Hazel smirked at the Wood Chipper, who still hadn't shed his coat. "Careful out there," she said. "It's hunting season."

Spilkes, who despised Brzezinski, added a withering glance to her remark. The guy had no business being here—he didn't take part in editorial meetings—and the managing editor wanted him to scram. Spilkes had no intention of bringing along this little operator the way Jimmy Gordon had tried to. Six months had passed since the Wood Chipper had written a word of *Bandbox,* and so long as

Spilkes was m.e., Brzezinski wouldn't be asked to do so much as a sidebar on "the perfect shoeshine," one of the magazine's perennials.

"I guess I'll go to my office and count paper clips," said Chip, turning his back on the line and heading down the corridor.

"You don't *have* an office," Spilkes reminded him, loudly.

Back in the bull pen of fact-checkers' desks, Chip decided that he *would* just count paper clips this morning, whereas his father, serving eight to twelve in Joliet State Prison for applying a tire iron to an alderman, was presumably counting the two hundred dollars he'd just made from Jimmy Gordon for photographing Leopold and Loeb to exact specifications. No one but Jimmy knew the Wood Chipper's father was doing time.

"Is Cuddles in?" Becky asked Hazel, as quietly as she could.

"Haven't seen him," said Harris's secretary over the scrape of her nail file.

Through the frosted glass, the assembled staff could see the boss standing near his window, still holding the telephone.

"I can't help it," he was telling Betty, as he looked down into Lexington Avenue, worried he might already see a bus carrying that terrible picture.

"Will you just put out your issue?" Betty responded from three flights down. "Why don't you let Jimmy Gordon's world revolve around yours for a while, instead of vice-a-versa?"

"What am I, living with Copernicus?"

"Give *who* a kiss?" asked Betty.

"COPERNICUS."

"Stop shouting. You're going to give yourself a heart attack. I have to go. Oldcastle's making me go to lunch with Helena Rubinstein. I've got another two coats of rouge to put on between now and then if she's going to think I'm serious about her product."

"All right," said Harris, replacing the receiver and finally shouting "Come in!" to the dozen of his hirelings beyond the door. "It's ten o'clock, for Christ's sake! You're standing there like we're a bi-monthly!"

The staff arranged themselves in two rows of chairs in front of his vast marble desktop. Its crystal inkpots and ornate fountain pens, bristling from brass holders, made it look like an ornamental sarcophagus.

"Where's Houlihan?" Harris asked Becky, once everyone was seated.

No longer Cuddles' keeper, she resented the question but lied for him anyway. "He's probably tied up in the subway."

Spilkes made a small notation, and Sidney Bruck issued a pitiless snort. Harris, who on occasion did some poaching of his own, had recently stolen this elegant young man, with his long Shelleyan hair and humorless wit, away from Crowninshield at *Vanity Fair*. For the past few months Bruck had been handling—or dismissing—most of the writers who'd fallen by Cuddles' wayside.

He sat, prodigious and calm, beside Andrew Burn, the magazine's publisher, a balding, thuggish Scot, probably the one who'd discovered the low road in and out of his native land. Burn had worked for Oldcastle in various fixer capacities for nearly a decade, before the owner gave him to Harris as a publisher. The Scot had been a major part of *Bandbox*'s turnaround, selling a vast acreage of ads against the magazine's new editorial formula; he remained the chief bulwark of Harris's security in the wake of Jimmy Gordon's desertion.

"We've got some holes in April," said the editor-in-chief, growling the meeting to order. "And May's half blank. What have you got going, ladies and gents?" He looked at Paul Montgomery. "Cobb about ready?"

"*More* than ready," said Paul. After this enthusiastic assurance, he clammed up, hoping to indicate that the stuff he'd gotten was too extraordinary to be shared yet even with his colleagues.

David Fine wasn't buying. "Sounds special, Paulie. What'd Cobb do? Beat some colored guy to death with his bat, right in front of you?"

"For starters!" Montgomery crowed, before sealing his lips with a finger gesture.

Becky exchanged a look of revulsion with Stuart Newman, and in the process noticed the dark rings under his eyes—something more, she felt pretty sure, than routine sexual exhaustion.

"I've got exactly two features in the May well," said Harris, at just below a shout. "Anybody got any ideas on how to keep this band-wagon rolling for another month?" The chronic paucity of on-hand copy was actually an indicator of the magazine's vitality. Harris kept next to no inventory to ensure topicality and solvency. And so anxiety reigned: the produce might be fresh, but the cupboard was always bare.

"I've heard that Peggy Hopkins Joyce is dating Chrysler," offered Spilkes. "Maybe there's a story there."

"And lose the car ads for three months?" asked Burn.

"He's right," said Paul Montgomery.

Suddenly, several voices, loud and indistinguishable, could be heard in the corridor outside. Richard Lord uncrossed his shined shoes and murmured, "The Columbia basketball team, I believe. Arriving for a shoot."

Harris looked confused.

"You signed off on it," said Lord. "Late one afternoon," he added, by way of explanation for the editor's lack of recollection. " 'Sky-scrapers.' The pictures will have tailors holding tape measures, with little office windows instead of inch marks, against the boys' legs. They're nearly all six-footers."

"That'll get Daisy out of her funk," said Nan O'Grady.

"What about Cuba?" asked Max Stanwick, returning to the business of story ideas.

"What about it?" responded Harris.

"Coolidge is there this week," said Spilkes.

"We don't cover treaty signings in this magazine," said the editor-in-chief.

"He means the food, I'll bet," said David Fine, sensing an invasion of turf by Stanwick. "You should see what the chinks down there can do with pork."

Harris looked puzzled.

"Chinks," explained Fine. "Cuba's crawling with 'em."

"I'm talking about the nightlife," Stanwick asserted. "The gambling, the goons. Hoods hacking up the honchos back at their haciendas. Señoritas stabbing their stogie-sucking suitors." Nan, her ears and teeth set on edge by Stanwick's staple alliteration, chewed a small hank of her red hair. Sidney Bruck, who had he been Adam would have found the Garden of Eden a stale cliché, put in his poisoned oar. "Oh, *wonderful*," he said. "*Here's* a way to use Peggy Joyce. Put her on the cover, maybe in a mantilla, or *dressed up like a matador*."

Before Stanwick could punch out his lights with a look, a great crash rattled the glass in Harris's office door.

"Perhaps I should have a look," said Lord, getting up from his seat.

Harris ignored the fuss to concentrate on Stanwick. "You're too busy to go down to Cuba."

"No, I'm not. We just closed Rothstein."

"Not quite," Nan corrected.

"You're not going," said Harris.

"You know," said Becky, "Japan presents some—"

"Japan?" asked Stanwick.

"Sure, Japan," interrupted Nan. " 'Slick samurai slices sailor with sword.' It's got possibilities for you."

"I wasn't thinking of it for Max," said Becky. "But I've heard that since the earthquake, the Imperial Hotel—"

"I could do it," Paul Montgomery rushed in to say. He was already grasping the lyric possibilities: delicate geishas who'd made teahouses from the rubble; little Hirohito struggling with Western dress. "The Emperor's New Clothes!" he blurted. "I could ship out in a week."

Paulie's long absence was a delightful prospect, but Becky had imagined the piece for a freelance, some young novelist with a bit of sensibility. She began to protest, but there was really no need. The Japan idea, like so many Monday-morning editorial notions, died out as fast as it had been uttered, drowned in the badinage of insult and conversational chaos created by the attempt to keep track of three different issues of the magazine in various stages of production.

"What about bank loans to brokers?" asked Spilkes. "They're way up. They could make things dangerous for the market."

"That's a theme," said Harris, "not a story. Come up with the guy who's lost his shirt or gone to the clink or left some blonde holding the bag, and *then* it'll be a story."

"I'm getting two short pieces from Nathan," said Sidney Bruck, like a weary magician extracting rabbits for his colleagues who couldn't even find the top hat. After a pause, he deigned to describe the two casual essays he'd just paid George Jean Nathan, the *American Mercury*'s drama critic, to write. "One on leisure versus loafing. Another on how wisecracks are killing conversation."

Cuddles Houlihan, who'd just entered the room, responded to Sidney as he looked for a chair. "Didn't we already *do* euthanasia?"

"Proving Nathan's point," said Bruck, whose words were lost in the still-growing roar outside the office. It seemed to be coming all the way from the Fashion Department.

"Siddown," Harris ordered Houlihan. Becky looked at her old boss and mouthed the words "Where have you been?"

"You might want to get out there," Cuddles said to Spilkes. "One of the Columbia boys just clocked Waldo."

"Lindstrom showed up?" asked Harris. "Good."

"If you say so," answered Cuddles, who at last found a chair next to David Fine.

Over the exterior noise, Harris told Montgomery he'd like something on Billy Durant, the motorcar manufacturer who'd lost all interest in making anything but stock-market killings. The head of Durant Motors now even lived in Deal, New Jersey, from which he engaged in marathon speculation. "We could pose him next to a rusting car," said Harris. "Have him sitting on a solid-gold ticker."

"Good," said Andrew Burn. "I can sell Studebaker against the pages."

David Fine, pouting over the offer of something this flashy to Paul Montgomery, leaned toward Cuddles and asked him what the hell was going on outside.

"Well, Waldo's *here*," Cuddles explained, "but not exactly all there. He looks like he just put two medicine balls' worth of cocaine up his nose. Eyes like Cantor's. He was getting made up and saw a couple of the court kings taking off their pants. He apparently thought he was somewhere else and dropped to his knees."

"The rusty car and the solid-gold ticker!" exclaimed Paulie. "That's swell."

An agonized cry and some animal howling—plus the fleeing shadows of two shrieking girls beyond the frosted glass of the office door—finally made it impossible to continue the meeting. Spilkes went out to the corridor and hastened past Chip Brzezinski, who was again lurking beside Hazel's desk. Once inside Fashion, the managing editor found the Columbia center holding his behind and screaming to high heaven. Gardiner Arinopoulos, being pulled along by some leashed creature of uncertain species, rushed past Spilkes while Richard Lord, with the merest suggestion of his fingertips, propelled Waldo Lindstrom in the opposite direction. Once both photographer and model were ten yards distant from the Columbia center, Daisy commenced the gentle application of what she called an old Italian remedy to the boy's rear end. While massaging him with her drug-store cold cream, she explained to Spilkes that the mishap had occurred when Mr. Arinopoulos's ocelot, which he'd brought from Queens for his shoot with Lindstrom, had attacked the center, but only after the hoop-shooter had attacked Lindstrom, of whom the animal seemed unaccountably fond. It would have been much, much worse, Daisy explained, had Allen Case, with some soothing words and fearless petting, not coaxed the animal's teeth out of the boy's behind.

In fact, as Daisy narrated these events to Spilkes, the young athlete was offering to buy Allen a thick New York steak as a token of thanks. The copyeditor appeared not even to hear him; he was staring in the direction of Gardiner Arinopoulos, with something like murder in his eyes.

"You can keep the suits," Spilkes told the Columbia squad. The boys would have been given them in any case, ocelot or no ocelot, but they seemed surprised, and placated, by such generosity.

"See," said Spilkes, satisfied he had taken charge of the situation. "Everybody wins."

7

—*Are you looking at my knees?*

—*No, I'm way above that.*

Cuddles listened to the two Burns and Allen imitators who were closing the first half of the Palace's afternoon bill. With half-blue stuff like this it was no wonder he hadn't had to dodge any scalpers on the way in. He'd escaped from the editorial meeting just half a minute after Gardiner Arinopoulos's noisy departure. The photographer and his ocelot had still been on the sidewalk waiting for their car when Cuddles exited the Graybar Building. Except for a quick detour to Manking, where Takeshi unlocked his vodka bottle for several fortifying snorts, he'd taken a direct route to the theatre.

Having slept through Taylor Holmes's monologue from *Ruggles of Red Gap*—the sort of thing, no, the *exact* thing Holmes had been doing here since '13—Cuddles now decided to drift off for the rest of the afternoon. He slumped further into his seat and cast his half-closed eyes up to the vast chandeliers and plaster rosettes that had once made this gigantic enclosure at Broadway and Forty-seventh a heaven beyond Brigham Young's most wingèd, wild imagining. Now, of course, every burg half the size of Schenectady was getting its own lowercase movie "palace," and you couldn't deny that some of them were the equal of this tired paradise. Cuddles began, once more, to doze.

It would be untrue to say he had neglected giving the picture of Leopold and Loeb any thought this weekend, but equally false to claim that the minutes he'd spent pondering it had yielded any approach fresher than the time-honored, though frequently fallible, if-you-can't-lick-'em-join-'em approach. He'd imagined hoisting Jimmy Gordon on his own petard in a first-thing-Monday-morning pitch to 'Phat: "It *would* make a great ad!" *So Good It's Criminal* was the line of copy he'd considered telling Harris to stick beneath the photo of the canoodling killers.

But as Saturday had worn on, with Cuddles sleeping through three showings of *The Wreck of the Hesperus* at Proctor's Eighty-sixth Street, and Kitty Sark, his unfed cat, greeting his homecoming with howls from beneath the coffee table, this strategy began to look less inspired. On Sunday, Cuddles managed to rouse himself from the couch only long enough to serve the creature some anchovy-topped kibble: "I'd say you're six down, three to go, sport." KS showed no sign of appreciating this jauntily dire *bon appétit*.

Today, sleep was the only nourishment Cuddles himself craved, but his current helping of it was interrupted by a sharp poke in the ribs. The sight that met his opening eyes was not the Palace's celestial ceiling fixtures but Becky Walter in a purple cloche hat. Too startled to give her the "look," Cuddles managed to murmur: "You can't be my Gibson girl without a brim."

"This style affords greater warmth," she said, mimicking the fashion boilerplate that had so often passed between their desks. "And greater peripheral vision," she added, as severely as she could.

"How'd you find me?"

"You may not have noticed, but you're not cutting too wide a swath these days. After Takeshi told me you'd already drunk and run, BRYant 4300 sounded like the number to ring." Beatrice, at the Palace box office, had confirmed Cuddles' presence in one of the two seats she always kept for him in row G, center right.

"Why'd you bother with the edit meeting at all?" asked Becky, taking off her coat to sit down beside him.

"I've been asking myself the very same thing," answered Cuddles.

"You're tight."

"You're right."

"Shaddup already," said a voice from row H. The play-on music for Miss Patricola had already announced the second half, and the popular violin-playing songstress was entering to strong applause from regulars wondering whether she would begin her return to the Palace with "Me No Speaka Good English" or "Lovin' Sam (The Sheik of Alabam')."

"Listen to me," Becky whispered to Cuddles. "You've got one last—"

He pointed in the direction of Miss Patricola's violin, whose E string had begun wailing toward a first comic crescendo. "I'm seeing a distinguished afterlife for Kitty Sark," he said to Becky. "As top-of-the-line catgut. Worthy of a Stradivarius. Delighting the masses and the longhairs both. It'll be a far better world than the one he's known with me."

Becky shook her head, trying to figure out why she even bothered. "At least I didn't bring Case with me," she declared, realizing that Cuddles' catgut fantasy would have further strained the copy-editor's nerves. What poor creatures laid off from the circus for the winter, she now wondered, had done the opening animal act here this afternoon? She looked down at her program: oh, Fink's Mules. She'd seen them once, years ago, with her father and mother, in Buffalo. An act benign enough for even Case, though not for the poor colored sap who had to get kicked by the supposedly high-IQ livestock.

Miss Patricola surrendered the stage to two aging precursors of Gallagher and Shean.

—I said goodbye to the train and jumped on my girl,
one informed the other, prompting Cuddles to mutter, "Jesus, this routine has hair on it."

Becky hissed: "Exactly what are you accomplishing here?"

"I *was*—more or less—waiting for Dr. Julian Siegel, official dentist to the National Vaudeville Association. But then you put your attractive backside into the seat I'd saved for him."

"Oh, really?" asked Becky. "When was he 'more or less' supposed to meet you?"

"Anytime this month. He's been pitching himself as a subject. Maybe Fine could write the piece, what do you think? 'This Guy's Act Is Like Pullin' Teeth!' "

"Tell me, are you going to put this story on Harris's desk before or after he fires you?"

Cuddles hesitated a moment before responding. "After, I think. It'll make him miss me."

Becky closed her eyes, trying to decide how to stanch the flow of quips and get him to concentrate. It was time to reach for the strongest tourniquet she had.

"*Aloysius?*" she asked.

Cuddles' given name had ages ago been replaced with this back-formation from an adjective offered, at a supper party, by Mrs. Theodore Dreiser to her husband: "Mr. Houlihan seems such a *cuddly* man." Months, sometimes years, now passed between utterances of "Aloysius," but Becky had waited a moment too long to shock Cuddles with the sound of his real moniker. The wheezing comic duo were gone; the houselights were down; and the afternoon's main attraction had stepped, all alone, into the next-to-closing spotlight.

"Soft," said Cuddles. "She speaks."

It was the great Nazimova. She had been playing the theatre, off and on, for almost as long as Taylor Holmes, inserting a cash-filled week at the Palace into her more stately schedule of Strindberg and Ibsen. With the first syllables from her throat, she reclaimed the house, stunning everyone from stagehands to Fink's most ornery mule into rapt silence. Her offering today was "India," a twenty-five-minute playlet in which she became a purple-saried young matron of the subcontinent, angrily mourning the baby trampled to death during a parade the local rajah had scared up for some visiting English prince. Assisted by two actors who might as well have been props, Nazimova proceeded, in less than half an hour, to make moving pictures seem a Coney Island contrivance, and their recent voice an unsynchronized joke. By the time she was through, everyone in the audience wanted to don a bedsheet and spin cotton with Gandhi, or just go out and pop the snoot of the first limey they found crossing Forty-seventh Street.

Cuddles was actually wiping a tear when the lights came up. "You know," he said, sniffling, "you could have brought Case. She really didn't blame the elephant."

The Watson Sisters, Kitty and Fanny, had the thankless task of following Nazimova and closing the show. Midway through the girls' duet, Cuddles leaned over to Becky and asked: "How about a late, late lunch at Manking? The boys looked like they were getting ready to do something special with a yak when I dropped in this morning."

"No," she replied. "You're coming with me." The moment the curtain dropped, she began propelling him, by his elbow, up the aisle. She was grateful for the help provided by the orchestra's peppy recessional march, a surviving feature of the Palace's shaky but still-in-place policy of only two shows a day. At almost any other vaude house, Fink's Mules would already be back on stage.

Becky hustled Cuddles past the lobby's electric piano and out the door, into air that over the weekend had gone from frigid to merely brisk. "Get that cab," she commanded.

"What for?"

"It'll be the most legitimate item on your expense sheet this month," she promised, pulling him into the backseat and directing the driver to Broadway and Sixty-fifth.

Alarmed by the apparent specificity of her plan, Cuddles started to squirm. He looked out the taxi's rear window and muttered: "I'd thought I might go and find Dr. Siegel, the molar jockey. His office is the other way." The cab was already clattering toward its destination, and Becky remained resolutely silent until it stopped, at her order, in front of the Macfadden Building.

Cuddles looked up and made a grim deduction. "You made an appointment for me in Personnel."

No serious editor wanted to work here. In the world of print, Bernarr Macfadden, the frizzily pompadoured czar of Macfadden Publications—crazy with crusading belief in exercise, eugenics, free love, and cole slaw; just as ululant against booze, tobacco, and censorship—made Joe Harris look more buttoned-up than Coolidge. But Becky said nothing as she maneuvered Cuddles through the lobby and into an elevator car.

He pointed to the white-gloved operator and feigned calm: "So where's the indoor aviator taking us?"

The car rose to the floor for *Physical Culture,* at which two muscle-men got off and three got on. It continued upward past *True Romances,* the magazine at which Becky sometimes feared *she* would wind up, should Joe Harris lose his war with Jimmy Gordon. Finally, the elevator stopped at the floor for the New York *Evening Graphic.* Becky tugged Cuddles forward.

"Jesus, Mary, and Joseph Smith," he whispered. "The Ninth Circle itself."

For the past four years the *Graphic* had been Macfadden's tabloid orgy of tub-thumping and titillation. Electric fans blew a sickly sweet smell toward Cuddles and Becky as they advanced, like Hansel and Gretel, onto the floor where it was produced. The *Graphic* had not entirely recovered from its experiment with perfumed ink, and even now persisted in publishing itself each night on pink news-print. At the far end of the newsroom—a term even the most loyal employee here used only loosely—Cuddles could recognize Emile Gauvreau, the respectable, constantly agonized managing editor Mac-fadden had hired to run the rag. Limping back and forth between two desks, tugging on his black forelock, Gauvreau was trying to decide which story to lead with tonight. Would the *Graphic*'s dis-tinctive vertiginous headline, each letter a skinny skyscraper unto itself, go to a missing Smith College co-ed or to the sixty-year-old Episcopal rector with marriage on his mind?

"She's five-five, a hundred and thirty. Busty," said the reporter ar-guing the Smith girl's case.

"The rev's temptress is thirty years old, half the geezer's age," came the opposing point of view. "And she's Catholic."

"The Smithie's father's a broker. They're Social Register. Up in Northampton they've got Boy Scouts *dragging a pond,* for Christ's sake."

It was a tough call for Gauvreau; Becky looked at the clock and decided there was no time to wait for him to make it. She pushed Cuddles along toward their final destination here. The *Graphic* had no foreign desk to block their way, but the two of them did have to pass the health-foods editor and the columnist who analyzed readers' handwriting before they reached the Photo Department.

"Mr. Wender, please," said Becky.

"Hey, Jerry!" shouted a boy at the department's first desk. "You gotta goil here!"

"Becks!" cried a slender fellow who, as he came running, looked not much older than the boy who'd summoned him. "Watch out for my hands," he said, managing to keep Becky free from inkstains while he gave her a hug. Cuddles, bewildered about his business here, made a jealous pout.

Jerry Wender, Becky explained, was a townie she used to date in Aurora, New York, when she was going to Wells. "He's the Composograph man," she announced. Jerry swelled with professional pride: the *Graphic's* notorious composite photographs, their fakery disclaimed in four-point type under the caption, were the tabloid's major draw.

"My masterpiece," said Jerry, rushing back to his desk to fetch a print. "At least until now."

The photo he brought out depicted Daddy Browning and Peaches Heenan, the city's most famous, if recently estranged, sugar daddy and gold digger. The once-happy couple were wearing what looked like harem outfits and awaiting the suggestive *à trois* attentions of a dancing girl.

"Too hot for Emile to run," said Jerry.

Cuddles and Becky nodded in unfeigned admiration, before she broke the silence to ask: "Jerry, you said something about this being your masterpiece 'until now'?"

"You bet, Becks!" He dashed back to his desk for a just-dried print that he triumphantly placed between her gloved hands.

What she saw in the picture was, she knew, monstrously false, and yet it had the appearance of absolute, Hogarthian truth. In short, it was better than she had dared to hope. The 1926 Christmas-party photograph of Jimmy Gordon that she had located at *Bandbox* on Saturday morning had been wondrously transformed in the forty-eight hours since she'd given it to Jerry with her confidential instructions. In the original photo, taken of Jimmy while he conversed with Richard Lord, the subject's facial expression had appeared argumentative. But now, Jimmy's head, seamlessly attached to someone else's body—and put beside a burlesque queen, whose hand rested in that body's lap—appeared to be expressing a sort of lubricious ecstasy.

"Oh, Jerry!" cried Becky, her face flushed not just from the air out on Broadway but a new hopefulness as well. "What do I owe you?"

"Nothin', kid," said Jerry. "Old times." He ran back for two extra prints of the picture.

Cuddles was too impressed by Jerry's latest work to notice, let alone begrudge, the kiss Becky now planted smack on her old boyfriend's lips.

"Okay," she said, wheeling around. "Let's go." Rolling up the photographs, Becky pushed Cuddles back into the *Graphic*'s newsroom. They dodged the staff's mandatory late-afternoon calisthenics on their rush to the elevator.

"Going down!" she cried.

"Could happen yet," said Cuddles.

8

"It's the scissors," said Harris, on the phone to Betty for the eleventh time that day. "Dmitri's in the office cutting my hair. I can't tell him to stop."

It amazed him that Betty could hear the shears but misapprehend at least one crucial word in each paragraph he spoke to her. Actually, it amazed him that she could hear *anything* at all with Mukluk yapping at her feet all the time, here in the Graybar and at home in the Warwick.

"Order up an early supper," he suggested. "I'm too jumpy for the Crillon." He'd been explaining the morning's fracas before Dmitri's scissors went into overdrive.

Dmitri, whose real name, never remembered by Harris, was Nicos, beavered away until his most important client got off the phone. Now the barber could give him the kind of stock tip he came in here with every two weeks. Today it was on a new company with a line of hair relaxants for Negro women.

"I tell you, Mr. Harris," said the barber, replacing the receiver for his customer. "It make these girls' heads look not even Italian. You'd think they was Roumanian or Polish. *Long,* straight hair I'm talking about. Down to their shoulders if they want."

After a long pause, Harris asked: "Did I ever tell you my old man used to cut hair?"

"No kidding," said Nicos, with a disappointed sigh. He'd heard about old man Haldeweiss's vocation at least a dozen times.

Other facts of Harris's life were conveyed with less regularity and truth during Nicos's office visits, but the barber had a good memory, and he'd learned to sort the more reliable pieces of autobiography into something like a chronological whole, the way he kept track of his margin purchases and all the mortgages he'd assumed over in Queens.

He could tell you how Harris had come to New York in the mid-nineties, after ten years on the Newburgh *Messenger;* how once on Park Row he'd done everything from the police beat at the *Recorder* to chasing down society items for Ward McAllister on the *World.* Theatre, books, City Hall: it had been a tiptop education for a writer and an even better one for an editor, which is what Harris really needed to be from the start, since he was prone to blowups with the editors he wrote *for.*

If his life at the papers had been a prolonged shouting match, his life at home had been—Nicos knew all this, too—perpetual silence. Harris would flee the company of his frosty wife, a Quaker school-teacher, for long, late-night association with his fellow reporters as well as the ad men, who kept the papers alive with their rate cards and column inches. All the oysters and beer he'd shared with them thirty years ago now allowed him to speak Andrew Burn's language—Oldcastle's, too.

Harris had switched over to magazines, and editing, around 1907, learning to ride each new publisher's hobbyhorse. Several years after the switch, at bellicose *Collier's,* he got his writers to beat the drum for American intervention in the Great War, editing a couple of pieces by TR himself, whose steel trap of a smile sometimes still flashed in his anxiety dreams. A few years later, at *Cosmopolitan,* he'd pretended the war didn't exist, since Hearst opposed it and felt sure it would end if his outlets ignored it.

Even as an editor, Harris had gotten into more than anyone's share of battles. His career at *Cosmopolitan* came to an end over an article about some Broadway composer whose name he couldn't remember today. He'd been sold on the guy by some writer, and so he went into Ray Long asking for plenty of space. "This fella is the next Berlin," he'd insisted. "He's not even the next Irving," replied Long, handing him back the writer's copy. Loud words and clenched fists followed. Ten minutes later Harris was out on the sidewalk.

He knew then that his only real hope in this business was an editor-in-chief's job, but at that moment, a half-dozen years ago, every top man had been firmly nailed to his masthead. And so, for a couple of years, already past fifty and finally divorced, Harris trudged through a dank professional wilderness—peddling pseudonymous pieces to old pals; toiling as a freelance adsmith for a half-dozen hatters and cigar-makers; even turning out that lucrative line of "French" postcards from an office down on Pearl Street. Only Fine and Houlihan knew the whole story of this last venture; even Betty still euphemized it as "that time you were between things." But Harris never disowned the enterprise. He kept two of its most shining pictorial productions— the unclad "Yvette" and the *déshabillée* "Claudine," actually two Irish sisters from Canarsie—framed on a wall to the left of his desk.

Right now, Nicos, finishing up the back of Harris's neck, took a fond glance at Yvette and listened for any sign that his customer might be approaching a mood for some two-sided conversation. Since getting off the phone with Betty, Harris had kept unusually silent. In fact, he was dwelling, however inwardly, on the triumphant climax of his personal epic—the advent of Betty and *Bandbox*. He had met the bubbling antithesis of his first wife through an old thespian warhorse whose musical he'd been nice to, ages before, in the pages of the *World*. That 1906 production had also employed a too-short chorine named Betty Divine. Seventeen years later, the ancient ac-tress's gratitude toward Harris, and her kindness toward Betty, led both of them to this Duse's dressing room for another opening night. And two weeks after that, Betty, fully briefed on Joe Harris's career, by Joe Harris himself, brought him to dinner with Hi Oldcastle.

Harris's sense that he owed Betty his big job and late success had never bothered him until now. It had actually been a part of the pride he took in his smart, doll-like paramour. But he could never quite believe the pride she took in *him,* his first wife having cauterized certain precincts of his ego. He was unable to shake the idea, which had draped him all this past weekend, that if he lost *Bandbox,* he might lose Betty, too.

Nervous again at this thought, he decided to get back to business. He reached for the unopened envelope full of Gardiner Arinopoulos's just-developed, just-delivered pictures, the ones the photographer had managed to take after hotfooting it out of here this morning with that freaky animal and dope addict. Harris would concentrate on the material, be resolute, decisive. He vacated his swivel chair before Nicos could even remove the bib, now covered with his gray and black hair. "No, thanks," he said, deflecting the whisk broom from his own shoulders; Mukluk would only be shedding all over him in a couple of hours' time.

"Hazel!" cried Harris, pulling Nicos through the open door. "Give Dmitri ten bucks." He shook hands with the barber, whose payment interrupted Hazel's attention to *True Story.* Harris was always too afraid to tell her that if she spent half as much time doing Oldcastle business as she did reading Macfadden's magazines, he might give her a raise. As it was, he gave her a raise whenever she asked.

Down the long hallway, just this side of Mrs. Zimmerman's desk, the countess was conversing with Max Stanwick, who had stayed around after the morning's chaos to bang an Underwood in somebody's vacant office. The two of them waved to Harris before he went back behind his frosted glass.

"As I was saying, Mr. Stanwick," breathed Daisy DiDonna, four inches from Stanwick's face. "I just adored your piece."

Max, who had just seen the third proof of his article on Arnold Rothstein, felt an instant, tumescent gratitude. "I thank you. And I thank you again for correcting my underestimation of Mr. Big's shoe size."

"Not at all," declared the countess, coming even closer, causing Max to wonder why he had spent the day banging the Underwood instead of Daisy. He knew, of course. Now living over in Brooklyn Heights with a wife and two little girls, he was reformed to the point of uxoriousness. But he had to remind himself of all this as Daisy blinked her lashes rather more than was necessary. For her part, Daisy had just begun to wonder why she had ever bothered unshoeing Rothstein when she could have been—could be even now—massaging Max's intrepid and no doubt equally large feet.

But then she recalled the new determination she'd begun feeling Friday night, and managed to retract her face a full two inches from Max's. No, no more lost, or even short-term, causes. She had to begin thinking of a future beyond her cramped little room on Beekman Place.

She didn't relax her smile, but she straightened her spine.

"I have such pleasant memories of the evening I spent in Mr. Rothstein's company," she told Max. "Perhaps especially of my ride with Mr. Diamond—Edward, that is, not Legs—who was kind enough to take me home."

Max wondered where this was going.

"But, silly me," continued Daisy. "I promised to send him a copy of my book and then misplaced the address he gave me. I don't suppose that *you* . . ."

Max smiled. So Daisy must be lovelorn; or just having a slow month. Well, if the old trouper in front of him could handle Rothstein himself, she could handle any of Mr. Big's lieutenants. But didn't she deserve somebody nicer than Eddie Diamond? "Sure," said Max, extracting a pen and small piece of paper from his breast pocket. "But, Countess, I can do better than that. *This* is a name worthy of an accomplished, wellborn gal like yourself." He wrote out the address of a recently widowed judge, one of Rothstein's most dependable possessions on the city bench, and handed it to Daisy.

Recognizing the name, she closed in on Max's face and purred, from an inch and a half away: "Wait right here." She went racing, on her tiny high heels, down the corridor and around the corner, returning half a minute later with a copy of *My Antonio* from her diminishing stash. "Could I have been more *rude*?" she said, while inscribing it. "I just realized I've never given *you* one of these."

Max regarded the frontispiece of this volume, widely known around the office as *Going Down for the Count,* and thanked her: "It will be a thrill to crawl between your covers, Countess."

Daisy rapped his knuckles and laughed a brave little laugh, tucking the judge's name and address into the top of her stocking while, with her free hand, she waved goodbye. Max, running late, rushed past the reception desk—"Gotta zoom zestily, Mrs. Z"—and boarded the elevator just as Cuddles and Becky were getting off it.

They were in an even greater hurry, but their double-timing down the corridor was stopped by a low-voiced greeting from Stuart Newman's office: "Becky?"

Politeness overtook urgency, and she halted Cuddles at the open door with a tug on his elbow. The two of them entered Newman's space, where a half-dozen bottles of cologne, all of them open, stood on the desk.

"Sorry about the stink," he said, woozily. "Harris has me doing this comparative thing on men's fragrances. I guess I reek."

What he reeked of most was implausibility. Becky knew from the more lucid moments of this morning's meeting that Stuart, in between "Bachelor's Life" columns, was supposed to be at work on something quite different from men's cologne. "What happened to your piece on Shipwreck Kelly?" she asked.

Newman appeared to have forgotten his assignment to write about the flagpole sitter. "Could I talk to you, soon, about Rosemary LaRoche? He's got me on *that* now, too." The screen siren, admired hotly from afar by Harris, had agreed to be *Bandbox*'s first female cover subject, a stunt the editor-in-chief hoped to spring on news-stand customers before Jimmy Gordon thought of doing something similar. "I don't know anything about the movies," Newman confessed, in his little-boy's voice.

"Sure," said Becky, deciding not to be annoyed that Harris had given this prime Hollywood subject to someone else. You couldn't reasonably expect him to have another woman writing about *that* woman, when the whole point of the article would be to have the slavering male scribe whip up the excited male readers—a bit like Boy Scouts in a shared tent, if she could believe the tales her little brother used to harrow her with.

"First thing tomorrow morning, if you like," she told Stuart, tugging Cuddles back into the corridor.

"What's with the field hand's workload?" asked Houlihan, once they were over the threshold. "Is 'Phat trying to drive this guy back to the sauce?"

"I think he's trying to keep him *off* it. If it's not too late already," Becky replied, considering the open cologne bottles and Newman's rheumy eyes. "But there's no time for that now." They had arrived at Hazel's desk. Becky asked if she might borrow an envelope. Hazel shrugged from behind *True Story:* "Be my guest."

"Now, listen," Becky told Cuddles. "You keep the third copy." She put one print of the photo into his hand and sealed up the other two for Harris. They would leave it for him, without explanation, like a foundling in a basket. Becky wouldn't dream of owning up to the authorship of this fraud she was perpetrating (if Daniel even knew she'd set *foot* in the *Graphic*'s offices!); and Cuddles' battered sense of chivalry would never let him take credit for what any girl—let alone herself—had done to pull his chestnuts out of the fire.

"Slide it under the door," suggested Hazel, without looking up. "Half of what's incoming doesn't exactly make it over the finish line. He's more likely to notice if he trips over it."

"Thanks." Becky motioned Cuddles back to his office. She then went to her own, and waited to see what would happen. She thrummed her fingers on the desktop and tried to look at the pile of press agents' letters that had arrived in the few hours she'd been gone, but she was too nervous to concentrate on their braying superlatives.

"W-w-would you like some r-r-raisins?" asked Allen Case, who, still grateful for her solicitude this morning, was now at her door.

"No, thanks, Allen. Have I missed much?"

Case was about to tell her something, but the first syllables of whatever it was remained locked on his palate while Harris came loudly bounding out of his office, sporting a smile even fresher than his haircut. Becky got up to join the copyeditor at her doorway.

"Mr. Lord!" cried Harris, summoning the art director into the hall, so that everyone could hear their conversation. He detested solitude when he was happy; any upturn in fortune demanded an audience.

"I don't want a month to go by without more animal pictures from Arinopoulos! That stuff he shot at lunchtime is unbelievable. What do you call the thing nuzzling Lindstrom's behind? A cheetah? A ferret? Whatever it is, it makes the coat look grand! Tell him we want rhinos, pterodactyls, whatever. Get the critters what they like to eat and keep 'em shiny with that spray. More snakes! More of everything!"

Allen Case had gone so white that Becky put an arm around his shoulders. She wished she could tell him that he needn't worry. She knew what photograph Harris was *really* excited over. The boss just needed something to crow about while he deployed the actual object of his glee on its delicate mission.

Spilkes had come into the corridor to give Lord and Harris "a well-deserved pat on the back." Becky edged past them toward Hazel's desk. The boss's secretary had already left, but Becky was able to confirm her hopeful surmise about Harris's elation when she saw Chip Brzezinski at Hazel's OUT box. He was carefully undoing the string on a manila envelope that was boldly addressed, in Harris's own hand, to JIMMY GORDON, *CUTAWAY*, 18TH FLOOR. Standing silently behind Chip, she, too, could read the bold strokes Harris had applied, from the fattest of his fountain pens, to the back of the incriminating Composograph: WOULD MAKE A GREAT SOUVE-NIR FOR JOANNA, MELVIN AND MICHAEL. Jimmy Gordon's wife and two boys out in Garden City. The boys were actually Mortimer and Monroe, but Jimmy would get the point.

Becky reached around Chip to pick up a rubber stamp from Hazel's desk.

"Oh!" he said, stuffing the picture back inside its envelope. "It's, uh, already marked," he told Becky.

"I know it is," she said, before she pressed the OUTGOING stamp against Chip's ever more sizable forehead. "So are you."

9

John Shepard had been traveling for twelve hours. After hitchhiking from Greencastle to Indianapolis, he had boarded an eastbound train. For most of the eight hours since, John had sat up straight in his cane seat while the train made stops in Anderson and Muncie and Union City and—rather to John's amazement—sped through big towns like McCordsville and Versailles without a halt.

"Another piece of pie, hon?"

"Thanks, but I'd better not," John told the waitress. Here in the Hotel Cleveland it was a quarter to three in the morning, and his stomach was too excited to hold anything more. His first sight of Cleveland's Public Square had so astonished him that for a moment he thought he might somehow already be at his final destination, New York City. The almost-finished Terminal Tower, still sheathed in scaffolding, was the tallest building John had ever seen. He had stood there at 2:30 A.M., counting its fifty-two stories. Through the window of the hotel's all-night coffee shop, he could see vast new excavations and steel skeletons all over the square, some of them flooded with electric light, although right now the world seemed to be inhabited by no one besides himself and the waitress putting away the apple pie.

Five hours remained until the first *Limited* left for New York. John looked across the coffee shop's big tiled floor and spotted the door to the men's washroom, no doubt a much cleaner jake than the one he'd visited on the train out of Indy. He imagined he must be needing a shave about now, though a manly stroking of his chin revealed, to his disappointment, no great growth since he'd last used a razor, so many hours ago in an entirely different state of the Union. Maybe he'd let any new whiskers go until he reached New York.

The train he'd be taking there was no *Twentieth Century*—it carried no barber, let alone a stock ticker—but there *would* be a valet to take care of his coat, and there would be stationery. The brochure he'd picked up along with his ticket promised all that, and John had hours ago decided that once he got hold of this writing paper he would use it to compose an explanation of his sudden flight. The *Cleveland Limited* letterhead would impress his mother, but be less brutal than the one-two punch of "New York, N.Y.," which by tomorrow—no, *this*—evening would be heading all John Shepard's communications to the world he had left behind.

He bet the seats on the Cleveland–New York run would be upholstered, and that his traveling companions would be a better class of person than the Hoosier salesmen he'd had to hear all night telling those awful stories about the unimaginable things they'd lately gotten girls from Fort Wayne and Gary to do. Recalling those men, John guessed they thought they were pretty smooth. But you wouldn't find Stuart Newman, who had ten times their experience with girls ten times as pretty, offering such loud confidences in what John's mother would call "language." He imagined Newman as he must be right now, asleep in some New York tower even taller than the one being built for the terminal here. The columnist's silk robe would be draped over a leather armchair, while he lay under the blankets in patterned pajamas covering a torso newly toned by an hour of boxing at the New York Athletic Club, probably with some fellow writer or young company president.

After a moment, with his eyes loosely focused on some crumbs of pie crust toward the edge of his plate, John realized that, inside his revery, it was now *he,* John Shepard, sleeping high atop New York, dreaming of a girl across town who could *not* sleep, so busy was she, looking at his picture in a silver frame beside her bed.

Worried that the waitress might close up if he appeared idle, John took a sip of his cooling coffee and opened up his magazine. Seeing the ad for Interwoven Socks, he curled his own toes with satisfaction. He had in his suitcase one pair of that very product, purchased this afternoon in Indianapolis. What he'd really wanted from the window of Lazarus's Department Store was a Kuppenheimer trench coat, but he could hardly afford one of those and had settled on the socks as a *bon voyage* present to himself. An excellent choice! he now decided, noticing the ad copy at the bottom of the page. *Stepping forth in his ribbed Interwoven argyles, our "Bandbox" man is ready for any place his feet may carry him to. . . .*

10

Stuart Newman reached through a hole in his union suit to scratch his stomach. He opened his eyes. Had he left the water running? No, the steady slurp of sound making itself heard above the radiator's clanging aubade was static from the radio, which he must have left on past the announcer's sign-off, before falling asleep here on the couch.

He rose and went into the bathroom, noticing as he pulled on the light that the circles under his eyes were darker than the last time he'd looked. He still hadn't had a drink, but he could no longer deny it: sobriety was killing him. The effort to stave off surrender, to sub-stitute the inhalation of setting lotion and cologne for the ingestion of bathtub gin, had exhausted his willpower and body. The other day he'd asked his masseur, three times, to slap on more witch hazel, and had sensed, over his shoulder, between hand chops, the look the guy was giving him.

Would he really, Newman wondered, be any worse off going around half-hammered, like Houlihan? Harris displayed only slightly more contempt toward Cuddles than himself, and Houlihan still en-joyed the tender ministrations of Becky Walter. Alas, when it came to booze, Newman knew he could do nothing by halves; once the sniffing of witch hazel gave way to the first sip of beer, he'd be a goner.

Newman had the smallest apartment in this old pile at the south-west corner of Gramercy Park. When the bishop who'd once owned it passed on, the building had done the familiar real estate divide into a half-dozen flats, including Newman's on the first floor at the back. With two fingers he now cracked open the kitchen blinds. Frost clung to the window, but the sunlight coming through it was strong enough to make him wince. Should he try to summon enough vitality to go out? Perhaps even attempt to sit in the park? Every renter got a key to that gated, cherished space, but Newman had received *two* keys from his widowed landlady, a few days after his arrival; the second one, he gathered, would open up her apartment.

Were he to go out and sit on one of the benches, what facts might he finally face, before they and the cold got the better of him? That he had just turned thirty-five, with less money and fewer prospects than he had had at thirty? That, these days, the elaborate courting rituals and male/female psychology that filled his column barely figured in his own romantic life—which consisted, more and more, of just picking up secretaries from Metropolitan Life as they walked past the statue of Roscoe Conkling in nearby Madison Square? The cushions of Newman's couch hid so many of their hairpins, powder puffs, and gumdrops that several times, after falling asleep there, he had dreamed he was clerking in a five-and-ten.

The telephone rang.

"Valentino," said the unmistakable voice of his boss. "Be in the Oak Room of the Plaza at two o'clock sharp. After my charm has thoroughly aroused LaRoche, I'll introduce her to you, the man who'll be explaining her to our supposedly discerning readers. *Two o'clock*."

Before Newman could say yes, Harris left the line. Newman groped for his father's pocket watch amidst a spillage of coins on the bedroom dresser and discovered to his relief that it was indeed only 7:20; he could now safely assume that Harris had called here not after failing to find him in his office, but from sheer lustful exuberance over the prospect of lunch with Rosemary LaRoche.

Newman rummaged under yesterday's *World* and socks, until he found the copy of *Motion Picture* he'd bought yesterday afternoon. Its long article about Rosemary LaRoche mentioned that she had been born Lucille Monahan in Hutchinson, Kansas. In any print profile, the star's actual name was always a permissible revelation (it encouraged a ticket buyer's own fantasies of re-invention), and even

Stuart, unaccustomed as he was to following the movies, already knew that the central, terrible event of LaRoche's life was her divorce from Howard Kenyon, filmdom's favorite pirate and swordsman. According to *Motion Picture,* the "grueling demands of a shared art" had "sundered the pulchritudinous pair," leaving Miss LaRoche to live alone in a modest new house in the Hollywood Hills. And yet, however bleak her romantic life, her professional outlook was brighter than ever: a sultry low voice assured her smooth transition to talkies.

But some of the magazine's facts didn't quite add up. Did a "Parisian music master"—just passing through Hutchinson?—really give her the proficiency in French that would one day deepen her performance as the soubrette in *Chanson*? Could she really be just twenty-three? Newman could swear he'd seen her take a pie in the face in some two-reeler more than a decade ago.

Becky would know more, he thought, closing his puffy, ringed eyes.

I I

"Mr. Brzezinski to see you, sir."

Use of the Wood Chipper's last name—let alone with an honorific—was sufficiently rare to make Jimmy Gordon wonder for a second who might be at his door.

"Let him in."

Once past the threshold, Chip noticed the phony Composograph on Jimmy's desk. But he also could see that it was off to the side;

Cutaway's editor was absorbed by a single sheet of paper, full of numbers and lines, right in front of him.

"Pour yourself some coffee," said Jimmy.

"I think I know what happened," said Chip, pointing nervously to the photo.

Jimmy Gordon waved his hand. "Not interested. You know, that's one difference between me and old Joe. I'm always interested in what somebody'll do *next* for me."

Chip stared at Jimmy and waited to hear what that might be. In some respects, he was looking at an older version of himself. At forty, Jimmy Gordon tended toward stockiness and, like Chip, had begun to bald. But the overall roughness, which the Wood Chipper came by naturally, was a matter of affectation in Jimmy, who was, in fact, the son of a judge. He'd gone to Princeton and stayed on two years past graduation to start a doctorate in English literature, even beginning a thesis on *The Faerie Queene,* whose title brought hoots of laughter from the tough-guy writers he now took out for steaks at Keen's. He'd quit the university upon realizing—as he explained years later to Joe Harris—that "there are no winners in philology." Leaving New Jersey for Chicago, he'd gone to work in 1914 for Colonel McCormick, editing a couple of correspondents posted to Mexico to cover the revolution. NO EVIDENCE OF ATROCITIES, one of them cabled home two weeks into Jimmy's tenure. YOU DISAPPOINT ME, he cabled back, knowing then he'd found his calling.

He would later put in several years at muckraking *McClure's,* but even there it was really carnage Jimmy craved, not crusades. Harris had found him at that declining journal, and decided he was just the man to put some thick slices of red meat between the gently rustling pages of the old *Bandbox*. Freed from uplift, Jimmy soon brought in bull after bull to bust up the china shop Oldcastle had given Joe. For almost four years they'd shared delight in the breakage and the noise, until Jimmy decided, inevitably, that the shop was too small for the two of them.

"For what it's worth," said the Wood Chipper, "I did bring you this." He handed Jimmy a galley he'd nicked from the *Bandbox* Copy Department: the Rothstein profile by Jimmy's onetime prize bull, Max Stanwick.

Jimmy swapped the sheet of figures on his desk for the galley. "Take a look," he told Chip. "These numbers ought to scare Joe more than Leopold diddling Loeb."

Having left school at twelve, Chip found the decimal-dappled columns hard to comprehend, but the two lines on a graph near the bottom were more scrutable. *Cutaway*'s trended up; *Bandbox*'s headed in the other direction.

Chip raised his eyes to see that Jimmy was muttering some of the best lines in Max's piece: the brutish *bons mots* from "Fats" Walsh, Rothstein's bodyguard, and the subject's own description of a Rubens he'd won in a card game as "a dirty picture of a fat naked woman." He chuckled when he came to Joe Harris's annotation of that line: *Can we get an illo of this gal?*

"So what's the old man up to?" Jimmy asked his informant.

Chip had hoped to be here today with a tale of Harris's desperation over the picture his own old man had sent from Joliet. That scheme having fizzled, he could offer Jimmy only an account of yesterday's chaos in the Fashion Department: the swing at Lindstrom's kisser, the bite out of the basketballer's can; Harris's bellowed pox on everyone involved—and his equally loud contentment once Arinopoulos's pictures came back. Jimmy Gordon smiled at the story's opening, and laughed out loud over its close, making the Wood Chipper realize that his patron, albeit in full battle dress, still *liked* his old boss.

"I guess you always hurt the one you love," said Chip, remembering something from that last year he'd spent in school.

"The word is *kill,* not hurt, Mr. Brzezinski."

The Wood Chipper nodded and made ready to leave.

"Let's go over to the Commodore," said Jimmy. "I'll buy you breakfast and tell you what you're going to do for me next."

12

"So what was that thing? Some kind of zebra?"

"An OCELOT, Mr. Harris," answered Gardiner Arinopoulos.

"Right. Spots," said Harris. "Anyway, the pictures are excellent. Now, how was Lindstrom? Cooperative?"

"MUCH better once he'd had his LUNCH. Your pal Roma sent over two silver tins of magnificent STUFF."

"Yeah," said Harris, who avoided thinking too deeply about the efforts Malocchio's owner had been making to get into Waldo Lindstrom's trousers ever since Harris had brought the model to the restaurant, for the first and last time, about six months ago. "He's, uh, an admirer of his artistry, I suppose. As I am of yours. Now I'll tell you what I'd like next. We've got to do some more neckwear soon. How about decking some ostriches out in ties and ascots?"

"A FINE idea," said Arinopoulos.

"See what we've got back there."

"A PLEASURE," declared the flamboyant photographer, already on his feet. Arinopoulos had much invested in his image as a great lover and artist, though his success with women and pictures tended to be as random as the accented syllables in his loud, rushed conversation.

"Don't forget your pith helmet," said Harris, handing Arinopoulos what was actually an Australian army slouch hat.

The editor-in-chief's afternoons usually got washed away by late lunches at Malocchio, but he made up for that by putting in a full day every morning. Now, at 8:00 A.M., Harris had already been at his desk for over an hour; and he felt fine.

Leopold and Loeb lay in pieces in the wastebasket, while the photograph with the showgirl's hand in Jimmy Gordon's lap lay face up on the blotter. Harris assumed it had been taken at some joint they'd all gone to after a sales conference, and that Houlihan had recalled it was lying around here on the premises. Well, fine, though one useful flicker of activity wasn't going to absolve Cuddles of the past two years of lovesick goldbricking.

He was about to dial Betty when Hazel's voice sawed through the closed door. "Go on in," she told the arrivals. "He ain't busy."

Andrew Burn and Norman Spilkes entered the office.

"Oh, Jesus," said Harris. "It was such a beautiful morning, too."

"No, no," said Spilkes, his mirthless smile coming and going as fast as a salute. "Everything's fine. Or certainly will be."

"You need to see this," said Burn, who never soft-pedaled. "Some numbers from GME."

Each quarter the Gotham Magazine Editors gathered up and distributed advertising and circulation figures throughout the industry. Spilkes was all in favor of this efficient innovation, but the GME had now begun making graphic, invidious comparisons, and when Andrew Burn handed Harris the same sheet of numbers Jimmy Gordon had just seen, the editor-in-chief could only grumble: "Why can't they stick to giving awards?"

He put on his glasses. Harris could read the figures with only a little more skill than Chip Brzezinski, but he felt the meaning of the graph like the point of a sword.

"There's nothing to panic over here," said Spilkes. "But as a precaution, just to keep from losing our edge, I've commissioned a little market research. We'll be getting together some groups of subscribers and asking them to discuss whatever they like or don't like about the magazine. It's what we did at the phone company a couple of years back. We talked to customer clusters in Fairfield County and New Hav—"

" 'Customer clusters'?" asked Harris. "And what precisely did you find out?"

"They indicated a near-uniform preference for lower charges."

"Thanks for the revelation. When I get back the monopoly *I* used to enjoy, I'll have you do your market research. Let me tell you something, Norman—there's only one way to edit, and it's not by sticking your finger into the wind. You've got to go by the seat of your pants, be decisive. You don't want Hamlet for an editor. Othello—now *there's* an editor-in-chief." Harris looked at Andrew Burn. "You, Iago, what's the story?"

"It isn't good," said Burn. "Marmon and Pierce-Arrow are thinking about doing business with Jimmy's man unless we drop the ad rate."

The doctored Composograph might already be yesterday's victory, but one more glance at it emboldened Harris to raise his voice: "Go back to each of the car guys and tell 'em to take *two* pages in *Cutaway,* if they want. Jimmy Gordon will be all they can afford after a few more ideas of mine kick in. Like this one. Remember?" He went into his top drawer for Rosemary LaRoche's perfumed, pink note accepting their lunch date. He held it up so that Burn and Spilkes could get a whiff. "Have a little patience, you two. Have a little faith. Once she's on the cover, our line on that graph will look like Rothstein's *schvantz*—on a very happy night."

A smile wiggled onto, and then off, Spilkes's face. "You're right, I'm sure. 'Rosemary and time' will take care of things."

Harris asked, after several seconds: "What the fuck are you talking about?"

Spilkes followed Burn out of the office, and before they could close the door, Harris yelled to Hazel: "Do you have my car ordered for the Plaza?"

"No," she said, before cracking a piece of hard candy with her molars. "Betty says you're too fat. You have to walk. She also says to keep your eyes above that floozy's neck."

"You look tired, my boy." Nelson Merrill, the magazine's lone surviving fashion illustrator, tried offering some grandfatherly comfort to Allen Case, as the two sat in Merrill's corner of the Art Department, sipping cups of lemon tea.

"I did work v-very late last night," said Allen, just above a whisper.

Their gentle exchange was interrupted by Gardiner Arinopoulos's loud, exasperated entrance: "Where IS Mr. Lord?" he asked.

"I'm afraid I've no idea," said Merrill.

"Well, then, WHERE'S Mr. ——, you know, the fashion fellow, the ONE that's skinny as a whippet?"

"You mean Brian K-Keene," said Allen.

"Yes," said the photographer, no less impatient. "Where IS he? I've got to find some damned ascots BACK THERE, when I need to be THINKING about bulls and bears." He left as abruptly as he'd entered.

"Is your tea too hot?" Nelson Merrill asked Allen. "You look flushed."

"No," said the copyeditor, whose color came from the alarm he was feeling over Arinopoulos's mention of two new species. "It's just . . . h-him." What humiliating plans did the photographer have for bulls and bears?

"Ah, yes," said the illustrator. "Mr. Arinopoulos—and all he represents."

Nelson Merrill, born in 1860, could remember seeing Lincoln's funeral procession come up Fifth Avenue when he was not quite five years old. Sixty years later, he was a roly-poly white-haired gentle-man, more or less the opposite of the young male ideal he still inked onto a few of the magazine's pages. His beautiful, attenuated draw-ings, much admired by the great Leyendecker, were sometimes made even more splendid with a color wash, but no longer did they ap-pear on *Bandbox*'s cover, nor even with much frequency inside. The office's only link to the pre-Harris regime, Merrill was allowed to come in late and go home early. A naturally cheerful man, he never-theless kept to himself, as if afraid of being singed by Flaming Youth. He had confided to only a few, such as Allen and Nan O'Grady, the sorrow he felt over his replacement by the camera.

Now, as always, he kept sketching, even as he kept up his end of the conversation: "Terrible business yesterday. I felt sorry for the Columbia boy."

"Yes," said Allen. "The p-p-poor ocelot bit the wrong behind."

Merrill smiled. Beneath his fast-moving hand, a soulful whippet was coming into view.

Allen went back to the Copy Department and asked Nan if she had heard anything about bulls and bears.

"It's on the lineup sheet," she answered. "Some Wall Street piece that's due in tomorrow. They're supposed to shoot a little koala bear being chased by some big Black Angus. Optimism overpowering pessimism, I gather." She rolled her eyes. "I heard Mr. Lord talking about it with the Greek shutterbug."

A bull could be obtained anywhere, Allen knew, but this meant that some illegally imported koala must now be tied up, with Arino-poulos's other exotic fauna, at that garage in Queens. *What is to be done?* he could hear one part of his mind pamphleteering to the other. He already knew what that was, but could not ask Nan for the help he needed; she would guess he was up to something. So he returned to the Art Department.

"Mr. M-Merrill," he asked. "You know Queens, don't you?"

"Oh, yes. It's what Miss O'Grady and myself have in common. Woodside and taking care of our mothers." In telling the story of Lincoln's funeral, the illustrator liked to point out that the now-eighty-nine-year-old Mrs. Merrill would have been old enough to *vote* for Lincoln, had the ladies had the franchise way back then.

"Right," said Allen. After a last moment's hesitation, he reached into his pocket for a folded slip of paper. "Do you know the easiest w-w-way for me to get to this address?" He had obtained it late last night by rifling through some invoices in the Art Department. The trucker who transported the animals to and from Arinopoulos's shoots listed their pickup point on his bill.

Merrill set the little sheet beside his penciled whippet. "That's a street in Long Island City," he said. "I should think I can give you pretty good directions."

13

"Of *course* she's not twenty-three," said Becky, struggling with her scarf and gloves.

Newman put a nickel into the codcake window for her.

"Put one into the pie slot," said Cuddles, "and I'll bet you she coughs up LaRoche's real name."

"Lucille Monahan," said Newman, as the three of them slid their trays along. "Born in Hutchinson, Kansas."

"Nope," said Becky.

Newman handed her a nickel, which she used to get a cup of coffee for Cuddles.

"Do I absolutely have to?" Houlihan asked, while Newman got a cup for himself.

Once the three were settled at a table, Becky brought Stuart up to speed: "She's at least thirty, and she was doing those two-reel comedies *more* than ten years ago. I heard all this from a friend who writes contracts in the Paramount Building. Lucille Monahan was her first *fake* name. She disappeared after a couple of years in Los Angeles. My friend thinks she was in the clink—maybe for shoplifting. When she got out, she rechristened herself *again*. She hadn't made enough of an impression the first time round so that anyone would notice."

"No Parisian music master?" asked Newman. "No French?"

"No Hutchinson?" cried Cuddles. *"Zut alors!"* He forced down a sip of coffee.

"Nobody," explained Becky, "knows where she actually came from or what her real name was." She turned toward Cuddles: "You look as if you're developing a theory."

"No," he said. "I'm just wondering about all these helpful old boyfriends. The *Graphic,* the Paramount Building—where else have you got them stashed? The boardroom of American Radiator? The Fulton Fish Market?"

"If I had one there, I'd tell him about *this.*" Becky pushed away the codcake. "The only other boyfriend I can think of is the current one," she said, looking straight at Cuddles. "The 'monk' at the Cloisters. Remember?"

Newman lit a cigarette and glanced at the clock. He was thinking how much simpler things would be if he were just starting another "Bachelor's Life" column: "When You Take Your Girl to the Automat."

"Are you running late?" asked Becky.

"The opposite," said Newman. "I've got another hour to kill before I'm supposed to present myself at the Plaza."

"Try not to bring Il Duce back to the premises until after four," Cuddles instructed Newman. "And make sure he's well oiled."

"So he won't notice you've gone to the 'home office'?" asked Becky, using Houlihan's term for his couch over in Brooklyn. "Nothing doing. Not after I hauled you back up over the rail yesterday." Putting on her scarf, she took a look at Stuart's handsome hollowed eyes and wondered how long it would be before someone had to throw him a life preserver, too.

14

"Yessir," said Harris. "He may be late, but there he is." He directed Rosemary LaRoche's attention to George M. Cohan, now sitting down at his regular corner table in the Oak Room.

"Yeah," said the film star, peeking through the smilax-wrapped trellis that shielded her from too much public view. "Give *my* regards to Broadway. *Fuck* Broadway," she declared, before putting a last bite of strip steak into her mouth.

Disappointed at the failure of what he had hoped would seem an authentic New York treat to this sun-bronzed captive of the film colony, Harris tried soothing her. "Of course," he said, recalling a fragment of autobiography she'd imparted during the soup course. "You're remembering those shortsighted rejections when you were trying to get started here." He sympathetically imagined the scene. "A beautiful girl being mistreated by those Broadway wolves."

"Wolves?" cried Miss LaRoche, tossing her napkin onto the remains of the steak. "In the whole six months I was up here, I never met *one* who wasn't a nellie. I practically shoved my melons into their kissers, but you'da thought they was live grenades the way those guys would flinch. Here," she said, extracting for a third time the small silver flask she kept in her garter. "You're still not completely thawed."

After his enforced walk from the office, and having puffed his way past the skaters near the fountain, Harris had arrived at the hotel exhausted. He now accepted a little dividend in what he and Rosemary and the waiter were pretending was his water glass. Her Hollywood hooch was a lot better than what he got from the countess back at the office, and when Rosemary swung her legs out from under the table to replace the flask inside her garter, there was the visual bonus of her splendid right thigh.

"Bingo," she said, upon accomplishing the storage. Once more Harris was face-to-face with her blond bob, stratospheric cheekbones, and blazing green eyes, which were bordered by the faintest tracery of wrinkles. He was more smitten than he had imagined, or Betty had feared. For the past hour and a half, the more profane this siren got, the more courtly and avuncular he'd found himself becoming.

"Terrible, isn't it?" he said, raising his glass. "The lengths the law makes us go to to disguise a civilized habit."

"Sounds like you're hoping for another flash," said Rosemary, snapping her garter.

"No, no," said Harris, innocently wounded. "I'm just remembering a time when you could see men come in here holding tumblers of whiskey, not pieces of ticker tape, when they sat down to their lunch." It would soon be a decade since the adjoining Oak Bar had been turned into an E.F. Hutton office.

"Don't knock the market," said Rosemary. "The week I dumped that no-good-nellie husband of mine I found out that his moneyman had quadrupled everything he'd been holding in the space of a month. Half and half? Hell, we split it double and double!"

Harris ignored these financial loaves and fishes. He could only marvel: Howard Kenyon—that cinematic sheik, that heroic screen doughboy, that movie-palace pirate . . . was a *feygele*? Why, he wondered, was she telling him this? Did she just assume that he'd be too scared to print any of the beans she was spilling? He tried looking further into those green eyes, and he hit an emerald wall.

"So let me tell you how you're gonna shoot me for your cover," said Rosemary.

Harris came out of his frightened revery. "Actually, Miss LaRoche, that'll be up to Mr. Lord, whom you'll—"

"You're gonna have me on a couch with just a fancy silk sheet covering my hoohah and melons. My wrists and ankles are gonna be tied together with pearls. I got a picture called *Chained* coming out around the time you'll be getting your show on the road, and I'm gonna need people to think this crummy masterpiece is a little hotter than it is."

"Was the director a nellie?" It was all Harris could think to say.

"Worse," said Rosemary. "A gentleman. Of course, you are, too. But in the best sense of the term. Which is why I know you'll be square with me. I get a nickel on each thirty-five-cent copy you sell above a hundred thousand."

Harris chose to concentrate not on the meaning, but the mere sound, of what she was saying. Where had he heard such a voice before? On the rodeo cowboy *Bandbox* had once let loose in the city for a babe-in-the-metropolitan-woods piece? No, it was too deep, and not quite twangy enough. On the old lady he and Betty had met last winter down at the Vinoy Park in St. Petersburg? The one who'd actually been *born* in Florida? No, not enough syrup. And the way Miss LaRoche said "term"—didn't it sound faintly like "toim"? Whatever head she might have for figures, this dame didn't add up.

"I'll have to talk with Mr. Burn, my publisher," Harris finally said.

"You do that, 'Phat. Otherwise we got no deal. Hel-*lo*," she then uttered, without a pause to mark the shift from business to pleasure. "What have we *here*?" She parted the smilax once again. Harris stretched his neck to get a look at the gentleman checking his overcoat with the girl at the entrance. A good-looking fellow, even if he was in need of a hair-combing and—

Rosemary LaRoche had him so agitated that it took several seconds to realize he was looking at Stuart Newman.

"That's your writer, Miss LaRoche. I asked him to join us for coffee."

Staring at Newman with her fierce green eyes and smile, the actress said to the editor: "You're goddamned right it is."

Newman approached the table, trying not to recall a long-ago bender that had ended here at the Plaza in a broom closet on the eleventh floor.

"Stuart!" cried Harris. "Come meet Rosemary LaRoche."

Newman took his last steps with a certain hesitation, trying to guess why the boss was looking at him as if he'd already accomplished something wonderful.

The actress put out her hand. Newman, uncertain for a moment what to do, finally took hold of it and brought it to his lips. Harris thought this tough-talking cookie might swallow his man in two bites, like a second order of strip steak. But in a soft little voice, creme-filled with vowels from yet another indeterminate part of the country, Rosemary LaRoche purred: "Mr. Newman is *très, très charmant.*"

15

Around other tables here at Lindy's, the showgirls outnumbered the fighters and newsmen and producers who were buying them supper. So Daisy felt grateful for the odds where she was: two to one, the one being herself, seated between Eddie Diamond and Judge Francis X. Gilfoyle. The numbers would only improve once Arnold Rothstein arrived at his usual spot, though perhaps it was the absence of his rather glum presence that had made this evening, so far, a little gayer than the one she'd spent at 912 Fifth Avenue a few weeks ago, shortly after Carolyn Rothstein's departure for Europe.

She knew that long-standing marital troubles had dictated that *bon voyage,* but she now decided to go ahead and ask if there had been any word on how Mrs. Rothstein was getting on over there. The response, from Judge Gilfoyle, was appropriately circumspect, since it concerned, as Daisy was coming to understand, his boss's wife.

"She's cabled that she's doing quite well," said the judge. "I'd say better than one might expect. You have to understand that Mrs. Rothstein is a nervous creature—" He paused to come up with a suitable softening. "Delicate. Refined."

"Oh, I'm sure she is," said Daisy, with a great deal of breathy sympathy.

"As he likes to say himself," the judge went on, "Mr. Rothstein usually keeps the lady 'in a glass case,' so perhaps this European excursion will prove liberat—"

Eddie Diamond's lungs erupted with wet, wheezy laughter. A tubercular past, thought Daisy; one found it in many men in his line of work.

"A glass case?" cried Eddie. "She's lucky he don't stop up the air holes!"

Noting the distress this remark provoked in the judge, Daisy pretended it had never been uttered. She liked Francis X. Gilfoyle. There was something reassuring about his florid face and advanced age. (The most dreadful revelation inside Max Stanwick's article was the fact that Rothstein was only two years older than herself.) She liked the whole ensemble that was the judge: the old-fashioned homburg; the three-quarter part in the thinning hair; the dandruff that needed a woman's cheerful brushing from the lapels. Put him in a lineup of her recent escorts—all those sharp-edged characters who came right to the point—and she'd have no trouble picking him out.

"And where *is* Mr. Rothstein tonight?" she finally asked.

"Out in Maspeth," said Judge Gilfoyle, who Daisy had learned was the third senior justice in Manhattan Criminal Court. "Looking over the progress on a grand housing development he's got a hand in. It's called Juniper Park. Two hundred modest homes—"

"That he's gonna have trouble sellin' to *coons*!" declared Eddie Diamond, who coughed his way so hard through the next couple of sentences that his two big ears shook. "You should see this 'development,' Duchess. They put the hot-water heaters in the front hallway! If 'The Brain' is out there, he's probably tryin' to keep the whole slum from bein' condemned before it opens."

Appalled at this sarcastic use of Mr. Rothstein's best-known nickname, Daisy looked toward her escort, who appeared positively frightened. Had she misjudged Eddie Diamond the night he drove her home from 912 Fifth? Had there perhaps been a deterioration in his business relationship with "The Brain"?

"Tell me how you know Max," said Daisy to the judge. "Now *there's* a brain! I daresay his books are touched with genius."

"Some friends of Mr. Rothstein had the misfortune to appear before me in court not long ago. Mr. Stanwick asked to interview me about the matter, but of course professional ethics forbade my commenting on it."

" 'Misfortune'?" cried Eddie. "I'd say they was pretty goddamned lucky to appear before *you*! 'Scuse my language, Duchess."

"Nonetheless," said Gilfoyle, struggling to continue. "I was very pleased to meet Mr. Stanwick. I count myself a great fan of his novels, particularly *Ticker Rape*."

It was now the judge's turn to apologize, for injuring Daisy's ears with that scandalous title. To make amends, he took out a dollar and snapped his fingers for the girl with the tray of paper gardenias.

Daisy cooed while he pinned one on her. "I should think Mr. Rothstein will be *very* pleased with the piece Max has written. Of course, *my* professional ethics forbid me from showing you an advance copy of it."

Eddie Diamond gave a thuggish snort over the word "piece."

"It must be fascinating," said the judge, "to produce a magazine about all that's new and unusual in this hundred-mile-an-hour world of ours."

Daisy's comment on the excitement and responsibility involved in such an enterprise was cut short by the arrival at the table of a skinny, shaking man in a checked jacket who asked Eddie Diamond when Rothstein was supposed to get here tonight. He was immediately pushed away, more forcefully than Daisy could imagine being necessary. Eddie responded to the inquisitive look on her face. "Some fourth-rate crooner who needs dough to pay his bookie. A parasite."

Embarrassed, Judge Gilfoyle explained to Daisy: "Mr. Rothstein often acts as a kind of banker for people unable to secure credit by more conventional means." The explanation competed for her attention with a wave from a tall, lately retired ballplayer at a table near the front of the restaurant.

"Do you know him?" asked the judge.

"No," said Daisy. "I suppose I remind him of someone."

"You couldn't possibly," said the judge, taking advantage of Eddie Diamond's current distraction by Leo Lindy himself, who had brought a pile of messages to the table. "You seem to me unique in all the world," Gilfoyle told Daisy.

"Oh, Your Honor!" she said, while Eddie straightened the little pile of paper and set beside it an ashtray and a book of matches.

"That's the 'out' basket," he explained to Daisy. "The boss don't like to keep a lot of files once he's through with readin' stuff."

Over the next quarter-hour, during which a policeman clapped his hand on the judge's back and a pockmarked lawyer came by the table to present his card, Daisy felt more and more certain that this poor, considerate magistrate was in over his head. The sweat pouring off his neck had begun to destroy his collar.

"Tell me about your late wife," she said, sure Judge Gilfoyle would welcome a sentimental shift in his mental focus.

"Oh," said the judge, immediately brighter. "My Charlotte was the most wonderful woman. A factory girl when I met her forty years ago, but anyone who knew her would swear she was a lady. Yes, Countess, a wonderful woman. We were never blessed with children, so she showered all her attention on me."

"No more than you deserved, I'm sure," said Daisy, whose own attention detected that the diners within a twenty-foot radius had fallen silent—over the arrival of three men who proceeded to sit down at her table. Judge Gilfoyle made the introductions. Arnold Rothstein—"The Brain," "The Big Bankroll"—was accompanied by Mr. Fats Walsh, his bodyguard, and a thin, blond-haired associate named William Wellman. Rothstein appeared even paler than Daisy remembered his being last month; the brown eyes were heavily ringed with fatigue. But he was dressed exactly as Max Stanwick had described him for *Bandbox,* with an all-white, spun-silk muffler done in an Ascot knot. While The Brain scowled at the stack of messages, the judge whispered to Daisy that Wellman was the man who had recommended the ill-starred Juniper Park venture.

"It's nice to see you again," Rothstein said to Daisy, remembering his manners and last month's foot massage.

Daisy's eyes went to bat, more for the judge's sake than her own. "Mr. Rothstein, I understand that you're camera-shy, but you really *should* have let my magazine shoot you wearing that muffler."

"Lady," said Eddie Diamond. "Never say 'shoot' around Mr. Rothstein." He hacked his way through another guffaw; an awkward silence followed.

Wellman eventually broke it. "I've been showing Mr. Rothstein the auto-racing track we're starting to build near the development in Queens."

Daisy, a natural encourager, nodded brightly.

"Yes," said Rothstein, cutting Wellman off. "The track goes round and round, just like the rest of the project." He then drilled the judge with a look that was all business. "I may soon be needing your—what shall we call it?" he said, glancing at Daisy with some wariness before he found the word. "Expertise."

Gilfoyle smiled nervously.

Daisy took the jurist's hand and made a last attempt to lighten the mood. "It's delightful seeing a bit more of your world, Mr. Rothstein. But isn't it time I showed you a little of mine? My magazine is hosting a party tomorrow evening, and I'd like to invite all of you gentlemen to come by."

"I'm afraid Mr. Diamond and Mr. Wellman and myself will have some business obligations to attend to," said Rothstein, "but I'm sure the judge'll be delighted to go." The Brain came the closest he had to smiling when he noticed the look of pleasure now invading Gilfoyle's sagging features. "In fact," added Rothstein, putting a match to the message he'd just read, "I'm going to let him see you home now, Countess."

16

Instead of asking for the Warwick Hotel, Betty told the cabdriver to take her the handful of blocks between the Forty-eighth Street Theatre and Malocchio. She'd left *Cock Robin* at intermission, upon realizing she'd missed half the dialogue and still figured out the rest of the plot. She was more than eager to go home, but had decided, having seen the same sheet of GME ad figures, to check up on Joe.

Arriving at Gianni Roma's detestable little bistro, she found Joe still in full swing, recounting the morning's victory over Jimmy to the small group of staff he'd shanghaied here hours ago. Gianni was on his way to get Betty a small plate of *spaghetti alla vongole,* her usual, before Joe even noticed she was there. "Hey, sweetie!" he finally said, his features in a visible war between pleasure and disappointment. Only Spilkes, on his right, betrayed unalloyed relief: Betty's supervision would mean a shorter night and the chance to catch a late train back to Connecticut.

"And you honestly think Houlihan accomplished this miracle?" asked David Fine, for the second time.

"Does it make a difference?" asked Harris.

Paul Montgomery, gathering that "no" was the right answer, vigorously said the word. Spilkes also shook his head in the negative.

"What a cover that's going to be!" said Paul Montgomery, toasting the air with his water glass. "Rosemary LaRoche! Jimmy's going to be green."

Green with money, thought Spilkes, if the ads kept moving in *Cutaway*'s direction. He looked at his watch and pressed upon the heartburn above his solar plexus, wishing among other things that Harris would get Montgomery out of town on another assignment as soon as possible. The managing editor could never take more than a couple of days of Paulie around the office, peeing all over the carpet like some exuberant puppy.

"There's plenty more great stuff in the pipeline," said Harris. "As soon as dawn breaks, Arinopoulos will be down on Wall Street shooting our bull and bear."

"You still haven't told us who's writing the text for that," said Spilkes, remembering to grin in tribute to the chief's slyness. "The lineup sheet still just has 'tk' for the scribe."

"You'll see," said Harris, leaning back and putting his arm around Betty. He scanned Fine and Montgomery's faces for signs of competitive anxiety. He knew how to keep his men on their game, and thanks to this morning's triumph over Jimmy, he was feeling very much on his own.

Giovanni Roma poured Betty some coffee and interjected a question: "So is Lindstrom gonna ride-a your bull?"

Harris answered: "Uh, we're going to give Waldo a rest after the last couple of days he's had."

"Good!" said Roma, flourishing the silver pot. "We *like* Waldo well rested."

"Gianni," said Harris, tugging the maître d's white towel. "Get us some grappa."

"Joe," warned Betty, "you've got another late night tomorrow."

"I do?"

"The bash for the fiction-contest winner," Spilkes informed him.

"Oh, right," said Harris. The affair had gotten bigger every year; this time Oldcastle was throwing open his own penthouse for it. "What you don't know is I've also got a big morning. Get the grappa, Gianni."

Betty, disgusted, removed Joe's arm from her shoulder.

He leaned back into the table. "Now let me tell you about this dame LaRoche," said Harris, forgetting he'd already apprised the males, at considerable length, of his lunch with the actress.

"I'm all ears," said Betty.

Harris's face froze. Exercising his gift for quick, strategic retreat, he said, gravely, "We're going to have to photograph her pretty carefully. She's not nearly the knockout I'd have guessed."

"If you drink the grappa," Betty pointed out, "you're not going to be able to keep lying this well."

The sound of a waiter's knuckles rapping sharply on the window above the checkered café curtains quieted the table. "A gawker," he explained, apologetically, when heads turned. The diners could see, through the glass, a sweet-faced, frightened-looking young man already beating a retreat to the other side of Fiftieth Street.

But just as quickly, Giovanni Roma headed out the door after him, scolding the waiter as he rushed past: "You never know *whose* son that might be!" Within thirty seconds, the boy was inside and getting warmed up in the vestibule.

The *Bandbox* party had already resumed listening to Harris's revised estimate of Rosemary LaRoche's looks, when Roma brought the pink-cheeked boy over to their table. "Mista Harris, I think you shoulda meet a very important subscriber. This here is—say your name again, *bambino*—from Greenpoint, Illinois."

"Greencastle, Indiana, actually," said the boy, scarcely believing the sound of his own voice, in *here* of all places. "My name's John Shepard."

"Hey, kid," said Harris.

Betty could see the boy's knees knocking. "Gianni, get the young man a chair. This is Mr. Spilkes, Mr. Fine, Mr. Montgomery. I'm Miss Divine. Sit down, sweetheart."

Harris was generally baffled by anyone between birth and twenty, and didn't relish turning the rest of his evening into some kind of kid's birthday party, but he could see Betty regarding the boy with a maternal gaze she ordinarily reserved for Mukluk, who had been delivered home to the Warwick hours ago by private car.

"John," asked Spilkes, "what is it you like about the magazine?"

Harris intervened: "Norman, let the kid drink some coffee before you turn him into a one-man customer cluster."

But Spilkes's question worked magic. John Shepard's jaw unlocked to pour forth a flood of consumer approval: "I must have read the January issue four times on the train! Mr. Fine, I loved what you wrote about that restaurant with the shish-kebab swordfights. I felt like I was in Constantinople!"

"His expense report looked like *he'd* been in Constantinople!" said Harris. "Where *was* that place?"

"Ho-Ho-Kus," said Fine, who was thinking this was one smart kid who'd come in the door.

"I missed seeing you in this issue, Mr. Montgomery, but I thought that article you did last month on the family of acrobats was completely swell. Especially the part at the end where the one who was paralyzed got all choked up saying goodbye to you—"

"Sorry about this month, John," said Paul, reaching into his pocket for one of the dozen Ty Cobb autographs he'd brought back. "Maybe this'll explain—and make up for—my absence."

"Tell me, kid," said Harris, waiting for the boy's mouth to close. "Do you ever read *Cutaway*?"

"I don't think you can get it in Greencastle," John Shepard replied, hoping the answer didn't make him seem like a rube.

"Gianni, get this kid a plate of your best veal!" cried Harris.

John, however overwhelmed, remained polite enough to turn to Miss Divine and say, "My sister always reads *Pinafore*."

"Gianni, get this boy a piece of cake," said Betty, glad the compliment had gone into her good ear. "Now, John, tell us where you've been today."

Before any of the food arrived, John Shepard downed several warm, and entirely unfamiliar, gulps of grappa, which caused him to narrate his adventures in a single loquacious rush. His dinner companions— companions!—were soon aware of everything that had happened to him aboard the *Cleveland Limited,* where he'd gotten no more than a couple of hours' sleep sitting up in the club car. They also learned how he'd found himself a room for a couple of nights at the Railroad YMCA, which he couldn't believe was actually on Park Avenue, because he knew all about Park Avenue, whereas the average person in Greencastle, even a professor like his father, still thought all the fancy people in New York lived on *Fifth* Avenue.

Harris and Betty and the rest of the table further learned about the hour John had just spent walking through Times Square, looking for the neon sign of the kitten with the spool of thread, which he'd seen pictures of but guessed must now be gone. He'd lost count of all the jewelry merchants and costume repairers and joke sellers whose windows he'd gone past—never mind the theatres!—before figuring out that New York, if you wanted to get a *real* idea of it, was better off seen from a distance than close up. So he'd ascended to the observation deck in the Shelton Hotel over on Lexington (he deliberately didn't say "Avenue," just "Lexington," so he'd sound more like a native), and he'd seen the whole metropolis spread out before him. Less than an hour ago he'd been floating high above the streets, and now here he was down in the thick of things in a way he couldn't have dreamed about! Except he *had* dreamed about it—a scene just like this—while he'd slept sitting up inside the *Cleveland Limited*.

Before long, in the presence of so much talkative innocence, Harris felt ready to call it a night. "Kid, why don't you come by the office tomorrow? We'll show you around."

"Really?" said John, gaping again, despite the speedy regularity with which these treats were coming.

"Sure," said Harris, getting up from the table. "Welcome to New York. I'm sure there're big things in store for you."

No one at the table had interrupted John's excited narrative to ask why he had come to the city, or what circumstances had preceded his departure from Indiana. It was, to these diners, a simple given that everywhere else was a place you left, that each person arrived in Manhattan like an appliance ready to be taken out of its box and plugged in. This nice boy was just one more shiny creature off destiny's assembly line.

There was another set of eyes peering into the restaurant's windows, with more accomplished stealth than John's had been able to practice. Ever since quitting time, Chip Brzezinski had been pacing Midtown, dogged by Jimmy Gordon's breakfast warning that *Cutaway* would lose interest in him if his next bit of sabotage didn't pan out. Looking obliquely through the glass, Chip was now wondering what truck this turnip had fallen off of, and why he was sitting at that table like he'd just made his First fucking Communion. Was the kid part of some new stunt by Harris? "Bandbox Junior"? A new feature, or maybe a whole new supplement? Chip made a note of the little fellow's kisser—so ripe for a pasting—before turning up his collar and heading into the night.

17

"Where are the goddamned HORNS?" shouted Gardiner Arinopoulos, rubbing his hands in the predawn cold.

The truck driver, standing in the gutter of Wall Street behind the live cargo he'd started to unload, looked from the photographer to the animal and back again. "*What* horns?" he asked. "He's a Black Angus."

"I ASKED for a bull! What KIND of bull has no horns?"

"The Black Angus kind," said the driver.

"Oh, Christ. SHEA!"

The photographer's assistant was standing beside a second, smaller, truck parked in front of the Subtreasury Building. He walked over to his boss.

"How are we GOING to get horns on this thing?" cried Arinopoulos—who soon had a brainstorm. "Get into a taxi and GO up to the studio. There's that pair of skinny megaphones STANDING in the corner. You know where I'm talking ABOUT? Strap them together and BRING them down here. Instantly!"

"What about the koala?" asked Shea, pointing to the smaller truck.

"I'LL watch the fucking bear," the photographer declared. "And YOU stay HERE," he ordered the driver of the Angus.

Looking a few feet down the sidewalk, Arinopoulos could already make out the time on the Seth Thomas clock that stood like a solemn lollipop on the sidewalk. Real daylight would arrive within fifteen minutes. After that he'd have perhaps another fifteen to get his picture, before the street's eager beavers started showing up to open their offices and get in his artistic way. So the moment Shea commenced his northward dash Arinopoulos began setting up his camera.

He took no notice of the young man standing across the street. About an hour ago, Allen Case, a cap pulled low across his face, had taken up position between two deep scars on the façade of the J. P. Morgan Building. These reminders of the 1920 anarchist attack had prompted Allen to look over at the now-famous spot where the bay horse got blown to bits by a bomb inside the wagon it had been forced to pull. It might be too late to save that poor creature, but it wasn't too late to save the koala, somewhere inside that second truck, from indignity, and worse.

Nelson Merrill had provided accurate directions to Long Island City, but when Allen got there several hours ago he'd found the warehouse of exotic animals protected by barbed wire, as well as a German shepherd even he couldn't charm into unbaring its teeth. Knowing Arinopoulos's schedule, he had retreated here, intent on rescuing one abused beast if not the whole imprisoned arkful. Shivering in his short jacket—he couldn't let a long coat get in the way of the maneuvers he was ready to perform—Allen looked across the street at the two different trucks, certain that the ordinary Angus had come from somewhere other than the Queens warehouse, whose strange, wonderful odors he could smell even now, as he wondered what sadists besides this photographer patronized that tragic menagerie. Its existence only confirmed Allen's belief that John Scopes had, in fact, been guilty, of at least presumption, since neither God nor nature would ever have allowed the evolution of charming monkeys into terrible men.

The sun had come up, if just barely. It was glinting off the face of the clock when Arinopoulos's assistant, still fashioning a ridiculous contraption from the two megaphones he'd fetched, got out of the returning taxicab.

"It'll HAVE to do," said the photographer, grabbing the fake horns. "There'll be a bit of a blur, in ANY case, once he's charging. Here," he ordered the truck driver. "Put THIS on him."

The Black Angus was soon snorting, more from bafflement than any real aggressive impulse. "Excellent!" said Arinopoulos, seeing the steam emerge from the animal's nostrils. "This goddamned cold is good for SOMETHING. Shea! Get the bear."

Idiots, thought Allen Case. It's not a bear; it's a marsupial.

"Tell me what exactly's supposed to happen?" the truck driver asked, once he'd finished crowning the Angus.

"As soon as my man sets DOWN the koala, your hornless wonder is going to CHASE it. Get the bull to the top of the steps and have him come down THROUGH two of the columns. With any luck I'll get old George into the shot, TOO." The trucker was already leading the Angus up past the statue of Washington. "Where's the koala supposed to end up?" he called back.

"Under a BUS? I couldn't care less. He's BOUGHT and paid for, not rented," explained Arinopoulos, now confident enough of success to be laughing. "I'm not exactly COUNTING on his survival. Shea! Get that jug-eared furball OUT here!"

Allen took the scrape of the panel truck's door as his signal. He dashed across the street. In a single movement he knocked down the photographer's assistant and scooped the terrified koala into his arms. Running toward the subway, as fast as he could with twenty-five pounds of marsupial clinging to his bony torso, he put a cough drop into the creature's mouth. It had been too late last night, and too early this morning, to get hold of any eucalyptus leaves for the animal to eat. Maybe the lozenge would satisfy until she was safely hidden and Allen could lay in a supply of the foliage from a flower shop he knew on Sixth Avenue.

The koala pulled on him as they descended into the Wall Street subway station. Allen looked down and could have sworn the animal was smiling.

"Here," he said, tucking a box of Smith Brothers into the marsupial's pouch. "T-take the pack."

18

Joe Harris looked again at the typescript in front of him. "What *is* this crap?" he muttered.

> For he snorts and paws the earth, yes *snorts and paws the earth,* inside the bloody Bourse. Oh, bloody *Bourse!!* Greenbacked *Pamplona!!!* where the meek and the cheap are trampled, where the meek and the cheap are *left behind—*

Christ, thought the editor, torn between disappointment and disbelief. It was like something written by Vachel Lindsay's drunken brother-in-law.

left out of the big bull's *big bull market!!!*
out of the big bull's *Big Bull Market!!*

"Hazel! Get me Harold Ober at the Reynolds Agency."

Always excited to get to the office, Harris had been looking forward to today as extra-special. Following his arrival at 7:30, almost three hours ago, he had waited for the Reynolds messenger to deliver this draft of the essay he'd commissioned, for a small fortune, from Henry Roebling, the thirty-year-old, big-game-hunting literary sensation, a writer so virile and hairy-chested, he looked, when his shirt was open, like something he might have just shot. In life, Roebling always had an aviatrix or girl reporter ready to kill herself over him; on the page, he boiled his sporting and amorous adventures down to a prose so spare it sometimes seemed he was being paid by the word for what he left out.

Harold Ober had promised that his client would produce a literary meditation, lean and manly, on the age's great bull market, an essay that, once published, would have the highbrows swooning and Jimmy Gordon sweating. Both *Bandbox* and *Cutaway* had been after Roebling for months, vying to be the first to entice him away from hardcovers and into magazines. What the messenger had finally arrived here with—this lunatic verbal discharge typed with the red part of the ribbon—was supposed to be Harris's first real burst of return fire at Jimmy. Now all he could do was look desperately at the booming, chanted, underlined letters.

"Mr. Ober's on the line," called Hazel, who managed as always to sound loud and bored at the same time.

Harris took the call.

The agent sighed through the wires. "I'm afraid he's not at the top of his game, is he?"

"Unless his game is incomprehensibility," responded Harris, more in sorrow than anger. "He's up for a gold medal in that department."

"Yes," said Ober, almost in a whisper.

That damned Yankee taciturnity, thought Harris. Ober was the same as Perkins: the two of them, agent and editor, baby-sitting a whole nursery of temperamental boy geniuses and never murmuring a word of impatience toward them. But this morning Harris thought he could sense, coming from Ober, a measure of apology, even anguish. He was sure the little squiffy sound he heard was one of the agent's bushy eyebrows colliding with the mouthpiece of the phone. Ober must be tapping its candlestick in frustration against his forehead; Harris did the same thing a half-dozen times a day.

"I'm going to be indiscreet here," said the agent. "The fellow's having a rough time. He's up in the Maine woods with only a satchel full of peyote for companionship. I'm afraid he was thrown over by a rodeo queen after his last trek through Mexico—not the sort of disappointment he's accustomed to. I'm willing to waive the kill fee."

"Let me get back to you," said Harris, still gentle with shock.

For the past month he'd been imagining an afternoon visit from Roebling, during which they would tinker manfully with a couple of participles and periods before toasting the success of the piece. Now he could only think, forlornly, of the moose he'd killed over Christmas week: its huge horned head lay on the floor of his office closet, covered with a tarpaulin, mounted to a plaque and awaiting placement on a wall. Harris had planned on putting it behind the couch prior to Roebling's arrival, surprising the writer with this evidence that he'd sold his prose to another woods-wise man of letters. Roebling need never know the moose had met its maker when Harris hit it with his Packard on a slippery road in Dutchess County. The car's front grille had been bashed to bits, and the one guy he and Betty could find to tow them, after a two-mile trek toward the lights of Poughkeepsie, would only do the job if they also let his underemployed cousin do some taxidermy on the moose. Fine, said Harris, who had forgotten all about the thing by the time it was shipped to

New York. The stuffing job wasn't the greatest—Harris had been able to make out the Packard logo pressed into the animal's neckline, like a brand, before painting it over with bourbon—and he feared derision from the rest of the masthead if he put the creature on the wall too far in advance of Roebling's arrival. So for the past few weeks he'd kept it in the closet, while he grew daily more eager for the editing session he would have with the celebrated young writer, just the two of them, *mano a mano,* under the buck he'd bagged.

Harris got up and opened the closet, pulling back the tarp to look into the glassy golf balls the mechanic's cousin had used for the eyes. He thought the moose looked disappointed, too.

"Lemme introduce ya."

At the sound of Hazel's voice, Harris rushed to shut the closet.

"It's a bad time!" he admonished her.

She turned to the blond boy beside her and smiled. "If I had a nickel for every time I heard him say that."

John Shepard smiled back, nervously. Miss Snow was perhaps a year or two older than himself, but within the two minutes of their acquaintance, during which he'd explained the amazing events at Malocchio that had led to his presence here this morning, she had already invited him to tonight's party in the publisher's penthouse.

"You'll like the mailroom," said Harris, who had no memory of the young man in front of him. "It's a good place to start," he continued, giving John the short spiel he imparted to any new hire that Hazel or the girl from Personnel ushered in here.

Hazel tsked, quite loudly. "Think," she said. "Veal *piccata.*"

"Oh, right," said Harris, unexcited by the ensuing flash of recognition.

John Shepard, trying not to stare over Harris's shoulder at the pictures of Yvette and Claudine, experienced his first moment of disappointment since stepping out of Grand Central last night.

"Come on," said Hazel, tugging him out of her boss's office. "You won't learn anything here."

She guided John down the hall, past a secretary who looked up from her comptometer to cry: "He's a cute little thing!"

"Let's see who's around," said Hazel, ignoring the girl, as well as John's mortification.

Sidney Bruck's door was the first they passed. It was open, a sign that he was getting ready to take a call from somebody with a big name. Now, alas, thanks to Hazel, he had to entertain this rustic-looking boy. With a certain disbelief Sidney soon heard himself asking the fellow about "school." Upon learning that he attended— or "used to go to"—Indiana University, Sidney's interest managed to diminish even further. Having himself graduated a few years ago from Brown, where he wrote for the campus magazine with his friends Sid Perelman and Nathanael West, Sidney could now only glance at his watch and ask John Shepard: "Exactly what are you doing here?"

John hesitated between telling the tale of last night at Malocchio—too long—and some brief remark like "I've come to try my luck in New York," which would make him sound too much like Dick Whittington.

"He's here to look around," said Hazel to Sidney. "So you be nice to him. I've got to run."

Startled that she would desert him so quickly after coming to his rescue, John gave her a pleading look.

"I've got a shopping date," said Hazel.

John looked at Sidney Bruck's watch, which was out on its owner's desk. "But it's not lunch hour, is it?"

Hazel waved toodle-oo and took off in search of the right lipstick to sport to tonight's party in Oldcastle's penthouse.

Left alone with Mr. Bruck, his own desperation equal to the

young editor's annoyance, John had no choice but to begin imparting his long story of how the *Cleveland Limited* and Mr. Giovanni
Roma and the veal *piccata* had led to his being here. He had reached
the part about his onboard haircut when Bruck began easing him
toward the door and, it turned out, into the path of Paul Montgomery, who'd been drawn to Sidney's office by the sound of John's
voice.

"Hey!" he shouted, clapping John's back. "It's our next editor-
in-chief!"

As soon as Paulie had gotten the look of admiration he craved, he
called down the corridor for Cuddles Houlihan and Becky Walter to
come meet this fine young visitor they all had. And once the two of
them had been introduced, John decided he'd better express interest
in some aspect of this office he'd succeeded in overcrowding.

"Mr. Bruck, what are those?" he asked, pointing to a tall stack of
manila envelopes.

"Rejects," said Sidney. "From our just-concluded fiction contest.
Perhaps Mr. Houlihan can enlighten you."

Cuddles dragged on his cigarette. "I was the first line of defense,"
he explained, exhaling.

"Yes," said Sidney, stimulated by a chance to inflict humiliation.
"As preliminary screener, Mr. Houlihan managed to read through
the contents of, I believe, four of those envelopes before higher authorities turned the remaining six hundred and ninety-three over to
me." Sidney decided to favor the boy with the wisdom of an old pro
twenty-eight years of age. "Mr. Shepard, what one really looks for in
magazine fiction is *less* of it. Today, too many short stories crowd too
many publications, prompting too many of the wrong people to buy
the publication at the newsstand."

John looked at Sidney, wondering who the wrong people might
be, hoping he wasn't one of them.

"It's a question of 'mass versus class,' " explained Sidney. "If one attracts a less-well-off reader, as magazine fiction tends to do, then editorial values plummet—along with the quality of advertisers. Mr. Harris runs a fiction contest because he likes contests. What he doesn't realize is that selecting one story from six hundred and ninety-seven submissions amounts to achieving just about the right ratio. If this magazine ran six pieces of fiction each year instead of twenty-four, we'd be drawing more of the right people to our party."

"I'm invited to the party tonight!" John exclaimed.

"Really?" said Sidney, who had not expected his figure of speech to produce this disagreeable piece of news. "Well, then, you, along with everyone else, will get to meet our lucky winner."

"Is Mr. Newman around?" asked John, so excited by this insider stuff he couldn't stop jumping from topic to topic.

"You might see him this evening," said Becky. "He doesn't seem to be in yet today."

"Getting ready for a hazardous assignment," said Cuddles. Newman had returned from the Plaza yesterday afternoon with evidence of his introduction to Rosemary LaRoche—an inch-long scratch mark on his cheek, her over-avid *au revoir.*

"Come on, John," said Becky, eager to get the boy away from Sidney Bruck as well as Cuddles, who might fill his ears with God-knows-what indiscretions. "Let me show you some of the other departments."

Just past Sidney's threshold, they were met by the magazine's most convivial researcher, drawn here, it would seem, by the scent of a newborn. Daisy was already tottering atop the party shoes she'd picked to wear this evening. *"Hello,"* she said to John, sweetly breathing into his unlined face, before remembering that her tutorial days were over, put paid to by the miraculous advent of Judge Francis X. Gilfoyle, who at the end of last night had not even demanded a kiss outside her Beekman Place doorway. Daisy retracted her visage from the new boy's, albeit with her own sort of tactile apology, a light rubbing of the young man's bicep. Before John could finish gulping, the whole claque, which Sidney Bruck was attempting to expel from his territory, fell suddenly silent—frozen by the fast, heavy approach of Jehoshaphat Harris.

He had Spilkes and Arinopoulos behind him. As he neared the cluster of employees blocking his path, he brandished the photographer's just-developed print.

It showed a lone bull, looking cold and confused, cocking its head at a statue of George Washington, as if to ask whether it was really necessary to cross the Delaware at such an hour on such a chilly morning.

"I've got a print-order meeting in two days!" cried Harris. "I'm supposed to be showing Oldcastle six pages of *wit* and *style* on the stock market. And what have I got? Some cockeyed, red-inked rant for a text and a bull with no bear for a picture! What are you all going to do about it?"

The question hung over the now-quiet hallway. Spilkes at last broke the silence with a soothing managerial pronouncement: "There's still time," he said.

Arinopoulos glared at the m.e. Did this commuting factotum have any idea how long it took to set up and execute one of these shoots?

Becky tried to position herself more directly between Harris and Cuddles. "Don't rise, Aloysius," she whispered, fearing he'd make some movement or quip that would thrust him into the boss's awareness.

Harris's eyes remained downcast upon the photographic fiasco in his hand. Finally, he asked: "Can we get Merrill to do an illo instead?"

"Of course," said Spilkes, in the all's-well-that-ends-well voice he tended to use in every phase of a crisis.

"Well," sighed Harris, his love of strategy and narrow escape kicking in. "I suppose that will take care of the visuals." He paused. "But there's only one thing to do about the words. Miss O'Grady!"

His roar drew Nan out of the Copy Department.

"Where's what's-his-name?" he asked. "The guy who looks like Harold Lloyd. The one who's always eating raisins."

"Allen Case," said Nan.

"That's the one. The kid who can write more like Fine or Stanwick than Fine or Stanwick when you're a couple of lines short. I've got a rewrite job for him."

"I'm afraid he's not here," said Nan. "He phoned in sick. He said he might make it in later."

"Tell him to lay off the twigs! Call him back and make him get in here!"

Thwarted for a moment, Harris scanned the faces in front of him, making some rural association when he got to John Shepard's.

"You know anything about livestock, kid?"

"Just my dog," said John, helplessly.

The editor-in-chief wheeled around. Spilkes and Arinopoulos followed suit and began piloting him back to his office. "Comb the berry bushes!" Harris cried. "Find Case!"

But there was no need to mount a search. The copyeditor, who always took the back stairs to avoid Mrs. Zimmerman's concerned clucking over how thin he looked, was coming into the corridor from the other end.

"Mr. Harris," Nan called out.

He turned around. "Case!" he cried, catching sight of the ventriloquial vegetarian.

Allen cautiously advanced toward this gaggle of his colleagues. Within a few seconds he was within the boss's bearlike clutch. Harris squeezed the fellow's left shoulder, discovering it to be as unfleshed as a ball bearing. "Jesus, kid," he said, removing his hand and sniffing the air. "You really *are* sick. You smell like you fell into a vat of cough syrup."

Allen shoved his right hand further into his pocket, trying to pull in any eucalyptus leaf that might be showing. He avoided Nan's suspicious glance.

"Not that I'd ever figure you for a malingerer, kid, not like these others. Come on," he said, once more putting Allen into his maw. "I've got something for you to do."

The two of them walked off looking like the number 10, and Allen could hear everyone behind starting to scatter. He took no pleasure in this strange new approval from Harris, but he did turn around long enough to take in the defeated expression on Gardiner Arinopoulos's carnivorous face.

"Hazel!" shouted Harris, now barreling forward in the direction of his long-gone secretary. "Go out and get some—what's your pleasure, kid? Lima beans? A bunch of bananas?" Ignoring Hazel's absence, he propelled Case into his office.

Within another few seconds, the corridor contained only Arinopoulos—recently so in favor, now so out of it—and John Shepard, who had a feeling he remembered from home, when a pickup basketball game would end as quickly as it began, with a fistfight, the asphalt swept clean of life and sound. Was *this* how the smooth, inevitable-looking magazine he relished each month came into existence? He had no idea what to make of the chaos he'd just witnessed, and no idea what to do next. He knew only that he never wanted to leave.

19

By 6:00 the floor appeared deserted, nearly everyone having gone home to primp for the party, or out to line their stomachs against the evening's impending alcoholic assault. Nan O'Grady was surprised when Norman Merrill entered Harris's office a moment after she went in to drop off a piece of copy.

The artist carried a large illustration, which he planned to leave for Harris's early-morning inspection. Nan asked him to flip up the bristol board's protective filmy paper and give her a look. Merrill obliged, revealing a gorgeous piece of pen-and-ink whimsy, in which a matinee-idol bull bore down upon a demurely frightened, eyelash-fluttering bear.

Nan shook her head in admiration. "Goodness, Mr. Merrill, it's better than Beardsley."

The artist's face went pink with pride. "Hazel passed my desk about an hour ago, and pronounced it 'the berries.' "

"Well," said Nan, "here's what the berries will be garnishing." Merrill read the first paragraph of copy that she handed him:

Inside his broker's office, the little merchant becomes a matador. He has come to buy on margin, to dye his cape in red ink and flash it at the bull—the great bull market he will no longer fear.

"Eerie," said Merrill.

"Isn't it?" said Nan. "I can't tell it from the real Roebling."

"Is Allen around?" asked Merrill. "I should pay him my compliments."

"I don't think so," said Nan. "He worked on this until about three. Then he put it on my desk and said he was going straight home."

"It's too bad he's not the sort to reward himself with this affair at Mr. Oldcastle's tonight."

"No, he's not," said Nan. "But what about yourself, Mr. Merrill? You deserve a bash for producing this illo."

The artist managed a sweet, tired smile. "I'll have to leave that to you young people. I'll be lucky to make it home to Woodside before my eyes shut."

Nan looked at Harris's clock. "I'll go with you, if you don't mind the company. I've got just time enough to get there and then back into the city. And to try fixing myself up in between." She rolled her eyes to indicate a losing battle.

"I'm sure you'll be a vision," said Merrill, who gave her his arm for the descent into Grand Central. After several minutes' straphanging under the East River and into Queens, the two of them were walking down narrow little Forty-first Drive in Woodside.

"You must stop in and say hello to my mother," declared Merrill once they reached his stoop. "She gets so little company. It would be a grand treat for her. Just for a moment?"

"Of course," said Nan.

Before Merrill's key could complete its turn in the lock, the front door opened from behind, revealing a tiny, stooped, ancient woman—who was already lit up with sociability.

"Come in!" she cried. "The boy's been here for some time! He's down the basement."

Merrill shot Nan a puzzled look. "Let me investigate," he said, wondering what intruder had conned himself past his mother's failing eyesight. "Mama, stay here with Miss O'Grady for a moment."

"Perhaps you could bring up some Vine-Glo, dear," said Mrs. Merrill. "It will be a nice treat for the four of us." A law-abiding soul who missed having spirits in the house, Mrs. Merrill had become devoted to these bricks of grape concentrate sold with the "warning" that two months in a dark, cool place would turn them into wine.

"Mr. Merrill," said Nan, "I think I should go down there with you." She and the illustrator settled the old lady in one of the front parlor's wicker chairs and headed, with quickness and caution, to the cellar.

Before they got fully down the wooden steps, they caught sight of two creatures hunched together near the coal furnace at the basement's far end.

"Now, Canberra," said the young man with his back to Nan and Merrill, "this door to the fire will be safely locked at all times. But you mustn't think of touching it, because it gets very hot."

The koala looked up, understandingly, into its companion's eyes and actually retracted one of its paws into its pouch. At last hearing the creak of the steps, Allen turned around.

"I'm sorry," he said, as soon as he saw Mr. Merrill standing in front of Nan. "I brought her here this morning. I couldn't think of anyplace else. My landlady's even threatening Sugar these days. She'd never understand."

Merrill nodded, before saying, with great delicacy, "But I'm afraid my mother—"

"She thinks it's a monkey!" said Allen, smiling more heartily than Nan had ever seen. "I told her there was an organ-grinder a block from the Graybar who'd just made a fortune in RCA stock and decided to abandon the poor creature who'd helped him earn a living for over ten years."

Merrill looked doubtful.

"It won't be for long," said Allen. "Canberra will be fine here until I can figure something out. I've gotten hold of more than enough eucalyptus, and as basements go, this one gets quite a lot of daylight."

Nan had been busy at the Vine-Glo apparatus. She now handed the illustrator a bucket of its runoff. "Mr. Merrill, why don't you take this upstairs and leave me with Allen for a minute or two?"

Once the artist departed with the beverage, she began speaking, as gently as she could, to this young man she'd been trying to supervise for the past year.

"Allen, this is quixotic. With a capital Q. And I don't add that as a matter of proper usage."

"I know," he said, finding it easier to look at the koala than his boss. "But if you could see what went on this morning, down on Wall Street with Arinopoulos!"

Nan listened to a soft but insistent recitation of the day's predawn events. Prior to seeing the bull, Allen assured her, Canberra had been dozing peacefully, thinking of her four brothers and sisters back in Queensland. But then "she was suddenly terrified. She'd never seen a dingo that big or that black, let alone wearing such a contraption on its head."

Nan was used to her colleague's animal fantasies, the dozens of weird creatures and habitats he could imagine himself into. But right now he seemed alarmingly separated from himself. "Allen, how much Vine-Glo have you had?"

"Two cups. It's very good!"

Nan rolled her eyes and looked unsuccessfully for a place to sit down. What was she going to do with this boy—or, for that matter, with herself? All day, ever since Spilkes had confided the latest ad figures to her, she'd been wondering if the magazine—such a showy, unsinkable success these past few years—might actually, having hit the iceberg Jimmy Gordon, be on its way to the bottom.

She looked at the koala, who maintained her adoring gaze upon Allen. The sight of such devotion acted as a reminder: before she could change her dress and get back on the subway, she had to walk her mother's Pomeranian.

"Allen," she sighed, looking at the watch that hung from her neck. "Couldn't you just get a dog?"

He looked at her, hurt; surely she knew his mission was bigger than that.

After starting back up the cellar steps, she turned around with a plea: "Promise me you won't try to walk that thing." She pointed to the koala. "Two brothers named Healy live down the block and you'll be in for the pasting of your life if they see you outside with that crea—"

"With Canberra," he corrected.

"With Canberra," she said, beginning a fast ascent, and feeling the need for something a lot stronger than Vine-Glo.

20

Hiram Oldcastle's penthouse at Park and Eighty-sixth occupied three floors and twenty-two rooms, nearly all with exceptional views, but an hour into the *Bandbox* party, the largest single cluster of guests could be found in a tiny space between a secondary pantry and the servants' dining room.

One of these guests was Hazel Snow, who while bending down to adjust her Holeproof Hosiery became the first to hear the rumble that signaled the light was about to blink. "Here we go," she said to Hannelore von Erhard, who stood next to her in such a short party dress she'd had to powder her knees, just like girls twenty years younger and forty pounds lighter.

"*Ja,*" said Hannelore, with some reverence. "Siegfried, *achtung.*"

Like everyone else in the group—even Mrs. Zimmerman, who left off smelling one of the huge flower arrangements from Armstrong & Brown—Siegfried now focused his eyes on the dumbwaiter. Its doors opened to reveal a shaking, clinking array of glasses—another four dozen old-fashioneds, sidecars, and vodka tonics—a crystalline miracle that the guests greeted as if it were Floyd Collins, come up at last, rescued from his cave.

If class versus mass remained the magazine's ongoing conundrum, tonight's party resolved those forces into the kind of giddy blend one was seeing more and more often on the city's social scene. Before the night was out, New York's big-domed literary mandarins—like John Farrar, poet-editor of *The Bookman,* over there with Paul Rosenfeld, saturnine music critic of the *Dial*—would be disporting themselves with everyone from *Bandbox*'s fashion assistants to its typists. This evening's shindig was so crowded and democratic that the owner of its venue couldn't stand to be there: Oldcastle was finishing up a holiday at his ranch in New Mexico.

The fiction contest's winning story had been printed up on thick, creamy paper and put between bright red covers. Swirling stacks of the production rose, mostly untouched, from a glass-topped table in the main salon. Nan O'Grady was one of the few guests who decided to have a look, since she'd soon be copyediting the story for the April issue. "Fair But for Fortune" was just eight pages long, and Nan managed to read it through in three sips of her whiskey sour. On page seven the tale's heroine chose to go off with the sarcastic young industrialist instead of the working-class yeoman, and on page eight the author, one Theophilus A. Palmer, made it clear that this was a happy ending, one the reader was supposed to like instead of lump.

It was, Nan supposed, an audacious twist. There was certainly no mistaking what its appeal had been to Sidney Bruck, who'd much prefer being at Oldcastle's ranch than inside this semi-hoi-polloi mob scene. Sidney couldn't even work his ticket tonight: having picked the winner, he was obligated to work Mr. Palmer's ticket instead. Nan could see her colleague on the other side of the immense room, introducing the new sensation to Horace Liveright. Watching young Mr. Palmer shake hands with the most important publisher at the party, Nan thought it odd that this tall, pompous winner looked more like a man discharging an obligation than collecting his big break.

She rolled her eyes and looked around, circumspectly, for the handsome figure of Stuart Newman, of whom there was yet no sign. She settled for gazing at Jeffrey Holmesdale, the blond, aristocratic-looking assistant to Alexander Woollcott, who was, someone said, tied up tonight, forty blocks downtown, reviewing a play. Nan took another sip of her drink and allowed herself a few seconds to imagine the willowy Mr. Holmesdale, more lovely than a Reynolds painting, as her very own. Well, there was no use barking up *that* tree; it probably belonged to the Fashion boys' part of the forest.

Daisy, of course, could confirm such a fact, but it would look too desperate even asking, Nan decided. Besides, the countess right now appeared caught up in calculating her own destiny. She could be seen, through the salon's doors, standing with her date on the apartment's glass-enclosed, heated terrace. From this distance, and by contrast with Francis X. Gilfoyle—whose gin-blossomed face was further flushed by a tight collar—one might assume Daisy still to be in the second or third blush of youth. She was beaming, lost for a moment in the thought of how Francis was even nicer than Sergei, the old Russian maître d' who'd given her all the vodka she still sold, a couple of bottles at a time, to Harris.

"Our own Daddy and Peaches," said Cuddles to Becky, pointing to the judge and countess.

"It seems like yesterday we were here for the Christmas party."

"I think it *was* yesterday," said Cuddles. "There's still a live poinsettia in one of the bathrooms. Redder than the judge."

"At least there aren't any of those horrible waitresses prancing around," said Becky, recalling the leggy elves and underclad Santa girls who'd served at the Christmas party, a typical Harris touch. "Tits the season!" Cuddles had exclaimed that night while clinking glasses with David Fine, who joined them now—to Becky's relief, since she still was waiting for her boyfriend to arrive from a function at the Cloisters. She would prefer not being alone with Cuddles when he did.

The food columnist drew Cuddles' and Becky's attention to Herbert Bayard Swope, the tall, redheaded editor of the *World,* whom Paul Montgomery was chatting up about his father. The elder Montgomery's death on the *Lusitania*—Siegfried and Hannelore had just paid Paul their usual tribute of a grave nod—was bound to interest the old war correspondent.

"Paulie's life is one big hedged bet," said Fine, a little enviously, since he himself was conscious of having put every chip he had on Harris.

"Max! Max!" they all heard Daisy cry. Max Stanwick was trying to reach one of the buffet tables, which fat Percy Hammond and big Heywood Broun were plundering like an old French farmhouse behind the lines. The crime writer gave up and allowed Daisy to show him what he'd accomplished for her and the judge. Max clinked his screwdriver against her highball.

Gilfoyle, despite the constriction of his dated duds, was no flat tire, and he fizzed with compliments for *Flaming Zeppelin* and *Ticker Rape,* the two novels Stanwick had managed to write since Jimmy Gordon hired him to report for *Bandbox.*

Daisy wanted to show off the judge to whomever else she could squeeze onto the terrace. But she had trouble catching the eye of either Richard Lord or the Wood Chipper, who were circumnavigating the salon in opposite directions—Lord in an admiring inventory of Elsie de Wolfe's decoration; Chip to overhear as many conversations as efficiently as he could. Daisy finally had to settle for summoning

John Shepard, who stood with Hazel behind the piano player as he banged out "Ukulele Lady."

Since his arrival here tonight, John had been uneasy about his baggy Oxford pants, hardly the right thing for a palace like this, but all he had until his trunk got to New York. Excusing himself from Hazel, he answered Daisy's excited wave by threading his way out to the terrace. En route he passed Burton Rascoe, who was taking notes for his newspaper column and watching Sidney Bruck introduce the contest winner to Andrew Burn. The publisher seemed unimpressed to the point of coldness. Mr. Palmer's winning story might be a forthright celebration of class over mass, but it undermined its own message by being a story at all. If Bruck wanted to limit the offerings of fiction in *Bandbox,* Burn wished to eliminate them altogether.

Despite their differing perspectives, the four men, as well as John, were soon unanimously distracted by the nearby sight and drunken sound of Waldo Lindstrom singing "There's Yes, Yes in Your Eyes" to a waiter he was making blush all the way to his patent-leather hair. Giovanni Roma, already contemptuous of the party's catering—these guinea hens from Longchamps—could now fume over this spectacle, too, until Lindstrom, failing to make headway with the waiter, began to display an alarming interest in the Afghan hound leashed to an actress from the *Follies.*

"What have you got, kid?"

Having reached the countess, John showed his glass of near-beer to this man on her right who'd asked the question. "It's swell!" he said. In fact, this third glass of it had put him on his way toward very mild, happy inebriation—and a loquacity that required no prompting. "This place is more ritzed up than O.O. McIntyre's, I'll bet!"

The man he was talking to nodded, then said in a smoky growl: "You've been checkin' out the chintz, shinin' an eye on the chinoiserie."

John's jaw dropped, and his glass of beer nearly dropped with it.

He realized this was Max Stanwick speaking to him, and suddenly all he could think to say himself was: "I, I don't know what to pay attention to first!"

The famous novelist-reporter leaned down to clasp John's shoulder and offer some advice about the business of observation: "You know what to listen for when you're someplace like this?"

John shook his head no.

"Everything," whispered Max.

"Everything," said John, lest he forget. He looked at Stanwick and nodded several times. He was still nodding when he at last turned to greet the countess and the judge, who drew him into a cozy foursome with themselves and Max.

A few feet away, at the same moment, Cuddles and Becky took note of Jimmy Gordon's entry into the salon. The triplex might be packed with editors from Hearst and Nast and all the other rival companies—even Frank Crowninshield's bobbing gray head was visible—but Jimmy's showing up did seem a bit much in the provocation department.

"Where's our boss?" said Becky to Cuddles.

"Relax," he replied. " 'Phat'll love this."

They watched Jimmy make his way across the room to shake hands with Spilkes and Andrew Burn. He backslapped both, and gave them a little razzing about the ad figures. "Nice to see you," he told Theophilus Palmer, who seemed to smile for the first time tonight.

Paul Montgomery, first standing on tiptoe to make sure the coast was clear, took hold of the Wood Chipper's elbow and propelled him toward Jimmy, as if doing the younger man a favor—making it okay for Chip to greet his former benefactor, since it was being done under the supervision of a current Harris star—i.e., Montgomery himself. Chip scowled during the brief forward march, unable to believe Paulie was so dumb as to think he hadn't been seeing Jimmy Gordon on a regular basis these past six months.

Of course, Chip was really protective coloring for Montgomery himself, who greeted Jimmy with a big handshake and jaunty question: "Everything copacetic at the competition?"

Becky and Cuddles recoiled from this scene, even if it was a good fifteen feet away, and threw themselves into the party's new, speeded-up phase of intoxication, which began with the arrival of three more cocktail carts—an angelus of Rob Roys, gin rickeys, and Presbyterians—as well as the piano player's rendition of "Let's Misbehave."

"They're playing our song," said Cuddles.

"They're playing your song," said Becky.

"You still seem to be singing solo."

"He'll be here," she replied. "Nothing wrong with working late hours. You should try it sometime."

"I'll bet he wears long underwear, too."

"Keep it up and I'll bet you get an old-fashioned in your lap."

"Excellent. You're an old-fashioned girl."

They were interrupted by the approach of Stuart Newman, whose right hand loosely held his date's, and whose left, more desperately, clutched a cream soda. The girl, with her peekaboo hat and Florida suntan, contrasted rather sharply with Stuart's openly haggard appearance. Becky was about to ask him how his first interview with Rosemary LaRoche had gone, but—as always these days—there wasn't enough time to gather the thought or complete the question. The party's center of gravity was shifting, suddenly, away from the terrace and into the salon, where Joe Harris had taken up position to perform the main business of the evening: introducing Mr. Theophilus A. Palmer to his public.

Harris stood with Betty on one side and, on his other, *Bandbox*'s sponsored contestant in the upcoming Bunion Derby, a massively promoted cross-country footrace that would begin in Los Angeles on March 4. "The next of these affairs had better be for you," said Harris, clearing his throat for a toast. The raw-boned, sandy-haired runner, a cousin of one of the ad salesmen, was much more Harris's sort of fellow than this vinegar-puss Palmer, whose story he'd read only an hour ago.

An excellent judge of fiction, the editor-in-chief was stewing about how this sour, pretentious story had passed muster with sour, pretentious Sidney—at whom he now glanced, skeptically. He shot an even stronger look at Houlihan, toward whom he felt newly furious. Cuddles was a better judge of fiction than either Sidney or himself, and in his not-so-long-ago heyday would have done a fine job with this contest, no doubt eliminating Mr. Palmer in the first round. At almost every editorial meeting, Harris liked to remind his staffers that the *Bandbox* reader had terrible values, which he expected them to cater to. And yet, Palmer's story of money trumping love left Harris's own sentimental heart quite cold. At this moment he wished they'd never announced the latest competition, which they'd done a few months ago, after he'd let Spilkes talk him out of running a story they'd received in the mail from Ernest Hemingway's thirteen-year-old brother Leicester in Oak Park, Illinois. NEW FICTION BY HEMINGWAY could have been the perfectly legal cover line. "We're better than that," Spilkes had said, and it was true. But what was the point of being any good at all if Theophilus A. Palmer was what you got instead of fun?

Harris at last raised his glass and came to life with a graceful joke about what might happen if the cross-country contestant and the short-story writer started playing each other's game. He did a less graceful job comparing the Palmer story's abrupt opening to Betty's choice of a plunging neckline for tonight's outfit. He'd pay for this last remark—if Betty had heard it—back at the Warwick. But for the moment Harris had the whole room with him. Whenever the center of attention, he blazed up warm and crackling, his deep voice a reliable bellows for his whole personality. Harris might look like a character actor, but in his world he was a star, and on occasions like these he had star power. With his glass aloft, he paid amusing, ribbing tribute to the other writers in the room besides Mr. Palmer, and he concluded by observing how "when it comes to fiction or nonfiction, this once mere fashion magazine is the one that figured out how 'prose makes the man.' " At which point he began staring at Jimmy Gordon, that thief of his own potent formula.

Jimmy smiled back and raised his glass along with everyone else. He knew that in another minute, in full view and earshot of everybody, Harris, unable to help himself, would come over and start something, a bit of repartee that would soon turn sufficiently loud and nasty to land both of them in Burton Rascoe's column.

As the applause died and Harris shook Mr. Palmer's boneless hand, the editor-in-chief never took his eye off Jimmy. His rage gathering, he issued, from the corner of his mouth, a summons to Stuart Newman, now only a few feet away. Was there any chance, he wanted to know, that Rosemary LaRoche might surprise them with a grand entrance, upstaging the night's honoree? No? Too bad. It would be worth spoiling the surprise of the first female cover just to wipe the smile off Jimmy's face.

At this same moment, Jimmy Gordon was making a sidelong query of his own, to Chip Brzezinski. "Find out who little Skippy in the Oxfords is." He nodded in the direction of John Shepard. "I smell a rat, or at least a gimmick." Chip had been trying all day to get the lowdown on this kid's supposedly spontaneous arrival in New York. Newly motivated, he went out to the terrace to investigate further.

Meanwhile, Andrew Burn tried presenting a Hickey-Freeman executive to Harris, who was too busy fuming to spare a word for this important advertiser. He was now fully furious—over yesterday morning's numbers; this sobersides of a contest winner; the apparent lack of vodka on the nearest drinks cart. He made do with a martini, and downed half of it before marching toward the terrace door with the first idea he came up with for alleviating his misery: he was going to fire Cuddles.

Seeing Harris pad across the Savonnerie carpet, as a dozen party-goers quickly cleared a path, Becky realized that the boss was up to something dire. She knew she must not allow his motive to meet its opportunity. So she pushed Cuddles into the nearest gaggle of guests, and then on through the next one and the next, until the two of them exited the enclosed part of the terrace and went out onto a stretch of it that was unprotected from the January air.

"You'll thank me for this," she said, shivering.

"I probably won't," he answered. "But it still counts."

It was too dark out here to see whether he was giving her the "look," but when he took off his coat and put it, along with his arm, over her shoulders, Becky realized she was too cold and too lit to protest—or even to mind.

Back inside, without Cuddles to bear down upon, Harris had been left with no real destination but Jimmy Gordon, who extended his hand to his former boss.

"Jimmy," said Jehoshaphat Harris. "You must be dog-tired from following in our footsteps."

Jimmy, saying nothing, sat down in an antique French chair, forcing Harris to lean over and pay him court.

"It's a little early for you to start playing Sun King," said the older man.

"You're off by one Roman numeral, Joe." Jimmy tapped the arms of the chair. "This is Louis the Fifteenth. One-five. The exact percentage our ads are up and yours are down."

"Yeah," said Harris. "I hear you're going to do a fashion piece on the correct rubber gloves to wear when you break into an old friend's place and rob him blind."

"If I do," said Jimmy, "you can be sure I'll get Stanwick to write it."

Monitoring the conversation, Spilkes decided to summon help from Gianni Roma and David Fine. Like a delegation from the League of Nations, the three men approached Harris and urged him to call it a night, at least here at Oldcastle's.

"Come on, Joe," said Fine. "Let's go to a speako. I've got all these paid-up memberships going to waste." He extracted a half-dozen cards for the "Pen and Pencil," "Artists and Writers," and the like. His suggestion proved indirectly effective: once Betty saw the cards come out of Fine's wallet, she decided to intervene herself. "Joe, you're boiled enough. Let's go. Home."

Looking, half-gratefully, like Jiggs after a swat with the rolling pin, Harris withdrew. Jimmy Gordon waved goodbye to his rival, his hand's dismissive flutter seeming to signal that, in any case, his levee was at an end. Baron de Meyer, the *Bazaar* photographer, never got the picture he'd hoped the onetime patron and onetime protégé would pose for together. Joe and Betty were out the door at 10:25, well before the party's population came close to peaking.

During the next half-hour, guests continued to come off the elevator onto the twenty-sixth floor; Jeffrey Holmesdale gave odds that his boss Woollcott would yet show up before midnight, after the curtain had dropped and he'd filed his review over the telephone. Someone put "O, for the Wings of a Dove" onto the Victrola, and the celestial, million-selling voice of Ernest Lough, that choirboy phenomenon, plunged the salon into cheerful absurdity. As eleven o'clock neared and the intake of alcohol accelerated, most of those present grew increasingly oblivious.

A few, however, became more purposeful: tired of trying to penetrate Daisy's foursome, where little Tom Sawyer still chattered away, Chip Brzezinski made off to the kitchen, where he'd earlier spotted the kind of girl he liked for a single night: one who was mopping her angry brow as she wiped the dishes. This was not a maiden holding out for Barrymore or Howard Kenyon.

Ever alert to the duties of reception, Mrs. Zimmerman had sub-consciously spent much of the evening near the elevator, and when three gentlemen got off it around 10:55, she asked if they were look-ing for anyone in particular. Only after inquiring did she recognize the youngest and best-looking of the three as Becky's boyfriend, Daniel Webb.

"She's out on the terrace, I'm pretty sure."

Daniel thanked Mrs. Z and ventured into the apartment's vast in-terior, leaving her with the other two gentlemen, each quite a bit rougher hewn than himself.

"I'm lookin' for the duchess," said the one who had trouble sti-fling a cough. "And for her daddy." After an explosion of hacking, he identified himself as Eddie Diamond. Mrs. Zimmerman never did get the name of his companion, but she led the two of them into the salon and pointed toward the terrace, where she remembered last seeing Daisy. Without even a grunt, the men ventured off in that direction.

On the way, they passed Nan, who'd been depressed tonight by each sight of Newman's pretty date. She was wondering if it wasn't time to catch the subway home, and curious whether the koala bear in Mr. Merrill's basement had gone to bed. The two men also brushed by Waldo Lindstrom, who was threatening to jump from the open part of the terrace if Gianni didn't give him the cabfare to go up to Small's Paradise in Harlem.

A few feet away, Max Stanwick was now huddled with Stuart Newman, who wanted to know how one went about securing some-body's police record from another state.

"For a story?" asked Max.

"No," said Newman, who hadn't mentioned Rosemary LaRoche. "For personal protection."

Eddie Diamond, far more boiled than Joe Harris had been a half-hour ago, finally noticed Daisy and the judge. It was the latter for whom he had a message. "Hey, Your Magistrate, you'd better get your carcass down to Centre Street, toot sweet."

Daisy's expression pleaded for further details.

"We got a problem," said Eddie. "And it needs immediate attention. Out at the Juniper development"—he couldn't name the project without sneering—"it seems that one of Mr. Wellman's contractors was just found very dead in a ditch. The foreman's been nabbed for it, and he's makin' noises about connecting The Brain to this little incident if he doesn't make bail pronto. Which is where you come in, Your Excellency." He poked the judge's shoulder. "We gotta get you downtown."

Gilfoyle gave Daisy's forearm a reassuring squeeze, but his face betrayed considerable anxiety.

"You don't get time to think this over," said Eddie, who nonetheless gave the judge a few seconds to squirm. Diamond used the time to take a quick survey of Oldcastle's lair, or as much as he could see of it from out here. Only when he directed his eyes to a griffin gargoyle jutting from the terrace's exterior did he notice what he'd up to now overlooked: a face as open and sunny as the gargoyle's was menacing.

"You been here the whole time?" Eddie asked John Shepard, who after seven near-beers had been steadying himself against the edge of a small metal table.

"Yessiree," said John, still happy to make one more improbable acquaintance.

"Tell me, kid. What'd you just hear?"

"*Everything!*" exclaimed John, raising his glass, proud of having committed Max Stanwick's lesson to memory.

It was the last thing anybody would have remembered him saying—if anybody besides Eddie Diamond and his colleague had heard him say it; but Daisy and Francis X. Gilfoyle were too preoccupied with urgent conversation about the judge's trip downtown.

And Becky and Cuddles, still unaware of Harris's departure or Daniel Webb's arrival, were far out of earshot, hiding in the library, which they'd been able to enter from the unheated stretch of the terrace.

John Shepard himself, still in love with New York and the magazine and near-beer, failed to understand how his simple reply to a straightforward question soon led to his being stuffed—quite discreetly—into Hiram Oldcastle's dumbwaiter, and then, a few minutes later, into the trunk of Mr. Diamond's car.

2 1

BUTTON UP YOUR OVERCOAT.

Harris read the cable from Betty and tossed it into the hotel-room wastebasket. It was curious how the two of them reversed behavior whenever he made the annual trip to London. Suddenly Betty felt the need to send two or three wires a day, in fair approximation of his own compulsive telephoning from floor to floor of the Graybar Building. When traveling, he liked to forget about everything back home, even her; for a week or two he relapsed into something like his bachelor days, surrounded on the upper deck or in the hotel bar by only his crew of male cronies. Good as Betty's advice could be— even about the overcoat; it was freezing over here, and the crossing had been worse—Harris decided he would once more let her telegrams go unopened and unanswered. This had become his standard practice while abroad, and she didn't object. The wires, which never contained much of importance, had performed their function as soon as she sent them: behaving like Joe made her feel he was still around.

Harris and his men always had to cross at this frigid time of year if they were going to fill the summer issues with the kind of English outfits even the new *Bandbox* reader wanted to see—all the garden-party and boating stuff that, in truth, didn't change much from year to year. While scouting it, the editors also had British motorcars and the Prince of Wales to catch up with, neither of which much impressed Harris.

But he liked being here. In London he felt exotic and secure all at once. The hotels, thank God, got more Americanized every year; on his first trip over he'd had a bathroom down the hall. This time out Andrew Burn had booked the *Bandbox* party into the slick, modern Berkeley—part of the relentless effort to keep the editor-in-chief up-to-date. The Berkeley's daily tea dance was filled with pansies and girls even skinnier than Hazel, and there was too much chrome everywhere, but even so, Harris was content.

As he waited for it to be 5:30, the time appointed for Fine, Montgomery, and Spilkes to meet him in the bar downstairs, Harris took a sip of hock and made a mental review of the last few weeks. The overnight editorial retreat at his house up in Dutchess County, held only five days after the party at Oldcastle's, had produced a few good ideas, marred though it had been by Malocchio's atrocious catering. Gianni had sent up less than half the food they required, and those meager rations had nearly poisoned those in attendance. They'd finally had to scare up a box of hot dogs and two buckets of beans from a roadhouse in Millbrook; David Fine had still been throwing up, not from the ocean but from Gianni, on the way over here.

Harris preferred not to imagine what had Gianni so off the beam. Most other matters had been on the upswing by the time they embarked from New York. Termagant though she was, Rosemary LaRoche appeared, from what little he'd seen and heard, to be smitten with Newman. Both text and layout of the bulls-and-bears piece had ended up in tiptop shape. And there'd been good ink in the trades and gossip columns for Mr. Palmer, months before his short story would even run. Oldcastle had sent a handwritten note congratulating Harris on the party's success, which he'd inferred from the amount of shrimp-tail and broken glass vacuumed up from his carpets.

Still, Harris was nagged by the feeling he'd forgotten to take care of something before setting sail. And yet what could it be? He'd settled Stanwick's contract for the coming year; had had a drink, at Burn's insistence, with the Hickey-Freeman executive; had even signed the industry letter to the Postmaster General protesting higher rates for printed matter. Damned if he could think of anything he'd missed; besides, if there really had been a loose end, Spilkes would have remembered to tie it up. They wouldn't be gone long, in any case. If you added up the voyage out and the one back, they'd be spending more time on the water than over here. In the mere several days they had, Richard Lord would buy up the clothes; Fine would compose a send-up of college dining; and Montgomery would write about having a bespoke suit made on Savile Row. He'd also interview some English skiers departing for the Winter Olympics in France.

Spilkes was along to make sure everybody did what they were supposed to be doing. And yet, at 5:30, down in the Berkeley bar, the managing editor was the only one missing. Lord might be excused from the nightly bonhomie, but for Spilkes it remained mandatory. Harris looked at his watch, scowled at Fine and Montgomery, and ordered a single-malt.

"Say what you will about this country," he pronounced. "A man can still order a drink here without committing a crime." This was his annual toast to John Bull, made as he sliced into a small wheel of cheese atop the table.

"Don't use a knife on that," said Fine. "Stilton takes a scooper. Let me get the waiter."

"For Christ's sake," said Harris. "It's cheese, not pistachio ice cream."

Fine, who hated having his gastronomic pedagogy cut short, frowned at the boss. "Just be glad we're not eating dinner here. I had a gander at the kitchen, and it makes Gianni's look like a surgical table. You know, I'm *still* not completely recov—"

"What's the matter with Gianni, anyway?" asked Paul Montgomery. "Does anybody really know?"

Harris and Fine both had their theories and fears, mostly centered on Gianni's sordid nightlife, but neither one said anything. Paulie did not reside in Harris's innermost circle, and thus it wasn't really his place to talk about Malocchio's owner. Letting him ask about Gianni would be like letting him ask about Betty; it was too weirdly intimate and, even worse, might create some expectation of reciprocity. Harris had no interest in the wives and children of his staff, and no record of ever asking about either. Did Montgomery even *have* a wife, let alone some towheaded Paulie Jr.?

The editor's momentary effort to recall this information was suddenly swamped by a wave of nostalgia for Cuddles and Jimmy Gordon, who both used to make this trip. God, would he have to invite Sidney Bruck next year, just to replenish the ranks? An awful thought. But what alternative existed? Newman was ineligible for obvious reasons, and you couldn't ask Burn: he'd be too close to having a home-court advantage when the conversation turned competitive.

Paulie never pressed his inquiry into Gianni's distraction. In truth, he was more worried about *Joe* being off his game. Maybe the magazine really *was* as shaky as it had begun to seem through most of January? Paulie had taken to wondering if his bridge to Jimmy Gordon was burnt or merely singed. He hadn't had enough time to test it at the Oldcastle party, but all the way across the Atlantic he'd been trying to decide whether he should have gone over to Jimmy last spring, right at *Cutaway*'s start-up.

Spilkes, ten minutes late, entered the hotel bar.

"Where have you been?" asked Harris.

"The National Gallery," said the managing editor, sitting down. "Sorry."

Harris looked at him as if he'd said he'd been held up at a convention of lepidopterists. On his four trips to this city, the editor-in-chief had never seen the inside of St. Paul's, or the Tower of London, or even a theatre, let alone the National Gallery. Spilkes, by contrast, had an almost touching devotion to the professed *Bandbox* ideal of well-roundedness and self-improvement—a sound mind in a sound body in a good suit—and he always squeezed visits to a museum or monument into those moments he was allowed outside Harris's clubland cocoon of hotel bars and hired cars. David Fine had once, on his own, wandered up to Scotland for a couple of days, claiming to be giving thought to a story about haggis. When he got back, Harris told him never to do it again.

Who needed Scotland? Right here in London they were all, more than ever, lairds to his king. Every long dinner stretched their waistbands and reaffirmed their fealty. Tonight, once the car had covered the distance between the Berkeley and the Strand, they settled down to eat at Simpson's. Harris declined the table beneath a plaque paying tribute to Dickens, apparently once as much a regular here as Cohan in the Oak Room; he preferred a spot by the open fire, where they could smell the chops and mutton saddles while eating a long, haphazard meal that included, along with the slowly sizzling viands, some hare soup, pudding, cheese, and trifle. Trifle of *what*? Harris always wanted to ask the waiter, but every year he stopped himself, lest Fine override the server with his own long lecture on the subject.

Finished eating, they loosened belts and braces and continued to sit beside what now seemed a campfire. Montgomery and Fine quietly argued over whether Dempsey and Tunney would fight a third time, Paulie taking Dempsey at his word that they wouldn't, Fine taking Dempsey's pledge no more seriously than he did Tunney's book-learning and pretensions to poetry. The argument might have ended in a draw had Paulie not thrown in the towel and proclaimed Fine "probably—no, absolutely—right." Spilkes predicted that the Fed would soon rein in the market, and Harris told him he was wrong, that Mellon would keep the party going. When the four of them had exhausted these topics, they embraced nostalgia, that traveler's refuge, retelling the stories of how each had come to join the others: the fateful lunch at Malocchio when Fine talked to Harris about Christy Mathewson and the 1912 cabernet; the first piece Montgomery wrote for the magazine, so full of similes Harris was moved to ask whether it was a story or a reversible raincoat.

This particular reminiscence had to be edited, not because it came at the end of the evening, but because neither Harris nor Montgomery could bring himself to mention that the raincoat question had been addressed to Jimmy Gordon, the story's editor and Paulie's original patron. As soon as Jimmy threatened, like Banquo's ghost, to invade the evening, Harris banished the thought of him and summoned the old carver back to their table to receive an enormous tip. With his rival now safely out of mind, Harris watched two skinny boys—New Year's babes to the carver's Father Time—bus the dishes. He fell into a memory of his own first job, washing plates at a hofbrau back in Newburgh when he was less than these kids' age and nearly as thin.

Once out in the cold air, Harris surprised everyone by dismissing the driver and announcing that they would walk back to the Berkeley. The mood of self-connoisseurship was fully upon him now, and he wanted to prolong it. As the group strolled home, it fell to Spilkes, the least drunk of the four, to remember which side of the street the cars here drove on. He heard Harris's voice, thickened with claret and the late hour, telling Montgomery and Fine, as if they'd never before heard the story: " 'Give me six months,' I said to him. And he said: 'Take a year.' And do you know how long it took me to turn things around?"

Paulie offered a well-educated guess: "One business quarter?"

"One business quarter!" said Harris.

At moments like this, Spilkes felt a genuine tenderness toward his boss, whose shrewdness was forever being trumped by his childlike lack of guile. Before they reached the hotel, amidst his war stories and some ominously irregular footwork, Harris declared, without abashment and to no one in particular: "God, I love my life."

Inside the Berkeley lobby, Spilkes gathered up and distributed everyone's messages. Getting into the lift, Harris flipped through the three or four for him, smiling at what he recognized as another wire from Betty. He gave the little yellow envelope a kiss, but true to his word put it into his pocket unread.

"And so to bed!" he exclaimed, getting out of the elevator, shielded from Betty's telegraphed news that PALMER CRIBBED STORY.

22

Whenever the boss and his lieutenants went to London, a slow-paced delinquency settled over the fourteenth floor of the Graybar, the sort of civilized languor Harris missed from his beloved 1890s. The employees, who came in late if at all, played golf with mailing tubes and pin cushions; bet sports pools; made margin purchases over the telephone; necked in the Fashion Department's capacious closets.

But the morning of Thursday, February 2, was different. The

news that Theophilus Palmer's prize-winning story was, in fact, pla-
giarized had broken in the previous afternoon's papers, and even
those shooting rubber bands into their wastebaskets now had eyes
peeled and ears cocked in the direction of Sidney Bruck's tightly
closed door. Would he decide to emerge, head held high, or wait for
aggrieved authority to come knocking with his punishment for having chosen Palmer? Who that authority might be, in the absence of
Harris and Spilkes, remained unclear, though it had been the subject
of much speculation around Mrs. Washington's coffee wagon.

According to the production schedule, Nan O'Grady and Allen
Case were supposed to begin copyediting Mr. Palmer's story today.
But now, in her unexpected idleness, Nan toyed with the temptation
to go knock on Sidney's door and ask whether, in light of what she'd
been hearing, she should prepare another piece of fiction as a substi-
tute. No, it would be more delicious to wait until Sidney was forced
to come to her. So she took off her shoes, adjusted her chair, and
leaned back, happy to read a novel until he came calling. The Copy
Department was, in any case, deserted; even Allen, normally consci-
entious, had been coming in later each morning. He'd told her he
was making the rounds of freighter companies, trying to book a passage back to Australia for the koala, but she feared he was actually
continuing to case that awful animal warehouse. She and Mr. Merrill
had pleaded with him not to go near it, warning him to think about
the dangerous types who could be running it, but the message failed
to penetrate some fundamental part of his logic, which held that all
humans were sufficiently dangerous to render moot any differences
of degree.

Outside Harris's office, Hazel and Daisy kept their own watch on
Sidney's door while trying to decide which movie to attend this
afternoon, *Buck Privates* or *The Student Prince*.

"So what's up with the judge?" asked Hazel, while turning a page
of the *Daily News*.

The question left Daisy flustered, and uncharacteristically discreet. "I have him smoking Dr. Blosser's Cigarettes," was all she could let herself say right now. "The medicinal herbs are good for the sinuses. He's constantly congested, from tension."

"Mm-hmm," said Hazel, who'd heard the rumors about Francis X. Gilfoyle, but pretended to be more absorbed by the list of movie showtimes.

"There's just an awful amount of pressure in his job," said the countess. "Messengers knocking at the door in the middle of whatever quiet dinner I've prepared. They pounce on the poor dear just after he's put his feet up on my hassock." She did not make clear that these messengers weren't exactly municipal employees. They brought news and reminders not from the judge's docket manager but from Eddie Diamond and Arnold Rothstein. Gilfoyle had succeeded in getting the Juniper project foreman out on bail, but was now expected to make the DA kick the charges entirely, for a supposed lack of what was actually overwhelming evidence. After a month in the judge's gentlemanly company, Daisy still didn't know exactly what Rothstein "had" on him, though she suspected it was gambling debts. The whole business had her worried and cross; the other morning she'd startled one of the fact-checkers (her last initiate) with a stern lecture against the horse-racing bet he was calling in to his bookie.

Giving up on the possibility of further revelations, Hazel changed the subject from the judge to Stuart Newman, and whether or not, given the much-discussed clutches of Miss LaRoche, he'd actually make it to Washington for a column he was supposed to write. Prediction from Daisy in a matter like this had considerable authority, but before the countess could speak, what everybody had been waiting for suddenly transpired: Andrew Burn was marching over the linoleum toward the office of Sidney Bruck.

He pushed open the door—and left it open.

"How bloody stupid can you be?" The short Scotsman, his bald pate red with agitation, somehow managed to bellow and burr at the same time.

"Who are you to interfere with the fiction pages?" replied Sidney, at half the volume but with equal indignation. He attempted to begin a lecture on the "church-and-state separation" of a magazine's business and editorial sides—a dynamic nearly as uneasy as "class versus mass"—but was cut short by Burn, who now stood only inches from his face: "I'm running this show until Harris gets back, buddy boy. I'm His Eminence and His Majesty all rolled into one."

Sidney could not bring himself to ask whether Harris already knew about the fiasco, but he winced, expecting Burn now to convey a transatlantic thrashing. When nothing more was uttered, Sidney could only ask, weakly: "How was I supposed to know the story wasn't original?"

"If Winchell and Rascoe could figure it out, *you* bloody well should have! Maybe you don't know how much trouble this magazine is in. A lot more than you think, buddy boy. Your portly boss sees a set of figures once a quarter. I get arithmetic every day, and the digits aren't dancing, Mr. Bruck. They're dropping, dropping, dropping. So don't tell me I'm not supposed to put out fires set by little piss-pants boys like you, playing with somebody else's matches!"

The publisher at last closed Sidney's door, shutting the two of them inside his small office.

Chip Brzezinski, who'd been listening from the closest safe position on the corridor, felt thrilled by Burn's tirade. It contained genuine news that he could drop at Jimmy Gordon's grateful feet. Once the door shut, he raced to the stairs at the back of the Art Department, hotfooting them two at a time up to eighteen, flying past Jimmy's secretary and straight into the office of *Cutaway*'s editor-in-chief.

Jimmy Gordon sat behind his desk, chatting calmly with Mr. Theophilus Palmer.

Chip came to a halt, breathing but not speaking through his open mouth. He struggled not to say "I don't get it."

"Did you two not meet at the party?" asked Jimmy, nonchalant as could be. "Brzezinski, say hello to Pierce Coleman. An old graduate-school pal of mine."

Chip wasn't exactly sure what graduate school was, though he knew it had something to do with Jimmy's "Fairy Queen," which he felt pretty sure was a book.

"How could you plan this?" he finally asked.

"Because," said Jimmy, "I understand Sidney and just what appeals to that slender nose he's got stuck in the air."

"American literature of the late nineteenth century," explained Coleman, "is now a 'field.' *My* field, as it happens. I found, in an issue of *Cosmopolitan* from 1887, exactly the sort of story Jimmy assured me Mr. Bruck would like. I updated the clothes and some of the slang and, more crucially, left generous chunks of it unchanged, before submitting it as the work of one Theophilus A. Palmer."

"And succeeding admirably," said Jimmy. "You, however," he said, looking at the Wood Chipper, "have so far only failed."

Chip moved his eyes from Jimmy to Mr. Coleman's beautiful alpaca coat, probably the reward he'd gotten for his sleight of hand. He'd likely fed Winchell and Rascoe the story himself, not in person but in a little note from Pierce Coleman, scholar-detective. The expertise involved in such an exploit put Chip only further into the shade; what he'd just overheard from Burn now seemed very small potatoes.

"So what have you come up here about?" Jimmy asked.

"Uh, it can wait," said Chip, slinking away. His energies were so depleted that he rode the elevator back down to fourteen, where even Mrs. Zimmerman realized she'd be better off not asking if anything was wrong. Once back in the checkers' bull pen, he threw his

IN basket onto the floor, even though Becky Walter was right nearby looking something up in the Dun & Bradstreet book.

"Gee," she said, "I wouldn't have expected you to feel so bad for Sidney."

Chip ignored her, which was fine by Becky. Unlike most of the deadbeats around here, she had work to do, a little what-to-buy piece on *Nelson's Loose-Leaf Encyclopaedia,* "the reference library that never gets out of date." Endorsed by Thomas Edison himself, this thirteen-volume production seemed the perfect embodiment of their whole frantic era. Every few months *Nelson's* sent subscribers printed "updates": all the newest developments in Refrigeration, Automobiles, Ultraviolet Glass, and Soviet Russia. The modernized articles then took their alphabetical place inside one of the encyclopedia's ring binders; the obsolete entries were extracted and thrown away. Even the Mayans and James Madison were subject to revision, depending on new finds by archaeologists, new judgments by historians.

This huge mutating enterprise, which at the moment took up much of her small office, perplexed and amused Becky, who couldn't quite summon the disdain she supposed she ought to be feeling for it. Yes, she should be wishing she were at Daniel's place, tucked into his window seat, reading one of his old, foxed editions of Malory instead. But the wish wasn't there.

Was she more a girl of her time than she liked to admit? Didn't she right now miss the customary noise and bustle of the fully staffed *Bandbox*? And hadn't she enjoyed her adventure with the Composograph a few weeks ago—relished its zany, flickering triumph? She might not suffer from the present age's worst nervous maladies, but could she deny the pleasure she took in being around those who did? As she snapped open one of the *Nelson's* ring binders to insert the latest on Iberia and Immunology, she wondered whether Stuart Newman would make it in this morning to give her the latest installment—awful but stimulating—of life with Rosemary. And she thought, with an actual sigh, about Cuddles, who for the duration of Harris's trip was choosing outright absence over on-site idleness.

23

Having earlier this week seen both *The Student Prince* and *Buck Privates*—the latter twice, out of a peculiar, better-left-unexplored case he had on ZaSu Pitts—Cuddles was spending the day at home in Brooklyn, sharing a tin of sardines with Kitty Sark and catching up on what the papers had to say about the missing Smith College co-ed: the state planned to search the pond one last time, using submarine lights.

He also noticed the little calamity that Mr. Palmer had created for Joe Harris.

'Phat's troubles did seem to be mounting, and while Cuddles retained a soft spot for the boss, he wondered just what use there was, to the world at large, in saving Harris from Jimmy. True, the two men weren't much alike—Jimmy lacking 'Phat's sweet, chewy center—and their magazines, for all that they followed the same formula, weren't indistinct. Jimmy couldn't keep *Cutaway* from hectoring its readers: every other page was a pronouncement about the best and worst of this or that, a list of rules the *au courant* reader had damned well better learn if he didn't know them already. If Joe made readers feel that they were getting away with something, that they'd acquired a worldly-wise rich uncle, Jimmy made them feel as if they'd been drafted. But even so: the war between the two men and magazines was still a matter of novelty jousting with novelty—in a time when novelty itself had lost its newness.

How he had once loved the game. Cuddles now thought back to the days when each issue of *Puck,* with its deeply watercolored covers and irreverent news from every precinct of the brand-new century, landed on the newsstand like the circus coming to town. *TRUTH JUSTICE BREVITY WIT* promised the motto atop special numbers on the tango or "The News in Rime." His own colors had begun to fade years ago, but as he considered things now, he realized it was only inside the hall of mirrors set up by *Cutaway*'s birth, last spring, that he had ground to a stop. An inner, final admission of the hopelessness of his feelings for Becky had come at the same time. (He'd given her, the month Jimmy Gordon's first issue came out, a book of Millay's poems, with the inscription, *"My candle burns at neither end."*) Since then, except for his reflexive mooning glances and the occasional crack about Daniel, he'd tried to call it quits, tried to free the two of them from this unattaching attachment that left her embarrassed and him miserable.

Having split the last sardine with Kitty Sark, he was now dozing off. His whole life had dozed off. No one would figure him for a seeker of El Dorado, but the churning forward movement of his father's wagon was still somewhere inside him, a muffled hum, background noise for this afternoon's couchbound dream, wherein Cuddles steered a team of horses through some cacti and falling rocks, toward a green-and-gold valley he'd just spotted below.

An hour passed before he woke. The sight of a Palace bill on the coffee table kept him confused for a second. No, he thought, looking up at the ceiling and failing to see any rosettes. He wasn't there, and he wasn't in El Dorado, either. He was just here on the couch, *hors de combat* and out of sardines.

The radio was softly playing "My Pretty Girl," and Kitty Sark's eyes looked wide with alarm. It took Cuddles a moment to realize why: his own eyes were moist with tears.

Surrender had brought him about as much peace as sobriety seemed to be bringing Newman. Another year like the last and he'd be ready for a jar inside Hubert's Museum of freaks over on Forty-second Street. No amount of chaste resignation was going to change the fact that he loved Becky Walter. The yearning for her had lived inside him almost since Coolidge started taking up space in the White House; she remained the possibility of love in the age of Mammon. *LET'S PUT THE CUPID BACK IN CUPIDITY,* he'd written across the last Valentine he'd sent her. Even now, still, he had to find a way of winning her. What was left of his instincts told him he couldn't make that happen by wearing his sad, barely jingling cap and bells. It was time to suit up and enter the lists in Joe and Jimmy's noisy, pointless tournament, because that was where, though she only half knew it, Becky wanted to be playing herself.

And if he could find a way to offer himself as an allied lover-in-arms?

A surge of something like hopefulness ran through him, but he groaned when he realized where all these King Arthur images were coming from: that prattling she used to feel obliged to do about Daniel-the-medievalist's work.

Even so, he was going to get off the couch.

"All right," he said to Kitty Sark, swinging his feet to the floor. "Make way for the Renaissance."

He stubbed his toe on the coffee table, but the cat, encouragingly, brushed his leg.

24

"I still think 'Harris Tweed' would have been a good story," said Spilkes to his boss.

"Nah," said Harris, who had vetoed the idea of a feature on *his* having a bespoke suit made. "Let it be about Montgomery. I like staying behind the scenes." Actually, he loved being present on the pages of his own magazine, in the occasional "editor's letter" or short endorsement of some gadget. But any tailoring story would have to include measurements and at least sketches of the customer, and Harris did not like to acknowledge the much-increased girth that had come with his late-life success.

Looking at Spilkes, who was wearing a just-acquired black bowler, hard as a construction helmet, he had to give his m.e. points for getting into the spirit of the thing; when it came to fashion, Harris himself did no more than was needed to preserve the formula by which *Bandbox*'s clothes-consciousness floated its journalism. Today's accommodation of the former had Harris and his companions at Henry Poole & Co., 37 Savile Row, where Paulie, who would soon be no sylph either, could begin chronicling the creation of a three-piece suit.

On the outside, lacking any window display, Poole's looked resolutely dull, more like a men's shop in Newburgh than New York. Inside, however, skylights drew down the morning sun onto dozens of bolts of cloth that had been unrolling themselves for a line of patrons stretching back beyond Lord Melbourne and forward past Edward VII. Now *there*, thought Harris, fingering a heavy houndstooth pattern, was a man who looked like a king—the opposite of the current feckless Heir, almost as skinny as that bark-eating copyboy back home.

"Is it true he once wore a sweater under his dinner jacket?" Harris asked one of the ancient, soft-voiced tailors. "The Prince of Wales, I mean."

"I'm afraid that's false, sir. But he has done quite a lot to 'boost,' if you'll pardon the expression, the Fair Isle Shetland sweaters made up in Scotland."

"He ever come in here himself?"

"We go to the palace, sir."

"Buckingham?"

"St. James'."

"I guess old George and Mary finally gave him the heave-ho."

Attempting to refract, if not change, the subject, the tailor informed Harris that "Sir Godfrey Thomas, the prince's secretary, makes all the arrangements for our visits."

Harris wondered for a moment, as he did with almost every male name that came his way, whether there might be a story in this Sir Godfrey, but his rumination was cut short by the sight of Richard Lord emerging from one of the shop's anterooms with a dozen brightly colored dressing gowns.

"I sleep raw myself," said Harris to the tailor.

"I see, sir."

Spilkes, who'd been standing on the edges of this colloquy, decided it might be a good moment to break away and join David Fine across the room.

Before he could move, however, the tailor, in an even-lower-than-usual whisper, said, "Sir?" to the managing editor, who he could see was actually trying to learn some things this morning. "If I may be bold," he continued, making a gentle nod in the direction of Spilkes's upper torso: "It's best not to wear soft-fronted dress shirts outside the privacy of one's home."

Spilkes thanked the man before heading over to Fine.

"Get a load of these," said the food writer, pointing to some framed royal warrants on the wall. "Even the Mikado's put his seal on this operation. And take a look over here," he added, propelling Spilkes toward a huge antique ledger, kept on display for ceremonial purposes. "I wonder what the salesmen here pull in. Do you think they ever take clients to lunch?"

If Spilkes liked information for its usefulness, its onward-and-upward applicability, Fine loved it as a simple possession, something to be avidly hoarded and compulsively shown off, like a collector's snuff boxes. "Did you know," he asked Spilkes, imparting a fact he had acquired minutes before, "that you can make one and a half suits with the material it takes to make a single kilt?"

"No kilts!" cried Harris, from several feet away, mistaking Fine's piece of tutelage for a story idea he was trying out on the m.e. Anxieties about losing his butch edge to Jimmy Gordon and *Cutaway* came rushing back. In fact, whenever he was inside a male clothier's, he could feel the old pansy *Bandbox* on the verge of reappearing, like some maiden aunt you thought was dead arriving for a visit.

Paul Montgomery chose this moment to emerge from another anteroom, clad in a dark blue woolen work-in-progress. Trying to take notes while he shuffled forward in the unhemmed pants, he looked at the tubular bolts of cloth and decided they would become "the organ pipes in this cathedral of clothes," once he started writing his piece. He'd been trying to win over the tailor all morning, to turn him into the sort of devoted character who always said a moist-eyed goodbye to Paulie in the last paragraph, but the man had offered only the dullest response to his blandishments, nothing but a dozen "quite rights" and "very well, sirs."

"It looks good," said Harris, who thought it would look even better in brown; but at least it was strong and solid, not one of those flimsy spun-sugar summer suits he'd seen Lord shopping for yesterday.

"Gentlemen!" he cried. "Let's wrap it up!" If the driver was on time, they could still get a good lunch table at Kettner's, a decent enough spot, though Harris could already feel a homesick craving for the security of his table at Malocchio.

25

"Can't you turn that down?" cried Gianni Roma through the bars of his holding cell. "It's enough like an igloo in here already."

The cop had his radio tuned to WEAF, which this morning featured the Eskimo Banjo Orchestra.

"At least *they're* just rubbin' *noses*," said the officer, otherwise ignoring the prisoner's request.

Gianni decided it was better not to try defending his masculinity. He knew, in fact, that it was best not to say anything at all. When he'd asked his cellmate—this poor, terrified shipping clerk—what *he'd* done, and the clerk said "Nothing," Gianni had realized, sickeningly, that it was true. The guy had probably been picked up off the street to fill some vice cop's quota.

He wished he could say the same for himself. He'd been arrested last night while closing up the restaurant. At first he'd figured the rookie officer didn't know the proper drill for settling the monthly trumped-up violation of the sumptuary laws, and that he'd be unhanded once he could make it over to the cash-register drawer. But as the young cop hustled him out onto Fiftieth Street, he was informed of the actual charge: selling narcotics to Waldo Lindstrom.

It was a lie; he had never sold drugs to Waldo. He'd given them to him for free, or at least not for money, and only for the last two weeks, since the night of the party at Oldcastle's, when he'd realized that's what it would take to get him—between the model's huge roster of other engagements—into bed. What, Gianni now wondered, had gone wrong? Had he purchased the drugs (from a connection of his bootlegging brother-in-law) with marked bills? Had he been set up? If your own bootlegger could be a stool pigeon, there was even less honor left in the world than he'd thought.

The only thing he knew for sure was that if his pals were here in New York instead of over in Europe he'd have been sprung inside of an hour, and they'd all have gone back to Malocchio to drink the expensive gin and have a laugh on the cops.

A sudden commotion made Gianni open his eyes. Waldo was being brought in, handcuffed to one cop and prodded by another. From the ensuing back-and-forth between the model and the booking officer, Gianni quickly gathered that the object of his desire had been arrested on a lower West Side pier.

"While sunning myself," said Waldo.

"Before dawn?" asked the arresting officer, who seemed glad to open the cuffs and detach himself. A young man whom they were both calling Waldo's "tanning partner" had managed to escape, but Waldo had spent the last few hours in the paddy wagon, almost ruining the vicuna overcoat he'd nicked from the *Bandbox* Fashion Department. Right now Gianni watched the second cop complete a last frisk; he pulled a thick money clip out of Waldo's coat—and pocketed it for himself.

"There goes my bail," said Gianni, as soon as Waldo joined him and the frightened shipping clerk inside the holding cell.

"It was worth it," said Waldo, faking a swoon over the just-completed search.

"I think you'd better get serious," said Gianni, who had noticed the steady disappearance of his own Italian accent in the long hours since his arrest.

"There's no chance I can bail you," said Waldo. "Not even if I still had the money clip. I might have to testify against you." Gianni looked at him in disbelief, but only for a moment, choosing to banish the thought of such treachery by concentrating on the arrival of a man he recognized as the fixer in this little drama that had ensnared him. Wearing a homburg—and dandruff so abundant he reminded Gianni of the platters of nonpareils he set out with his guests' coffee—the man approached the cell.

"I can set you up with an excellent bondsman and the finest attorney," he promised.

Gianni rather doubted it. The finest attorney, now being pointed out, was a palsied septuagenarian leaning on a cane. But Gianni didn't see what alternative he had. He nodded to the fixer and went to sit, head in hands, on the bench at the back of his cell. On the other side of the wall he could hear what sounded like someone getting the third degree. The shipping clerk shuddered, until Waldo said, with disgust: "Oh, please, I've *paid* to be slapped harder than that."

The remark left Gianni feeling jealous, but there was no time right now to explore his emotions toward Waldo. The cop listening to the radio was calling for both of them: "Okay, Gina and Ingemary! Upstairs!"

The bondsman had done his work in a matter of minutes; the lawyer was already splitting his fee with the arresting officer. Satisfied with his take, Gianni's new attorney tottered over to the cell and told his client, in a heavy Greek accent, that everything would now be fine.

"Is there any chance," asked Gianni, "that we could get this case to come before Judge Gilfoyle?" He had met Daisy's new boyfriend at Oldcastle's party, where he'd heard from Max that the guy had a seat at Rothstein's table over at Lindy's.

The decrepit barrister shrugged. "He's a very busy man."

Being handcuffed to Waldo, however indifferent the young man seemed to their enforced proximity, would be Gianni's only pleasant memory of this experience. The two of them, linked at the wrist, were brought upstairs to stand before a visibly drunk judge who slurred his way through the cut-and-dried arraignment. Amidst his lawyer's continuing assurances that everything was all right, Gianni kept looking nervously around. A bailiff chatted up a prostitute; a numbers runner with a receding hairline loudly protested that he could prove himself a juvenile; and the court reporter, who took down nothing, read last night's *Graphic*.

Gianni wondered what this morning's papers were saying about his arrest, and as soon as he and Waldo, unshackled from each other, emerged into the day's still-early light, he got his answer. A blind item in one of the gossip columns was asking:

> *Which prominent Gotham mag editor appears to have skipped a fiscal "civic obligation," stirring up dire consequences for a midtown spaghetti-slinger with more of a strut—or is that a swish?—than Mussolini?*

Gianni, who knew about the vice-squad payoffs necessitated by Waldo's unfortunate past, groaned. Now it was clear. Once Joe had missed his monthly payment, the cops had started watching Waldo. And once they made their arrest, Jimmy Gordon—who along with Cuddles and himself and no one else, not even Spilkes, knew about the payoffs—had tipped the papers.

"*Porca la luna!*" Gianni cried. How could Joe have been so careless?

Waldo, fluffing his coat, just yawned, wondering who was going to get him a cab.

26

"Guests typically sit in the sub-stalls, sir."

The term was sufficiently unfamiliar, and its delivery by Ian Hopkins—a young physics tutor at St. John's College, Cambridge—so sincerely pleasant, that for a moment Harris didn't realize he and his colleagues were being ushered into the cheap seats. Not that the house was packed. The college chapel stood perhaps one-tenth full for Sunday evensong.

"It's even worse, I'm afraid, at morning prayer," said Hopkins. "Ever since the abolition of compulsory chapel."

Besides Harris and Mr. Hopkins, the front row of the first sub-stall contained only Spilkes and Fine. Lord had been allowed to go off and visit his family in Surrey, Paulie to nip down to Dover and see his skiers off to the Olympics.

Weeks before sailing, in preparation for Fine's piece on English college dining, Harris had asked Hazel to locate an Oxford or Cambridge subscriber, and she'd come up with Mr. Hopkins, a dapper young man with nothing of the absentminded don about him. After ten minutes in his company, Harris felt quite comfortable with this "fellow-with-a-capital-F," as Fine had just described him in his notes. Even so, the editor-in-chief was concentrating on the choir, filled as it was with so many potential readers. Hopkins was a rarity, willing to wait two months for each issue of *Bandbox* to make its slow swim across the ocean. But what about transatlantic airmail? thought Harris. It would soon be a fact; once he got home he should tell Burn to look into the possibilities.

Harris had remembered to pack his earplugs—Lord having warned him against early-morning birdsong in the college courtyards—and right now, while the choir soared through the "Magnificat" and on into "Hail, Gladdening Light," he gave a fond thought to them, lying unused in his overnight bag. It could have been worse: at least the audience was being treated to the "men's voices" and not some squad of prepubescent altar boys like Ernest Lough.

"Nice job," said Harris, getting up while the last note of "O Worship the King" still hung in the upper reaches of the stained-glass chapel.

"Yes," said Mr. Hopkins. "It was, rather, wasn't it?"

Once outside, the young tutor led the *Bandbox* party toward the dining hall. Smells from the college bakehouse, detectable along the way, seemed promising, but after Mr. Hopkins settled his guests at the half-full Fellows' table, the meal they were served proved a great disappointment, or—if looked at with David Fine's satiric purpose—something close to perfection. The meat had the same shade of gray as a pair of dress trousers they'd seen in Poole's, and the vegetables were worse.

"What's your guess?" Harris whispered to Fine. "Brussels sprouts?"

Fine expressed amazement over what appeared on his plate. "It makes you wonder who won the war. Four years bogged down in France. You'd think they'd have learned *something*."

Mr. Hopkins leaned across the table and said, apologetically: "Mr. Harris, I can arrange for something else to be sent round to your rooms. I happen to know there's still some quite good shepherd's pie back in the kitchen."

"Excellent, kid," said Harris, who searched his mind for some suitable thanks he could make. "I'll send you a tie," he said, taking inspiration from the neckwear visible under Mr. Hopkins' unfastened academic gown. "That thing you've got on makes you look like you're working for some dragon-slayer."

As soon as the port was uncorked, Mr. Hopkins introduced Harris to the Master, who was wearing the same crested college tie. Having only half-attended to the words of his most junior Fellow, the St. John's head man persisted in thinking that the visiting American was a manufacturer, not a magazine editor. "Ah," he said, topping up Harris's glass, "over here to sink some money into the place? You think Hopkins over there can figure out the formula for launching your man Lindbergh all the way to the moon?"

The Master and the editor-in-chief had nothing more in common than their high authority and a shared enthusiasm for port, but with Spilkes and Mr. Hopkins operating more or less as translators, the two managed a cordial hour in each other's company. The old don spouted some Latin motto about temperance, and Harris assured him that he'd said a mouthful. Before the hour was up, each man was inebriated two or three steps beyond anything that had been achieved at Simpson's the other night.

Mr. Hopkins made sure Harris was safely up the ancient staircase leading to his set of guest rooms before finally bidding him good night. Harris clapped him on the shoulder and promised he wouldn't forget about that tie once they all got back to New York.

He opened the door slowly, finding the light switch and checking for mice before he stepped into the room. Someone had lit a log fire for him, and when the draft sent a few sparks sailing in his direction, he looked nervously at the ancient wooden beams overhead.

He had begun searching for the earplugs in his valise when he heard a knock at the door. It was the college porter, carrying, sure enough, a dish of shepherd's pie covered with a green baize cloth, atop which sat a small envelope. Betty had managed to find him even here, with the news—tossed unread into the fire—that NEWMAN FELL OFF WAGON AND ONTO COOLIDGE—SERIOUS.

27

Over the past few weeks, in conversation with Becky Walter, Newman had played down the extent to which he'd been at Rosemary LaRoche's glandular beck and call. He had also sanitized his enforced adventures. Rosemary had so worn him out that, once or twice, while descending in the elevator from her rooms at the Plaza, he'd thought longingly of the broom closet where he'd once passed out in that same hotel. Being trapped there in the clutches of drink now seemed less of an ordeal than being pinned, by her fiery red talons, to Rosemary's four-poster.

Out in Hollywood, the studio kept putting off the start of production on her next film, the follow-up to "that limp little stinker" she'd be promoting with the *Bandbox* cover. Each day that she remained in New York, the star would summon Newman to her lair, where he'd sneeze from the flowers and nervously peel the fruit sent up in competitive quantities by her admirers. On each visit Newman would actually attempt to interview the actress, a task he never managed to accomplish or even really commence before she cranked him up for a long-duration round of lovemaking. He performed with a combination of physical technique and emotional absence that left Rosemary more delighted than a rise in the market. Newman once had the idea of getting his interview in the course of some postcoital conversation; the star played along for a few minutes, until she tossed his pad across the room and challenged him to a game of Hide the Pencil, which she won in a burst of anatomical creativity. "Yep," he could still hear her saying. "That's why they call it a goose chase."

Newman was determined to go through with a trip to Washington, where he'd made plans to interview a couple of young congressmen and female reporters for "The Bachelor's Life." He would stay with Fitz O'Neal, an old college pal who covered the capital for the Philadelphia *Bulletin* and had a little gingerbread house in Foggy Bottom. Together he and Fitz had each spent two years at Lehigh, which they liked to think equaled a whole college degree between them. Fitz had suggested he come down the first weekend in February, when the new National Press Club building would open, with Coolidge himself in attendance.

"You know," said Fitz, as he and Newman got ready to set out on Saturday night, "you could bring a girl. It's not like the Gridiron."

"Nah," said Newman, as lightheartedly as he could manage. "I've had enough dames for a while."

"Jeez, Stu, how many things can a guy swear off?" Fitz had never understood his pal's inability to manage anything between stone-cold sobriety and falling-down drunkenness, but he'd always envied his excesses with women, and been grateful for the overflow.

The new Press Club building had risen at the corner of Fourteenth and F streets. The club itself occupied the top two of the structure's fourteen floors; tiny out-of-town news bureaus tenanted most of the offices below. As the elevator ascended to the banquet, Fitz pointed to the indicator needle and sang: "I hang my hat, rain or shine, felt or straw, on number nine."

Newman, too, was beginning to feel a song in his heart. As the car rose, he could sense himself being released from Rosemary's gravitational pull. Normally indifferent to politics, he found himself eager to watch a different game in a different city. Fitz ushered him into the noisy, predinner festivities—thanks to Coolidge's impending arrival, there wouldn't be a hint of hooch.

"Is that Dawes?" he asked.

"Nah," said Fitz, who explained that the businessman-turned-vice-president hadn't been out of the doghouse since his first day in office, when he'd decided, after taking the oath, to give the assembled senators a little lecture on productivity, specifically theirs. As the Senate's new presiding officer, he said they could quickly increase it by overhauling the body's 125-year-old customs and procedures. "Honest," said Fitz, "he finished himself off worse than Andy Johnson did getting sworn in dead drunk back in '65."

"Yeah," was all Newman said.

Fitz hoped he hadn't been tactless. But his buddy was busy enjoying the scene, whose overwhelming maleness was diluted by only a handful of women correspondents and wives. Released from Rosemary's Circean spell, Newman was delighted to observe the strut of these duded-up news jockeys from Duluth and Tulsa and Mobile, each swollen with his significance as a transmitter of tidings from the world's new center. He and Fitz had just been seated between some young fellows from Salt Lake and Houston; if one of them proved to be single, Newman might already be on the way toward having his column.

"Sir," said a waiter tapping his shoulder. "A note for you. Sent from across the street."

"Hey," said the Salt Lake correspondent. "That handwriting looks like a dame's. Go get her and bring her back here!"

The newsman had just been told, during Fitz's introduction of his pal, about Newman's legendary cocksmanship; the Houston reporter, who read *Bandbox* each month, was already enviously aware of it. Both men, along with Fitz, now good-naturedly thumped their knives on the white tablecloth in a drumbeat of lustful encouragement. They were having too good a time to notice that Newman had gone quite white.

He rose from his chair, faking the jaunty discretion of a gentleman. "I'll just have a quick look to see what this is about."

A few minutes later he was across the street inside a dark chophouse. A new plaque inside its door advertised the place's pride in having inherited its brass rail from the old Ebbitt House, which had been torn down to make way for the Press Club's new building. This polished relic was about the only sign of light amidst the chophouse's wooden booths. Newman put his foot on it in a kind of steadying link to the past, and ordered a glass of ice water.

Maybe the note was just a practical joke, her way of saying, Enjoy your weekend off, but don't think Mama isn't watching. There was, after all, no sign of her actual presence that he could detect when he dared to turn his head and look at the row of booths. In fact, the only female he could see in here had red hair, not blond, cut so that two sharp triangles of it thrust downward from an especially low-drawn cloche hat. Not like Rosemary at all, except that—

It was Rosemary. As soon as he realized it, the temperature of Newman's stomach fell to that of the ice water. He now remembered the half-dozen wigs he'd seen in the trunks at the Plaza.

"I was wondering how long it would take you," said Rosemary, once he'd gathered the courage to approach her booth. She was not smiling.

"How did you find me?" asked Newman, like a fugitive returned to the chain gang.

"I've got a press agent, sweetheart. They're better at finding stuff out than all those reporters you're sitting with across the street. You want to learn how to uncover secrets? Take a job helping people to *keep* them. Anyway, *everybody* knows where you are, lamb chop. They've got those line-up sheets of story assignments posted on every wall of that rag you work at."

Newman noticed that she had no food in front of her, only an ice-filled tumbler.

"Do you want to come back to the Press Club with me? They're sitting down to dinner." It was all he could think to say.

Rosemary snorted. "Honey, I'm a lot bigger than fucking Coolidge. I don't appear nowhere for free."

In a terrifying shift of mood, she got up and came around to his side of the booth. She smashed her lips against his and shoved her left hand into his right pants pocket—from which she extracted the key to Fitz's house. He feared another game on the order of Hide the Pencil, but Rosemary had something else in mind.

"A simple exchange," she said, putting his key into her purse and handing him one to her room at the Willard.

"Okay," said Newman, with what he supposed passed for gallantry in this situation. "But why do you need the key to Fitz's?"

"You'll get it back if you're good," said Rosemary. "Don't stay out too late with the boys. And think about bringing one of them home with you. Just a suggestion."

With one last tug on the cloche hat, she was gone, leaving Newman to feel like the fallen, hopelessly enslaved girl in some novel by Crane or Frank Norris. There was nothing he could do: lose this cover story and Harris would can him for sure. Besides that, he was just plain afraid of Rosemary, whose reprisals would more likely target his anatomy than his job. He continued to sit in the booth, making a circular assessment of his predicament, until the waiter came over with a large coffee cup.

The crockery was camouflage. Newman could tell from the aroma that the mug was full of Bushmills.

"Compliments of the lady," said the waiter.

Newman could hear Rosemary's voice, about five days ago at the Plaza: "You know, every great stick man I've been acquainted with has been even *better* on booze. Honey, I'd love to have known you before you went off the sauce."

He looked down into the cup's two inches of amber liquid—as terrifying as a monsoon, as inviting as a warm bath.

A moment passed.

"Another, pal?"

So great was the shock to his system, he didn't realize, until hearing the waiter's voice, that he'd already downed the liquor in two gulps.

"Yes, please," he said, at which point he felt unaccountably normal.

An hour and fifteen minutes went by before he returned to the Press Club.

"You just made it," said Fitz, pointing to the dais, where Coolidge was now rising to speak. Fitz was less peeved than slyly proud—hadn't he told the guys from Salt Lake and Houston what a Lothario his highly paid magazine buddy was?

The president cleared his throat.

"He looks better in his redskin headdress," whispered Fitz, an ardent Democrat. Newman smiled.

Those in the audience anticipating some genial after-dinner fare were soon disabused and dozing. The president began his remarks by droning through statistics about the Press Club's new headquarters: the library's five thousand books; the property's ten-million-dollar valuation; its 270 feet of frontage on F Street.

"Christ," said Fitz. "He's like some general-store owner counting up the cereal boxes."

But the president went on to launch a lyric paean to modernity and money:

"The construction has transformed your Press Club into a great business institution. It is possible to see in this spacious building, so magnificently equipped, a symbol of the development of the whole United States. The old, the outworn, the poorly adapted has been discarded to make place for the new. . . ."

"Jesus," hissed Fitz. "He *does* want to run again. I'd almost swear it." He craned forward, wondering if Coolidge had picked this moment, with the whole of the nation's press before him, to retract last summer's retirement announcement.

Newman, meanwhile, could feel a thoroughgoing change in his own body politic. The three Bushmills doubles had finally effected a revolution. The Wets had returned to power on a flood tide of scotch, repealing Newman's two years of Prohibition. He sat quietly, but smiled broadly, wondering if Fitz had noticed the shift in administrations.

But his pal was still leaning into Coolidge's speech, listening for whatever newsflash might be lurking amidst the inventory and the bromides. The president, however, soon began a severe nasal scolding: "The constant criticism of all things that have to do with our country, with the administration of its public affairs, with the operation of its commercial enterprises, with the conduct of its social life, and the attempt to foment class distinctions and jealousies, weaken and disintegrate the necessary spirit of patriotism."

Newman nodded vigorously. Fitz whispered "Class, my ass" to the man from Salt Lake.

"In no small degree," continued Coolidge, without looking up at his audience, "you are the keepers of the public conscience."

"Or, in my case," said Newman, rather loudly—as he thought of his own magazine and how much, he was surprised to realize, he loved his job—"the arbiter of the necktie!" He reached over and good-naturedly tugged the Windsor knot beneath Fitz's throat. His friend looked confused.

"The spirit of mankind," pronounced the president, "is more and more asserting itself, more and more demanding that the affairs of government and society be conducted in accordance with the laws of truth. The people who neglect that precept are bound for a moral explosion."

Newman, whose insides and brain were now popping like one long glorious Fourth of July, found himself astonished by the Chief Executive's eloquence. How had he for so long missed the Periclean wisdom in this dour little Yankee they took so for granted? The man was Lincoln; he was Jefferson; he was the two of them rolled into one. As the speech concluded, Newman applauded more lustily than anyone in the huge room.

"Thanks, I'll take two," he said, when the waiter came around with a box of Havana cigars from the president's recent trip to Cuba.

The Associated Press man began offering a sort of benediction, during which Fitz, who knew the drill, said "On your feet" to his tablemates. They were close enough to the dais to be part of the group allowed to approach Coolidge, who along with the club president had begun conducting a quick receiving line.

Newman was hustled along between the man from Salt Lake and the fellow from Houston. He felt part of the crowd, a sensation he hadn't had for years—and with it came another old, once-familiar feeling. He was like a rubber tree that had just been tapped; loose-limbed, unburdened. Yes, he was a *tree*! And his leaves were on fire! He was brilliantly aflame—experiencing the "explosion" which Coolidge, that Solon, that sage, had prophesied a minute ago!

"Mr. Stuart Newman," said Fitz, presenting him, the next in line, to the President of the United States.

"Mr. Newman," said Coolidge.

"Fucking well spoken, Cal!" cried Stuart, who grabbed the president's hand, and then his lapels, before falling face first into his stuffed shirt.

28

Joe Harris sat, overcoat buttoned, under a tartan blanket, on an enclosed portion of the ship's upper deck, not far from the second of its four great funnels. He sipped his lobster cocktail and finished a six-month-old issue of *Punch,* imagining what he could do with *that* moribund franchise.

For more than three years, between the time *Bandbox* had really hit its stride and the moment Jimmy left, Harris had more than once thought of his magazine as a big liner just like this, sleek and punctual, sliding into subscribers' mailboxes the way the ship docked to the pleasure of all awaiting her arrival. The boiler room below might be a sweaty, even chaotic, affair—Jimmy shoveling ideas so fast that half his coals spilled onto the ground instead of going into the furnace—but none of that showed on deck, where everything was bridge games and balloons.

On this actual ship he gave his travel companions more freedom of movement than they had in the London hotel—Spilkes signed up for rhumba lessons and lectures on the Boer War; Fine played billiards and haunted the kitchens—though Harris insisted on their unanimous assembly for dinner. He shunned any invitation to the captain's table, preferring each night to be the captain of his own.

Through the glass enclosure he could now see Paul Montgomery standing alone out on the deck, staring at the freezing February sea. Poor guy, thought Harris, imagining how Paulie must be thinking of his old man, still lying full fathom five in the vasty deep.

Whereas, in fact, Paulie was thinking about Billy Durant, the Jersey manufacturer who'd given up making motorcars to concentrate on stock deals. The rusted jalopy and the solid-gold stock ticker: the story he'd be starting work on once they got home. Might, Paulie wondered, a book come out of it? He really needed to talk to Harold Ober. But wait: Ober was in a bad odor with Harris over Roebling's bulls-and-bears fiasco. Better not approach him just now. Maybe Stanwick would have some good advice about getting a deal through some other agent?

Writing a book would be personal insurance against whatever fall the magazine could be getting ready to take. Throughout this whole trip he'd wanted, hopelessly, to talk with *somebody* about how far off his game the Big Guy seemed. Those advertising numbers: Would they be even worse on their return home? Would Jimmy Gordon be lapping up ever more press and subscribers? Paulie still wished he'd been able to spend more time with Jimmy at Oldcastle's party, just to get a feel for what sort of welcome might await him on the eighteenth floor.

He gazed out at a tiny whitecap. Once he was back on dry land, wouldn't it be time to jump ship?

And yet, for now, they were still on the bounding main. He should be spending some time with the chief, he decided, so he turned around to send Harris a big smile through the glass.

Alas, Fine had just sat down in the deck chair to the editor's left.

Well, that still left the one on his right, to which Paulie now beat a path.

"Colder than a witch's!" he cried, clapping his gloved hands. "Boy, that looks great." He pointed to Harris's cocktail and took off his coat.

Fine was reading aloud from the mimeographed summary of shipboard and international news. Grand Duchess Anastasia had arrived in New York three days ago, and Fine had a brainstorm: "How about a two-page cartoon spread on 'Famous People You Only Thought Were Dead'? You know, a ninety-year-old John Wilkes Booth playing *Lear* in Kokomo? Woodrow Wilson, recovered from the stroke, grab-assing some girls on the Riviera?"

It wasn't the world's worst idea, but once Harris thought of how good Cuddles used to be at executing this sort of thing, he had to banish the proposal.

"Nah. Ignore her," he said, meaning Anastasia. "The Commies may turn out to be the coming thing. We shouldn't keep pissing them off." He paused for a minute. "What do we really know about those guys? Do they include any regular Joes?" He meant potential readers.

"I could go on campus," said Paulie, whose thoughts of defection from the magazine couldn't drown out the siren call of a potential assignment. "Attend a few of the young guys' meetings, interview some of the big Bolsheviks behind the lecterns."

Fine sank into silence. Harris closed his eyes, imagining their arrival in New York on Monday. He would spend that night at his place in Murray Hill and hold off seeing Betty until the following morning, Valentine's Day. He'd burst into her office with two armfuls of flowers and chocolate.

Her telegrams had stopped altogether, the shore-to-ship variety remaining somehow beyond her, and their little spell apart had done them good, thought Harris. Maybe he'd be less dependent when he got back, less in need of making those dozen daily phone calls, which he knew were an object of sport to his staff.

The ship continued west at twenty-five knots, and the lobster cocktail had begun its work. The editor-in-chief was now at least one half-sheet to the wind.

Maybe, he thought, last month's clouds had really lifted.

"We could put the younger guys, the students, into red sweaters."

He realized Paulie was still talking about Communists.

"Right," he murmured. "Red sweaters."

Closing his eyes, he tried concentrating on blue skies.

29

Mrs. von Erhard gave Chip Brzezinski a dirty look. He was walking past her with a newspaper he'd bought somewhere else this morning. Hannelore kept track of her Midtown competitors no less carefully than Oldcastle and Nast kept an eye on each other's magazines, and she guessed that the Wood Chipper had gotten his *Daily News* from Kid Herman, the onetime lightweight contender who sold papers at Forty-second and Broadway.

Chip gave Hannelore a tip of his hat—another loan from the Fashion Department. She ignored him and muttered something to Siegfried, who gently urged her to cheer up. The same events that had left Chip unable to postpone buying the paper on his walk from Ninth Avenue to the office had raised the von Erhards' own sales this Monday morning, February 13. None of the Oldcastle and Nast employees could stand sitting down for work without reading the latest on the swirl of plagiarism, narcotics-selling, and public drunkenness that now threatened to engulf *Bandbox*.

Theophilus Palmer's real identity remained a secret. Today's papers could still say only that he was "missing"—same as Waldo Lindstrom. The police were warning the model not to skip bail, but the gossip columns were rife with speculation that Lindstrom had already made a deal with the DA and was being sequestered by the cops themselves. His absence, for whatever reason, suggested further legal peril for Giovanni Roma, though it was conceded that the restaurateur's moral health would now improve without Lindstrom around to lure him into further unprintable acts.

Patrick Boylan, a spokesman for Commissioner Warren, said that payoffs were not part of the way the New York Police Department did business, but even so, in light of the newspaper rumors, investigators would "be asking Mr. Harris some questions upon his return from the so-called Mother Country."

Mentions of Stuart Newman's unfortunate evening in the nation's capital continued to contain more misinformation than the column inches about Gianni or Mr. Palmer, thanks mostly to Fitz O'Neal, who for Newman's sake had fabricated as favorable an explanation as he could. There was "a woman involved," Fitz told his colleagues in the press. The code of a gentleman prevented him from saying more, but people had to understand that Newman was not himself— was, frankly, in despair over a romantic disappointment.

Newman had, in fact, spent three nights in a Washington jail, charged only with being drunk and disorderly ("B'BOX SCRIBE: D&D IN D. OF C."), though he was thought to be the first man ever to have assaulted a President of the United States by accident. His current whereabouts remained, like Lindstrom's and Mr. Palmer's, unknown.

Harris's demise seemed to be approaching so fast that Chip worried there might not be time for him to contribute to it. He also feared that the whole remaining staff of *Bandbox* would soon be lined up at Jimmy Gordon's door asking for jobs.

Half the magazine's offices remained empty on this last morning of Harris's absence. Outside Fine's door, baskets of fancy comestibles, sent over from purveyors hoping for a write-up or mention, were now piled waist high. A frozen brisket, dispatched by an over-excited butcher who'd gotten wind of the Williamsburg versus Williamsburg piece, had been carted to the icebox by Hazel once she'd noticed the dripping. The grooming products in front of Newman's office—an array of shaving brushes, nail clippers, and tooth powder—seemed curiously forlorn, as if keeping vigil against his uncertain return. Cuddles' entryway was blocked by hopeful books, tickets, and sheet music, though in his case the space looked much as it did on days when he was present.

As a contract writer, Max Stanwick did not have an office of his own. He'd been using Paul Montgomery's for the past couple of weeks, waiting out a dry period. Until the right new lurid subject came along, he'd decided to do some work on *Boop-Boop-a-Dead,* his new novel. At the moment, however, his attentions were taken up with Daisy, who reported Arnold Rothstein's pleasure with Max's profile, which had finally reached newsstands. "He thought it dignified. Or so I've heard," said Daisy, who was more interested in finding out the meaning of some dire-sounding slang—"jelly" and "onse"—that the latest group of messengers had been using in front of the judge last night.

Back in the Art Department, Norman Merrill was deriving nostalgic satisfaction from a couple of illustrations he'd begun preparing just in case Waldo Lindstrom really had gone on the lam and would be unavailable for the next shoot.

"I'm sure the poor creature will be all right," said Merrill, soothingly, while he inked a jut into his pencilled man's perfect jaw. He was speaking not about Lindstrom, but of Canberra, the koala, who was due to leave tomorrow on an epic journey, through the Panama Canal and across the South Pacific, to a natural habitat in her native land.

Allen Case, knowing this was all for the best, still couldn't find a reply.

"Of course, Mother and I will miss her terribly," said Merrill, "but you've done the right thing. You've been heroic, really."

It was, from Allen's point of view, a paltry accomplishment. That whole evil warehouse, full of suffering animals, remained just as it was, protected, he now realized—in light of recent events involving Giovanni Roma, that hateful trafficker in veal calves—by bribes paid to the police. Despite the success with Canberra, whose passage was being financed by some of Mrs. Merrill's Spanish-American War bonds, Gardiner Arinopoulos continued to flourish: you could see a lemur on the lawn in a picture he'd shot for this month's *House & Garden*.

No product or perquisite languished outside Harris's door. Hazel made a point of taking them home for herself during each night of his trip, just as she intended to take the brisket with her this evening. Right now she was idling through the list of words in an ad for the Enunciphone Company, whose phonograph records promised to cure the listener of embarrassment over mispronunciation: *Noth-*

ing reveals your culture—or lack of it—so surely. Well, she wasn't so sure of that: the great big purple hickey on the neck of the approaching Wood Chipper, a giant love bite from some all-night hash-slinger, told you more about *his* culture than any inability to say "table d'hôte." But to make conversation, she showed him the ad when he reached her desk.

He wouldn't take the bait. She could tell he no more knew whether "canapés" was can-o-peas or ca-napes than she was sure, even after hearing about that treaty since the ninth grade, whether it was Ver-sigh or Ver-sails. But Chip wouldn't risk pronouncing a single one of the words. It was a sorry era (erra? ear-a?) they lived in, thought Hazel, everybody so scared of being found out or suckered or just of falling behind. It exhausted you after a while. Shouldn't a girl be able to find a decent husband without knowing, for sure, how to pronounce "pianist"? And yet, before Chip arrived, hadn't she been thinking of ordering these records for herself?

"Hey," she called to Allen Case, who was coming down the hall. "Help us out. How do you pronounce p-i-q-u-a-n-t? And what's it mean?"

Allen proceeded with caution. Hazel had always seemed only slightly less dangerous than the Wood Chipper.

"A p-p-pungent flavor or taste," said Allen. "Pleasantly so. L-l-like eucalyptus."

Hazel asked him to repeat the definition, so that she could write it down. While she did so, Chip began fingering the stack of unopened mail on her desk.

"Keep your mitts off that," ordered Hazel, however uninterested she herself might be in reading the letters, most of which were reader questions about the right hair tonic or shoelace to use.

"Thanks, Allen," she said.

The copyeditor could now complete his errand for Nan: getting one of the buckram cases that the editor-in-chief kept on the floor of his closet. Twice a year Harris had the Copy Department arrange the binding of *Bandbox*'s latest six issues for his personal shelves.

"Be my guest," said Hazel, after Allen explained his presence here. "It's unlocked."

She slit open a letter, if only to justify keeping Chip away from the pile of envelopes. While she read its contents, he pretended to busy himself reading Harris's copy of *Time*.

"Jeez," said Hazel, surprisingly engrossed. "Do you remember that kid from Indiana? The one who came to the office that day— maybe a month ago? This letter's from his mother."

Everyone had long since forgotten about John Shepard, though the Wood Chipper was the only person on the masthead who'd *deliberately* dropped him from his mind, after failing to get any dope on the Hoosier brat that might interest Jimmy Gordon. But he made himself listen to Hazel now, as she read from Mrs. Thelma Shepard's urgent appeal to Jehoshaphat Harris:

. . . the last we've heard from him was a letter he wrote on Wednesday, January 18, at suppertime, from the YMCA on Park Avenue. How excited he was to have seen your offices! He was even more thrilled to be going to a party, that very night, at your kind invitation. His letter to me was postmarked at 6:30 P.M. from the post office at Grand Central Terminal. We have telephoned the YMCA, as well as my husband's cousin in Brooklyn, the only person John knew in New York prior to his arrival. You can imagine how heartsick we are. If there is anything at all that you might be able to tell us . . .

"He's such a sweet kid," said Hazel. "What do you think's happened?"

Chip took the letter and examined the headlong flow of Mrs. Shepard's ink. "He probably got white-slaved to South America. Where they chopped his head off."

"You're a heartless crumbum," said Hazel.

"Oh, relax, Snow," said the Wood Chipper. "He probably just ran away."

"He'd *already* run away," said Hazel. "That's how he came to New York. He told me."

A cry—"Oh, n-n-no!"—came from Harris's office.

Hazel leapt to her feet, imagining that Allen Case had somehow found John Shepard's body on the floor of the boss's closet. She dashed into the office.

"Oh, God," she said, sighing with relief. "I'm never going to read another one of Stanwick's goddamned books. You can take that home with you, Allen. He'll never miss it."

"I w-will," said Allen, looking into the huge, sad eyes of the stuffed moosehead. Newly appalled, he staggered out of the office under this huge piece of taxidermy. Once he left, Chip came in, still holding the letter.

"Give me that," said Hazel, who grabbed it and put it face up on Harris's empty blotter.

"What do you expect *him* to do?" asked Chip.

"I expect him to go to the police with it," said Hazel. "He can file a missing-persons report and pay his overdue bribes. All in one trip."

30

On the morning of Valentine's Day, the skies were dark, plump with impending rain and thunder. Despite some red Cupid silhouettes pasted to the walls, the atmosphere on the Graybar Building's fourteenth floor was less amorous than it had been for most of the past two weeks. Clothes that had cushioned trysts inside the Fashion Department's closets had been hung back up. The girls had returned to their typewriters, the young men to their layout tables. Even last week's indoor-golf equipment had been restored to its proper shelves and purposes. Keyboards clicked; razors trimmed photographs; fresh proofs ejected themselves from the pneumatic mail tubes—even though Harris probably wouldn't be in for another hour. On their first day back from England, custom dictated that Spilkes, Fine, and Montgomery first make a series of late, individual entrances. After they'd each served up a couple of anecdotes about the boss's behavior abroad, it would be all right for Harris himself to sail down the main corridor.

At 10:05, it was still only Nan O'Grady, Norman Merrill, and Allen Case getting off the elevator.

"Nope," said Mrs. Zimmerman, with a reassuring smile. "He's not here yet."

"I knew it," said Nan, still clutching some of the *bon voyage* streamers she and her companions had flung toward the caged little koala, who'd departed from a dock at the end of West Forty-fourth Street.

"Jesus," said Chip Brzezinski, noticing the colored ribbons. "What'd you do? Go down to the pier and welcome them home?"

"That's stupid even for you," said Nan, who with the possible exception of Hazel was less of an apple-polisher than anyone at the magazine.

"Hey, O'Grady," cried Hazel. "Come look at somethin'." Nan tucked the streamers into her pocket and approached Harris's office. Hazel, who was chatting with Daisy, pointed through the open door to the boss's desk: "Tell me what you think."

Nan went in and read the letter from John Shepard's mother.

Hazel called to her. "You remember him, don't you?"

"He came up to me at Oldcastle's," said Nan. "He asked whether I thought Stuart would be offended if he introduced himself."

"I *know* he spoke to the judge," said Daisy. "But all I can recall for sure is that the poor thing had never really kissed a girl."

"Did he tell you that?" asked Nan.

"No, but I remember noticing how he ate one of the shrimp. You could—"

"Please," said Nan. "I'll use my imagination." She turned to Hazel. "Are you showing that letter to everybody?"

"Yeah. If people like you and Becky know, then Himself may feel shamed into doing something."

"He wouldn't be shamed by us?" asked the countess, wounded that Hazel didn't credit her with the same moral persuasiveness.

"No, not by us," said Hazel, untroubled by her own exclusion.

"I'll needle him about it," promised Nan.

Daisy went back to reading a newspaper story on John Nicholas Brown, born America's richest baby in 1900 thanks to the death of his father while Nicky himself was still in the womb. Now a young man of extreme eligibility, Brown was combining in Daisy's mind this morning with the lost John Shepard, and the two were stirring up memories of her own rich young count, the lovely, wheezing Antonio. Despite her sympathy for Mrs. Shepard out there in Indiana, Daisy knew how important it was for these sensitive boys to be pried from their mamas. She wondered for a moment whether John hadn't taken the extreme measure of disappearance to elude an over-zealous maternal grasp.

"Could you take a look at this?"

The Wood Chipper had once again come up to Nan, before she could start back to her own desk. He handed her a brief fashion piece—two badly typed pages about the advisability of a short man's wearing a low, narrowly pointed collar. Nan took less than thirty seconds to make her way through the text's shaky grammar and ask Chip why he'd produced this effusion.

"Just trying to pitch in," he answered. "I figure we need all hands on deck with everything that's going on here."

Nan narrowed her eyes, knowing his motives had to be as mixed as his metaphors.

Chip looked away, hoping she wouldn't guess that the squib was something he'd worked up for Jimmy Gordon. This was going to be his week, he felt sure. At least one of the crises facing *Bandbox* should provide him a chance to be so useful to Jimmy that Chip Brzezinski would finally be invited aboard *Cutaway*. He would hit the ground running with this little piece of copy on collars.

"Maybe I should show it to Case," he muttered, when Nan failed to say anything more.

"Don't," she responded. "He'd be able to make it sound even more like you."

Norman Spilkes, still wearing his overcoat, came suddenly into view. He made a fast approach to Hazel's desk. "Is he in?" the m.e. asked.

Hazel shook her head no.

"How was your trip?" asked Nan.

"I learned to rhumba," Spilkes answered, before noticing the Wood Chipper. "I'll tell you more later."

Once left alone with Hazel, he tried again: "Has he *called*?"

"Nope," she answered.

Spilkes wondered when he'd be able to tell Harris about yet another problem that Andrew Burn had just imparted in the elevator: Wanamaker's was shifting three-quarters of its menswear ads from *Bandbox* to *Cutaway*.

A couple of the catastrophes that Spilkes had become acquainted with since arriving home last night seemed soluble enough. First, put an end to the fiction contests: treat the fiasco of the current one as a big boy-are-we-embarrassed joke, and hold it in reserve against Sidney, a weapon to be deployed once he again got too big for his fancy flannel britches. Second, realize that the solution to Newman's problem was even easier: fire him. But there was nothing easily done about all these numbers. Jimmy's magazine had made it past the dangers of infancy. It was now another mouth for the economy to feed, and even in this boom there were only so many readers and advertisers to go around. *Cutaway* needed to be strangled in its playpen, but the tot seemed well on its way to committing parricide before that could be accomplished.

Hazel's voice halted Spilkes's dark train of thought. "If you find him before I do," she said, "give him these." She handed the managing editor two powder-blue slips of paper—one message asking Harris to report to the police commissioner's office "as soon as possible," and another requesting that he visit Hiram Oldcastle "IMMEDIATELY."

3 1

"Mukluk!" cried Betty Divine. "That's too loud even for me!"

The dog had begun barking once he smelled the familiar aroma of Joe Harris's shaving lather. Harris himself was still outside the closed door to Betty's office, giving a box of candy to her secretary and smiling at the two girls in matching jumpers on their way to be photographed for *Pinafore*. If his English journey had been a men-only interlude, he now found himself the only male inside another single-sex paradise. There could scarcely be a more charming place to spend Valentine's Day than Betty's magazine. From one end of the eleventh floor to the other, girls were untying candy-box ribbons, opening envelopes, and plucking eyebrows in anticipation of their evening dinner dates.

"Baby," said Harris, once Betty figured out the cause of Mukluk's yapping and opened the door. "Happy Valentine's."

She kissed him quickly and took her presents, putting the enormous heart-shaped Whitman's sampler onto her desk. She hushed the dog, asked her secretary to find a vase for the roses, and sat Joe down in a chair in front of her desk. Then she closed the door once more.

"Jesus, baby, did you miss me? You're acting like you've got some efficiency expert eyeballing you through a peephole."

"Have you been to your office? Have you spoken to Norman?"

Harris stretched his arms in animal contentment. "Came straight here from my place. The salt air must still be in my lungs. I slept eleven hours—that's more than even Coolidge can manage."

Betty could see how rested he was. She hadn't had the heart to call his apartment in Murray Hill last night; she'd called Spilkes at his home instead.

"Speaking of Coolidge," she said after a deep breath, handing Joe the first newspaper story, clipped eight days ago, about Stuart Newman's misadventure.

As he read it, Harris's shoulders slumped, and his stomach poured forward in a long, defeated exhalation.

"I'll can him," he finally said, without relish. "This is worse than his being sober. Christ, our model of the single gentleman."

Betty waited for some aggression to overtake mere weariness and disgust. But Harris just sat there, shaking his head.

"Joe, you can't fire him. Not right now. Hazel told me your precious LaRoche has such a case on him she'd never put up with it."

Harris's eyes flared. After an extended silence, he muttered: "She's one cover I can't lose."

Betty could make out the alarm in his expression, but not what he'd just said. "She's got a lover who can't booze?"

"SHE'S ONE COVER I CAN'T LOSE."

Betty felt shaken, not by the volume, which she was used to during these auditory clarifications, but by the realization that he still had almost no idea how deep his troubles were.

"Jehoshaphat," she said, using the name Harris heard even less often than Houlihan heard "Aloysius." She leaned forward and looked straight into his eyes. "You need to start worrying about losing the whole book."

Betty laid it all out: the tale of Mr. Palmer's plagiarism; the scandal of Gianni's arrest, and Harris's own crucial role in it. If she'd known the news about Wanamaker's, she would have thrown that in, too. Once finished, she couldn't tell whether she'd brought Joe to his senses or thrown him permanently into shock. He'd gone so white and silent that Mukluk, observing from a corner, began moaning low.

"You never opened the telegrams, did you?" she asked.

"Get me a drink," he said at last, knowing there were two bottles of everything in the bottom drawer of Betty's filing cabinet.

She stared at him, fiercely. "You're not getting so much as a Drambuie-filled chocolate. Here," she said, tearing open the Whitman's sampler and tossing him a caramel. "Eat that. It'll give you energy."

Harris meekly accepted the candy, popping the little cube into his mouth while Betty selected a coconut creme for herself. For several seconds they chewed in silence. When she saw Joe's tongue trying to pry the sticky caramel off the roof of his mouth, she practically wanted to sing "Can't Help Lovin' That Man of Mine." But she was too short and too cute to pull off Helen Morgan; besides, she'd never be that needy. She *could,* however, be like Winnie Winkle, that plucky female breadwinner of the funny papers, which lay open under Mukluk's water bowl. Why couldn't Joe just retire and let *her* keep at it for a couple more years until they could both call it quits for good up in Dutchess County? Because, of course, inside of two weeks he'd be drinking applejack and talking to the moosehead. No, she realized, seeing all the fight gone out of him, neither Helen Morgan nor Winnie Winkle was called for now. It was time to hardboil herself into a pint-sized Lady Macbeth.

"Joe," she said, pitching her voice as deep as it would go. "When Hi gave you *Bandbox,* a magazine with no ads, no readers, and no future, how long did it take you to turn it around?"

"One business quarter," Harris replied, with more reflex than gusto.

"And tell me, Joe," asked Betty, getting up from her chair and going over to his, where she sat herself on his lap. "Who do I always say is the smartest man in the Graybar Building?" Her hands were streaked with chocolate, not blood, and a little of it was getting on Joe's shirt front, but she knew, if there were no interruptions, that she could make him screw his courage to the sticking-place. Aside from all else, sitting on his lap made it easier for her to hear.

"I am," said Joe.

Betty nodded, and kissed his nose.

"But I'm also the oldest," said Harris. "I don't know if I can hoist myself up out of all this. I'm fresh out of presto-changos."

Before Betty could say she'd rather have him back in the postcard business than sounding like this, the intercom buzzed. She got up and went back to her desk.

"Mr. Spilkes on the line," said her secretary.

She handed the receiver to Joe, who only listened and said yeah, three or four times, before hanging up.

"Wanamaker's is moving most of their ads to Jimmy."

Betty wanted to get back on his lap and resume her pep talk, but the mood of connubial conspiracy had been broken.

Harris continued, tonelessly: "Norman says I've got messages to go see the police and Oldcastle."

"Do the easy one first," Betty advised. "Go see the police."

32

Hazel was getting what she wanted. In the bathrooms, at the water fountain, and beside the contribution box for the sponsored Bunion Derby contestant ("Don't Let His Dogs Get Tired!"), staffers were devoting some of their morning conversation to the disappearance of that bright-eyed fellow from Indiana, who, in truth, most of them didn't remember.

Becky and Cuddles had both seen Mrs. Shepard's letter, but by 10:45 they'd yet to discuss it. Inside Cuddles' office, Becky was helping to scoop up the complimentary clutter that had accumulated during his absence.

"Disgraceful," he said, looking at his pocket watch. "Ten forty-five. The idea that senior people can still be absent from their desks at such an hour."

"Do you want tickets to *Rio Rita*?" she asked, before tossing them into the wastebasket.

Cuddles' only response was to begin humming a Latin tune, an effort quickly interrupted by Paul Montgomery's arrival at his door.

"Cheerio, guv'nor!" cried Paulie to Cuddles, adding something about "this lovely bird" once he noticed Becky.

"Been to England, Paulie?" Cuddles asked. The returning writer carried a ski pole autographed by his Olympic subjects; a half-yard of worsted left over from his bespoke suit and speared to the pole; three oversized menus from the ship; and six boxes of English toffee, *noblesse-oblige* presents for the secretaries and messengers. "You know," continued Cuddles, "the only way you could get any worse is to be an actual Englishman. No offense intended."

"None taken!" said Paulie, who clattered down the rest of the corridor, noisy as a junkman, toward Hazel's desk.

"Is Rudy Vallee a pansy?" asked Spilkes, whose grave face replaced Montgomery's in the doorway.

Cuddles waited a moment before replying: "That's carrying Valentine's Day awfully far, Norman. I wouldn't send a card."

Spilkes was trying, despite his current anxiety, to practice business as usual. He was seeking information that would allow him to decide whether the Connecticut Yankees' saxophone player, who'd created a sensation when he sang a couple of numbers at the Heigh-Ho last month, might be a suitable *Bandbox* story, maybe even a cover.

"I hear he likes girls," said Cuddles, "but not so much that they'd notice. Sort of like me." He instantly regretted the joke—it belonged to his old, motley-wearing character—but Becky ignored him and went on tidying. "Get Sidney to handle a piece on Vallee," he suggested. "That should be punishment enough for him."

Max Stanwick was the next to enter.

"Any good rubouts last night?" asked Cuddles, who'd heard about Max's current drought.

"Nah," said Max, too discouraged to alliterate more than a pair of initial consonants: "Every tommy gun's drilling a dry hole. This

Hammer Slayer they've just arrested is no good; he'll be in the chair before our lead time is up."

"What about the Subway Slasher over in Brooklyn?" asked Becky.

"So far he's only slashing coats," said Max. "Besides, it's too local."

"Maybe he'll start working the Express," suggested Cuddles.

"You know," said Max, "the Hammer Slayer would have been a good story if the woman had disappeared for a while, instead of just turning up dead with the guy's fingerprints all over her and the ballpeen."

Cuddles had a thought: "Has Hazel shown you this letter to the boss? From the distraught mother in Indiana?"

"No," said Max, but as Cuddles laid out the handful of facts, he began to display a clear interest and new signs of life: "I remember him at that party. A happy little Hoosier hoisting his first hooch. I gave him some reporting tips."

"Do you think he's playing a trick on his parents?" asked Becky. "By disappearing, I mean."

"No," said Max, shutting his eyes and concentrating like a police psychic. "It's something bad. The kid's giving me the heebie-jeebies." Closing his eyes even tighter, he tried seeing whether he himself had followed the advice he'd imparted at the Oldcastle party: notice *everything*. Could he recall anything peculiar?

"Max," asked Cuddles, "if you were an actual cop, instead of our consonantal connoisseur of crime, what would you do first here?"

"Talk to Lindstrom," said Stanwick, without hesitation.

"Why so?" asked Spilkes.

"He'd know who might be in the market for boys like our little Hoosier."

"Oh, *God*," said Becky, who went on to point out, hopefully, that Lindstrom himself, a different sort altogether, had also disappeared.

"Maybe it's Peaches and Daddy in reverse," suggested Cuddles. "Maybe our boy has found himself some seventy-year-old Mrs. Astor who's got him on a divan up on Park Avenue."

"I suppose," said Max, "that if Gianni Roma's crowd *is* involved, any story here would be off-limits to *Bandbox,* by fiat of 'Phat. Of course, the issue might not be flesh. The kid could have come up against anybody from rumrunners to the Klan."

"If you *were* to write about this for the magazine," said Cuddles, with an ardor that took the others—and himself—by surprise, "maybe you could take a different approach entirely. Make the hunt itself be what's important."

"Yes," said Spilkes, thinking there might be something fresh here. " 'In Search of a Subscriber.' Something like that." A story that would build brand loyalty among readers by showing *Bandbox*'s loyalty to *them.*

Cuddles watched Spilkes consider the possibilities for the magazine, while Stanwick thought through the opportunities for himself. Within half a minute they were leaving his office, discussing the angles in low, intense tones.

"I don't know if this can actually work," said Spilkes.

"Norm," replied Stanwick, who was by now truly enthusiastic, "what you don't realize is that I *invented* Mrs. Shepard."

He meant only that more than ten years ago, for a novel called *McCormick's Grim Reaper,* he'd created the character of a grief-stricken midwest farm wife whose son got murdered with a piece of automated agricultural equipment; he understood the psychology of such a mother, and its appeal to the reading public.

Alas, before the writer and the managing editor entered Spilkes's office, Chip Brzezinski, who'd been following them in the corridor at a prudent distance, succeeded in hearing only that Max had "invented Mrs. Shepard."

33

In sight of the domed Police Building, which looked a little like that London church Spilkes was always trying to get him to visit, Harris reflected that it only made sense for the NYPD to have its headquarters in Little Italy. Who needed more policing than the *paisans*? Even so: poor Gianni, being treated like some murderous gangster when he was just an enterprising pervert. How would he face him tonight at Malocchio?

A police matron ushered Harris into Patrick Boylan's second-floor office and told him he'd have to wait a few minutes for the commissioner's spokesman. Left alone, Harris picked up a ceremonial baton and gently shook what appeared to be some ancient noisemaker. This last item was still in his hand, making a surprising little racket, when Boylan entered.

Everything about him was steel gray: the old suit; the wires of his spectacles; the hair above his gaunt face. "Mr. Harris," he said, not offering a handshake. The brogue, Harris noted, was substantial.

"Mr. Boylan."

"It's Captain Boylan, actually."

Harris smiled, and nodded toward the thing in his hand. "It's a little early for New Year's, I guess."

"That object you're holding is nearly three hundred years old. It's what the Dutch Rattle Watch once employed while on foot patrol to warn the good people of New Amsterdam about any sign of trouble. A first defense against the community's undesirables and malefactors."

"Clever race, the Dutch," said Harris, who replaced the rattle onto Boylan's desktop. He thought of adding "Nearly as clever as the Irish," but decided against it after another look at Boylan's expression.

"We arrested your friend Mr. Roma while you were out of the country."

"Yes," said Harris. "A prince of a guy. I'm sure all that will prove to be a misunderstanding."

"A prin*cess*, perhaps. Maybe one of the 'horticultural lads' who seem to enjoy your magazine."

If Harris had been uncomfortable before, he was plain angry now. What rock was this guy living under? How many years had it been since he'd picked up *Bandbox*?

"We're actually concerned," continued Boylan, "with what preceded Mr. Roma's arrest. A reliable informant tells us that you had been offering illegal monthly gratuities to a uniformed officer of this department in order to keep concealed certain facts of Mr. Waldo Lindstrom's past, thereby allowing him to continue working for your publication. I would like the name of that officer."

Harris tried, quickly, to figure out Boylan's angle: Did he want to shake down the cop for a portion of the take? Maybe scapegoat him to reduce the newspaper heat on higher-ups? Or maybe—the worst possibility—this guy was on the level? Maybe Boylan was some high-strung Savonarola trying to clean up his church right here in Little Italy? Whichever, Harris decided it was better not to offer him the free pair of *Show Boat* tickets he'd discovered in his pants pocket on the way downtown.

"I may have made *contributions*," he said, finally.

"To whom?" asked Boylan.

"An officer who comes into Mr. Roma's restaurant from time to time, soliciting for the police widows' fund."

"Let me suggest that this officer comes into the restaurant once a month."

"That sounds about right."

"Let me suggest that it's exactly right. What is this officer's name?"

"I don't know," said Harris. "He's a tall friendly Irishman." He knew he would regret this last remark, but allowed it to escape his lips nonetheless.

Boylan glared. "You're telling me you never asked this officer his name. Well, I'm telling you that the Widows and Orphans Fund does not go about soliciting donations in restaurants."

"This one did," said Harris, who once a month, out of sight in Gianni's kitchen, would hand over the payoff envelope.

"So," said Boylan, "if I were to find this officer, he would tell me that these payments had to do with charity and not with Mr. Lindstrom?"

Harris, speaking what was only the truth, replied, "I would hope so."

"And you have no idea where Mr. Lindstrom is?"

"None," said Harris, eyeing an antique, knobby nightstick that was mounted on the wall. He wondered if it, too, was Dutch, or maybe Indian. "This informant of yours," he at last made bold enough to say, all but mentioning Jimmy by name, "have you asked him *how* he knows what he says he knows? Have you given any thought to what ax he might be grinding?"

"We leave axes to Major Campbell and the federal boys," said Boylan. Harris took this to be a reference to the overzealous bust-up of Helen Morgan's nightclub, around New Year's, by some Prohibition officers. "But I *will* tell you something about grinding, Mr. Harris. I shall grind into sawdust anyone who helps diminish the reputation of this department."

By that standard, Harris couldn't understand why Boylan's real quarrel wasn't with Jimmy Gordon, who was flinging around all these aspersions. Nor could he understand why the cash he paid to Officer Michael O'Flynn, always extracted from a "Special Projects" box kept beneath Hazel's desk, was any more tainted than the public money with which the police department regularly paid its stool pigeons.

"I suggest that you explore your memory, Mr. Harris. That you give it a good ransacking before Mr. Roma comes to trial next month. You know, we don't break down doors with axes, but we might take a sudden interest in looking around your offices. It would be a shame if any liquor, or large sums of money, or questionable 'fashion' photographs were found on the premises. You, by the way, have a history with photography, don't you?"

Boylan reached into a drawer for two poses of "Yvette" and "Claudine." He laid the postcards on the desktop, facing Harris, who had never been arrested in connection with his previous venture but could, even now, the sweat breaking out on his neck, recall some of the "warnings" he'd received. Boylan might not be current about some things—would it help or hurt to comp him a subscription to the renovated *Bandbox*?—but his thoroughness seemed otherwise to rival Spilkes's. Oh, why, Harris asked himself, had he not told Norman about the payoffs to O'Flynn? The m.e. wouldn't have liked the idea, but last month's envelope would at least have gotten there.

The police matron—who was no Yvette—came in to summon Boylan to an appointment.

"Good day, Mr. Harris," said the captain. "Don't travel too far."

Harris exited into the severely overcast day. He wandered through Little Italy for several blocks, stopping in front of a bakery window that displayed a picture of Mussolini. Envying the Duce's absolute power, he sighed. A pretty girl in a white apron came out to offer him two *biscotti* fresh from the oven. So delicious were they, compared to what got served at Malocchio, that Harris had to wonder, munching and walking away, whether Gianni didn't belong in jail after all.

34

Newman had been sprung from the District of Columbia jail a week ago today. The charges against him had, by some miracle, been dropped. After two days hiding out at Fitz's, he'd been bundled onto a train for New York, where he quickly resumed the drinking he'd begun at the chophouse across from the Press Club. In the five days he'd been back in his own place, he had remounted the wagon every twenty-four hours or so, until the weaker side of his nature once again took over and had him reaching for the Bushmills instead of for Dew-ol's nerve-strengthening tonic.

The carpet was littered with ten or twelve pages of notes—interviews with the Washington bachelors Fitz had brought to the house in Foggy Bottom, in the days after Newman's release, as occupational therapy. Work had not, alas, proved especially strong medicine. Newman could barely read the notes, let alone write from them. He had, however, succeeded in pulling the telephone out of the wall, so he wouldn't have to hear himself be fired by Harris or Spilkes. As it was, he expected to see news of his dismissal come slithering under the door in the form of a telegram.

Disconnecting the phone had also cut off the terrifying prospect of a call from Rosemary, who'd now returned to Hollywood, where production had finally begun on her new film.

Newman knew she would at some point exact punishment for his desertion, or for the bad publicity any association with him might yet bring. He had the blinds drawn as much against her as the sunlight. The one time he'd made himself go out and sit in Gramercy Park, he'd spent no more than a quarter of an hour there, all of it looking over his shoulder.

"Stuart?"

Newman jumped at the sound of a voice beyond the door. Up to now, he'd believed not even his landlady knew he was home. With caution, he rose from the bed, put on his slippers, and soundlessly approached the peephole. Looking through it, he saw the unexpected face of Nan O'Grady.

"Hey, kiddo," he heard himself saying, before simulating a cough and trying to remember if he ever even called Nan by that name. Was he drunk or sober today? On the wagon or off? He was honestly unsure.

"Do you need a minute or two?" asked Nan. "Take your time."

Allen Case, watching some squirrels from the hall window, was out of the peephole's range, but he'd come here from the office with Nan, listening to her on the subway trip down as she tried to interest him "in a *human* rescue." While conceding that Newman was nice enough as humans went, Allen had changed the subject to the animal warehouse in Queens and what he was sure the lemur had told the ocelot after enduring the *House & Garden* shoot with Gardiner Arinopoulos.

Nan now waited with whatever patience she had left. Behind her she could hear Allen whispering to the rodents; through the wooden door she detected the sound of Stuart's panicky, circular movements. She shook her head. Three years ago she would have been behind her desk at Scribner's correcting some New England dowager's spelling of wistaria. Now, for a few extra dollars a week, she was caught between one guy full of sunflower seeds and another full of booze, neither of them with the slightest interest in her.

"Stuart," she said, knocking again. "You really don't need to fuss for me. I'm here with Allen. We want to help." She tried the doorknob. "May we come in?"

Newman, who had certainly not fussed, managed to open up. Nan noticed the clothes, loose papers, and movie magazines featuring Rosemary LaRoche all over the floor. She also couldn't help noticing how beautiful Stuart looked, unshaven and slightly haggard, in his undershirt. He was no longer just handsome, but poetic, the way the young men in *La Bohème* should have looked, instead of being so operatically fat, when she took her mother to the Met.

She tried for a lightness of touch. "We've given up on Harris *ever* arriving at the office," she said, laughing. "We decided we'd rather see you instead."

"Do I still have a job?" asked Newman, quite bewildered.

"There hasn't been *time* to fire you," said Nan, still bundled up against today's weather. "And there's no need to, Stuart. Your column can still make it into the issue if we have a draft by tomorrow. Were you able to do any work on it before your"—she paused for the right word—"mishap?"

Stuart tried to gather lucidity, and at last said, huskily: "I did a little work *after* it, actually." He bent down to pick up the notes scattered across the floor; he felt ashamed handing them to Nan, whose whole life, he knew, was a matter of order.

But she took them with a smile, consciously checking the reflex by which she would ordinarily have rolled her eyes. "Wait just a minute," she said, before crossing the room to confer with Allen, who'd been checking one of the nerve-tonic labels for mineral content and, he hoped, an absence of animal fat. He took the notes, straightened them into a stack, and nodded in response to Nan's whispered instructions. He waved goodbye to Newman and left the apartment, observing, before he crossed back over the threshold, that Nan had begun to throw away the empty whiskey bottles.

Despite the weather, Allen decided to walk home to Cornelia Street, down Sixth Avenue, whose soaked excavations for a new subway line had the Stygian appearance of those Somme Valley photographs that had shaped him long ago. He half expected to see a dead horse float by the wooden pilings.

Tonight he would easily accomplish what Nan wanted done with the notes. Before he went to bed they'd have bloomed into a whole column in Stuart's trademark Lothario style, which was already, Allen knew, an unnatural impersonation on Stuart's part. Even so, he could hear his own parody beginning to take shape inside his head: *If you're courting a gal on Capitol Hill, let me give you some advice for getting her consent . . .*

Hopping a puddle, Allen decided that under certain circumstances it was probably all right to help out a human. Still, he knew that when he turned out the light and said good night to Sugar and to Freddy and the new moosehead, he would lack any sense of achievement. What he'd still be feeling, even as Canberra spent her first night on the high seas, was his terrible failure to have accomplished the liberation of that warehouse across the East River. What use were his perfect grammar and talent for mimicry when it came to effecting what had become his one object in life?

If you're trying to free a Long Island City lemur, let me give you—

All at once, as the rabbi he was passing struggled with a broken umbrella, the solution had flown into his head. If he could impersonate David Fine and Paul Montgomery and Stuart Newman when need be, why couldn't he also write in the voice of Gardiner Arinopoulos?

35

Hiram Oldcastle's blandly agreeable manner was supplemented by a few pronounced eccentricities. Uptown he might live in sleek modernity, but he often came to his sixteenth-floor office in the Graybar dressed in flannel shirts and dungarees. The robust Americanism that he imposed on his magazines—each Oldcastle title, even *Band-*

box, had to do a Fourth of July cover—sprang not from his deep native roots (he came from one of the country's oldest families) or any love of democracy, but from a violent bout of homesickness he'd suffered as a child. When young Hi's mother deserted his father to marry an English actor, she'd inflicted on the boy several miserable years in the Cotswolds. Several decades later, any subject of George V still had a hard time getting hired at Oldcastle Publications: Andrew Burn and Richard Lord had been exceptions, the first for his iron Scottish nationalism, the latter as part of the *carte blanche* Joe Harris enjoyed after *Bandbox*'s miraculous turnaround.

"Sit down, Joe," said Oldcastle, smiling into the middle distance. "Did you have a good trip?" The owner tolerated the annual London pilgrimage as a business necessity, but he still didn't like it.

"As good as you can expect," said Harris, who always knew how to play this. "But what an awful place. I couldn't find a cigar worth smoking."

"I'm not surprised," said Oldcastle, before he announced, in the same cheerfully flat tone: "I've had some more disturbing numericals, Joe."

Harris nodded. "I know, I know. Wanamaker's. Norman told me."

"I'm afraid it's more than that, Joe. A different set of figures entirely. Advance word from the GME."

"*More* numbers? I feel like I'm working for Burroughs."

Oldcastle appeared perplexed.

"The adding machines," said Harris.

"That's a good one, Joe." Without hesitation, or any change in expression, the owner continued: "You remember that *Cutaway* ran a special subs promotion for women buyers before Christmas."

"Yeah," said Harris. " 'Please the Man in Your Life.' I guess I can't get Jimmy to stop being the man in mine."

"They had a big success with it, Joe."

"All right," said Harris, sighing. "I'm sure that's slowed our rate of growth. But how could we have kept it at the same level after the four phenomenal years—"

"Your subscriptions have dropped, Joe. Not the rate of growth. The actual numbers."

Harris looked as if he'd just been told the sixteenth floor was plummeting to the sidewalk.

"The GME reports that Jimmy's up 43,215 for October through New Year's. That's not surprising, since *Cutaway* is still a start-up. But you're down 17,690 for the same period, Joe. Which may suggest that this town isn't big enough for both you and Jimmy."

"Hiram, what are *you* suggesting?"

"That if Jimmy looks like he's winning the game, it might make sense to sell."

"I don't follow you," said Harris. "Sell what? More subscriptions? Believe me, we're trying."

"No, Joe. Sell *Bandbox*. To Nast. Let Jimmy absorb it into *Cutaway* while the subscription list and masthead are still worth charging him real money for."

Harris's face turned as gray as the rain falling past the window. "And what do you expect me to do? Go to work for Jimmy?"

"I don't expect anything, Joe. I'm just saying that we need to be realistic if present trends continue."

"*Trends?* It's one set of numbers!"

"Joe," said Oldcastle, not a decibel higher than he'd said anything else. "When I hired you, how long did it take you to turn *Bandbox* around?"

"One business quarter."

"That's right, Joe. And it can head back in the other direction just as quickly."

"You let the *old* version languish for twenty years!"

"That was a sentimental gesture, Joe. Something for the family." Oldcastle was now old enough that people sometimes forgot he'd in-

herited the first of his several millions, as well as the company, from
his childless uncle, who had started *Bandbox*.

"Now, Joe," the publisher continued, "no long faces. During this
wait-and-see period I'd like to talk about some things we really
can't have going on. Let's start with your employment of this fellow
Lindstrom. . . ."

From Waldo, it was on to Gianni, and then Newman, and then
Mr. Palmer. Fifteen minutes passed before Harris, having done little
more than nod, could get up from his chair and, with Oldcastle's permission, leave the office.

Right now Paul Montgomery, hidden behind two potted palms at
the elevator bank, felt confident that with a little scrutiny of Harris's
facial expression, he'd be able to infer just what had happened behind Oldcastle's door. Paulie had been up here on the sixteenth floor
four times today, ever since noticing the summons to the boss on
Hazel's desk. And now, at last, after getting a good look at Harris
watching the elevator arrow, he had the information he'd come for.

It was time for him to quit.

36

"This is the first year I haven't had a Valentine from Daisy," said
David Fine, sitting across from Spilkes at Malocchio. They were close
to finishing the main course.

"She must be serious about this judge."

"Yeah, but I didn't figure she'd cut me off. She never did during
the polo player. Or the wrestler."

Harris finally entered the restaurant, an hour late, so ashen and unsteady that a waiter helped him toward the table. Spilkes and Fine could scarcely conceal their shock.

"Thanks," said Harris, relinquishing the waiter's arm. "It'd be something if the one time I actually fell on the floor in this place I turned out to be sober." He managed to unfold his napkin. "Where's Paulie?"

"He telephoned," said Spilkes. "He's not feeling well."

"I hope he doesn't catch what I've got."

Spilkes wondered whether this dinner, which he'd proposed during his call to Betty's office this morning, was still such a good idea. "You sure you're strong enough for a war council, Joe?"

"I'm not even strong enough to eat," said Harris, who signaled the waiter back. "Just a small plate of calamari. And bring the special olive oil. The golden-brown kind."

"Yes, sir," said the waiter, who recognized the code for scotch, which he'd now bring to the table in a glass cruet.

"Is Gianni around?" Harris asked, nervously.

Fine pointed to the kitchen door. "He hasn't come out the whole time we've been here."

Spilkes added: "It may be just as well, Joe." He wanted to review the whole series of disasters, one at a time, in his orderly way. "I've found out a little more about Wanamaker's—"

Harris, who'd never made it to his own office today, cut him off with a laugh. "Let me restore your sense of proportion, Norman." He then told all that had happened in Oldcastle's office, from which he'd gone straight to the Warwick to lie down with a hot towel across his forehead, waiting for Betty.

Spilkes, badly shaken by this new information, noticed that Harris was already refilling a coffee cup with "olive oil." "Joe," he warned, "you need to be on your toes."

"Norman, I'm not training for the Golden Gloves."

"Start simply," Spilkes urged, remembering a day when the whole

AT&T grid, from Greenwich to Norwalk, had gone down. "First off, you need to repair things with Rosemary LaRoche, even if we have to sober Newman up and send him to California. You've *got* to tend to that first thing in the morning. Jimmy's clearly up to something there. Hellinger's running an item that says *Cutaway*'s preparing a portfolio called 'Ladies We Worship.' Jimmy promises Rosemary will be at the top of their list."

"Who's feeding Jimmy all of our troubles?" cried Harris.

Spilkes, who now knew that the Newman-LaRoche story was all over the fourteenth floor and could have traveled up to *Cutaway* as simple gossip, just moved to the next matter. "You're going to get a heavy pitch from Max first thing tomorrow morning." He explained the disappearance of John Shepard, of whom Harris had no memory at all. "In some ways this is a very good idea," Spilkes said, arguing how the story of a search might cement the bond between *Bandbox* and its readers.

Harris was baffled. "Why don't we just start rescuing cats from trees? No, Norman."

"I have a few doubts myself," said Spilkes, "but it's worth considering."

"Norman, I'm worn out. Don't even ask about the half-hour I had to spend with this sanctimonious mick, Boylan." Harris took a breath. "The only thing I've got to deal with tonight is Gianni."

"You've got to keep him friendly, Joe. We can't have him saying anything about those payoffs on the witness stand. In the meantime, I should tell you that the money in your 'Special Projects' strongbox has been put into a passbook savings account. You know, I always had my suspicions . . ."

Fine had explained the payoffs to Spilkes this morning. "You know, Joe," the columnist now said, "things aren't going to be smooth between you and Gianni. I called him this afternoon. He didn't even want to talk to *me*."

"Why not?" asked Harris.

"Because, he says, five years ago I introduced him to *you.*"

Harris reached for the olive-oil cruet. Pursing his lips, Spilkes rose to his feet and signaled Fine that it was a good time for them to go. The editor-in-chief, deciding he didn't need their disapproval, waved them off. He was happy to keep sitting for a time, while a rainstorm blew outside the restaurant, in something close to solitude. Not noted for romantic atmosphere, Malocchio was always empty on Valentine's Day.

A waiter approached with a piece of paper.

"What's that?" asked Harris.

"The bill."

It was the first time he'd ever been presented with one here. Sighing, Harris reached for his money clip. After putting nearly all the cash he had onto the table, he got up and walked to the kitchen.

Gianni was seated alone at a wooden table near one of the sinks. Harris came and stood over him, unable for a moment to do more than stare at the tiny coffee cup in front of his former friend. He'd never understood it: however strong the brew might be, these thimble-sized Ginny cups were such an affectation.

At last, pointing to a rain-lashed window, he said: "Every time I'm in here lately it feels like the end of the world."

"So," said Gianni. "You go off to England, fiddling while Roma burns." He'd stolen the line from a subhead in the *Mirror.* "Siddown," he continued, snapping his fingers for the grappa bottle. "You letta me down." His accent had returned since his release on bail.

Harris said nothing.

"You *forgot?*" asked Gianni. "You *forgot* to make the payments to that fat paddy bastard O'Flynn? Do I *forget* to go to fish market every morning? Do I *forget* my mamma's birthday?"

"Okay," said Harris, sitting down and pouring himself a grappa. "I forgot. But how was I supposed to know the cops' going after Waldo would lead them to you?" He paused. "Did you sell him stuff?" This was easier to ask than whether Gianni had actually slept with Lindstrom.

"I no sell! I *give*! Like I *always* give!" He jumped up and went to a sideboard. "Here! Take a free *boconnotto*!" he cried, slapping down the pastry. "Here! Take some more grappa!" he shouted, pouring from the bottle until Harris's glass overflowed onto the table. "I give and I give! And now I probably lose my restaurant. Thanks to you! Well, now you and your friends won't have no place to go when you finished with your workday."

Harris mopped up the grappa before it could reach his lap.

"*Goombah,* we soon may not have any place to go *during* the workday."

Harris was too keyed up to return to the Warwick, so when he'd finished with Gianni, he took a cab to the Graybar and paid the driver with what cash he had left. The Negro watchman let him into the building and brought him up in the elevator to fourteen. Lights were on all over the deserted floor. All right, he thought: he would start *very* simply, with a memo to the staff about all this midnight oil being burnt for nothing.

He kept an ancient Remington in his office, using it when he thought its distinctive typeface would add a note of personal authority to his communications. Unfortunately, his two-fingered hunting and pecking was so hit-and-miss that Nan had once compared it to man's discovery of fire. Tonight, on top of all else, his hands were too shaky to get the mimeograph paper into the roller. He'd have to dictate to Hazel in the morning.

Sinking into the cracked leather of his desk chair, he tried to feel at home again. But glaring up from the blotter was a letter from Rosemary LaRoche, messengered over by the Paramount Building after a three-day air trip from Hollywood.

What kind of magazine are you running? This was her opening, in a penmanship so unadorned it might have belonged to an engineer instead of a movie actress. The letter proceeded to indict the magazine's "phony made-up stories" (presumably a reference to Mr. Palmer), the "drug crowd" its people ran with, and the "gross indecencies" that Stuart Newman, "a public dipso," had tried inflicting on her person. She would hate having to tell *Cutaway* the details of these offenses. "But listen, 'Phat,'" the letter went on—and Harris *was* somewhat thrilled by her use of his familiar—"I'm willing to let Mr. Newman come out here and redeem himself, so long as a third party stays in the room at all times, alongside the two of us, so as to keep an eye on things. You need to get in touch with me about such new arrangements, which I hope will save the reputation and face of everybody involved. In the meantime, on account of the embarrassment and suffering your magazine has caused me, I'll be getting seven cents, not five, on every copy of my issue that you sell."

Harris did a rough mathematical calculation while, through the frosted glass, he watched the bright, bankrupting glow of electric light. Forget her endearments and diminutives! He would put Max Stanwick on this vulture's tail; he'd have him find out who this dame really was and what skeletons she'd buried on her trek from the wheat fields to Grauman's Egyptian.

He made a note to telephone Max in the morning, and then picked up the next item on the blotter: that tear-jerking letter from the mother in Indiana. He read it and frowned: aside from all else, how was the magazine supposed to scour the country for this milk-fed kid? It'd be like looking for hay in a haystack.

He put the letter on the bottom of the pile and took a break to commune with his familiar surroundings: the pictures of Yvette and

Claudine, who looked so much more at ease here than in Captain Boylan's office; his quiver of pens and their massive crystal inkwells; his EDITOR OF THE YEAR cigarette case; and all the photographs of himself—with Dempsey, Valentino, Walker, Mae West (when they did the piece on her, Oldcastle had approved the title "Vitamin Mae," but vetoed a picture of her sucking some healthful concoction off a spoon). Another wall photo, from his regime's earliest days, showed Harris inside Malocchio with Fine and Houlihan and Gianni. A last one, from the old offices, had him and Jimmy Gordon with that lawyer Oldcastle always assigned to the closing of Jimmy's more audacious pieces.

This was his world, and he was not leaving it.

He looked again at the clock. Betty would soon be worrying, so he got up and went in search of some money he could use on a cab back to the Warwick. Rummaging beneath Hazel's desk, he remembered that, thanks to Norman, the Special Projects fund was now locked up at the Irving Trust earning three percent. Where else might he find—

Suddenly, from behind Houlihan's door, he heard a noise. Oh, Christ, thought Harris: don't tell me Cuddles has been evicted and is bunking on his office couch. With surprising daintiness, he tiptoed toward the door, which was open a crack, and listened to the particular sort of raised voice that signified long-distance telephone conversation.

"Yes, ma'am," he heard Cuddles say between pauses. "Yes, Mrs. Shepard, we're very concerned. . . . We'll be sure to cooperate with the police in every way. . . . No, we don't know anything about the trunk. . . . That's why we're going to try something special. . . . No, I'm sure John would never do anything like that." He listened and spoke with great patience before the line was relinquished back to an operator in Indianapolis.

"It's not enough everybody's running up the light bill," said Harris. "We've got to squander the long-distance budget, too."

"Official business," said Cuddles, not the least bit startled, as he turned around in his chair.

"Unauthorized business is more like it. Listen, I know about this let's-find-Fido idea, and it's a stinker. Besides, I want Max for something else right now. I'm going to get him to dig up three bushelfuls of dirt on our gal LaRoche. We're going to climb through every hole in her negligee."

"Yeah?" said Cuddles, cocking an eyebrow—a gesture that had once supplied Harris with a bigger dose of reality than any well-reasoned lecture from Spilkes. At this unexpected reprise of it, Harris's eyes nearly glistened. If there were any justice in the world—if Cuddles hadn't betrayed him by *losing interest*—the two of them would be back in his own office right now, huddled around the bottle of Stoli as if it were the last grenade in their foxhole.

"Turn Max loose on the kid," Cuddles calmly advised. "Readers want to imagine ravishing Rosie on a pile of money. They don't want us telling them she's got a social disease."

"You know," said Harris, after some hesitation, "it scares me to hear you thinking like an editor." He waited some more. "Tell me what's so damned important about this Shepard kid. Why are *you* so interested in a mother's tears?"

For much of the day Cuddles had been wondering that himself. Maybe the question required a head doctor: Was he really trying to find his *own* lost carcass? Or was he just hoping that here, somehow, might lie the opportunity to crank himself back to life in front of Becky? All he knew for certain was that the story had stuck to him even before Stanwick and Spilkes began confabulating about it this morning.

"Norman and Max have their reasons," said Cuddles. "That should be enough for you. Me agreeing is only like some exception proving a rule."

"I don't follow you," said Harris.

"I don't either," replied Cuddles. "Just do the story. It's a good one."

Maybe it was, thought Harris. Maybe they should go ahead and find the kid and thereby stick it to Boylan and the whole NYPD, so busy taking graft they had no time to concern themselves with the nation's missing young men, its future Lindberghs being swallowed up by urban evildoers. Harris felt himself warming to the idea. He tried picturing his readers like those folks who sit around the radio until the trapped miner is pulled free. They'd be watching their mailboxes waiting for news of John—no, the magazine would call him Jack, or even better, *Shep*. Maybe there *was* something here. And besides, who knew how many chances against Jimmy he had left?

"Okay," said Harris. "We'll do it, but if it fails, it was your call."

Cuddles smiled. "Delighted to know my head's still worth platter space."

"Now lend me two bucks," said Harris, who took the cash and went back to his office, leaving Cuddles to reflect that he might as well get fired over something instead of nothing.

From the boss's office, he soon, almost nostalgically, heard a clatter of hangers and some good-night bellowing: "And while he's at it," cried 'Phat, pulling his topcoat from the closet, "tell Stanwick to find my goddamn moose!"

37

To guard against using it in a moment of romantic desperation, Daisy had rarely taken, or even allowed herself to know, any man's phone number.

But this was a moment of *real* desperation, and she thanked her stars as soon as she located the number for Chip's horrible rooming house on a crumpled piece of paper inside an old purse. Dialing with the tip of a trembling fingernail—which even now she could see needed new polish—she prayed that Chip's huge Norwegian land-lady wouldn't pick up and yell at her about the lateness of the hour.

"Yeah?" said a rough male voice instead.

"May I please speak to Mr. Brzezinski? It's an emergency."

"Sure, lady," said this other tenant. "It'll be a pleasure to wake him." He went off to bang on Chip's door down the hall. The whole sordid place came back to Daisy as she heard the footsteps and knock-ing through the phone. At last Chip took the receiver on his end.

"Listen, Mabel, I told you to stop—"

"Chip, it's Daisy." At the sound of her own name, she burst into self-pitying tears. "He's dead!" she cried. "Please come over right away! I need you!"

Chip's thoughts, few and far apart tonight, began to multiply; they required a moment's collection. He'd heard that this judge of hers wasn't on the level. If there'd been a rubout, did he want to be around while the countess decided whether to call the cops?

"Are you alone?" he asked.

"Yes—except for the body!" said Daisy, with a gasp. "Please take a cab!"

Chip liked to hold as many markers as possible, and this one, he realized, might be worth plenty. Maybe riding off to the damsel in distress would net him some piece of juicy, damaging information on Harris, which Chip had always suspected Daisy of possessing. Of course, like everyone else, he had a soft spot for her; that *he* was all she had to call at a moment like this struck even Chip as sad. Some Valentine's Day.

"Give me ten minutes," he finally said.

It took him no more than that to get from Ninth Avenue to Beekman Place. On the third floor, Daisy stood, shaking, behind her apartment door, which was open a few inches but still chained. As soon as she let him in, even before he could spot the twisted form under a sheet on the Murphy bed, a narrative flood started to pour out of her:

"I knew I'd be alone tonight, but I didn't mind: I had things to do." (Remembering the bottle of Wyeth's Sage Tea and Sulfur Compound, with which she'd been planning to dye her hair, she moved to hide it from Chip's sight.) "The judge had told me he'd be attending a Bar Association dinner, which did sound a bit unlikely for Valentine's Day, but as you know, dear Chip, I don't believe in being a clinging vine. I knew he really had some business at Lindy's, and I wouldn't pry into it." More tears began escaping, but she managed to continue: "I never open the door these days, not with all the suspicious characters who have been coming around—a jurist makes so many enemies! But I recognized the voice, even the knock, and I let him in."

At this point she sat down in a club chair and gave way to sobbing.

"Right," said Chip, as he wondered, given her emotional state, whether the two of them might not wind up knocking off a piece before the cops showed up to haul away the judge. He looked over at the sheet but couldn't see any blood. They must have strangled the poor bastard. Where'd she hide when they did? And why'd they let her go? "So they forced their way in behind him . . . ," he said, encouraging her to complete the story.

Daisy, looking perplexed through her tears, asked: "They?"

"Whoever did this to the judge," said Chip.

"The judge is at Lindy's."

"Then who—?" With more exasperation than squeamishness, Chip lifted the sheet on the Murphy bed, revealing the contorted form of Siegfried von Erhard. No wounds of any kind were visible, not even at the neck; in fact, were Siegfried lying face up instead of down, Chip was pretty sure there'd be evidence the newsstand owner had died smiling.

"It didn't happen often," said Daisy, who was calmer now. "But sometimes when his wife was cross, preoccupied by the business and being a bit of a scold, he'd come here for a sympathetic female ear, a softer touch. He'd tell Hannelore he was going out for a bottle of milk. She'd be sleeping when he got back. Perhaps they had some unspoken understanding. You know, in today's modern world—"

Even the Wood Chipper, whose ear was not the best, realized that Daisy, too, now talked like a magazine. It happened to a lot of people in the trade. He decided to stop listening to her and get down to business. Having once seen his father do what had to be done with a corpse in far worse shape than Siegfried, he went about dressing the news slinger, starting with his socks. "Don't worry," he told Daisy, "we'll find some spot to set him down in. Someplace they'll find him fast. It'll look like his heart blew a gasket while he was out for a walk. Which is pretty much what happened, no?"

Chip nicked a dolly from the basement of Daisy's building and trundled Siegfried's still-warm remains (covered by a *Bandbox* garment bag that Daisy had around) almost twenty blocks south. He unzipped his cargo at the darkest point between two streetlamps, remembering Daisy's suggestion that he put a quart of milk not far from Siegfried's right hand—a consoling fiction for Hannelore's benefit.

38

THE DAILY NEWS,

FRIDAY, FEB. 17, 1928, P. 7.

MAG PUTS CRIME SCRIBE ON TRAIL OF MISSING HOOSIER

Yesterday afternoon, Jehoshaphat ("Joe") Harris, editor-in-chief of the embattled "Bandbox," announced the assignment of novelist-cum-crime-reporter Max Stanwick to investigate the disappearance of John Shepard, an Indiana subscriber not seen since the night of January 18th, when he appeared as a guest of the magazine at a party in publisher Hiram Oldcastle's Park Avenue penthouse.

"Shep was like some Horatio Alger kid and Frank Merriwell all rolled into one," said Harris, fighting back emotion in his midtown office (see NEWS foto, facing page). "We thought— did I say that?—we *think* the world of him, and are sure he's destined for great things once he's back among us." Harris insisted that if he had known about the young man's disappearance sooner, he would have cancelled his recent trip to the British Isles.

"In an age of fair-weather friends and high-speed trends," the editor-in-chief declared, "our subscribers are loyal to us, and we're loyal to them." Recent circulation and ad figures—see the NEWS' Business Page—cast some doubt on the fidelity of "Bandbox"'s readers and advertisers, but Harris was having none of it when confronted with the numbers. He would say only that the deployment of Stanwick's imagination and investigative skills would lead to the safe return of young Shepard, who had apparently been in the middle of a spontaneous trip to New York.

Asked to comment on the Hoosier's disappearance, Captain Patrick Boylan, speaking for the police commissioner, told the NEWS: "Yes, we got a report only the other day about this young fellow of no fixed address who left a suitcase and an unpaid bill at one of the city's YMCAs—the sort of thing that happens a dozen times a week. We've been told that a trunk was sent from Greencastle, Indiana, to New York a few days before Mr. Shepard went missing, but so far nothing has turned up."

Boylan speculated that the young man "may have taken off from the city just as impulsively as he came here," and suggested, if that was the case, that he "call his mother."

As for Joe Harris, the captain said, "If he really wants to help our Missing Persons squad, he'll assist them in finding Mr. Waldo Lindstrom."

Lindstrom, the magazine's most popular cover subject, has reportedly jumped bail after a recent arrest for possession of narcotics. Giovanni Roma, proprietor of the Malocchio restaurant and a crony of Harris', allegedly sold him the dope. Other "Bandbox" staff and associates have recently been nabbed for plagiarism and a drunken assault on the nation's Chief Magistrate.

One observer of the magazine industry expressed surprise that in the midst of such troubles, Harris would let himself be distracted by "some woe on the Wabash."

Reading the story behind his desk at 8:00 A.M., Harris scowled, annoyed that the circulation figures and Boylan's skeptical quotes had been thrown in. Stanwick *was,* in fact, pursuing Lindstrom, if only in connection with Shep, and he was also looking for the trunk the cops had been unable to find. Max had pledged not to show his face in the office until he'd located both "the fled flit and the vamoosed valise."

Harris turned the page with an angry snap. He made breakneck progress through the rest of the paper, pausing only to read, in its entirety, a small obituary of Siegfried von Erhard—run as a professional courtesy of the newspaper fraternity. The small type took note of Siegfried's birth in Dusseldorf; his peacetime service in the Kaiser's army; and his unsuccessful butter-and-egg business, which had collapsed just before his proud emigration to this country in 1914. The notice declared that the vendor's death had come from a coronary suffered only a block from his home in Kips Bay. His spouse, Hannelore, was his only survivor.

Well, thought Harris, that fishwife frau had driven the poor guy to an early grave.

Actually, thirteen floors below, Siegfried had just, in a manner of speaking, returned to work. Having kept the newsstand shut for two days, Hannelore was opening its scissor-gate and removing the counter displays of pipe cleaners and Life Savers in order to make room, beside the cash register, for her husband's ashes. She turned the urn so its Iron Cross wouldn't face customers, and then she sighed. Life had to go on. She had been thinking this same thought half an hour ago, while soaking her Post Toasties in the last of the milk Siegfried had gone out for Tuesday night. Right now she was rereading his obituary, though keeping one eye on the stenographer thumbing through an unpurchased copy of *Harper's Bazaar*.

"This is a newsstand, not a 'view stand'!" cried Hannelore, already back in form.

Preceded by Mukluk on his pink leash, Betty Divine entered the Graybar lobby. She was earlier than usual. Thanks to Joe, her sleep patterns were all off. During his nights at the Warwick, he got up half a dozen times to pace; and when he stayed home in Murray Hill, he'd call her after midnight or before five to rehash his anxieties about Hi and Jimmy. This morning, never expecting Hannelore to have reopened, Betty had bought her paper at the corner. Startled by the retracted scissor-gate, she approached the newsstand to pay her respects: "Mrs. von Erhard! Shouldn't you be giving yourself a little more time?"

"Thank you, Miss Divine," said Hannelore, bowing her head to a depth befitting conversation with an editor-in-chief. "But Siegfried would have wanted me back to normal as soon as possible."

Betty missed two or three words of this, but heard Mrs. von Erhard tap her wedding ring, with a sort of prideful affection, against a glazed urn that looked quite a bit like a beer stein. After a moment Betty understood that Siegfried now resided within it.

"I'm so sorry for your loss," she said.

"Few have been so kind as you," replied Hannelore.

"And I'm sorry to hear that," said Betty, who wondered how Mrs. von Erhard expected the pity normally due a widow when for years she'd been tearing into potential mourners, like that poor girl eyeing the *Bazaar*.

"That nice Mr. Montgomery," said Hannelore. "From your gentleman friend's magazine? He has been an exception."

"Oh," said Betty. "Then he's back."

"No, still at home under the weather. But so kind as to send a telegram to my apartment when he heard the news."

"He's very thoughtful," declared Betty. She was running out of things to say, but Mrs. von Erhard more than kept up her end with some chatter about Siegfried.

"There was nothing old-fashioned about Mr. von Erhard, you know. Back in Dusseldorf he was the first one to put air tires onto his bicycle, and over here he saw to it that we were the earliest in our building to have a radio. So, you understand, I couldn't have him moldering under the weeds up in Woodlawn. It didn't seem *twentieth-century*. Whereas the Rose Hill Mortuary and Crematorium are right up-to-date."

Betty was losing the auditory thread, since Hannelore was not only talking fast and with her accent, but addressing some of her remarks to what was left of Siegfried himself. Launching into a description of her husband's fiery, up-to-date *Dämmerung,* the news vendor remarked to Betty, and reminded Siegfried, that "Mr. von Erhard's remains were untouched by human hands. While the soul ascended to heaven, the ashes proceeded straight from the furnace to the urn. Via a stainless-steel spout," she explained. "The 'Felicity Shunt,' the Rose Hill man told me it's called."

With Mrs. von Erhard tapping the urn again, Betty had missed nearly all of the last few sentences, and misunderstood her to say "publicity stunt."

"Yes," said Hannelore, no longer tapping, and looking straight at Betty now. "How Siegfried got here has been written up in the newspapers." She meant a recent article on Rose Hill's modern methods, but having heard "publicity stunt" and then, more clearly, this last business about a write-up, Betty concluded that Hannelore had been trying to draw attention to the newsstand by means of a feature about Siegfried's new dwelling place here on the counter. She recoiled, and pretended that Mukluk was tugging on his leash. "I should be getting upstairs. My sincerest sympathies, Mrs. von Erhard. I hope that Siegfried will be happy here."

"Danke," said Hannelore, back in her forelock-tugging mode.

Betty and Mukluk walked off to the elevator bank—followed closely by Chip Brzezinski, who did a fast skulk past the newsstand to avoid the Widow von Erhard's notice. He entered the elevator, returned Betty's smile, and took a position at the rear of the car. Mukluk, always overexcited to be on board, yapped so loudly that Chip imagined trying to squeeze the thing into the shaft once someone got on at another level and created a gap in the flooring.

As they ascended, Chip looked over Betty's shoulder at her *Daily News,* which she had open to the story of *Bandbox*'s search for John Shepard. Though he could see only the back of her head, Chip assumed she was concentrating on the article, especially Joe Harris's quotes, whereas in fact she was looking over the top of the paper, toward nothing but the metal gate of the car, and continuing to marvel, distastefully, over Mrs. von Erhard's conversation.

"A publicity stunt!" she muttered, louder than her poor hearing let her realize.

The elevator operator just smiled, but Chip—hearing the remark, and seeing the back of Betty's head shake from side to side while she seemed to be reading about Harris's hunt for that awful hick kid—was prompted to remember Max Stanwick's recent remark to Spilkes: *I invented Mrs. Shepard.* Trying to suppress his excitement, he managed to put two and two together and come up with three grand—the salary he'd be able to command from *Cutaway* once he told Jimmy Gordon this whole "search" was a big con designed to increase the circulation of his dying rival.

39

An impending strike by the city's tailors concerned Jimmy more for its potential effects on his own closet than on the fashion pages of *Cutaway.* The latter had already been sketched and photographed for the next several months, but Andrei, his personal, high-end Russian threadsman, was Bolshy enough to walk out with all the poor

Jews down on Seventh, leaving the gray silk suit he was making for Jimmy in some uncuffed limbo until who knows when. So, having planned to spend Friday in the city but out of the office, Jimmy decided he would drop in on Andrei prior to boxing a few rounds at the Athletic Club, after which he'd head back to Garden City on a mid-afternoon train. With Joe so satisfyingly on the run, he could afford to spend a few hours shoring things up at home.

Informed of Jimmy's absence by the *Cutaway* receptionist, Chip felt like he'd been thrown on the rack. Now he'd have to spend the weekend holding down this giant canary of information he'd swallowed in the elevator, a frustration that would get all the worse when it combined with his nervousness that some cop who'd noticed him deposit Siegfried on East Thirty-second Street might still show up at his door.

"Have you seen Siegfried?" All morning long the question lilted across the fourteenth floor, as one person after another reported making a stop at the newsstand and spotting the tall ceramic urn. Daisy owed him big, Chip decided once again, as he listened to this chatter. And he wanted to collect: any dirt on Harris—and he felt sure she had some—would be ice cream atop the slice of pie he was ready to serve Jimmy. But Daisy, claiming a cold, hadn't returned to the office since Siegfried's amorous demise.

What a bunch of weak sisters, thought Chip: Newman absent with his drunkard's shattered nerves; Paulie out with the flu. But waiting for Jimmy made Chip feel like an invalid, too. By 3:30 he could take no more: he left the office and went across town to Penn Station to get a train for Long Island. Jimmy was now grand enough to be unlisted from the latest phone book, but once Hazel went out for lunch, Chip had found she still had his Garden City home address in her file box.

He arrived in the fancy suburb as it was turning dark. Walking up Stewart Avenue past some huge mock-Tudor spreads, he figured

Jimmy would trade up to one of these before long. For now, though, his future boss could be found in a modest frame house whose sidewalk Chip paced four or five times before deciding he'd get arrested for casing the joint if he couldn't bring himself to ring the bell.

"Well, hello!" cried Jimmy's wife. "This is certainly the day for unexpected visitors!" She told him to come inside, where she was letting her sons spoil their supper with cookies and milk. Chip remembered her from two Christmas parties ago. Prettier than she should be; sweeter, too. She made him feel even more thwarted and angry.

"He's in his den," she said, "behind that door on the right. I'll let you take yourself in there, since my hands are full with these two." She laughed, tilting her head in the direction of the noisy boys.

Now that he was here, Chip didn't care if he interrupted Jimmy clipping his toenails or talking to his bookie. He strode up to the door of this "den" and knocked twice. A moment later it was opened—by Paul Montgomery.

"Welcome to dry land," Jimmy called out from a chair at the far end of the room.

Chip looked perplexed.

"He means congratulations on deserting the sinking ship," Paulie explained. "Guess we know what that makes us!"

Chip wanted to bust him on the beezer. Why wasn't he home sick in bed?

Jimmy broke the silence. "And what are *you* selling, Brzezinski?"

Unable to answer in front of a third party, Chip just looked at Paulie, who was wearing the suit he'd had made in London; all day Tuesday he'd been waving around that swatch of fabric, bragging.

"We're trying to decide," said Jimmy, "whether I can run Montgomery's article about getting his suit made if I cut Joe a check for his trip expenses. It's a little unorthodox, but it might keep Oldcastle's lawyers away."

"It's your call, boss!" said Paulie.

Chip finally spoke. "Oldcastle's lawyers are going to have more than that to worry about!"

"Right," said Jimmy. "Joe's payoffs." He smiled over his part in their disclosure.

"Payoffs nothing!" yelled Chip. "He's now in on the biggest fraud since Aimee Semple faked her kidnapping!"

Jimmy waited a minute, pretending to be unexcited. "Tell me more," he then said.

"Can I sit down?" asked Chip.

"You can even have a drink," said Jimmy.

Chip declined, but he could feel those mere words welcoming him to the company of gentlemen. His future had finally stretched itself out like a red carpet.

"This John Shepard business is a fake," he said.

Jimmy smiled again, but managed to keep his teeth hidden, as if they were his cards in the negotiation. He was going to make Chip earn it. "I'm listening," was all he said.

Without further interruption, Chip proceeded, until his narrative had covered both Betty's muttering about a "publicity stunt" and the "I invented Mrs. Shepard" remark from Stanwick to Spilkes.

"So," said Jimmy at last. "They're going to try and 'rescue' the kid, like Tom Sawyer from the cave, to make readers believe the magazine would do the same for them, be their selfless friend in a cutthroat world."

"This is a disgrace!" opined Paulie. "Think of how Joe's always priding himself on the 'real journalism' they run."

"Oh, shut up, Montgomery," said Jimmy Gordon. "If this thing is a fake, it's the best idea Joe's had in six months."

"It's pretty ingenious all right," said Paulie.

"But *is* it a fake?" Jimmy wondered, as he looked toward his bookshelves and tried to figure things out.

"Of course it is!" shouted the Wood Chipper. Had he given away this bonanza for nothing? Was Jimmy going to say, Thanks, I'll think about it, and just let him go back to the city?

"Well," said Jimmy. "I'll tell you what we'll do. I'll set Mr. Montgomery to find out if it's true or not. That's your first assignment, Paulie, after the article about your suit. Expose the story behind Joe's story."

Paulie gave him a thumbs-up.

"What about me?" asked Chip, with more menace than he could conceal.

"You're going to hope like hell that Paulie succeeds," said Jimmy. "If he finds out this story's a phony, it's the *coup de grâce* for poor old Joe. You'll be a rat with a *new* ship—the jolly, bobbing *Cutaway*."

Chip's expression turned so hopeful that he would have looked almost sympathetic to anyone seeing him.

"And we won't keep you in the hold," promised Jimmy. "We'll let you scurry right up the masthead—long tail, twitchy little snout, and everything."

"Welcome aboard!" cried Paulie.

Chip smiled so wide he didn't care if his two cracked molars showed. For the first time in eight hours he didn't feel like hitting somebody.

40

"Thanks, Betty, I'll be down in a few minutes."

Hanging up the phone, Becky could scarcely believe that today— February 20th, another awful Monday in this raw, endless winter—

she had just agreed to browse the *Pinafore* dress racks for outfits she could take with her to sunny southern California. Late Friday afternoon Harris had stunned her with an assignment: go out to Hollywood and report on Blanche Sweet and Dorothy Gish, two nice-girl actresses now struggling to get racy vehicles, *The Green Hat* and *The Constant Nymph,* past the Hays Office and into production. The decency czar would soon be in Washington to testify about all the money he'd once scooped up for the GOP—in Liberty Bonds, no less—from a big oil man who'd later gotten some choice Teapot Dome leases. Becky felt shaky on the politics but understood Harris wanted her to keep the focus on two pretty girls caught in the hypocrisies of flesh and finance. The as-yet-unreported, unwritten piece was already on a lineup sheet with the title "Temptations and Teapots."

She crossed the corridor to Cuddles' office carrying a plant she hoped he would water while she was gone. Relying on him for this task wouldn't win her any commendation from the Botanists' League, but maybe Cuddles would see the request as a sign of confidence.

"Would you mind?" she asked.

Cuddles stroked his chin, considering. "It'll be risky. But okay. I'll borrow one of Kitty Sark's two remaining lives for it."

Harris made a sudden entrance. "You all ready, kid?" he asked Becky. "Come into my office for a pop at five o'clock. We'll see you off."

She smiled, not quite believing how, after a cocktail, she'd be escorted downstairs to Grand Central for the 6:00 P.M. departure of the *Twentieth Century Limited,* just the way it happened for Paulie and Max and David Fine.

"Betty's lending me some things to wear," she told the boss.

"Have her pick out some schoolgirl stuff," Harris replied.

Becky blanched. What was *this* salacious fantasy? Just when she'd been thinking so well of him for the shot at something big!

"To wear in front of Rosemary LaRoche," he explained. "So she won't think of you as vampy competition—devastating though you may be, Miss Walter." Seeing her puzzled look, Harris elaborated: "I'm sending you out there with *two* assignments. You're the new writer on our Rosemary cover story. I'd say congratulations, but I'm still not sure she'll agree to go through with it. Actually, I'm not sure I'd say congratulations even then—seeing as how in order to *get* the story you'll have to be in the same room with that tramp."

Becky, flustered but determined not to blush, said, "I'm not sure—" and then stopped, uncertain of what to add.

Cuddles finished her sentence: " 'That I could live without this opportunity.' " He looked straight at her. "Say thank you, Gracie."

"Thank you," said Becky to Harris. "But what's happened to Newman?"

"He's announced he's taking a leave of absence. Not that he could be bothered to tell me personally, of course. I've been informed of it through Miss O'Grady, who's apparently trying to keep him off a cot at the Salvation Army. She says LaRoche is the last thing he could handle at this point. By the way, he's the last teetotaler I ever let work at this place."

"Which means," said Cuddles, "that Miss Walter will be in your office at five for that pop."

"Good," said Harris, who now gave Becky the only real marching order she was going to get. "It won't be our usual angle on a Duse. A girl reporter can't be the stand-in for the reader's desire. But maybe the idea of two beautiful girls *together* will get something going in him." He tapped her on the behind with a file folder.

Please don't say anything more, thought Becky, who remembered the persistent rumor that—undisplayed, in a drawer in his office— there were pictures of Yvette and Claudine *à deux.*

"They're putting you at the Roosevelt?" asked Harris. "Good. We'll wire you contacts and locations once you're out there. Meanwhile, I'll be trying to soothe LaRoche's feathers through some back channels at Paramount." He paused, and turned his gaze toward Houlihan. "The truth is, I'd have preferred a somewhat rougher approach to her. But with Stanwick taken up by other obligations, we'll have to go this route." It seemed clear that Cuddles would now be responsible for any failure with Rosemary as well as on the Shepard story.

Harris's abrupt departure brought Becky's worries to the surface. She wanted to talk things over with Cuddles, but he'd turned toward his typewriter.

"Will you be coming in for that farewell cocktail?" she asked.

"It's a pretty busy day," he answered.

Becky looked at his Underwood, which rather to her amazement contained the draft of a tribute to Eddie Foy, who'd died the other day.

Cuddles leaned into the roller and made an elaborate erasure, whisking off the shavings and hoping that his sweet, smart Becky would just *go* and make things easier. However much he hungered for her presence, he right now needed her absence even more: he'd never come up with a new plan for winning her if he kept looking for her face across the corridor. This California assignment had been his doing; he'd actually sent a memo to Harris's IN basket Friday morning, headed "AT THE RISK OF SCARING YOU AGAIN," and signed off "Thinking like an editor."

"Our own little Adela Rogers St. Johns," he said now, still not turning around. "Well, write if you get work. Which is to say, if you get past Rosemary's Dobermans."

"Okay," said Becky, confused, now that it had arrived, over this new distance she'd so long been hoping he'd put between them. "See you." She reached over to touch his shoulder, but found herself unable to complete the gesture.

Walking back to her own office she felt almost as lost as the Shepard boy. In Hollywood? By herself? She'd never been anywhere but upstate or here, and all of a sudden the fourteenth floor, this greased pole of fads and one-upsmanship, seemed snug and eternal, like Main Street in Aurora, each office a familiar shop. She looked down the hall toward David Fine's. Between now and St. Patrick's Day, while he covered the Golden Gloves at the Garden, it would be full of autographed towels and blood-flecked ring cards. He was doing a column on what fighters eat during three weeks of elimination bouts, and Becky could already imagine the illo: a picture of Fine himself holding a small fork in the padded maw of a boxing glove, the way he'd worn a chef's toque and red suspenders when he did the piece on firehouse cooking.

Enough. She needed to be organized, not sentimental. She picked up the corrected proof of her squib on *Nelson's Loose-Leaf Encyclopaedia* and walked it to Copy.

"How is Stuart?" she asked Nan O'Grady.

"Coming along," said Nan, a bit uncertainly. "But not ready to be back here." She was blushing, afraid for it to appear she was giving chase to the fallen glamour boy. "I really don't know that much," she added, especially worried she'd look foolish to Becky, so dewy and so nice, a kind of abstract competition that left her feeling devoid of any real hope in the matter of Stuart.

"They've given me Rosemary LaRoche," said Becky, anything but boastful.

"Really?" asked Nan. "I *think* I'm pleased for you."

They both laughed. "You know," said Becky, "Paulie's the one who should be doing this. But I guess he's really sick. They're saying it's something serious he picked up aboard ship."

"So I hear," said Nan, tucking a pencil behind her ear. "Sounds a little odd, though, doesn't it? I'd think the northern latitudes in the middle of winter would be pretty germ-free. But who am I not to take him at his word? Listen, Becky, I can ask Stuart if he has any notes to give you." She had thrown away the movie magazines when straightening up his apartment down in Gramercy Park, but could recall seeing some scratchings about Rosemary not far from where they'd found the mess of pages that Allen had turned into "Billing and Cooing: Making Laws and Making Love on Capitol Hill."

"Thanks," said Becky.

Nan, beset by a new collapse of confidence and another surge of blushing, rushed off to the fact-checking department with the encyclopedia proof.

Left alone in silence with Allen Case, Becky began to experience the odd sense of invisibility that's sometimes the first stage of homesickness: the feeling that one's already departed the place one's actually still standing in. She wished Allen would say something, but he was never a sure bet for conversation, especially not now, hunched over proofs of what Becky assumed to be the column he'd salvaged from Stuart's visit to Washington. She lingered a moment, scanning Allen's little bulletin board, bare but for two wheat-germ coupons and what appeared to be a very new snapshot of a koala bear boarding a ship.

Allen's own mind was on two letters inside his drawer, the first a carbon copy of what he'd sent, in the voice of Gardiner Arinopoulos, to a Mr. Boldoni, who according to the bills he'd seen ran the animal warehouse in Queens:

The zebra shoot went very, VERY well, and I must NOW proceed with plans for late-spring work for Vanity Fair. And yet, so busy am I with other matters besides, I MUST ask you to allow Mr. Allen Case, my assistant, to BROWSE the creatures for me, and to select what HE deems suitable for my VF assignment. PLEASE reply to HIM at the Graybar Building.

The second letter, Mr. Boldoni's answer, had arrived only this morning:

Mr. Case—

I heard from G. Arin-etc. I'm not running a zoo with visiting hours here. But you can come out a week from Friday, around three. By the way, the llama died.

B. Boldoni

Who could he bring with him that Friday? An honest cop? Maybe the one friend he'd made at the *American,* a reporter he might convince to write an exposé? If only there were someone *here* who could help. But Fine would just be interested in whether the wombat went with string beans, and Stanwick in seeing if the ferret could take the lemur in a dark alley.

Giving up on the possibility of a chat, Becky began her exit of the Copy room.

"I'm on my way to California," she said, waving goodbye. "I'll see you in a few weeks, Allen."

He finally looked up. *"B-b-bon voyage."*

41

Somewhere between Eighth Avenue and Fifth, Max Stanwick sat in the back of a cab reading the paper, which informed him that Mayor Walker had gone down to New Orleans for Mardi Gras. The item prompted nostalgic envy in Max, who long ago, during an ideal bachelor summer in the Quarter, had begun and failed to complete a novel called *Jambalicepick*. Did he still have the unfinished manuscript somewhere? The book's premise had been pretty good, if he remembered right, maybe better than what underlay the disappearance of Hoosier Boy. He was beginning to have doubts about this story.

After two hours at the Post Office, rooting around General Delivery, he'd found the trunk—stored under "J" instead of "S" by some Hungarian civil servant with a third-grade education. He'd given the guy a second fifty bucks to bust the lock, and had found inside a bunch of schoolbooks and enough clothes for a whole term at college—just where the first address label had indicated the kid was going, before he pasted it over with "GENERAL DELIVERY NEW YORK CITY." Seems Shep had had exactly the hasty change of heart— Gamma Gamma greenfields for gaudy gritty Gotham—that his ma and pa had chewed Max's ear off about this past weekend on the phone.

For a third fifty bucks the Hungarian put the trunk back in the wrong place. Boylan's cops wouldn't find it if they decided to take an interest and compete with Harris's vigilante 'vestigation.

Well, thought Max, he might as well get on with it, and do his bit to keep *Bandbox* from turning up as dead as Siegfried at the newsstand. He had no desire to wind up working for Macfadden at *True* (sic) *Detective*, although he'd go there before he went to work for Jimmy Gordon. Loyalty counted for a lot with Max, and while you could argue Jimmy'd been the one who brought him to the dance, the way Jimmy had bolted from Joe seemed shamelessly shabby. Besides, thought Max, Joe's the one who signs my checks: I take the king's shilling, I am the king's Shep-finder.

Once the cab stopped, Max looked up at the Sherry-Netherland. It was almost brand new, too new for any history of stolen jewels and blood-soaked towels, of embezzlers and adulterers who'd hurled themselves and one another out the windows. Every hotel, in Max's eyes, was an historic four-walled crime spree, but this one stood like some gleaming electric chair that had yet to be fouled with its first fried follicle. If the place was ever going to sizzle, it needed time to soak up slime, suck in secrets.

He took the elevator to the twentieth floor and turned the knob of room 2008. Open. He shook his head over the inhabitant's sheer stupidity—the inhabitant being Waldo Lindstrom, who lay naked on a sofa, eating an ice cream sundae and listening to the French lesson being broadcast over WNYC.

"I didn't figure you for the self-improving type," said Max.

Waldo, calmly recognizing this person from the Graybar Building, took a moment to recall what facts he knew about him. Deciding there was nothing to be gained in this instance by remaining naked, he got up and put on a long terry-cloth robe with a fighter's hood. So bored he could use the company, he indicated a chair where Max should feel free to sit down. "I can get them to send up a second spoon," he said, nodding toward the sundae and not bothering to stifle a yawn.

Max declined both the seat and the snack. He pointed to the radio's wire-mesh speaker, from which the words *bouton, brique,* and *brouillard* were being defined, in a fast alliterative succession he had to admire. "Sounds like maybe you're planning a trip? Fluffing up your fluency in Frog?"

"How'd you find me?" asked Waldo, still not terribly curious.

On Saturday night a vice cop Max knew had sent him up to Seventh Avenue and 126th Street, to a rough bar where Waldo, tired of sitting in champagne baths drawn by panting pansy plutocrats, was known to seek out his own, more strenuous pleasures. Sure enough, once Max festooned the place with fifties, somebody told him Waldo had been stashed at the Sherry-Netherland by a play producer who'd be taking him off to Haiti once his latest revue closed down. Without even asking, Max had also learned about a ten-year-old son, fathered when Waldo was thirteen, back in Kansas—or, as Max still called it, *Sinflower State,* which had followed *McCormick's Grim Reaper* when his bibliography went on a binge of rural inspiration.

He mentioned none of this purchased information to Waldo. "I know you're earning your freight here. Has the guy on WNYC taught you the French for 'It hurts sitting down'?"

"If only it hurt a little *more,*" sighed Waldo, as he sucked some whipped cream off the spoon. "So you found me. Why, and so what?"

"I'm not even looking for you," said Max.

"I know. You're looking for that kid from Iowa."

"Close enough. You sound interested."

"I can read, you know," said Waldo. "I look at the papers same as everybody else."

"And what do you know about the kid outside of what's in them? You were there at Oldcastle's party that night. Did you drag him off somewhere with you? Maybe up to that place on 126th?"

"Him?!" cried Waldo, laughing so hard he spit a pistachio nut.

"Or maybe you passed him off to one of your buddies. One of them got a taste for jam?"

Max watched Waldo lick the back of his spoon and remembered why he'd abandoned *Banana Split,* a novel with undercurrents of homosexual sadism, even before his publisher had to tell him it was beyond the pale. He could see that Waldo's face was handsome enough to move thirty thousand Arrow collars with a single photograph, but too blank and lazy to hide even a small lie, let alone one as big as knowing anything about Shep's disappearance or demise. Waldo had room in his mind for nothing more than a handful of French words and the good sense to keep his head face down in the pillow until Flit Ziegfeld could ship him off to Port-au-Prince.

This was one row Max could stop hoeing.

"Anything you want me to tell Gianni?" he asked, while straightening his hat.

"Tell him he owes me," said Waldo.

"How do you figure that?"

"Because by the time I'm supposed to testify against him, I'm gonna be down in the Caribbean."

"So sensationally selfless!" scoffed Max. "Knowing that if you *do* testify, the guys who actually sold Gianni the drugs might beat you beyond even *your* tastes. For causing all these difficulties." Max looked at this degenerate Adonis while a dribble of vanilla ice cream slid down Waldo's square jaw. He thought about how much he'd like to drop a nickel on him, call his buddy down at vice to have them come here and pick him up. But then Waldo would be around to rat Gianni, who had torn up at least a hundred restaurant checks for Max.

"Give my best to the boys down in Haiti," was all Max said as he made for the door, hoping Waldo would wind up a shrunken head.

42

Inside her purse Becky had a Garden-of-Allah napkin and a Garden-of-Allah matchbox, the first for Daniel, who'd tease her about them, the second for Cuddles, who'd love the items. She'd done the souvenir gathering in the nervous moments prior to Blanche Sweet's arrival and her own mortifying first words: "I loved you in *The Ragamuffin!*" Blanche, hitting thirty-three, would surely have appreciated mention of a movie she'd made more recently than a dozen years ago.

But the actress gave no sign of being annoyed. For twenty minutes her conversation had been jolly as could be. Though born to show-biz, Blanche liked straying from the topic at hand to talk about her feckless, funny husband, Mickey, with whom she'd had a swell time for years, though by Blanche's cheerful admission they probably had Reno in their future. Mickey was show-business, too, of course—a director—and the way Blanche spoke about him made Becky picture Cuddles standing beside a camera with a megaphone. In fact, the star's breezy, confidential manner soon inspired Becky to impart her own worries over how the real Cuddles was getting on back at the office in this time of crisis.

Blanche sighed sympathetically: it was always one thing or another, wasn't it? Whatever happened with *The Green Hat,* she expected to be back on stage, or even in vaude, a year from now—not because she didn't have the voice for sound; it was the whole style of talkies acting that seemed wrong for her. "And you know what?" she said to Becky. "If I wind up behind the girdles counter a couple of years from now, that'll be okay, too!"

She was still laughing when the maître d' brought Dorothy Gish to the table.

"Thanks so much for coming!" said Becky, standing up to offer the second actress her gloved hand.

"You really want to be with a couple of whores?" asked Miss Gish, in quite a deep voice, provoking laughter from Blanche, who understood the reference to their having played both Anna Christie and Nell Gwynne.

Becky had read that Dorothy, who'd lately been working in England, was the more raucous of the Gish sisters. She lived up to this billing throughout lunch, razzing Blanche when the other star elaborated for Becky on the difficulty of acting in sound pictures. "Oh, crap, Blanche. Lillian says they've *never* been able to act over at MGM, not unless they had music on in the background. I'm not joking, dearie," she added for Becky. "The phonograph would be going round the clock just to put an expression on the actors' kissers."

Miss Gish ordered two bottles of white wine for the table. Blanche, noting Becky's Prohibition-induced surprise, reassured her: "Oh, no one worries about such things out here, darling." Two movie queens and their companion could have whatever they wanted, even at high noon. So Becky set her glass to the right of her reporter's pad and asked what Hays's men had against *The Constant Nymph* and *The Green Hat*.

"We need the ladies to be running things," declared Dorothy. "You know, my sister directed me once. Either of you ever see *Remodeling the Husband*? It was like doing a play in a girls' school. *Marvelous* time had by all. Frances Marion did the script. You know, she'd be good with your *Hat*, Blanche."

Miss Sweet topped up her own wine glass. "All girls? I'm all for it. On both productions. How about you, honey?" she asked Becky. "Want to come in on it? You can handle the press."

From Frances Marion and script girls and censors the conversation moved on to Pickford and Griffith and the actresses' favorite leading men: Ronald Colman for Blanche, William Powell for Miss Gish.

"You've both also worked with Howard Kenyon, haven't you?" asked Becky.

The two fairly fizzed with approbation of that brawny swash-buckler.

"Such a darling man," said Dorothy Gish.

"Of course," added Blanche, "he could fly *without* a trapeze."

Dorothy nodded. "Kissing him was like kissing your brother."

"Your sister, actually," argued Blanche. "Not Lillian. You know what I mean."

Dorothy paused before exclaiming, with a full silent-screen shudder: "Oh, that dreadful woman!" She clarified things for Becky. "Not Lillian. That awful LaRoche person he married."

"A beast," Blanche concurred. "Where were Fatty and his Coke bottle when we needed them?"

Becky, a bit stunned, succeeded in saying: "I'm supposed to try to see her while I'm out here. My editor wants her for one of our covers."

"Ask her about *The Warrens of Virginia*," suggested Blanche. "She was an extra on it—in nineteen *fifteen*."

"Ask her about blackmailing poor Howard," said Dorothy. "When she wanted his name and the publicity that marrying him would bring."

"I'm afraid those aren't questions that would get me onto the set where she's working," said Becky.

"What's the picture?" asked Dorothy.

"Wyoming Wilderness."

"She plays the wilderness," said Blanche.

"Always above the title, always under the director," added Dorothy.

"Can we help, honey?" asked Blanche.

Becky smiled and said thanks anyway, but a couple of hours later, back at the Roosevelt, lying on her bed and actually having to run the electric fan against the afternoon heat, she decided that Miss Sweet and Miss Gish *had* helped, by providing inspiration. She'd fallen in love with both of them and their gumption. They made her want to get to the bottom of Will Hays's dirty Teapot Dome dealings, and to save this cover story on the horrible Rosemary. Becky realized she was excited the way she'd been that afternoon at the *Graphic,* though this time she was out not to save Cuddles' bacon but to bring home her own. And that was a perfectly fine end in itself, she decided, still feeling the effects of the wine and wiggling her just-polished toenails in the breeze of the fan.

She reached for Newman's notes on Rosemary, which Nan had airmailed to the hotel ahead of her train. They weren't much, mostly questions to himself ("Lost Years—1904–06?") and lists of Rosemary's rough, idiosyncratic slang, but you could see him sketching out some vision of the star who'd laid him low:

> Rosemary LaRoche—the Rock?—An alabaster cliff—Biblical temptress—shopgirl goddess—secrets in her voice—origins unplaceable? Athena from the head of Zeus?

Oh, these college men and their one classics course. Stuart wouldn't have gotten very far with this, drunk or sober, thought Becky. But at a second glance, she decided *she* might get someplace with it. She took a pair of manicure scissors from her purse and clipped this paragraph of fragmentary musings away from the even less coherent notations that surrounded it; and then she took a Hotel Roosevelt envelope from the desk drawer. She would messenger these handwritten variations on the theme of Rosemary to the set of *Wyoming Wilderness*—and make the actress think that Newman was staying at the return address. She would even put a date and time on the envelope, and the word *LOUNGE* as the location for an assignation "Newman" was proposing. If Rosemary showed up, Becky would come clean and play on the star's mercies, however small an orchestra those might comprise. She would recite the dire facts of Newman's current condition. If Rosemary was still as smitten as rumor had it—and if renewal of Newman's attentions could be made to depend on her assent—she just might agree to do the story and cover shoot after all.

43

On Friday, March 2, Paul Montgomery began setting up his office at *Cutaway*. He'd ordered himself a new monogrammed desk calendar, and after personally picking it up at Dempsey & Carroll decided to detour past Malocchio on his way back to Lexington Avenue. Sure enough, peering in over the café curtains, he could see Harris and Spilkes sitting down to lunch. Paulie looked at his watch and figured he had just enough time to make the stop he needed to at *Bandbox*, so he hotfooted it down to the Graybar.

"Pssst," he called to Chip Brzezinski from the stairwell at the back of the fourteenth floor. Daisy, sitting on the other side of the fact-checkers' bull pen and looking rather wan, gave no sign of hearing anything.

"Hey, Chipper," whispered Paulie to the approaching Brzezinski. He clapped him on the back. "Getting ready to have your own office?"

Chip grunted. "We'll see."

"The right surroundings are important," said Paulie, easing into his avuncular mode. He'd cleaned out his *Bandbox* office on Monday night when nobody was around. Before leaving the building, he'd put his letter of resignation on Harris's desk. Its text was full of gratitude and sorrow—about how terrific the last few years had been; how wonderful the opportunities he'd been granted; how, alas, his own gifts were too modest for what lay ahead: "I'm not sure I can pull my weight over the threshold of achievement this magazine is approaching." So, he told Joe, he would retreat to more modest ventures while remaining a happy, awestruck subscriber to Harris's monthly miracle.

On Wednesday, Jimmy Gordon had announced his hiring at *Cutaway* and offered to pay his English travel expenses.

"Here," said Paulie, handing Chip two keys. "You should encourage Max to use my old office, not Newman's, when he's around."

Chip looked puzzled.

"My old desk can be locked," said Paulie. "Newman's can't. Give Max this key and tell him it's because you know what sensitive stuff the Shepard search may turn up."

"What's the second key for?"

"A duplicate. For you. So you can check on what he puts into the desk."

The Wood Chipper was wondering exactly how much more spying he was going to have to do for Jimmy before he got his reward. It didn't surprise him that the answer seemed to be plenty, but he wouldn't have figured Montgomery had the balls for this sort of thing.

Paulie read his look. "I know it *seems* underhanded, but Chip, I'm doing this as a *citizen*. One who's concerned about how Joe and the rest of them may be defrauding not only readers but the police department, too."

Chip snorted, before shoving both keys into his pocket.

"Good man," said Paulie.

There was a second reason for Montgomery's stealthy appearance on fourteen. Knowing what his shift from one side to the other must look like, Paulie needed to convince himself that he still possessed the admiration of each editor, secretary, and messenger at what was now his old magazine. Calculating that he still had some time before Harris and Spilkes returned, he beat a quiet path to the Art Department, where Norman Merrill was executing a beautiful sketch of some socks and garters.

Paulie shook his head. "You're Daumier and Rockwell Kent rolled into one, Mr. Merrill."

The illustrator said nothing for a moment, just went on drawing, while Paulie wondered, with some upset, whether Joe had issued an edict against anyone here even saying hello to him. But then Mr. Merrill identified the source of his mute consternation, by pointing toward the open door of the Fashion Department, where three Waldo Lindstrom lookalikes, all large, blond, and lantern-jawed—though lacking the hint of depravity that made Waldo such a success with the reader's subconscious—were preening and posing like motorized sculptures.

"It's a sort of audition," said Mr. Merrill. "For the replacement."

Richard Lord and Gardiner Arinopoulos circled the young contenders, whose aura of Michelangelene masculinity faded a bit when one of them was heard informing another, with high-pitched excitement, that his "*best best* friend" had just gotten a part in the chorus of *Rain or Shine*.

The other responded in an equally tremulous register: "That's such a darb!"

Paulie squeezed Mr. Merrill's pencilless hand and said: "This magazine doesn't need any of 'em. All it ever needed was your imagination." He waited for the illustrator to say thanks, as well as something by way of congratulation on this new job at *Cutaway* that everyone had been talking about. But Mr. Merrill only smiled. Unseen by Paulie, who was already looking around for other sources of approval, he began drawing a long water moccasin beside the human ankles he'd just sketched.

Paulie thought about going into Copy, but his better instincts made him doubt the reception he would get from Nan. So he decided it was time to ascend the stairs from fourteen to eighteen, and after one last quick look around he was gone.

Had he summoned the courage to enter Nan's department, he would have found Allen Case nervously watching the clock. It was almost time for him to slip across the East River for his appointment inside that warehouse of cruelty. His friend from the *American* wouldn't pledge to do a story, but he'd at least promised to be waiting for Allen outside the place's wire fence.

Allen paid no attention to Nan, who was on the telephone with Stuart, telling him not to bother with any more Dew-ol's tonic but to make sure he had some of the milk and pie she'd brought over late yesterday afternoon. "And I've got some really good news," she added. "Art Murphy over at *Catholic World* will be happy to see you next week. He says they can use somebody for a couple of months to fill in for a man who's having a gallstone removed. The atmosphere there is very quiet, and I said you'd be wonderful at the work."

After Stuart's weakly grateful reply, she asked if he'd like her to bring down the last pass of page proofs for his Washington column. She could come straight from work on the subway; it would be no trouble. Waiting for him to respond, she tried to convince herself there was no risk of disappointment. Even if Stuart didn't reciprocate her feelings, worrying about him was nicer than worrying about the subway strike (pending), the subway slasher (caught), or the subway fare (soon sure to go to seven cents).

"You would?" said Nan, rather surprised. "Oh, grand, I'll bring them."

The prospect of this errand was still not so delightful as what occurred next: Stuart's asking how her cousin, the one with the new baby, was getting on. Blushing with pleasure over the personal, cozy nature of the question, Nan answered: "May's just fine. The two of them come home from the hospital tomorrow." She chatted on for a few minutes about the baby's prodigious lung power and May's older boy, almost ready for school, and how she still couldn't—could he?—get used to the idea of hospital-born babies. She was amazed by how at ease she'd begun to feel talking to Stuart, almost as comfortable as she felt talking in *front* of Allen, who even when not preoccupied, as he seemed to be today, tended to ignore words emanating from a species he regarded as largely unimportant.

At this exact moment, however, his ears pricked up, not over Nan's spoken goodbye to Stuart, but at the sudden noisy passage through the hall of Gardiner Arinopoulos and the new It Boy apparent. "Meet the NEW face of YOUR magazine!" the photographer was telling Sidney Bruck's secretary. "THIS is Mr. Bonus Corer, whose face will SOON launch a HUNDRED THOUSAND subscriptions."

Mr. Corer, who spoke with a soft, rural accent, in deeper tones than the competition he'd just defeated, matched Arinopoulos's enthusiasm, if not his volume. "I've got to tell you, sir, I just love animals, and I thought that picture you did of the fella wearin' the snake along with the tie just about beat all. I can't wait for the chance for us to do somethin' like that."

"No, NO, Mr. Corer," the photographer said. "My vision for myself—AND for YOU—is not mammals but MACHINES. I've been seeing them in my dreams for WEEKS now: pylons instead of pythons. New York Edison coils! RADIO TOWERS to mimic the LINES and CONSTRUCTION of the clothes you'll be wearing. Which is to say, no more CRITTERS! I told their landlord, just yesterday, on the phone: I'm CANCELING the rest of my shoots with them. No NEED for him to supply them with any more SPACE out there in Queens once their room and board's UP at the end of the month. Maybe between now and then somebody PASSÉ will discover a need for them, but I told him he WON'T be hearing from me or anyone HERE. No, Mr. Corer: MACHINES! Vroom-VROOM!"

Arinopoulos pushed the new, nearly deafened model down the corridor, while Allen Case looked at Canberra's photo on the bulletin board and realized he would never be gaining entry to the warehouse this afternoon. All of the koala's old friends would probably be dead by the thirty-first.

44

"Smile, honey!" shouted the *Mirror*'s photographer.

Here at the bottom of the courthouse steps on Friday, March 9, a suddenly springlike day, Hazel had just opened her coat to reveal a pretty checkered jumper.

"What was the 'Special Projects' Fund for?" asked the reporter. "Did you ever see Mr. Harris take cash from it himself?"

"No," said Hazel, answering the second question first. She held her pose, keeping the coat open with a white-gloved hand on her hip. "He'd just ask me to take out whatever amount he needed. I didn't always know what it was for. Sometimes to pay some poor freelancer who had the wolf at the door and couldn't wait for a check, sometimes just to pay Nicos."

"Nicos?" asked the reporter, as he scribbled down the name.

"Mr. Harris's barber."

"Oh."

Cuddles Houlihan nudged Hazel along by her posed, jutting elbow. Inside the courtroom, in a row toward the back, the two of them joined the rest of a contingent—including Fine, Nan, Spilkes, and Sidney Bruck—who had been ordered by Harris to attend Giovanni Roma's trial. The editor-in-chief couldn't reasonably go himself, but he wanted Gianni to realize that he still had friends at *Bandbox*. He also wanted Gianni to shut up.

Even the Wood Chipper was present, feigning solidarity with the rest of them, though he was actually here to keep an eye on things for Jimmy Gordon, who didn't want *his* name to surface during the proceedings, either.

Judge Francis X. Gilfoyle—picked, surprisingly enough, by routine, legitimate means to preside over the *State of New York v. John
Roma*—was carefully watched by Daisy, here doing double duty as
Bandbox staffer and loyal girlfriend, as well as by a man wearing
tinted glasses and a chalk-striped suit. This second observer did not
bother to remove his hat or even rise when Gilfoyle entered the
courtroom, a violation of judicial decorum that failed to earn him a
rebuke from either the bench or the bailiff. Even with his dark
glasses Daisy could recognize him as one of the "messengers" who
continued to show up at the oddest hours on Beekman Place.

Everyone expected the trial to be a quick affair, no longer than a
day or two, and it got going at a pace that guaranteed an even swifter
conclusion.

The arresting officer testified that he had received an anony-
mous tip about suspicious activity at Mr. Roma's restaurant. The
informant—no, he didn't know who it was; yes, it might have been a
fellow officer—also suggested that he question Mr. Waldo Lindstrom, whose information eventually led to the arrest of Mr. Roma.
"Yeah, the guy sitting right there in the green tie."

A scurrying of reporters and sketch artists signaled Waldo's arrival on the stand. He was here not because Max had decided to
drop a nickel on him after all, but because the management of the
Sherry-Netherland had had to call the police one recent night when
he and his producer began to argue and throw things at each other.
A radio and, less explicably, an egg beater had landed on the sidewalk of Fifty-ninth Street and nearly injured two pedestrians. The
officers arriving at the hotel had recognized Waldo, and there went
his trip to Haiti, at least for now.

Even more bored than he'd been the day Max visited, Waldo testified with a blank, straight face that Mr. Roma had tried to sell him illegal narcotics and caused him even greater shock by asking that

payment be made through the performance of "certain unnatural and unlawful acts with my person," a term Waldo had learned from the district attorney several minutes before.

Cross-examination was conducted not by the legal stumblebum Gianni had hired the morning after his arrest, but by Lawrence Goodheart, the lawyer Oldcastle used to keep on hand when they were closing Jimmy Gordon's riskier pieces at *Bandbox*. Harris had gotten hold of him and was paying his fees—further reason, he hoped, for Gianni to keep his mouth closed.

Mr. Goodheart began by inquiring about whether the prosecution had offered the witness a deal in exchange for his testimony here today.

Waldo merely shrugged. Judge Gilfoyle instructed him, almost apologetically, to answer with an audible yes or no, if only for the sake of the court reporter.

Once Waldo uttered in the affirmative, Mr. Goodheart continued: "How is it, Mr. Lindstrom, that on the morning of February third you were found with narcotics on, as you might put it, your 'person'?"

"Gianni put them into the pocket of my overcoat. He said I could try them and see if I liked them before I had to give him what he asked for."

"A sort of no-obligation-for-thirty-days arrangement? The kind one might make with Montgomery Ward?"

The prosecutor objected; Mr. Goodheart went on to other matters.

"And is it your testimony, Mr. Lindstrom, that you never sampled any of these narcotics?"

"Of course not," said Waldo.

"Of course not," repeated Mr. Goodheart. "Wouldn't it, however, be true that you showed no such hesitation some years back, in the state of Kansas, about experimenting with public drunkenness, shoplifting, and animal abuse of a kind more unnatural than anything Mr. Roma allegedly proposed for your precious 'person'?"

Waldo shrugged again; Mr. Goodheart asked the court reporter to make a note of the gesture.

"Mr. Lindstrom, did you not, in the summer of 1925, escape from the Kansas State Penitentiary in Lansing?"

Waldo paused briefly before answering: "It was my understanding that I'd been paroled."

General laughter followed, even from the man wearing dark glasses and a hat.

"Did the Manhattan district attorney's office, as part of the arrangement for your appearance here today, promise to help straighten things out with the Kansas authorities?"

"Oh, termites and Topeka!" Waldo, exasperated only by the idea that he was expected to keep all these things straight, sighed loudly before Mr. Goodheart permitted him to step down.

He was followed on the stand by the defendant's brother-in-law, Benjamin Harrison Gattopardi, at whom Gianni appeared to mouth the words *Et tu, brutto?* before Mr. Goodheart put a restraining hand on his forearm.

Yes, this new witness testified, he would occasionally supply Mr. Roma with wine for his restaurant. But he worked full-time in the electrical-supplies business, and when his brother-in-law urged him to procure narcotics, he had been stunned and disappointed. He'd introduced him to the man who'd provided them—no, he actually couldn't recall the gentleman's name—only because of family pressure. (Mr. Gattopardi, too, had received what he called "consideration" from the prosecutors.)

A few others, including a hopped-up police chemist, took the stand in quick succession, but Gianni himself never testified, a fact from which the jury was supposed to draw no inference, according to both Mr. Goodheart, during his summation, and Judge Gilfoyle in the course of his charge. Throughout these last phases of the proceedings, David Fine sat by Gianni at the defense table, and Daisy sent the judge supportive nods. Between encouragements she spared a wave of greeting to Cuddles, who she suspected was missing Becky. Once the jury had retired to deliberate, she went over to ask if he'd like to join her and the judge for lunch at Go-Lo's, on Lafayette Street. He accepted.

At the restaurant Gilfoyle took obvious pleasure in Daisy's chatter—much of it about the insights she'd been acquiring from Dr. Horne's philosophy program on the radio—but he still appeared mighty nervous to Cuddles, who tried to keep things light: "Well, Judge, I see the Irish Vigilance Committee's approved *Mother Machree.* Guess you won't have to worry about any rioting Hibernian filmgoers being brought up before you."

Gilfoyle smiled, and as the three of them waited for their food, he remained a model of jurisprudence, keeping conversation well away from Gianni's case. He asked instead about "how your remarkable Mr. Stanwick is coming with his investigation of that boy's disappearance. I enjoyed meeting him—not only Stanwick, as it happens, but the boy, too. A bright lad, eager to take everything in." The judge seemed to be trying to concentrate on the happier portions of the occasion he was recalling. But his face soon turned grave. "That was quite an evening," he said, nearly in a whisper.

"I missed a lot of it myself," said Cuddles. "Huddled away in Oldcastle's library."

"Romance?" asked the countess, batting her eyes and imagining him on a leather sofa with Becky.

"Protection, mostly. From threatening presences." He remembered how Becky had hustled him away from 'Phat.

"We were surprised by some unappetizing company ourselves," Daisy told Cuddles.

"And who was that?"

Suddenly cautious, Daisy only let herself add: "People who do business with a friend of ours." The judge restrained her with a gentle tap on her wrist. "There, there, dear."

Cuddles figured they were talking about Rothstein. But he was only now realizing, from what the judge had said about Shep—*Jesus,* thought Cuddles, *even I'm using the name now*—that the kid might have been around the judge at the same time this "unappetizing company," probably Rothstein's goons, had shown up at the penthouse. Did the kid do something inconvenient in their presence?

Cuddles made a note to ask Max what tactics The Brain was inclined to employ in such a situation. (A few aspects of Rothstein's behavior had been prudentially soft-pedaled in the *Bandbox* profile.)

Meanwhile, Cuddles tucked into his *moo goo gai pan,* a dish he'd had many times at Manking but only now realized was supposed to be made with chicken.

By 2:30, he and the judge and Daisy were back in court for the guilty verdict on Gianni, whose only real crime, most of the spectators thought, had been developing a case on a miscreant like Waldo.

45

Through the door, open a couple of inches, he could hear the radio reporting the last stretch of the six-day bicycle race at Madison Square Garden. The action was being relayed minute-by-minute over the Teletype. Except for the local announcer's twangy accent, and in spite of the static, which indicated that listeners like himself were in some remote, blocked place, probably a valley, it was almost possible for John Shepard to entertain the fantasy that it was still January and he was right there in New York.

He could hear the cowboys on the other side of the door. Half a dozen were always out there, playing cards and singing songs and not paying much mind to whatever got broadcast. With them, always, were men in suits—three of them tonight—who gave more attention to the radio, especially when the announcer read the news. John had heard them talking a little earlier about Hoover, who'd said he'd stick with Prohibition if he got elected president this year, a promise that made one of them joke how the Commerce secretary was "always good for business—even *our* business."

Once in a while John was allowed to go out and join them, but most evenings, even at dinner, he was kept in here by himself. The remains of tonight's barbecued beef still sat on the desk a few feet from his bunk. Through the small chicken-wired window, in the evening's first moonlight, he could see the leaves of the sycamores; and it was just late enough for him to hear the first distant cry of some coyote or mountain lion. The nightly noise had scared him at first, but by now he was used to it.

He felt as if he'd been here forever, though he knew it still wouldn't even be midterms week at IU.

He'd had a lot of time to think about how he got here. During the first, short ride, the one he'd made in the trunk, he hadn't really been too terrified—thanks to the near-beer. He had worried more about getting to a bathroom than whether he'd suffocate. When they stopped at a garage and let him out, he knew they were somewhere outside Manhattan; he had felt the car going over a long stretch of different surface that had to be a bridge.

Inside the windowless garage he'd gotten knocked around a little bit, until somebody with more authority told Eddie Diamond and the other guy who'd rushed him out of Mr. Oldcastle's penthouse that they were jerks. "Tell me exactly what you heard, kid," this man then asked him. Confused by the beer, he'd been scared *not* to tell them, though he soon realized that keeping quiet would have been the wiser course. As it happened, with an almost word-for-word fidelity that Max Stanwick would have admired, he repeated everything he'd heard Eddie say to the judge about the killing at the Juniper development.

They'd kept him locked up in the garage for two nights, until another two men, different from any he'd yet seen, drove him out of the city on the first leg of a long, long trip. Before it was over, he'd felt as if he'd crossed the whole country. By now, so many weeks after, he realized that he had. The journey had included stretches inside private train compartments and hundreds of miles, usually at night, in the backseats of cars. He'd been able to follow where they were going from the license plates outside the window. The guys transporting him gave him plenty to read, and that was a good thing, since their conversation was worse than anything he could remember hearing back in January from those salesmen on the train between Indianapolis and Cleveland.

He came to understand that all the men minding and chauffeuring him—the dozen shifts and relays that took over from one another at small-town intersections or the end of dirt roads—had at least one thing in common: none of them seemed to know who he was or why they were moving him around in the first place. You could see some of them trying to figure out whether he'd done something wrong or was maybe someone important. Since it might be the latter, they tended to treat him pretty well. He'd felt a gun at his back only once or twice, though a couple of times he had heard one fellow in the front seat ask the other if it seemed likely they'd be asked, at some point, to kill their cargo. This speculation occurred when the drivers were leaning to the theory that he'd done something wrong. They would also wonder out loud—as if he *were* cargo instead of a passenger—why no one had killed him before now, or just let him go after they'd scared him silly. This last possibility would have been swell by John, but his minders clearly lacked the standing to implement any alternative plan. And so, even now, he remained like a product they couldn't sell and couldn't quite afford to discontinue.

After all these weeks, he still couldn't say for sure where he was, except that it looked like a real ranch, overseen by the men in suits and worked by the cowboys. He'd long since settled into a daily routine: mornings began with *huevos rancheros* and buttermilk pancakes, followed by a long hike through the groves of sycamores and cottonwoods, under the eyes of the cowboys, who sometimes allowed him to ride along with them and the cattle. Animals were everywhere: not just the horses and bulls, but deer and bobcats and even bears. Whoever actually owned the ranch had set up a wild-animal preserve, a sort of open-air zoo, on the other side of its highest ridge. John hadn't been there but he'd heard the men in suits joking about it.

He had never been more brown and fit in his life, but he felt like one of the horses—not exactly ill-treated, but not recognized as having any needs of his own. When he asked if he could write to his mother and father and sister, without a return address, he'd been refused. He'd begun to wonder if he'd grow old here, and sometimes, out of anyone's sight, he cried. He remembered reading, years ago, "The Ransom of Red Chief," but he knew it wasn't in him—he was too scared and too well-mannered—to secure his release through sheer obnoxiousness.

The noise beyond the door was dying down. The card game had broken up and somebody was switching off the radio. John pulled the Navajo blanket up to his chin and looked at the designs painted on the ceiling. Lately he needed to convince himself that he hadn't just dreamed those thirty hours he'd spent in Manhattan. In fact, most nights now he *did* dream them, like a wonderful movie he was seeing for the thirtieth or fortieth time. It would probably happen again tonight, but in the event he couldn't sleep, he decided he would reread, once more, an eight-month-old *Bandbox* that he'd found, his first week here, in the main room of the ranch house.

46

"Miss LaRoche?"

"Am-scray," said the movie star from behind her giant menu in the Roosevelt's dining room. "Keep bothering me and I'll have you put out on your caboose."

"Miss LaRoche," Becky persisted, "I believe I'm the person you came here to see."

"Well, *I* believe—and believe you *me*—that you're nothing *like* what I came to see." She raised her fingers over the menu and snapped them for the maître d'.

"You're hoping to see Stuart Newman, aren't you?"

Rosemary lowered the menu a tentative two inches. "And how the hell would you know that?"

"Because I sent that note to the set," said Becky. "I mean *his* note, about you."

"Siddown," said Rosemary, closing the menu at last, but refusing to look her new lunch partner in the face.

"I'm his colleague," said Becky.

Rosemary guffawed. "Is *that* what they're callin' it these days?" More encouragingly, she waved off the just-summoned maître d'.

Becky pressed forward. "I'm hoping that you'll accept me in his place."

Rosemary hated being puzzled. *In his place?* As in "alongside" him? Had 'Phat Harris so misunderstood the nature of her hint about a "third party" that he'd sent this moist little *frail* out here instead of Newman and another gentleman?

"Listen, honey, you're a little confused. If you're lookin' to play field hockey with the girls, I can give you Miss Garbo's phone number. Now where's Mr. Newman?"

"He's in New York," said Becky, who nervously munched a roll while trying to explain just how she came to be here.

Rosemary waited for her to finish the story before saying, quietly, "You took all this upon yourself?"

Becky nodded, hoping the star would admire her moxie, maybe see her as the kind of girl Dorothy Gish often played.

"Of all the goddamned stupid nerve! Take your mitts off that roll! You're not gettin' so much as a cup of coffee here!" Only when she saw that other diners were turning around did the star replace the roar with a hiss. "Exactly *what* did you expect to accomplish?"

It was a question Becky almost hadn't dared ask herself, so new was the thrill of ambition—and accomplishment—that had been filling her. Over the past two weeks she had played the Ouija board with Blanche Sweet, gone for drives in the desert with Dorothy Gish, and pried several damning admissions about the actresses' censorship problems from a man in Will Hays's office. The article she was trying to write needed to be a grand slam if she didn't want to get knocked back to doing squibs on *Nelson's Loose-Leaf Encyclopaedia*. Her confidence had been rising with each longhand draft composed in her room upstairs; she reminded herself that even the *Spirit of St. Louis* had bumped the runway three times before lifting off.

But right now, face-to-face with this implacable siren, she could feel her propeller starting to sputter. Her hopes of turning a little miracle for Harris were headed into the drink, and she had no maneuvers left to execute. She had even considered calling Howard Kenyon, but Dorothy had assured her that the star's ex had "no more pull than he used to have push" with Rosemary.

Looking into the actress's eyes, Becky knew she'd better give up. Back in New York she'd simply have to take a deep breath and tell

Harris she'd done her best; then she'd go shopping for an Easter dress, something less *jeune fille* than the *Pinafore* loaner she had on now.

Rosemary was back behind her menu, snarling once again. "I'll count to three and you'd better be lost."

Becky could feel her right foot lifting, getting ready to beat the first step of a retreat. "You know," she said, "Stuart's job depends on your doing this story."

"Four, five, *six*," said Rosemary.

"He's more handsome than ever," Becky added, as she finally stood up.

Rosemary's knuckles tightened to an extreme whiteness against the menu—out of desire or impatience, Becky couldn't tell. But when nothing further happened, she had no choice other than to leave the dining room.

Back up in her room, she began to pack, laying a program from Grauman's Chinese beneath several writing tablets and a straw hat. Tomorrow she would start the long journey home aboard the *Chief* to Chicago, passing through all that western territory she still had trouble imagining as the scene of Cuddles' boyhood. On the trip out she'd tried to picture his younger self as a merry little fossil, not so much petrified as suspended, awaiting reanimation, inside one of the rocky canyons' geologic layers. She had written him twice and cabled once from out here, all to no response. Daniel, by contrast, had written every other day. She now put the rubber-banded stash of his letters under the straw hat, remembering as she did how one of them contained a list of things she should be sure to see at the Huntington Library. Between all her outings with Blanche and Dorothy, she'd never got around to going.

The Roosevelt kept a big Kelvinator at the end of each hall. At 3:00 P.M. Becky was taking some fresh pineapple from it and thinking about how hard she'd find going back to her leaky icebox on Seventeenth Street. It was then she heard the telephone ringing in her room. She hurried back down the hall, assuming the front desk had just received her tickets from the Oldcastle travel agent.

"Amazing what they can do with electricity these days," said the voice on the other end.

"Cuddles!" It was the clearest long-distance connection she'd ever been on.

"Ah, those crystal-clear sibilants. Norman must have pulled a few strings with his old pals at AT&T. Got our lines routed under nothing but widows' porches from Midtown to Malibu. Pretty quiet, no? So how are you? It's almost quitting time here."

"You sound—" said Becky, hesitantly.

"Sober?"

"I didn't want to use the word."

"It's the war footing we're on. Concentrates the mind. 'Don't give up the Shep'—that's our slogan. He's the Rosetta corncob at this point."

"I've seen the papers." The *Los Angeles Examiner* had picked up the story, and even run news of Gianni's conviction in a sidebar summary of *Bandbox*'s woes. "Any more news?"

"Yeah, actually," said Cuddles. "From a surprising source."

"What is it? Who from?" Becky was surprised by the avidity of her own questions.

"It'll take too long to tell on the horn. 'Phat says we've got to act like we're down to the budget's last nickel. I'll wait and give it to you in person. When I get there."

"When you get here?"

"Book yourself another week in that pleasure palace."

"Cuddles." She tried, with a stern tone, to snuff whatever desperate romantic gesture he might be planning.

"This is business," he informed her. "I won't even stay on the same floor."

"On what basis am I supposed to extend my stay here? I'm done with Blanche and Dorothy, and I struck out completely with that hateful LaRoche."

"Well, I guess she's not a lez."

"She thinks *I'm* a lez."

"If you are, you're lez majesté."

"Lez change the subject."

"Lez misbehave. No, scratch that. We have business. Expect me by the nineteenth at the latest."

Becky sighed. "That's a long way to travel just to read my Blanche-and-Dorothy piece. Which may actually be good. Oh, gosh, Cuddles, it's *got* to be good."

"We can edit out by the pool."

"Will you *stop*? Listen, I'm happy to hear your voice, even with the practical joke. And I *will* see you by the nineteenth. At the latest. Since that's when I'll be back in the office."

"No. You've got to stay put."

"You're beginning to exasperate me, Mr. H. I'm going to say toodle-oo now."

"No, you're going to find Shep. Next week. With me. Stay where you are, because you're already getting warm."

He went on to reveal just enough to make Becky realize he wasn't kidding, that he'd be coming out on a train headed in the opposite direction from the one Oldcastle's travel agent was still booking her on. In the end, she could only say okay.

After he'd hung up, she stared out her window of the Roosevelt into the blazing sun. And then she went downstairs to extend her reservation. Cuddles' word had always been his bond. Sometimes the bond turned out to be Confederate—worth only its weight in sentiment—but she couldn't say no to whatever long shot he was trying to play, not when for so many months she'd been urging him to play any shot at all.

Three thousand miles away, Cuddles, too, was staring out the window, not into the sun, which in New York had gone down, but at the steel shell of the Chanin Building, now risen past the top of the Commodore Hotel and visible from even the Graybar. Its rapid ascent seemed a reminder to make haste, and after another moment Cuddles got himself down to Grand Central to make his reservations for Los Angeles. He'd take the *Twentieth Century* to Chicago and, from there, a *Chief* to L.A. His departure from here a couple of days from now would occasion no collegial sendoff; he was determined to keep absolutely mum about what he'd learned.

Which was this: Max had told him, when he asked what Rothstein tended to do with bystanders who'd stumbled into his more delicate business affairs, about several places where the gang kept people on ice before returning them to New York or sending them to a more permanent nowhere. He'd mentioned a farmhouse in New England and a ranch in California—"There's corpses under the copse, stiffs beneath the sand"—while Cuddles tried to seem no more than moderately interested, withholding what he'd learned from the judge about their little pitcher and his possibly big ears. If he sent Max down the wrong path in search of Shep, that would truly be the end of Harris & Houlihan. But if his secrecy led to a surprise heroic payoff in the eyes of BW? Well, then, Shep really might be the Rosetta cob.

Late Friday afternoon, joining half the staff inside 'Phat's office to toast the absent, just-convicted Gianni at a wake that felt more mick than mama mia, Cuddles had gone back to his best source. Whisking Daisy aside—who ever was more whiskable?—Cuddles asked if any of those "messengers" had ever said anything about a New England farmhouse or a California ranch. Maybe the judge himself had been threatened with a sojourn at one of them?

No, Daisy had said, after a bit of cogitation. But one of the messengers, an especially well-built man, had recently arrived at Beekman Place with a new tan, which, he told Daisy, had been soaked up in California. He'd also mentioned horses.

Cuddles had then asked her if she could arrange to see this fellow again, quickly. On Sunday she managed that, while the judge was visiting ninety-one-year-old Ma Gilfoyle at the Little Sisters of Mercy home in Jackson Heights.

And this morning Daisy had come into Cuddles' office, practically purring: "Go west, young man."

"You're two generations late," he'd replied. But Daisy's tryst with the tanned specimen of Rothstein's muscle-squad had produced amazingly precise directions to a sort of half-working, half-dude ranch in the San Rafael Valley. Cuddles had to wonder why Daisy had wasted her war years on the late Count DiDonna, when she could have been Uncle Sam's own Mata Hari. But he just thanked her, and figured that her Sunday-afternoon assignation had been its own reward.

Until she'd shyly added a request. "I won't ask what this is about," she whispered, blowing her perfumed breath toward Cuddles, "but if what I told you is useful, well—could you see if there might be something in it for the judge? A way to get the dogs called off?"

47

Five days later, Daisy still had the judge on her mind and in her sights. "I don't care if he *is* out of fashion. Don't you think he looks *distinguished* up there in his high hat?"

"Like a regular judge," said Nan, stamping her feet as she tried to keep warm on the sidewalk near Sixty-fourth Street, on the other side of Fifth Avenue from the St. Patrick's Day parade reviewing stand. Francis X. Gilfoyle stood with a dozen other officeholders and Tammany chiefs, all of them come to watch Acting Mayor McKee ride past on his white charger while Walker continued his vacation in Miami.

The Rainbow Division marched by to full-throated cheers. Nan saw Daisy make a fast, expert appraisal of the best-looking physiques in the ranks, but once the long line of shaving-bowl helmets had passed, the countess's eyes returned to Gilfoyle. She really did seem to cherish her corrupt, kindly jurist, thought Nan.

"A man *can* change," said Daisy, tugging on her colleague's sleeve. "No matter what pressures he's under. You do believe that, don't you?"

She meant for the remark to encourage Nan's pursuit of Newman. Its truth had been demonstrated by her own romance: Daisy had the judge eating well and drinking less. If he'd been wearing today's green carnation when she'd met him two months ago, the flower would have entered into a Christmasy combination with his nose. By now the judge's prominent proboscis was barely pink, and even that hue came mostly from the noontime cold that was freezing the high-school trumpeters' lips.

Nan was too shy to talk about Stuart, so she tried shifting the subject of reformation to Cuddles Houlihan: "A man can *relapse,* too." Cuddles had been absent since Wednesday, assumed by everyone to be home in mid-bender.

"He seemed so sharp when I talked to him Monday afternoon," said Daisy, who went no further in expressing her bafflement, though she wondered what he could have done with the information she'd imparted. Lost his nerve and started drinking? The thought made her sad, but only for a moment. Daisy loved all parades, especially this one, whose crush of observers, prone to impulsive kisses, made it one more piece of the mistletoe under which she lived her life.

Nan was the one truly worried. She had carried another pot roast and another pie down to Stuart's Wednesday night, and been there when the first of the telegrams had come—from Needles, California. Stuart had called her the following afternoon, when he got home early from *Catholic World* and found two more wires: one from Albuquerque and another from Dodge City. The *Chief* was making its way east with Rosemary LaRoche, who'd deserted the set of *Wyoming Wilderness* for another crack at the columnist.

By 4:00 P.M. on Thursday, Nan had felt like some New Woman angel, determined to defend her fallen, fallible man from this Lilith. Before she left the Graybar that day, she began her chancy counterattack with a telephone call to Helen Hatfield in Emporia, Kansas. After the failure of Helen's novel, *The Wheat and the Chaff*—which had been tightened up by Nan at Scribner's—the author had quit New York and gone back to her home town, to work for William Allen White on the *Emporia Gazette*. But she would do anything for Nan, including the very odd favor her old copyeditor was now asking.

All day Friday, with a utopian air swirling around the city—the ticker running thirty-three minutes behind on buy orders; a conference of diplomats in Paris close to outlawing war, at least on paper— Nan had chewed her nails and waited. But no word came from Helen.

Now, on Saturday, Nan clapped her gloves against the cold and let her glance stray southward, down Fifth Avenue, toward the hotel where that bottle-blond succubus would probably soon check in.

On Sunday, sure enough, as soon as she called Stuart, Nan found out that there had been additional telegrams from Toledo and Albany and, finally, the Plaza. The last wire informed Stuart that Rosemary would give herself one night to freshen up and him one night to hesitate. If he wasn't at her room by Monday at 8:00 P.M., she'd be at his place by 8:30.

After sharing this dire news, Stuart expected Nan to invite him out to Woodside on Monday night for a hideout and a homecooked meal. Instead she urged him to stay home and meet Rosemary's assault head-on. "Until you do, she'll just keep after you," said Nan.

"But," Stuart asked, despairingly, "what if she brings liquor?"

"Be strong" was all Nan would add to her advice.

All Sunday evening, she forced herself to wait. She sat by the radio, listening to Madame Schumann-Heink and rereading what the papers had to say about the wedding of Nancy Ann Miller, an American girl, to the Maharajah of Indore. All the details about the 25,000 spectators and sacrificial tree bark helped get Nan to Monday morning, when at the office a telegram finally arrived from Helen in Emporia.

CAN SEND BIRTH CERT. IN MAIL; YOU SHD. HAVE END OF WEEK. MEANWHILE INFO. BELOW. CAN'T IMAGINE WHAT IT'S FOR BUT HERE 'TIS. MISS YOUR TOUCH WITH SEMI-COLON . . .

Bless her heart: the telegram must have cost Helen more than she'd gotten in royalties for *The Wheat and the Chaff,* while the information on its second page was worth above rubies to Nan, who whispered "Jesus, Mary, Joseph" by way of thanksgiving.

Nan double-timed it from Copy to Fashion, where Richard Lord was trying several pairs of socks on Bonus Corer, the new main model. When Nan casually asked if either of them knew what might have happened to Waldo Lindstrom now that Gianni's trial was over, Lord said that the cops had been warning Waldo not to leave the city just yet—something he couldn't do anyway, now that his rich producer was out of the picture. According to Bonus, Waldo was such damaged goods that *Cutaway* wouldn't touch him either. He'd been reduced to looking for work at *Physical Culture.*

Armed with this knowledge and too restless to settle for telephoning, Nan flew uptown to the Macfadden Building. She arrived during the mandatory afternoon calisthenics, which on the floor for *PC* were conducted a rigorous notch above the other magazines' performance level. Nan was hoping only to come away with a temporary, post–Sherry-Netherland address for Waldo—something the models booker might have in her notebook—but there he was himself, behind a pillar, hiding from the exercise.

"I guess there's no action for me here," he explained to Nan, once she said hello. "I might have a shot at some forearms portfolio they're doing, but that's it." He made a rueful little snigger. "Might as well be a damned *hand* model."

Apparently, Waldo's physique, so beautiful in a Kuppenheimer suit, lacked the heft and muscle required by Macfadden's anatomical monthly. If truth be told, Nan could see that *Bandbox*'s former cover boy, sitting next to her in just a T-shirt, was beginning to sag a little.

"That's terrible," she said. "Waldo, would you consider coming around to see Stuart Newman this evening? At his apartment?"

Nan explained, with a complete lack of truthfulness, that Stuart, reduced to freelancing by a scandal similar to Waldo's, was thinking of writing an article about Waldo's plight. Would he consider being interviewed?

"Sure," said Waldo, guessing that a little piece of Newman might be in this for Miss O'Grady.

A measure of Waldo's career straits could be found in the punctuality of his arrival at Newman's place that evening. He was startled to see Nan standing in front of the closed apartment door, listening to a din from inside. Bursts of female yelling rolled over the occasional male murmur. There was a crash of china, too. Nan looked to be doing everything she could to restrain herself from intervening; so great was her concentration that Waldo had to tap her on the shoulder.

"Oh!" she cried, wheeling around. "Thank you for coming, Waldo.

I guess we're ready now." She took a deep breath and knocked on the door.

"Take a powder!" yelled the woman inside.

Nan decided just to turn the knob. Once the door was open she motioned to Waldo and the two of them entered.

Stuart Newman sat slumped on the couch behind a half-empty tumbler of whiskey. His tie was off, and smears of lipstick covered the left side of his face. Standing over him, in a black slip, Rosemary LaRoche pursued a spirited line of questioning about his manhood, at one point driving her shiny little fist into his ribs.

Nan said nothing, just closed her eyes and prayed for the exact exclamation that, a second later, emanated from Waldo Lindstrom: "Termites and Topeka! *Mama!*"

Startled by some distant familiarity in the cry, Rosemary drew away from Stuart to look at the equally handsome but much further dissipated man across the room.

Recognition dawned.

"What's the lousy idea?" she screamed. "Get outta here, you little bastard!"

For Stuart's enlightenment, Nan took Helen Hatfield's telegram from her purse.

" 'WALDO LINDSTROM,' " she read. " 'BORN COLDWATER, KANSAS, JANUARY 10, 1905, TO ROSE ROCK, FOURTEEN YEARS OF AGE. FATHER UNKNOWN.' " After a pause—to give poor, dazed Stuart a chance to grasp the situation's essentials—Nan declared: "I thought a little family reunion might be nice. Considering how far you've traveled, Miss Rock."

The penny had dropped ten days ago, when Waldo testified at Gianni's trial and used that oddly local termites expression. Nan had recognized it, from Stuart's hash of notes, as belonging to Rosemary; it was then that she'd been able to put her finger on a physical resemblance that had nagged at her from the moment Waldo ambled up to the witness stand. *He,* Nan wildly surmised, had been the principal event of what Stuart's notes called Rosemary's "Lost Years—1904–06."

The thirty-seven-year-old film star managed to throw on her fur coat over her black slip. She had already reached the door by the time Waldo could extract a Brownie snapshot from his wallet and call out to her, with considerable sincerity: "Don't you want to see your grandson? He's real big for eight."

48

The road wasn't exactly unpaved, but so many stones and branches lay across the broken asphalt it might as well have been. The Ford Becky had hired took another sharp bounce and Cuddles issued a low moan before once more focusing on *Balto: The Hero Dog.* Unique among automobile passengers, he claimed that he could fend off car sickness by reading. But when the car jumped another bad rut, he put his book on the floor and murmured: "I don't think this rattletrap is going to make it."

Becky, who'd learned to drive at college, dismissed the idea: "Will Rogers says Henry Ford could make a farm pay. We'll get there." She patted the steering wheel.

"The rattletrap I was referring to," said Cuddles, "is myself. And I would rather sit through two hours of Fink's Mules than twenty minutes of Rogers."

"Relax," Becky ordered. She glanced again at the map Cuddles had drawn from Daisy's information, then gunned the engine, pushing them a little further into the San Rafael Valley.

"You know," said Cuddles, "Spilkes and Burn would tell you our means of transport isn't in keeping with the Oldcastle image."

"That's the idea, isn't it?"

Once at their destination, she and Cuddles would be trying to pass themselves off as geologists with the state's Department of Public Safety, charged with spot-checking land formations within fifty miles of the St. Francis Dam, which had collapsed last Monday night only hours after Cuddles called the Roosevelt. Four hundred had died, and a small army of typhoid inoculators was now on the move. The California papers were shrill with cries for investigation.

Cuddles had arrived in Los Angeles only yesterday, and immediately argued with Becky over what movie to see before dinner.

"*Two Lovers,*" he'd suggested, with peculiar confidence. "Colman and Vilma Banky."

"Pass," said Becky.

"*Love Happy*. Lois Moran."

"Pick another, Aloysius."

"*Love*. Garbo and Gilbert."

They'd settled on seeing *Wings* for the third time each. Afterwards, over a Mexican dinner, Cuddles spiritedly explained the chain of clues—from the judge to Max to Daisy and her messenger—that had led him to come out here without telling anyone back at the office. Maybe it was the derring-do of *Wings,* or the two tequilas Becky drank on top of an Orange Julius, but by the end of the night she'd begun to feel that Cuddles' plan to scout the whereabouts of John Shepard might not be so preposterous. And, all things considered, she would rather be dodging rocks and brush and maybe even snakes with Cuddles than trying to wake him up inside the Palace Theatre.

Cuddles himself, despite his pouting, continued to seem energetic, even hopeful this morning. He'd seen a good omen in their having found a Mexican restaurant as awful as Manking.

After making two more of the turns on Daisy's map, Becky noticed a change in terrain—fewer wildflowers and more chapparal.
She could also see a line of fir trees atop a distant ridge. Before long
she and Cuddles spotted the ranch house, a big split-log pile with
mortar like the chalk stripes on one of Rothstein's suits. The whole
effect was so native that one instantly knew it belonged to an East-
erner who'd never been on a horse. Two German shepherds on the
porch looked as imported as the architecture. One of them slept while
the other—with a suggestion of bared teeth—barked to beat the
band.

"Well," said Cuddles, "I've got a pretty good idea which one's
Hannelore and which one's Siegfried."

Her hands shaking a little, Becky managed to park the Ford. A
minute later the door was answered by a handsome cowboy in dungarees and a Stetson. He took off the hat to say, "Ma'am?"

Cuddles made note of Becky's little swoon. "So that's what it
takes," he muttered.

Becky thanked the cowboy, who went to get his associate, "Mr.
Jones." Dressed in an expensive suit—maybe one of the two-hundred-
and-fifty-dollar numbers from Wallach's that Rothstein had made
his men wear after getting a grip on that haberdashery—Jones
approached Becky and Cuddles while straightening the polka-dot
handkerchief in his breast pocket.

Becky explained their geologic purpose.

Mr. Jones smiled. " 'Course, you don't never know how many
bodies was inside the dam *before* it busted."

Becky and Cuddles each responded with something closer to a
gulp than a laugh.

"You and your friend don't make small talk?" asked Mr. Jones. He
seemed to be weighing suspicion of them against the prudence of
complying with the state's rock cops. "Okay," he said, finally. "But
don't take too long. And no wandering inside the house."

The "equipment" Cuddles and Becky had brought along consisted of several beheaded knitting needles, two slide rules, a package of litmus paper and a few small, impressively labeled bottles that actually held sarsaparilla and ginger ale. Cuddles had counted on the ranch-house occupants' being less than highly educated, and his assumption seemed borne out by their lack of any questions about the "soil sampling" he and Becky now performed in close proximity to the house. The two of them managed a glance or two through the windows, but saw nothing of interest except an old copy of *Bandbox* inside a small room at the back. Even that probably signified nothing more than what Andrew Burn liked to call the magazine's "excellent penetration" of the western states.

Becky once more started to think the whole mission might be crazy—Cuddles was starting to display unmistakable signs of belief in his geological efforts—but then, halfway up the closest ridge, only a couple of hundred yards to the north, she could see a young man, clearly not to the saddle born, sitting wobbly atop a bay horse. She nudged Cuddles.

"Yep," he said, shading his eyes and taking a look. "Yonder." He regarded the cowboys and cattle just ahead of the boy they now both recognized as Shep. "Jesus, that longhorned thing at the head of the parade would scare even Case." He and Becky quickly turned away from the riders, though there was little chance Shep would recognize the two of them, clad as they were in a pith helmet and wide-brimmed gardening hat.

"Shouldn't we let him know?" whispered Becky, beginning to feel guilty about their plan.

"Nope," said Cuddles. "Can't risk his blurting stuff out before the real cavalry gets here." That, as he'd explained last night over dinner, would be Max and Gardiner Arinopoulos, whom they now could summon to write and photograph a piece that would prove Shep's whereabouts and make *Bandbox* his heroic rescuer.

Back inside the ranch house, Cuddles pronounced its surrounding earth "tiptop topsoil, rock-solid safe," to Mr. Jones, who responded by saying, with a snort, "Yeah, a regular fuckin' Gibraltar," perhaps a reference to Rothstein's shaky current affairs.

A few hours later, back in Los Angeles, Cuddles and Becky wired Max, in his own idiom, at the Graybar Building in New York:

SHEP SHIPSHAPE. RESTING, RESTRAINED ON RANCH. TELEPHONE
HOULIHAN AND NELLIE BLY. HOTEL ROOSEVELT, L.A., CALIF.

49

By late morning the following Monday, the radio was forecasting the biggest-volume stock session ever; General Motors, the lead bull, looked ready to crash past $200 a share. Harris listened to the news in his office, wishing that Oldcastle Publications were publicly traded. A dizzying run-up of its stock might distract Hi from the corporate soft spot *Bandbox* had suddenly become. Burn had just been in to report that Knox Hats was forsaking *Bandbox* for *Cutaway*. And before that, news had arrived that Jimmy was about to land Tunney for a fashion spread. Christ, down here on fourteen, Fine was still fooling around with those Golden Gloves amateurs.

Throughout his frustrated musings on these events, Harris's face—with walnut shells over his eyes—remained under the ultraviolet lamp Betty had installed to the left of his desk. His troubles were giving him a bad pallor, she insisted, which would only compound his troubles by its suggestion of beleaguerment and weakness. Harris himself had always thought he'd look better with a beard, but sporting one would only further mark him as a man of the past, an appearance to be avoided at all costs right now.

"Mr. Harris?"

He could hear Nan O'Grady knocking on the frosted glass. Where was Hazel, who should be out there saving him from such a thing? Oh, if only the copy chief were coming in to complain of a *schvantz* in Max's latest piece! Such an objection would mean there was a piece to complain *about,* whereas Max had so far been everywhere— from Shep's old frat house to the New York recruiting office of the French Foreign Legion—and come up with nothing. A few days ago he'd disappeared altogether. How much time could be left until the magazine publicly had to give up on the kid and look even more foolish than it did already?

Harris at last raised his head; the walnut shells fell from his eyes. "Yes, Miss O'Grady?"

Nan entered but did not sit down. "You may want to put in a call to the Plaza. Rosemary LaRoche has been there for a week."

Harris turned off the lamp. "Our dealings with Miss LaRoche are finished. Miss Walter struck out with her in Hollywood, trying to pinch hit for your friend Mr. Newman."

Nan fought to control her blushing. "Miss LaRoche has agreed to do the story and the cover."

Harris raised a skeptical eyebrow in the direction of his newly tanned forehead.

"I'm not at liberty to tell you why," said Nan, who'd decided it was best not to reveal the family history that had brought Rosemary low, or the several days of moping the star had done before realizing there was no way of refusing Nan's demands—not without having herself and Baby Waldo all over the pink pages of the *Graphic.*

"Okay," said Harris, slowly. "Get Newman back here from the *Presbyterian Post* or wherever he's gone. Tell him we can wipe the slate clean."

"*Catholic World,*" said Nan. "And I'm afraid he's not quite ready to return here, certainly not for Rosemary LaRoche. Who, by the way, has agreed to let Becky write the story. Is she on her way back?"

"I don't know where *anyone* is!" cried Harris. "*She's* disappeared. *Houlihan's* gone. *Stanwick* is gone. And your own Romeo can't bring himself to write about a movie goddess who won't keep her hands off him!"

"If you still want this story——"

"Of course I want this story!"

"Then hold Stuart's job for him. And send Becky to the Plaza whenever she gets back. Miss LaRoche won't be going anywhere, believe me."

At the same hour, out in California, Mr. Jones was banging on a cuckoo clock. "Sing, ya bastard," he urged the tiny mechanical bird, once he'd coaxed it to emerge, twenty minutes early, from behind the little handcarved doors. But the artificial creature held its tongue, and the house-proud Mr. Jones had to propose an alternative delight to his two visitors: "How about gettin' a picture of the best rug?" The Mexican housemaid, he explained, kept their polar bear pelt, which lay on the floor of a bedroom once used by Rothstein himself, absolutely snow-white.

Max had been acquainted with Mr. Jones (real name Ivan Jacobs) even before doing his profile of The Brain. Until this morning's conversation turned to interior decoration, they'd been chatting about "Diamond Joe" Esposito, whose murder was being investigated in Chicago. The coroner's office said he'd sustained fifty-eight shotgun wounds; a police source put the count at sixty-one. Either way, it was a shame.

Max had arrived here at the ranch house with Gardiner Arinopoulos and informed Mr. Jones that Rothstein was so pleased with the story about himself in *Bandbox* that he'd agreed to allow some of his domains—the Fifth Avenue apartment, this ranch, a farmhouse in New England—to be photographed by Mr. Arinopoulos for Old-castle's *Manse*. Max would supply a little bit of text, strictly atmospheric, to run alongside the pictures.

"You know, you really nailed him," said Mr. Jones, full of admiration. "Right down to his shoe size." Far from seeing any reason to doubt Stanwick's stated purpose in being here, Mr. Jones was eager to get into the pictures Arinopoulos was already shooting of the tasteful, rustic decor. When the photographer mentioned his new penchant for man-and-machine shots, the obliging host asked if he could pose with the automatic weapon behind one of the couches.

He pointed out that the ranch also had "some nice animals who could say cheese for ya." Arinopoulos emphatically declined the opportunity.

But Max overruled his colleague. "Sure he'd like it." He shot Arinopoulos a stern glance, reminding him of the actual, documentary reason for their trip here. Miffed, but compliant, the photographer announced that he would look at the creatures "RIGHT now." A cowboy named Daryl was summoned to take him up to the little wildlife preserve over the ridge and introduce him to Mr. Mazzaferro.

"Neither one of us will need much time," Max assured Mr. Jones. "Mr. Arinopoulos works fast, and if you can give me the run of the place for about an hour—I might even drive around—I should be able to soak up the scene, ignite my impressions."

"Absotively posilutely," said Mr. Jones. "You're the master, Max." His hospitable manner clouded over for only a moment, when he seemed to remember something. "Daryl," he called out to the cowboy, who'd started shouldering Arinopoulos's equipment. "Is the kid around?"

"He's out for a walk with one of the dogs. He ain't goin' nowhere."

"Okay," Mr. Jones said to the visitors. "Knock yourselves out."

Back outside, Max could well believe from the look of the fencing that Shep wasn't going anywhere, at least not without a little help. For the next forty-five minutes or so, the writer was all business—seriously surveying the sage, no shilly-shallying in the chaparral. He wasn't bothered that Houlihan had been the one to crack the case, so long as the rescue and the writing were left to himself. Meanwhile, Arinopoulos took pictures of the topography and the animals and then nearly every cranny of the ranch house. Max was glad to get away from the photographer, whose random fortissimos had effected a queasy-making syncopation with his own alliterations on the long days of train travel out here.

The shutterbug had required no persuasion to accept the assignment, when Max advised him he was needed in California. Arinopoulos had gotten tremendously excited, dashing off for a minute and then returning to Max's office (Paulie's, actually) with a fistful of tearsheets from an old *Manse* article on Oldcastle's ranch in New Mexico. The photographer had shot the rustic retreat a couple of years back, and thought he could produce something even better with another crack at another ranch house. Max took the pages and stuffed them into the drawer, reminding GA that on this new assignment, for all that they'd like some vivacious visuals, proof trumped artistry. What's more, until they got what they were going out there for, 'Phat and Spilkes were to be kept in the dark, by Houlihan's say-so.

Now, a week later, Max drove the ranch's pebbly paths with great care, looking back every so often to make sure nobody went into the house without his noticing. It was wearying work, until suddenly—just ahead, on a sandy stretch Max had already been over twice—thar she blew: a boy and his dog. Shep and a German shepherd.

Max pulled the car even with him. "Kid," he said, "tell the pooch to make a beeline back to the bunkhouse. You're coming with me."

When neither creature, two-footed or four-, seemed ready to budge from its confusion, Max addressed the dog directly: "On, King! Go see what's churnin' on the chuck wagon."

John had been figuring he was in for one more pointless ride or roughing up. But when he heard the stranger's canine command, he realized this wasn't a stranger at all. "Mr. Stanwick?" he cried, struggling to hold down the volume.

"Sssssssh," said Max, at some length, enjoying the sound's extended action. "Yeah, kid, it's me."

The young man began babbling out his story at the same giddy clip he'd spoken during his days in New York. But Max managed to shut him down: "Not now, my heroic little Hoosier. Tie your tongue and take the trunk."

With John packed inside, just the way he'd departed Oldcastle's penthouse, Max drove the car back down to the ranch house. Making sure they were alone, he gave the high sign to Arinopoulos, who was in the process of shooting a chromium thermometer fixed to a windowsill. Max let Shep out of the trunk for no more than a minute, just long enough for Arinopoulos to photograph him beside the house, and then against a backdrop of mountains, each time holding a copy of today's newspaper. Max trusted that the pictures' elements would combine into something more convincing than Macfadden's Composographs.

He and Arinopoulos didn't again let their prize out of the trunk until they were twenty miles from Los Angeles, at which point John was permitted to ride up front with Max, who told him that for the foreseeable future his name was Shep. "Kid," he added, after hearing the circumstances of the penthouse snatch, "I hope you really *have* noticed *everything*. 'Cause I've got to write one sensational slam-bang story."

50

Three days later, for the first time in more than a week, the Wood Chipper used the key to Paulie's old desk drawer, though he wondered why he even made the effort. So far as he could see, Montgomery had made zero progress in exposing the big fraud, while Stanwick, AWOL for the last week, had before that just gone through the motions of trying to "find" the little Hoosier, telling everybody about his trips to Indiana and the Jersey City morgue, but never coming up with anything. He'd probably, Chip figured, gone off to work on one of his novels while Harris and the rest of them kept up the hoax until they decided it was time to produce the pipsqueak. For all the reward he'd gotten so far, Chip wished that the little rube *had* been snatched, and maybe ground up in some cement plant.

He gave the desk drawer a vicious little yank and for the first time, to his surprise, found something in it. Two items, actually. The first was a telegram from Houlihan to Max, sent from the Hotel Roosevelt in Hollywood; the second was some tearsheets out of *Manse*— a long-ago spread on Oldcastle's New Mexico ranch.

Wait a minute. How far was that from Los Angeles? Not very, Chip thought, his heart going like it had the day he heard Betty Divine say "publicity stunt." If this "shipshape" Shep was "resting" and "restrained" on a ranch, like the telegram said, you could bet it was on the one belonging to the publisher. That's where the kid had been all along, biding everyone's time in voluntary luxury. This thing went all the way to the top!

Excitement so banished surliness that Chip considered just saying the hell with Jimmy and marching this incriminating haul over to the *Daily News*. But what would that bring him besides a single day's fame? He needed to think long-term. And yet, he couldn't bring himself to run the items upstairs. He jammed them into his pockets instead. Tonight he'd pound the pavement, thinking. And then he'd sleep on it.

That same afternoon Spilkes sat in Harris's office, proudly relating the details of his visit, the day before, to AT&T's headquarters on Broadway, where one of his old pals had invited him to a demonstration of the first telephone link between New York and Paris.

"Pershing talked to the president," said Spilkes.

"Coolidge was there?" asked Harris.

"Not him. Gifford. AT&T's president. Pershing was in Paris." The m.e. tapped the copy of the *New York Times* on Harris's desk.

The editor-in-chief was not impressed. "Have you been keeping track of the phone bills around *here,* Norman? Before he went on the lam, Stanwick was calling fortune-tellers, coroners, and traveling circuses from Kokomo to Cucamonga. With no result. And Houlihan was running a tab of calls to his imaginary girlfriend out in California. Well, *she's* now overdue, and everybody else, along with Newman, has disappeared. The way Jimmy's luck is running, there'll be a Nairobi edition of *Cutaway* in another two weeks. And one of us will be editing it."

"What about Rosemary?"

Harris was about to express a lack of faith in even that one supposed bright spot—Nan's assurances still struck him as too vague to be true—when the steep soundwaves of Hazel's voice came through the open door.

"Hey, how are ya?" she was shouting from coast to coast. "We'd given up on you." Short pause. "I must say you don't *sound* plastered. Hold the line, I'll get him. *It's Mr. Houlihan!*"

"Not interested!" cried Harris.

Hazel communicated this to Cuddles before resuming private conversation with him.

"See what I mean?" Harris asked his managing editor. "This is how they run up the bill here."

"Mr. Spilkes?" called Hazel. "Will *you* talk to him?"

Made curious by what seemed to be Houlihan's own insistence, Spilkes picked up Harris's telephone.

"We're making tracks," said Cuddles in his familiar murmur. "Gotten as far as Chicago already. So be ready for us when the *Twentieth Century* gets in. Tomorrow morning. Nine-thirty."

Spilkes transmitted this news to Harris, who responded: "He wants us to watch him walk down the red carpet after he's been on a cross-country binge?" He said it loud enough that there was no need for the m.e. to repeat it.

"Actually," said Cuddles, "my companions and I would appreciate something like the opposite of fanfare for the special guest we're bringing with us. If you can arrange a hood for him, that'd be good."

"I'm going to give you to Joe," said Spilkes.

Taking the telephone, Harris could feel the words rising to his lips at last: "Houlihan, you're fi—"

"Aboard is my Shepard," said Cuddles. "I shall not want."

Harris was silent.

"Nine-thirty," said Cuddles. "And you'd better have a place to stash him."

At ten o'clock that night the *Twentieth Century* rolled east through Ohio. John Shepard had an upper berth, complete with a radio, all to himself, and he was listening to the Dodge Brothers' nationwide variety hour: John Barrymore reciting Hamlet's soliloquy; Dolores Del

Rio singing a Spanish song; Charlie Chaplin telling Pat-and-Mike stories in an Irish accent. Put it all together and it was like listening to a magazine!

Earlier, in the dining car, John had paid more attention to the glamour all around him than to Mr. Houlihan's explanation of what had happened to him these past couple of months. Supper had been a feast, more food and heavier cutlery than you got at Grandma Chilton's on Thanksgiving. And they'd let him have a cocktail, even if near-beer had started so much of the trouble that night at Mr. Oldcastle's penthouse. John had forgotten all about his recent terrors, not to mention the one piece of corroborative evidence he'd managed to hide in his pocket against the faint hope of a rescue like this. Everyone in the dining car had sung "When That Midnight Choo-Choo Leaves for Alabam' "—twice, in fact, even though Mr. Ari-whatsisname's odd way of hitting some of the words threw people's rhythm off. Over dessert, John had asked if he could call his mother and pa as soon as they all got to New York, and the answer was yes, so long as they could keep a secret.

The Negro porter woke him at seven in the morning to ask if he wanted a shave before they got to New York. The hot towel was still across his face when Mr. Stanwick came up to the barber's chair with a fedora he'd bought in Chicago and asked him to try it on.

"Pull it tight, kid. Better bury the whole brow."

Which is what he did when the train pulled into Grand Central and they all rushed down the concourse to the Graybar Building. He knew they must be passing under those ceiling paintings of airships and locomotives, but he kept his eyes on the ground, as he'd been told to. Once inside the building, Mr. Houlihan, Miss Walter, and the photographer were allowed to take the elevator, but Mr. Stanwick asked him if he could manage all the flights of stairs up to fourteen. They didn't want anybody seeing him in one of the cars.

"Silent as a soundproofed sarcophagus, *sí*?" said Mr. Stanwick as they climbed the stairs together. Unsure of what he meant, John nodded. And at the tenth floor he took off the fedora, because he was beginning to sweat.

At that moment, Paul Montgomery, coming down the stairs between eighteen and fourteen, was surprised to hear noise from below. Without letting himself be seen, he decided to halt until he could recognize who was coming up. Paulie was in the stairwell because, five minutes before, the Wood Chipper had called with the news that he'd better take the stairs to the rear door on fourteen if he wanted to see all the proof of a hoax that he'd ever need. "I'll come out to the landing as soon as you knock," said Chip, who had gotten over his own Hamlet-like indecision about the telegram and clipping.

Paulie, who'd come up dry in his own investigations, had developed enough doubts about Chip Brzezinski to start thinking that Shep, who was now called that even at *Cutaway,* might really *be* missing. But those doubts vanished as he looked down and saw, through two iron rods of the banister, the ascending figures of Max Stanwick and John Shepard.

"Won't be long now," he could hear the older man saying, not much above a whisper, to the boy. "Fame and fortune are fixed on fourteen, friend."

5 I

During the first week of April, the papers were full of news about an apocalyptic collision, in some distant reach of the galaxy, between Nova Pictoris and another star. And as *Bandbox* prepared its Shep story and waited for some sort of counter-strike by *Cutaway,* a feeling prevailed that the universe was no longer big enough for both of them.

John Shepard, comfortably sequestered in a room at the Commodore, squeezed his memory during long sessions with Max, who pressed for any vivid detail of his cross-country detention, while Hazel squiggled every one of John's utterances onto her steno pad. Over in the Graybar, illustration and layout of this captivity narrative proceeded under conditions of strict secrecy: the door to the back stairwell was now locked, and Mrs. Zimmerman had received instructions not to let anyone past Reception without an escort.

Since returning to New York, Cuddles and Becky had barely left the building. Even on Sunday afternoon, April 1, when Daniel had wanted her to go with him to a St. Cecilia's Society concert, Becky had stayed here, working on the Hays Office piece. Monday then brought an amazing encounter with Rosemary LaRoche up at the Plaza. She'd been sweetness itself! She might have been lured back to New York by Becky's dangling of Stuart Newman, but some team of pixies seemed to have transformed her disposition en route. She'd offered Becky chocolates and tea, and put forth a version of her life story that, if almost certainly false, was still full of usable material, especially if Daisy, lenient in these matters, did the fact-checking. When Becky asked Blanche's question about the star's having extra'd on *The Warrens of Virginia* in '15, Miss LaRoche stayed nice as pie ("Blanche is mistaken, I'm afraid"); and when she questioned the actress as to why she'd left the set of *Wyoming Wilderness*, Rosemary insisted it was only "so I can be at your disposal." The sole subject that made her bristle was Stuart Newman, whose accidental mention by Becky made Miss LaRoche ask *"Who?"* in a voice two registers lower than the rest of her conversation.

On Wednesday, in his office not far from Becky's, David Fine tried to hide his disappointment over not being involved in the high-stakes Shep piece. He paraded Joseph Siclari, the 112-pound flyweight

Golden Gloves champ, before the rest of the staffers, and regaled them with predictions of how timely his Williamsburg-versus-Williamsburg piece would be, what with all the Ford and Rockefeller money now pouring into the Colonial restoration down there. Fine then canvassed everybody on whether or not they thought there'd be a good "Groaning Board" column in this vegetarian hotel somebody was opening up in Atlantic City. Maybe he should take Case down there?

Allen was too depressed to react to the suggestion. By Wednesday morning three days had passed since Arinopoulos was supposed to stop paying for the care of the animals out in Queens. Nothing could cheer Allen up, not even Mr. Merrill's new pencil drawing of Canberra (cavorting among some Aborigines) or his invitation to lunch with some of the old illustrators in the Beaux Arts Building.

There was no talk on the floor of Paul Montgomery, though now that his piece on Ty Cobb had been killed, Fine was pitching a baseball profile of his own: something on Eddie Bennett, the Yankees' little mascot, whose humped back got touched for good luck by every player heading to the batter's box. Sidney Bruck, whose fumble of the fiction contest had not been forgotten amidst *Bandbox*'s more pressing troubles, made no direct objection, though he thought this exactly the kind of tasteless piece that would put the magazine into an eccentric dotage. Behind his now-always-closed door, Sidney was still trying to get Ring Lardner to write about Waite Hoyt, a ballplayer so civilized he could also paint pictures and compose fiction.

Individual anxieties were reaching a zenith. Daisy, happy to have helped Cuddles and Max, tried not to imagine the consequences to herself, but she did fret over how the information she'd supplied, traced back to its source, might kill the messenger. And the messenger was, she'd decided, not such a bad fellow. (She'd seen him twice more.)

Nan, whose pencil holder now contained cuttings of palm that she'd gotten at church this past Sunday, continued, for all her success with Rosemary, to worry about having tricked Waldo Lindstrom, whose only payoff so far had been Nan's sending his son one of the autographed Eddie Bennett baseballs that David Fine had in his office. Tense over this and Stuart, she flipped through the newspaper as she drank her coffee, dodging the avalanche of advertised remedies against dandruff, constipation, cough, rupture, cramps, weak blood, sore gums, coated tongue, and gas. Burn and Harris had tried to keep these unappetizing products out of *Bandbox*—who wanted the wheezing and the ruptured among one's readers?—but if the magazine survived the current crisis in some badly wounded state, Nan supposed they'd have to start running notices for this stuff in the back of the book. Editors like Sidney would have to get used to a little less class and a little more mass.

Nan had been seeing such ads all her life, but the current run of them was different from the depressing displays that used to fill the papers during her childhood before the war. Back then each remedy promised the purchaser only enough relief that he could rejoin, for one more day, the losing battle of life. Today the touted elixirs seemed intent not only on alleviating the targeted malady but—more important—on masking the affliction from everyone who might discover the sufferer's breath to be as imperfect as his knowledge of current events or the turkey trot.

Here she was in a world of appearances, trying to win the heart of a fellow prettier than she was. The thought compounded her nervousness with despair—a mortal sin, she reminded herself. She decided, for the sake of calm, to attend the noon Lenten service at the Palace. Heading out to it, she joked with Cuddles about the theatre's ecclesiastical transformation whenever the calendar took a religious turn.

"By the way," she asked, "what have you given up for Lent?"

"Giving up," he answered, after a couple of seconds' thought.

———

That same day, over lunch at Malocchio, Spilkes had to talk Harris out of an idea the boss had to dress up some bums who'd recently been rousted from "Mr. Zero's Tub" on St. Mark's Place. (The city's health commissioner had developed some momentary zeal about flophouse conditions.)

"Have Lord put 'em in tuxedos and we'll run their pictures next to some guys from the Yale Club," Harris had proposed. "Challenge the reader to pick out the real swells from the down-and-outs. We'll print the answers upside down, in small type, at the bottom of the page."

Spilkes dissuaded him with an argument that the magazine's more "sensitive" readers might find a certain cruelty in all this. Harris asked him just who could be called sensitive in this day and age, and while Spilkes had no real answer for that, his use of the word had served to remind Harris that *he,* in fact, beneath the bombast and the current blood sport with Jimmy, still retained an earlier era's spirit of fair play. Soon Harris was thinking: Why humiliate those poor Sterno-drinking souls? Even if there was a free suit in it for them.

What Spilkes really needed the boss to change his mind about was Max's article-in-progress. The m.e. had developed a considerable fear over one aspect of the situation. "If the police department sees us making ourselves out to be heroes," he argued, "Boylan may be all over you. Only five days ago he took the head off that reporter who asked him how come there'd been no progress finding Shep."

"Norman, I'd like to point out that we *did* find him. Even if Houlihan was heading up the 'we.' " With things still so uncertain, Harris had decided there was no reason yet to forgive Cuddles, though he'd had to take back his pink slip. "So what would you suggest?"

"Let the cops go out there and capture Rothstein's guys. Make that the climax of Max's story."

Harris poured himself more olive oil and asked if Spilkes had ever heard of such a thing as a calendar. "We've accelerated the print run. I begged Oldcastle to change the schedule for every magazine in the company so that we could have an earlier press time this month."

Calendars being more or less his specialty, Spilkes took one out from his wallet. "The pages go to the printer on the thirteenth. If you act today, there's still time. Tell Boylan the situation. His men will have three days to get out there, three days to get back—and three days in between to make arrests."

"The thirteenth is a Friday," said Harris, looking at the tiny calendar. His mind went back to Leopold and Loeb. "How the hell does that happen twice in four months?"

Spilkes ignored the objection. "You can still be on the stands by the twentieth. The issue'll leave the printing plant on the nineteenth."

"Keep your voice down," said Harris, hearing mention of this other unpleasant date—the one for Gianni's sentencing. The restaurateur had given the editors no more than a curt nod this afternoon, before retreating into his kitchen.

Spilkes waved away this problem, too. "The nineteenth is also one day before the GMEs. But so what? You need to concentrate on what's important here."

Harris was so concerned about the magazine's collapse that he *had* in fact forgotten all about the GMEs. Since that day on the sixteenth floor, Oldcastle had been more silent than Coolidge, offering only his knife blade of a smile whenever the editor saw him in the elevator.

"All right," said Harris, willing to consider Spilkes's approach. "But suppose California lets Boylan's cops make the collar, and suppose it even extradites Rothstein's thugs. What's to say Boylan'll keep it out of the papers until we can get onto the stands?"

"Because that's the arrangement you'll offer him: he gets credit, but from us. He'll take the deal."

"Now tell me how you keep Rothstein from killing Max, once his guys are in a New York jail."

Spilkes sighed. "Max seems willing to take the risk. You know, sales for *Ticker Rape* weren't up to his usual level. His publishers have concluded that no one can associate the stock market with pain. He's ready for the new burst of publicity this will give him. He'll hide in plain sight."

"If he's not hidden in some landfill first." Harris took another sip. He'd also been wondering what might happen to the kid—and, for that matter, to all the rest of them, too.

He consoled himself with the thought that these gangsters might settle for an atrocity against Mukluk. And he told Spilkes okay.

Up on eighteen, Paul Montgomery was preparing the short counter-article wanted on newsstands at exactly the moment *Bandbox*'s Shep story hit. What Paulie had been asked to compose—a straight-forward exposé, deduced from the chain of the Wood Chipper's evidence—was not at all suited to his talents. In place of his usual lyric enthusiasm there would be numbered points, as well as photographs of what Chip had taken from Max's desk (and then put back, before Max could find it missing). Jimmy still hoped *Cutaway* might somehow get a picture of the Shepard kid on the *Bandbox* premises, maybe lounging against the water fountain, but he could do without that if need be. More important was knowing Joe's speeded-up production schedule, which he did, now that the Wood Chipper had seen it on Hazel's desk. It was the last thing, Jimmy promised, that Chip would ever be required to copy, swipe, or even overhear.

Down on fourteen everyone was too busy to notice how little Chip was around. Sick of waiting for his reward, he'd gone on an extended shopping spree, running up bills for French ties from

Sulka's, a half-dozen silk shirts, and a fur-collared overcoat like the mayor's.

When Hannelore saw him in this last garment, she knew it hadn't come from the *Bandbox* Fashion Department. She gave Mr. Brzezinski a long look that mixed skepticism with—rather to her own surprise—lust.

John spent Wednesday afternoon in his room at the Commodore, ordering another hamburger from the kitchen and almost beginning to miss the walks and horseback rides he'd had on the ranch. Outside his window, the Chanin Building, growing higher every day, resembled a craggy mountain ridge he would never be allowed to wander past. He told himself he'd just have to be patient and consider the plus side: Miss Snow, who was really pretty, kept treating him like a fellow who'd just come back from the war, bringing over more magazines and crossword puzzles than he could handle. He'd also been promised Sunday dinner at Mr. and Mrs. Stanwick's in Brooklyn, and a late-night movie in Times Square after that. And he'd finally gotten to make that telephone call to his parents, who were overjoyed to hear from him but unable to understand why they had to keep news of his discovery a secret. "Is this quite on the level, young man?" his father had asked, making John wonder, for a moment or two, whether he might not be in worse trouble now than before.

52

"Bellissimo!" cried Mrs. Pandolfo from the top of the stoop. At this early hour on Cornelia Street, her husband was carrying a just-purchased lamb, its feet bound and ready for Easter slaughter, toward the patch of yard at the back of the building.

Walking past, Allen Case kept his eyes on the sidewalk and tried to ignore this grim reminder of Sunday's approach. But he did make a mental note to pick up some carrots, a holiday treat, for Sugar.

Arriving at the office before 8:30, Allen looked around for the next piece of Max Stanwick's closely guarded draft, which had been reaching the Copy Department two or three paragraphs at a time. As the text grew and rearranged itself according to Max's latest inspiration, the layout and photographs kept changing with it. And this morning there was something different.

That had to be a mountain lion. And in the next photo on the pile: wasn't that the wingspan of a condor?

"NO," said Gardiner Arinopoulos, bustling in. "Those are already OUT." He took the prints from Allen's hand. "We MAY use that little QUAIL instead. See it looking so HELPLESS on that sandy PATH? An analogue to our CAPTIVE SUBJECT."

Allen thought about driving a no. 2 pencil into the wrinkled patch of skin between the photographer's eyebrows.

"So WHAT do you THINK?" Arinopoulos asked Allen, drawing his attention back to the prints just snatched from his hand.

"I th-think they're all w-wonderful."

"THANK you."

Allen had meant the animals, not Arinopoulos's artistry. He let his gaze linger on the eight-by-ten image of a wolf pondering its apparent freedom out there in California; just across the East River, he knew, the photographer's own no-longer-wanted menagerie must be in the early throes of starvation.

Arinopoulos chuckled as he put the pictures back into his portfolio. "They're as PAMPERED as FOLLIES girls, these ones."

"Who t-takes care of them?" asked Allen.

"Some CRAZY old dago Jew," explained the photographer. "Mr. Isidore Mazzaferro. He used to KILL people for Rothstein when he wasn't running diplomatic missions between the Ginny and Hebrew bubbles of crime's MELTING pot. NOW he PURRS over every HAIR on these CREATURES." Arinopoulos tapped the portfolio. "Rothstein's PENSIONED him off to this little NATURE preserve. Along with the cattle, he takes care of these NOT-quite-indigenous PETS."

This was all news to Allen; Max hadn't written a word about the ranch's animals, at least not in the bits of copy he'd seen so far.

"Not that Mr. M's KILLER instincts have disappeared ENTIRELY. You should have seen his RAGE when this cowboy named DARYL dug one of his HEELS a little too hard into his horse."

Allen spoke carefully. "I imagine M-Mr. Mazzaferro would h-hurt anyone doing something b-b-bad to the creatures in his pr-preserve."

"WORSE harm than came to Diamond Joe Esposito," Arinopoulos assured him, with a loud laugh.

"I imagine," said Allen, "that he'd want to h-hurt anyone doing h-h-harm to animals anywhere. Even in Qu-Queens?"

Arinopoulos narrowed his eyes. "What are you TRYING to say?"

"Take me out to that warehouse," said Allen, with a force that broke through every consonant.

The photographer tried laughing off this sudden request. "I have a COVER shoot THIS afternoon. I need to get ready."

For a moment Allen said nothing, just continued looking straight at Arinopoulos, who realized with a chill that this gaunt, bespectacled boy might be crazier than Mr. Mazzaferro.

"You stopped p-paying the bills five days ago," said Allen.

"YES," said Arinopoulos. "I DID. The creatures had SERVED their purpose. Let somebody BUY them and EAT them. WHAT business is it of YOURS?"

He was almost out the door when Allen blocked his path into the corridor.

"Mr. M-Mazzaferro w-will be seeing this article. He'll be m-m-mad enough already. Th-then wait until he finds out about that w-warehouse in Queens."

"And YOU'RE going to tell him that?" With contempt, the photographer scanned the boy from head to toe. He was as skinny as . . . a fuse. Arinopoulos swallowed hard.

"Take me there," said Allen. "N-now."

They were over the Queensboro Bridge within fifteen minutes, the photographer doing his best not to appear afraid. When they arrived at the warehouse property in Long Island City, Allen made a fast survey of its torn wire fencing; the weeds strewn with car parts; the broken little factory windows. From somewhere inside the low brick building a radio played "Make My Cot Where the Cot-Cot-Cotton Grows."

"Don't move," Arinopoulos instructed the taxi driver. "We'll PAY you to WAIT."

No growling dogs were in evidence this time, perhaps because it was daylight. Allen and Arinopoulos had a clear path to the overhead garage door, which went up seconds after the photographer knocked on it.

"I thought you were through with all that," said Mr. Boldoni, the manager, with a vague hand gesture toward some distant but, even from here, pungent precinct of the interior. Allen leaned forward, trying to find the little zoo inside this vast and filthy expanse—half auto body shop, half indoor junkyard.

"C'mon," said Mr. Boldoni, in a weary tone. He led them inside at last, wishing that Arinopoulos would make up his mind about these smelly beasts. "You're lucky any of them are still around."

The sight of a half-dozen scrawny caged animals, without even straw beneath them, just sodden newspaper, seared Allen's vision. A wild-eyed ram weakly bleated, while the lemur who'd done the *House & Garden* shoot shivered violently, trying to sleep through its slow starvation. Through one of the broken windows Allen could see what appeared to be an open pit for burning trash. God only knew how many creatures had been flung into it.

A blue vein bulged through the thin skin of his neck, as he turned toward Gardiner Arinopoulos: "Mr. M-Mazzaferro would be very m-m-mad."

"Oh, for Christ's SAKE!" cried Arinopoulos, who reached into his wallet for a wad of small bills that he handed over to Boldoni. "Here's their MEAL ticket for ANOTHER month."

Imagining the long days and nights that Canberra had spent here, Allen told the photographer: "I'm afraid that's n-not going to be good enough. For m-me *or* Mr. Mazzaferro."

53

At lunchtime that day, Nan stood in Harris's office going over a piece of Max's story. She had, at least so far, no obscenity problems to raise, only a concern that Max's cowboy dialect sounded less than wholly accurate. She was reading Harris some examples of it when Mrs. Zimmerman rang Hazel's desk to announce that Rosemary LaRoche had just arrived on fourteen with her own hairdresser, chauffeur, and secretary. Hazel took only enough time to repeat the information before dashing off to Reception for a look.

Nan had a suggestion for the boss. "Tell Miss LaRoche to send all her flunkies back to the Plaza. Order her to wait for the photographer, right there by the elevator, and don't even offer her a glass of water."

Harris looked incredulous.

"Try it," urged Nan. "Honest."

Harris buzzed Mrs. Zimmerman and dared to convey the instructions. After a long moment, during which the receptionist covered the telephone's mouthpiece, Mrs. Z replied: "It's all right. She'll wait."

Harris still had no idea what they had on this Hollywood dame. Newman might be handsome, but surely something more than a good-looking juicer was keeping LaRoche in that chair out there.

The film star waited a full hour and a half for the photographer to show up. Harris never went out to greet her, just checked with Mrs. Zimmerman every so often to see that she was really still there. Finally, at 3:15, Gardiner Arinopoulos, looking quite white, arrived back at the office. "I'm sorry," he said, with none of his usual volume or any of the deference Rosemary LaRoche's presence ought to generate. "I'll go set up in Studio Two."

"Are you all right?" asked Mrs. Z.

"Yes, it's all settled," said the photographer, with cryptic haste.

It was four o'clock by the time Harris walked into the studio to watch the setup. With all the trouble she'd caused these last two months, he had forgotten how blindingly beautiful—and *hard*—Rosemary was. Like a silver hood ornament. Even under the hot overhead lamps she seemed lit more from within than without.

"Hello, Mr. Harris," she said.

What, he wondered, had happened to " 'Phat"?

"It's a pleasure to see you again," he replied.

"Yeah," she said, quietly. "A barrel of laughs." Something had gone out of her, Harris could tell; the remark was a papier-mâché imitation of her old nasty confidence. But even now, nothing could melt the exterior of this broad. Arinopoulos kept ordering his assistant to move the lights even closer, but Rosemary never blinked or broke a sweat.

Only Bonus Corer, whose cover debut had been pushed back a month, was disappointed by her appearance here today. Everyone else on staff, even Sidney Bruck, found an excuse to enter Studio Two for at least a glimpse of the film star—who, to everybody's surprise, made no objection to the gawking.

Andrew Burn was the only ogler to arrive with actual business on his mind. As the setup continued, he whispered to Harris a reminder of the outrageous seven-cents-per-copy skim the actress had demanded.

Harris tapped him on the arm and whispered, "Watch this." Over the groaning movement of stanchions and dollies, he called out to Rosemary: "Wonderful of you to do this for nothing more than the chance to promote *Chained* with our readers."

Rosemary kept gazing straight into the lights. She didn't say a word.

Harris, like a fascinated matador, tried to see if he could provoke her.

"It's a good arrangement, isn't it?" he asked.

"Yeah," she said, not shifting her eyes. "It's swell."

Burn was impressed.

"Gardiner," called Harris, "are you almost ready?"

"Yes, I believe I am," said the distracted photographer, without a syllable of emphasis.

"Good," said Harris, "because I've got something to add to your composition. Clear the studio! Everybody not needed here get out!"

Arinopoulos looked perplexed, but not the least bit violated artistically.

Harris picked up the telephone. "Hazel, get the kid."

It took just five minutes to bring John Shepard from the Commodore up to the Graybar's fourteenth floor, during which interval Rosemary managed to hold both her tongue and her pose. But then she saw Harold Teen come in, wearing Hart, Schaffner & Marx, a six-dollar pair of blue-striped suspenders, and a cowlick.

"Okay, Shep," said Harris, "stand next to her."

"What *is* this?" Rosemary at last allowed herself to say.

"I want you to kiss his cheek," said Harris, "while with your left hand you muss his hair, and with your right you pull on one of his braces. Get ready to shoot on the count of three, Gardiner."

John Shepard, thinking of how his mother would scold his pa whenever his suspenders even *showed* in front of a woman, swallowed nervously. Rosemary had the expression of a beautiful, lethal beast whose tranquilizing dart was beginning to wear off. A couple of spectators actually took a step backwards.

But Harris ignored her look of imminent refusal. "Shep," he ordered, "remember to let your eyes show your excitement." Then, to guarantee the necessary result, he used the line Nan O'Grady had delphically suggested for this moment: "Remember, you're being kissed by a movie star, not a grandmother, right?"

Rosemary narrowed her eyes.

"DILATE!" cried Gardiner Arinopoulos, whose professional reflexes were at last responding.

With her right heel Rosemary gave the stool she was sitting on a little kick. "This isn't what—"

"One, two, *three!*" shouted Harris.

And then it was the turn of Rosemary's professional reflexes to respond. As Arinopoulos's assistant lit the flash powder, she gave it everything she had—a full, one-hundred-percent blaze of authentic beauty and false passion—the same as she would for any nellie director who stood between her and a paycheck. She leaned in and planted her blood-red lips on Shep's cheek. The boy's eyes popped with more candlepower than the blazing magnesium.

"Again!" cried Harris, six times, until the air was full of fumes and they had the shot. By the time Arinopoulos came out from under the camera's hood, Rosemary had covered Shep's cheek with more lipstick than she'd smeared over Stuart two weeks ago, prior to Nan's rescue.

The smudges gave Shep a look of dissolute innocence, and Richard Lord decided to keep them, unairbrushed, on the cover that was soon laid out to proclaim:

THAT'S OUR BOY!

FILM STAR WELCOMES B'BOX SUBSCRIBER
HOME FROM KIDNAP ORDEAL

A Special Investigation by Max Stanwick

54

President Coolidge threw out the first baseball of the season four days later, but a week after that, on Tuesday, April 17, it seemed as if the long, implacable winter had returned yet again: snow flurries were falling in New York.

Inside the Fifth Avenue Child's, Stuart Newman ate breakfast and read the paper with his overcoat on. Halfway through his bacon and eggs, he found an item about Rosemary LaRoche. She'd finally returned to the *Wyoming Wilderness* set, and agreed to pay a fine. Her recent absence was being attributed to romance, the most crowd-pleasing rumor of which involved a possible reconciliation with Howard Kenyon, who was thought to be in the East, "pining for her in an off-season Provincetown hotel."

Newman was still smiling over this last bit of intelligence when he heard his name being called.

"I was on my way to the library," said Becky, who came in flushed with the cold. "I saw you through the window." She had promised to look up something on the Scottish Chaucerians for her boyfriend, but she accepted Newman's invitation to sit down.

He looked awfully well, thought Becky, if not quite so glamorous. The circles were gone from under his eyes, and he'd put on some weight. The tabletop might even be hiding the beginnings of a paunch. In any case, he appeared more relaxed than she could remember seeing him; the cup of coffee beside his scrambled eggs seemed for once like coffee instead of an antidote.

"Things pretty frantic over there?" he asked.

Becky laughed. "I take it you mean the magazine, not the library. Yes, they are," she said, though she was sure Nan had kept him informed of everything going on. "I'm not certain what's holding up Max's story," she added, her expression turning grave as soon as she mentioned it. Harris and Spilkes had said nothing about the delay and, unwilling to let their western caper become the basis for renewed daily proximity, Becky hadn't allowed herself to ask Cuddles about the latest developments—though in fact she'd been hoping he'd invite her to Manking, where over two plates of what he liked to call the "feline duck" they could ponder the great Shep gamble he'd set in motion.

"Well, at least you got your cover shot," said Newman, whose voice startled Becky out of her revery. "I still don't know how you managed that," he continued, smiling through his fib while silently reflecting on all Nan had done for him. He was so grateful, so proud of her; it seemed a shame not to be able to reveal the story of her sleuthing. He settled for telling Becky how the two of them had gone last night to see the *Greenwich Village Follies* at the Winter Garden. "Blossom Seeley sang, and Dr. Rockwell was the comic," Newman explained. "I thought he'd be a little broad for Nan's taste, but I've never seen her laugh so hard."

He looked like a hearth-happy man, daydreaming of home. Becky hadn't guessed that things had moved quite so fast and favorably for him and Nan, but her deduction of it now made her feel less happy for Newman than anxious about herself. The space around her own half-established hearth had seemed a little too warm last night— stuffy, in fact. Daniel had put Palestrina on the Victrola, and the two of them had listened to the set of four records straight through with- out speaking a word to each other—not, in her case, from music ap- preciation; just from having nothing to say. Hearing about Newman's night at the *Follies,* she knew she would rather have been there, though it wasn't the sort of thing to which one easily invited Daniel.

"I've got to run," said Becky, as soon as she found herself thinking of just who *would* have been the ideal date for such an occasion.

Daisy sat by herself in the fact-checkers' bull pen, reading the same item Newman had about Rosemary LaRoche. Oh, to abscond from the stage-set of her own life, if only for a week! But there was no escaping the terrible pressures she was under. On Thursday the judge would have to sentence Gianni Roma, and right after that—having failed to get the prosecutors to drop the case—he'd have to begin getting ready for the trial of the Juniper Park foreman. Poor Francis was now like a crooked referee waiting for the opening bell. The messengers had made it plain that the judge's securing of bail for the defendant was regarded, by The Brain himself, as a less than sufficient effort.

The messengers had also been talking about events "out in California," which she assumed had something to do with Cuddles' interest in that ranch hideout and the rediscovery of that attractive boy from Indiana. But she didn't know much more about the situation. Max's current piece, said to be about all this, would not, she'd been informed, be passing through the Research Department—on account of its "special sensitivity." Daisy had seen no sign of it, or for that matter of Max himself. Well, she already had too much to do for the May issue as it was, what with Chip always off shopping, instead of being at his desk.

She looked around for him now but saw only Allen Case, who was passing through the corridor and, to her amazement, *whistling,* without the least bit of faltering between notes. He was also eating a doughnut, food she'd once heard him condemn, at Mrs. Washington's coffee wagon, for being "f-fried in others' f-fat." He appeared to be on some sort of holiday from himself.

Allen was, in fact, still so happy that he'd quite forgotten any culinary crimes to which the doughnut might be accessory. Last Monday, Arinopoulos had furnished proof that the surviving warehouse animals were on their way, via trucks equipped with the latest in ventilation, to the San Rafael Valley, where they would be cared for inside Isidore Mazzaferro's nature preserve. The photographer had arranged, in a series of telegrams, for the superannuated mobster to take charge of this little group of creatures he claimed to have discovered living in APPALLING conditions when he was out in Long Island City to shoot the mechanical marvel of the Silvercup sign.

At the other end of the floor, Joe Harris sat in a state of nervousness beyond any Daisy was enduring. Chewing his nails, he still waited for news of what had happened out in California. So far there had been only an abundance of rumor: the cops had made arrests and were on their way back to New York with Rothstein's henchmen; no, the local authorities had not allowed extradition; actually, the police had gotten all the way across the country and then failed to arrest anyone; in fact, despite Boylan's promises, they'd never gone out there in the first place. Every hour it was something else. Had he been double-crossed? All Harris knew for certain was that the May issue, already printed, included a picture of Boylan and a vaguely phrased but still declarative paragraph about how his boys in blue had made masterful use of Max Stanwick's detection and brought Shep's tormentors back to the bar of New York justice.

If the cops *had* gone to California, and *had* made arrests, and *had* gotten extradition, there were now three days left for them to get back here. Actually, only two, until Harris would no longer be able to stop the issue from leaving the Connecticut printing plant for newsstands all over town.

He was looking up at his picture of Yvette, whose countenance offered no odds on the outcome, when the telephone rang.

"Congratulations," said Betty.

"Thank God!" responded Harris. "I don't think I'd have survived waiting till Friday."

"What do you mean? You've got to."

Confused, Harris said nothing.

"You and Jimmy are both nominated for Distinguished Achievement in a new men's category. The awards breakfast is Friday. Read the memo. It's got to be somewhere on Hazel's desk."

"Oh," sighed Harris. "The GMEs."

"That's all you can say?" Betty, who remembered his up-all-night cravings for these awards, hardly knew what to do. "You need to call Jimmy and offer congratulations" was all she could think to suggest.

Harris barely heard her. No GME was going to provide relief. Old-castle wouldn't be impressed with a whole row of the silver-pencil trophies now that the competition, and maybe the cops, were closing in on Joe Harris.

"Why can't Jimmy call *me*?" he finally replied.

Accustomed to pretending that she'd heard correctly, Betty decided to make this one of the rare moments when she would pretend to have *mis*heard. "That's better," she said, kissing Joe through the telephone before hanging up.

Harris's line rang again as soon as she was off.

"It's nice that the GME committee still considered the portion of last year *before* we came along," said Jimmy Gordon. "I guess that's how you squeaked by."

"Nice of me to have invented a whole new category of magazine for you to fit into."

"Actually," said Jimmy, "we're doing some uniquely pioneering work—in crimefighting. But in my acceptance speech Friday morning I *will* give you credit for providing the crime. I've asked them to put us at adjoining tables. See you at the Biltmore."

REALTY PERIODICALS CORP.

BUREAU OF NATIONAL LITERATURE, INC.

EVANGELISTIC COMMITTEE OF NEW YORK CITY

Just before lunchtime, waiting for the elevator, Becky mused upon the obscurity of some of the smaller tenants listed on the Graybar's wall directory. What did they have in common with one another? Nothing, it seemed, except Becky's own feeling that she wouldn't want to punch a time card at any of them. She was happy, she now knew, working right where she was. She had done the best she could making this sheaf of notes for Daniel, and she would get them all typed up before the end of the day, but only if she drank two extra cups of coffee to stay awake.

The Scottish Chaucerians, really! And all this respect for obscure history—which had been what, after all? Just the ephemerality of its own day, disdained by those like her own dear Daniel until it could congeal into the past. But somebody had to put things into the world in the first place. And wasn't that what she and her colleagues were doing each day on fourteen? Whipping up the silly faddish here-and-now of life itself so that someone could pronounce it, eons later, the spirit of its vanished age? Why shouldn't she be at the foamy, evanescent moment of creation itself? Why not keep dancing in and out of the ring binder that could hold *Nelson's Loose-Leaf Encyclopaedia* for only a month or two at a time, instead of gluing herself, for eternity, into the *Britannica*?

Stepping into her office, Becky noticed a bottle of prewar wine and a half-dozen roses that had been set down on her desk beside the not-yet-filed-away galleys of her piece on Rosemary LaRoche. "NICE JOB, KID," said the card from Harris. "GOD WILLING, WE'LL ACTUALLY ISSUE THIS ISSUE." She smiled, and put the Scottish Chaucerians on a chair by the wall. The Rosemary profile might already be closed, but right now she felt an impulse to reread the proofs of her own words, to revel in having gotten things stylish, if not (thanks to Rosemary's mythmaking) completely right. The actress's mendacity was her own affair; but she, the Rebecca Walter of the byline, had succeeded in putting things across. Could she do it again, maybe even better, next time? She kicked off her shoes and kept reading until Cuddles materialized in the doorway.

"*I* didn't get a cactus. Not even a bottle of seltzer."

Becky could no longer keep herself from asking: "Do you know any more than I do? About what's going on?"

"Volumes."

"Oh."

"We're all catching frostbite from Spilkes's cold feet." The m.e., having grown direly nervous about the restraint he'd imposed on Harris, had this morning confided to Cuddles what the delay was all about.

"So what do they *think's* been happening out there?" Becky asked.

"It's all rumors," said Cuddles. "One is that Mr. Jones tried to *use* his tommy gun, not just pose with it." He paused to drag on his cigarette. "As for the facts: we know Max has gotten a little skittish. He's home in Brooklyn, peeking out through the shutters. But Shep's life is still one big cherry phosphate from room service. Want to come out with me?"

"To Manking? I shouldn't. I had a big breakfast before I—"

She decided against mentioning the Scottish Chaucerians, but not because she feared Cuddles would make a crack about Daniel. She feared *she* might.

"Not to Manking," he said. "On an errand. Slightly adventurous."

"Okay," she said, right away and not even against her better judgment. If she had to sit here typing Daniel's notes—and imagining what it would soon be like to type his dissertation—she'd wind up rummaging in her desk for aspirin to go along with the extra coffee.

Only when they were in a taxicab did she ask Cuddles where they were going.

"You'll see," he said, as they started up Lexington. The outing felt like a strange reversal of the afternoon she'd hauled him unawares to the Macfadden Building. Since when was he supposed to be rescuing *her*?

"Give me a hint," she asked.

"I'm packing," said Cuddles.

"For where?"

"No, *packing*. Heat," he explained, extracting a .22 pistol halfway from his suit coat. He noted Becky's shocked expression. "Relax. I don't think you can make a citizen's arrest for a mere violation of the Sullivan Act."

"My God, are they after *you,* too?" she asked. "Along with Max?"

"Nah," said Cuddles. "As soon as we get the wagon through the pass, I'll give him back his gun."

"Are you going to tell me what this is about?"

"Want to turn back?"

"No."

"Good. It's really just a simple delivery."

Becky knew, once the two of them reached its headquarters inside a Fifty-seventh Street walkup, that the Rothmere Investment Co. was not what it claimed to be. A lone secretary occupied the outer office, and a monastic quiet suggested that no one else was on the floor. Becky recalled from Max's profile that Arnold Rothstein rarely rose before mid-afternoon, and she was now pretty sure she also remembered a description of this secretary—MISS FREDA ROSENBERG, the nameplate said—from the article.

"Good afternoon," said Cuddles. "May I leave this for Mr. Rothmere?"

Miss Rosenberg, organizing some long ledger sheets marked BOX-ING and BASEBALL, responded with a studied neutrality that convinced Becky and Cuddles of her indispensability to whatever went on here: "Mr. Rothmere does not accept deliveries at the office."

"This one," said Cuddles, proferring a thin envelope, "should definitely be opened before Christmas."

Miss Rosenberg allowed herself the slightest of frowns.

"It's a greeting from Mr. Jones," said Cuddles, who pulled open his overcoat to show the bulge in his suit jacket.

Miss Rosenberg rolled her eyes, in the manner of Nan O'Grady. She had seen this sort of male protuberance many, many times and was not much impressed. But she finally sighed and accepted the envelope from whoever this amateur was.

On the cab ride back, even though she was sitting down, Becky could feel her ankles shaking. She and Cuddles were nearly at the Graybar before she at last managed to press him for enlightenment: " 'A greeting from Mr. Jones'? And you're only delivering it *now*?"

"Actually, it's a greeting Jones doesn't know he's making. Something transmitted by Shep. Remember our little pitcher's big ears at the party?"

"Yes," said Becky, excitement making her sound angrier than she was. "They're what caused all the trouble in the first place."

"Well, they were up and alert back at the ranch. What's in that envelope might get us all home before dark."

Waiting for the elevator on still-unsteady legs, Becky looked for the second time that day at the wall directory listing the Bureau of National Literature and the Evangelistic Committee of New York City. She could almost swear she saw the Scottish Chaucerians on the board with them.

Once inside the elevator, ignoring the white-gloved operator, she whispered to Cuddles: "Kiss me. Just once, but kiss me."

55

Francis X. Gilfoyle was never free, even on his own bench, from the watchful eye of a "messenger." But on Thursday afternoon, with nothing much at stake for Arnold Rothstein in *State of New York v. John Roma,* the judge could follow his own lenient instincts.

Gianni, called upon to make a statement before sentence was pronounced, looked around and found the audience pitifully small. Waldo was of course nowhere to be seen, but not even Daisy Di-

Donna? No, a couple of columnists had made mention of "the countess and the judge," and she'd thought it better not to appear in her lover's courtroom on a day he had to send someone from her circle up the river. And aside from that, what with *Bandbox*'s more pressing woes and the current newsprint-devouring story of the *Bremen* aviators—found stranded but alive up on Greenely Island—Gianni's little drugs-and-degeneracy episode had lost any head of steam in the press. The only viewer the defendant could recognize was David Fine, who'd shown up as the eyes and ears of Joe Harris, preoccupied by the approaching climax of the Shep venture.

A look from Mr. Goodheart, his top-notch lawyer, reminded Gianni that he needed to be contrite. Just *admit* it, he'd been advised; put in a dig at Prohibition if you want—it'll go down well with a Tammany wet like Gilfoyle—but let that be the extent of any contempt for the court.

"Your Honor," said Gianni, after clearing his throat, "itsa hard to tella right from wrong these days."

Goodheart gave him a second stern look.

"But I didda wrong." Gianni paused to look around at Fine. "I coulda used a little help and guidance from my friends, but"—he turned back to the bench—"even so, I didda wrong."

Judge Gilfoyle looked as sympathetic as his sweet, ancient mother, and pronounced a sentence of four months in the state prison at Fishkill—as little punishment as the law would allow.

Both Gianni and the judge were then led from the courtroom— the latter not by his bailiff but the ever-watchful messenger.

Fine sat for a moment by himself, thinking about his good old days as Gianni's sommelier, even before Joe Harris came on the scene. He had an awful feeling that it was all coming to an end. Joe had looked plain terrible this morning, trying to decide whether to hold the issue back or let it go—a quandary he had only hours left to think his way out of. Boylan would not return the editor's calls, whether just to torture him or because there'd been a double-cross, no one could be sure. And tomorrow, whatever happened, Joe would have to sit through the GME breakfast with a smile.

Fine decided to go up to Yankee Stadium and rub Eddie Bennett's hump.

Norman Spilkes sat alone in his office, fingering the tie tack he'd been given the other week at AT&T: a tiny Statue of Liberty and a bejeweled little Eiffel Tower attached by five links of the thinnest possible chain. Between his index finger and thumb, the managing editor worried the object as if it were the string of beads Harris's barber always carried.

He meditated upon the marvel that had once been the focus of his own employment: the telephone. Before long, everyone, not just General Pershing, would be able to call from Paris—or dial directly from Norwalk to New London—all on his own. Harris's helpless bellowing of "Hello, Central!" when Mrs. Zimmerman and Hazel were away from their desks had already begun sounding antique. During his days at AT&T, Spilkes had never seen the numbers drop; people only wanted more of a product being continually improved and purveyed by no one else. Whereas desire for his current wares, after a long juicy waxing, had begun to wane so fast you could hear the air escaping.

Why, he tried to remind himself, had he come here? Because he'd grown tired of administering too sure a thing? Because he'd been so dispirited, a few years ago, by the discovery of his own early middle age? Back then an improbable dinner-party encounter with Joe Harris had seemed a chance to throw his own gearshift into a fast, giddy reverse. He loved Joe's *Bandbox*—its pages were a flashing nickelodeon of all the images he'd desired for himself as a young man—and in many respects he loved Harris, too. The fun catering to his moods when that outsized creature was soaring! And the pleasure of being the calm traffic cop to all the colliding racehorse personalities on the fourteenth floor! The clattering racks of suits; the athletes; the steakhouses; the girls and the gadgets—what would he have done without them? Jazzed by his new job's tonic, but still happily tethered to his pretty wife and children, Spilkes had made it successfully into his middle years. Which only—right now—put him at another crossroads. The career change that had been a matter of rejuvenation was turning, suddenly, into a terrifying self-indulgence.

Ever since Harris told him about Jimmy Gordon's taunting phone call, Spilkes had felt seized by something like panic. What did Jimmy mean about *Bandbox* "providing the crime"? What did he know? That the rumor of arrests out in California was false? Had Boylan set a trap—his way of getting back at Harris? And had Spilkes's own cautionary calculation been the undoing of what might have been a great success?

Maybe he and Joe would both wind up in the clink with Gianni.

Instinct now made him reach for that embodiment of everything once steady and secure in his life: the phone.

"Mrs. Zimmerman," he heard himself saying, "please get me James Lauder at AT&T headquarters."

While he waited for the connection, he consulted his New Haven Rail Road timetable and took out an empty Brooks Brothers shopping bag from the bottom drawer. Could he get out of here, with his personal possessions, *this afternoon,* without anybody noticing?

Just before 5:00, Cuddles came in from a short walk to the Commodore to pay Shep's weekly bill. Across from the Chanin Building's construction site, he'd looked up at some Indians strolling the girders twenty floors above the street. Strange that they should be the group most at home atop the city's new vertical essence; stranger still that New York had been home to *him* from the moment he first ferried into Manhattan more than twenty years ago. He had rarely made a surefooted way across any beams—he'd more usually felt like he was hiding in the bucket that dangled from the crane—but even now, as Brigham Young had said to Grandpa Houlihan about somewhere far away, This was the Place.

And from what he'd learned just before his walk, it might be that for a while to come.

Back inside his office, Cuddles removed his raincoat and found Harris taking up position in the doorway. The boss was in a state. "Where's Norman?" he asked.

"I've no idea."

Harris shook his head. "The pictures on his desk are gone. Is Fine around?"

"Not back from the courtroom," said Cuddles. He realized that 'Phat was looking for friends, and that he himself still hadn't been redeemed to the point where he was eligible to serve.

"How about your girlfriend? Is she here?"

"Do me a favor," said Cuddles. "Tell her that's the role life has thrust upon her."

Harris, all need, stood there waiting. Cuddles refrained from giving him the look he deserved, and added only: "She left early."

Harris moved his eyes to the clock, whose second hand kept falling and ticking, falling and ticking.

"You know," said Cuddles. "You can find Jimmy and Paulie up on eighteen."

Stung by the remark, and the realization that on this crucial evening of his life it was coming down to him and Houlihan, Harris finally asked: "Have a drink?"

Cuddles hesitated, and tried to pretend his delay came from something other than pride, but Harris persisted: "There are two bottles of pre-Prohibition Stoli still standing—at the back of the closet, where my moose used to be."

Once the two of them got settled on opposite sides of the big marble desk, under the gaze of Yvette and Claudine, Harris could no longer hold it in: "I've got twenty minutes left to pick up the phone. I haven't heard from Boylan, and the trucks leave the plant at five-thirty." He looked at his EDITOR OF THE YEAR cigarette case, and the buckram-bound back issues, and the pictures of Mae West and Walker and all the rest of them inside their simple black frames. "I'm damned either way. What am I supposed to do? Hold it back and *skip* an issue?" He knew that would be like asking the rain cycle to skip a step; the sudden downward lurch of the sales graph would resemble the thunderbolt immediately hurled by Oldcastle. "Even Betty's taken a pass," said Harris. "She claims she'll love me either way."

"Sounds good to me," said Cuddles.

"Not to me," Harris responded. "I'll hate myself if I pick wrong. And hate myself worse if she still loves me after that." He took a frustrated pause. "Christ, we came *so close* with this. I don't know whether to kill Jimmy or kill Norman."

Cuddles thought a moment before asking, "You know that second bottle of czarist Stoli? Wrap it up for Jimmy. And put in a thank-you card—for forcing you to the top of your game."

Harris looked at him blankly.

"Has my judgment ever been wrong?" asked Cuddles.

It was an astonishing question. Cuddles' absence of initiative had for so long been so total that one would no more ponder the matter of his judgment than one might worry over the walking skills of a man who'd stopped breathing.

"Call the plant," said Cuddles. "Tell the trucks to roll."

Harris was sweating. His own judgment and initiative were top-notch, but what he'd always had in huger measure than anyone else was nerve. He now peered at Houlihan, the last man around the campfire. To bet everything on the look in *his* eye, which hadn't been clear since long before *Bandbox* began its slide, would take the last dollop of guts the editor-in-chief could find.

"Mrs. Zimmerman," he said, not even realizing he'd picked up the phone. "Get me the printing plant."

56

The following morning, at five minutes to six, Mukluk was barking so loud even Betty could hear him. Taking off her sleep mask, she sat up in bed and noticed that Joe was gone. She went to the window and peeked through the blinds to see whether the sun had even come up. Sixth Avenue looked barely awake. The Italian news vendor hadn't yet opened his stand in front of the Warwick, and Betty could see a lone, too-early customer trying to extract a magazine from a bundle dropped off by a delivery truck.

She realized it was Joe, who'd been up most of the night hoping for a call from Boylan. She sighed, and stepped away from the window. "Do you think you'd like it if we all went to live in the country?" she asked the highly indifferent Mukluk.

Out on the sidewalk, dressed in his best suit for the GME breakfast, Harris continued his struggle with the bale of magazines, until he felt a tap on the shoulder.

"I was going to leave the money!" he protested.

"Hasn't the all-night newsstand made it to Manhattan?" asked a familiar voice. "We've had 'em in Brooklyn for years."

Cuddles Houlihan handed his boss the latest issue of *Bandbox*. In another hour Rosemary LaRoche would be kissing Shep on a thousand magazine racks across New York City.

"Jesus," said Harris, startled more by the horrid fact of the magazine than by Cuddles. He asked if Betty had somehow dispatched him to the hotel to provide moral support.

"No," Cuddles explained. "I knew you'd be out here. I'm just glad you're not in your slippers. Come on, you've got an appointment downtown."

Downtown! It sounded to Harris like news of his arrest.

"Trust me," said Cuddles, who put the two of them into a taxi he directed to Centre Street.

Traveling along Broadway, Harris couldn't stop himself from looking into the magazine's new issue. He winced at the picture of Boylan next to the crucial, now-erroneous paragraph.

"Try the piece on *Nelson's Loose-Leaf Encyclopaedia*," Cuddles suggested. "It's really got something."

It was still not seven when they walked into Judge Gilfoyle's courtroom—so odd an hour they couldn't be sure whether night court or the regular daytime version was in session. Then Daisy DiDonna, glowing with maximum wattage, rose from one of the spectators' benches to greet Cuddles with a kiss on the lips.

"He feels like a new man!" she cried, struggling to keep down the decibels of this remark about the judge.

"I knew you two had something in common," replied Cuddles, as he sat Harris down beside the countess.

The whole scene had a disturbing, dreamlike quality for the editor-in-chief, who felt he might at any moment discover himself to be wearing pajamas or standing on a ledge. The three of them in this back row were, aside from the bailiff and two lawyers, the only ones in the courtroom.

"All rise!"

In walked Francis X. Gilfoyle, who seemed newly magisterial, a lofty, independent jurist on the order of Charles Evans Hughes, not some small-time robe rack co-owned by Tammany and the gangs.

Daisy could not stop effervescing. "Look at him!" she whispered to Cuddles. "Not even a speck of dandruff. Those Listerine scalp rinses really work, just like the advertisements say!"

The judge banged his gavel and Daisy came to order with a smile, as if he'd given her a love tap.

"Bring them in," Gilfoyle ordered the bailiff, with a great deal of volume and sincerity.

Captain Patrick Boylan himself led in three men for arraignment. Within two minutes the judge had read out kidnapping charges against the fellow who'd helped Eddie Diamond hustle Shep out of Oldcastle's apartment, and assault counts against the one who'd roughed him up in the New York garage. The third man, Mr. Ivan Jones, aka Jacobs, had participated only in the California phase of this crime, but had been arrested out there by Boylan's men on a series of outstanding New York charges.

Gilfoyle banged his gavel a second time, refusing to let the men's lawyer—with whom he was well acquainted—say anything on their behalf. He denied the defendants bail before they could even ask for it, and kept them standing for a crisp, eloquent denunciation of the evils wrought by organized criminality in the realms of loan-sharking, sports-fixing, and even "the construction of substandard housing for the colored and the poor." He made sure this last, pointed complaint had drilled the ears of Rothstein's foot soldiers before actually crying, "Take them away!"

Everything the judge had said reached Harris's ears, too—without, however, being absorbed by his understanding. He watched the prisoners as they were led off by the bailiff and Boylan, who locked eyes with him and glared—half in anger, half in triumph. No, he hadn't had any choice but to make the arrests, not if he didn't want Harris's publicity machine depicting his department as hopelessly off the ball; but Boylan could see, in the editor's still-drooping countenance, that he'd extracted at least a pound of flesh by the torturous waiting game. Before disappearing from the courtroom, the captain narrowed his eyes still further, sending a message that he would get Jehoshaphat Harris yet.

"It all fits together!" cried Daisy. "Just like Scanties!" It was unclear to Harris which part of this puzzle corresponded to the panties, or the girdle, or the brassiere of that detestably unseductive piece of modern apparel. But then Cuddles told him what he'd told Daisy and Becky late last night—that Tuesday's noontime delivery to Rothmere Investments had been a single sheet of paper Shep had heard about and then taken from Mr. Jones's desk out in the San Rafael Valley: a few columns of spectacularly incriminating facts and figures that Shep then kept hidden on his person at all times, including the moment of his rescue by Max. Amidst the glamour of the dining car and the Commodore, he'd forgotten, until Sunday night, about this piece of paper whose handful of details made most of Rothstein's better-known operations, from the Black Sox to Juniper, look like a summertime chautauqua.

Yesterday afternoon, just before his errand at the Commodore, Miss Freda Rosenberg had called to thank Cuddles for the document, in exchange for which, Mr. Rothstein agreed, Max Stanwick could live out his life in good health and Judge Gilfoyle consider his judicial independence restored.

That everything had bounced like a double-play ball from Tinker to Evers to Chance began to dawn on Harris even more brightly than the morning sun, now established in the sky above the courthouse.

"We'd better get to the Biltmore," said Cuddles, once they were out on the sidewalk. "You don't want the porridge getting cold."

Harris didn't hear him. Fully reanimated, he was striding toward Patrick Boylan, determined to reach the captain before he got into his squad car.

57

Holding aloft his silver-pencil trophy, Jimmy Gordon looked down from the dais and decided that the applause, sweet as it might be, couldn't compare with the sight of the empty *Bandbox* table down front. Its only occupant was an identifying centerpiece, a fishtailed stack of the magazine's brand-new mendacious issue. Jimmy had imagined what it would feel like watching Joe listen to his speech, but the absence of his vanquished rival—*too scared to show!*—felt even better.

He looked out across the whitecaps of napery in the ocean-sized dining room. Everyone was here: the bespectacled old brass of the *Saturday Evening Post* and *Century;* the upstarts, nearly as young as himself, from *The New Yorker* and *Time*. Four years working for Joe had kept him one of the crowd; eight months on his own had him up at this lectern.

"*Cutaway*," he intoned, "will shine its light not only on the fashionable and famous, not only on the achievers and the record-breakers, but also on the sad overreachers who drag down our age with their dishonest graspings."

As he ladled these words over the industry assembled at his feet, a squad of well-tailored young men infiltrated the four dozen breakfast tables, passing out the just-printed May number of *Cutaway*, which Jimmy had not wasted on a centerpiece, but held in reserve for this moment.

THREADBARE!

shouted the cover line.

JOE HARRIS AND *BANDBOX*
CREATE A TAILOR-MADE FRAUD

A Special Investigation by Paul Montgomery

Jimmy continued his slow, sonorous remarks while the diners flipped to the opening graf of the lead article, which read:

> *For a good part of our dapper, kinetic decade, Joe Harris' revital-*
> *ized* Bandbox *has been filling up the American man's mind along*
> *with his armoire. Only lately, faced with a stiff breeze of compe-*
> *tition from this magazine, has* Bandbox *resorted to pulling some*
> *thick lamb's wool over its readers' eyes.*

Jimmy took a long pause to let everyone scan the accumulated evidence, as well as Paulie's brief peroration against "an alliterating fantasist's corruption of youth, and a whole magazine's mockery of the once-proud NYPD."

The susurrus in the ballroom became a loud buzz; editors sprinted to the *Bandbox* centerpiece to see just what Joe Harris had perpetrated. Jimmy watched the commotion and felt he was making commercial and artistic history. People would be talking about this occasion years from now, the way they still recalled the Armory Show and *The Rite of Spring*'s premiere. He waited for the noise to die down enough that he could tell everyone how *Cutaway* now stood as "the *only* magazine in this new awards category." And while he waited, he could see, just outside the room, through two open doors, the smoke from a photo flash.

The buzzing did not abate, but the smoke quickly cleared, and once it did Jimmy's eyes were greeted by the sight of the Shepard kid leading a three-man parade through the ballroom, all the way to the *Bandbox* table, which had been denuded of its May issue. Behind the kid marched the unmistakable form of Joe Harris, and behind that a figure recognized from the newspapers as Captain Patrick Boylan.

"There's no centerpiece," said Joe. He was taking note of an opportunity, not a lack. "Shep, get up there."

John Chilton Shepard, by now accustomed to orders of the most inexplicable kind, bounded up onto the tablecloth in his newly shined shoes. The crowd, not knowing what to think, began to quiet down.

"Captain?" said Joe, pressing his luck. "Want to make Commissioner someday?"

Boylan, who'd already been persuaded against his better judgment to come uptown with this man, narrowed his eyes.

"If you want to," advised Harris, "you'll stand up on that table and hoist the kid's arm into the air."

Boylan glared at this detestable Barnum for one moment longer, until ambition once more overrode caution.

The crowd, noting that something had gone very wrong with Jimmy Gordon's expression, fell almost silent when Boylan's feet joined Shep's somewhere in the small space between the water pitcher and the coffeepot. And then, accustomed by the age to throwing ticker tape and applause at a new hero every day, it began to clap, first in a slow, rhythmic wave, and finally—once Harris, rising like Tunney from the Long Count, joined Boylan and the boy atop the table—in a thunderous, whooping storm of half-comprehension and complete delight.

With one arm holding Boylan's wrist, and the other pulling Shep's hand even higher, Harris looked out into the audience, where he saw Betty mouthing the words "Felicity Shunt" to a confused reporter, and the figure of Cuddles Houlihan, leaving the hall like a man who'd completed his work.

58

Four hours later, still limp with victory and disbelief, Harris was summoned to Oldcastle's office. Getting off the elevator on sixteen, he consulted his reflection in the shiny leaf of a giant potted plant. He was combing his hair when he felt the footsteps of Jimmy Gordon coming up behind him. The two men looked at each other and then at the clock, realizing they'd been asked to appear here at the same time.

"After you," said Jimmy, pointing to the door.

"That's your problem," answered Harris. "You always are."

Oldcastle calmly greeted the two of them. "Joe, Jimmy, come sit down." The owner sat behind his desk in a blue plaid flannel shirt and bolo tie and spoke, despite the wrangler's getup, in the emollient tones of a trusts-and-estates lawyer.

"Did you see Condé on your way in?" he asked both men. "He was just here for a little discussion."

Harris said nothing. He was remembering his last visit here, when Nast's name had been so chillingly raised. He was also waiting for a word of congratulations.

"I'll be seeing Mr. Nast this afternoon," Jimmy said. "We've got to go over some projected fig—"

"Actually, Jimmy, you won't be seeing him," Oldcastle declared idly, as if observing that a train was a little late, or it looked like rain.

Jimmy frowned, hoping to remind the publisher that he was here as a courtesy, since Hiram Oldcastle hadn't been Jimmy Gordon's boss for almost a year.

"Condé's just sold me *Cutaway*," the owner at last explained.

Jimmy tightened his grip on the armrest of his chair. The whole day was starting to feel like some colossal practical joke.

"Tell us more, Hi," said Harris.

Oldcastle went on at his own pace. "It seems, Jimmy, that your Mr. Montgomery got everything about Joe's subscriber wrong. That's bad enough—and of course I'm only telling you what Condé feels—but your writer made things very troublesome by suggesting that the New York Police Department is letting the citizenry down. You know, Jimmy, neither Condé nor I can afford to antagonize Captain Boylan's men. There are delivery trucks that need protecting, outdoor photography shoots that need permits, and business dinners at which the service of certain beverages shouldn't be interrupted."

"It was *one story*," said Jimmy.

"Joe," said Oldcastle, "how long did it take you to revive *Bandbox*?"

"I believe it was one business quarter."

"There you go," said the publisher. "Well, after one business quarter I hope we'll have achieved a smooth amalgamation of the two magazines. Make 'em go together like bacon and eggs," he added, pleased to be throwing in this bit of Everyman's argot. "*Cutaway*, I've decided, will be the name of *Bandbox*'s fashion section—a supplement, really. Detachable along a perforation. As its name implies. You see? Cut-away, meaning—"

"I *get* it," said Jimmy, gripping the other armrest.

"Some of your current staff can stay and work on it. And you,

Joe, can concentrate more on the journalism you do so well. By the way, Mayor Walker wants to give the boy from Indiana—what's his name?"

"Shep," said Harris.

"The mayor wants to give Shep a little decoration on the steps of City Hall this coming Monday."

"We'll get him there," said Harris. "And I'll get Arinopoulos to shoot the ceremony."

"Good," said Oldcastle, actually smiling. "You know, gentlemen, Condé was actually quite happy to make the sale. Even during this short-lived success you brought him, Jimmy, his attention had really been moving toward some new idea he has for a travel magazine. He's got this notion that everyone's soon going to be traipsing around much more often and more quickly. He thinks we're going to see more clothes packed into trunks than on people's backs." Oldcastle looked directly at Harris. "I suppose that'll be a challenge for you, Joe."

Like an aging Dalmatian hearing one last fire bell, Harris was already deciding how he could beat this new book. He'd take a few pages away from sports and food; hire a full-time travel writer who could flit from Tokyo to Timbuktu.

"Joe?" asked Oldcastle.

"Sorry, I was lost in thought." After a moment's pause, Harris amended the explanation, with a certain peevishness: "Actually, I was *working*. And if you don't mind, I'd like to get back to my office." He hoped his rudeness would serve as some small retort against the publisher's earlier lack of faith, but Oldcastle had always been oblivious to any display of manners, good or bad, by the men he employed. He said nothing while Harris rose to his feet.

Jimmy Gordon's expression had turned cool and faraway. Revenge, he was thinking, would come slowly. He'd take a year or two off, maybe finish his dissertation on *The Faerie Queene,* and then return to town atop the masthead of some start-up. Coming back would be even more exciting than coming up had been. But for now he could feel only contempt. He rose from his seat, nodded to Old-castle, and followed Joe out to the bank of elevators.

The two men waited for their two cars, one heading up, the other going down. Jimmy began to pace, a sulking Achilles without a tent, whereas Harris, realizing that he had a tale he'd be telling his men for years to come around the London campfire, allowed the sentimental broth of his nature to bubble up. His eyes glistened with tears.

"I once told you," he called out to Jimmy, "that I think of you as a bastard son."

Jimmy returned to the elevator's call button and punched it again. It didn't matter that he still liked Joe and always would. "The Bastard never gets to be the Heir," he said, showing Harris his back.

"Right," said the older man, genuinely hurt. "He becomes the Pretender."

Jimmy Gordon had a desk to clean out, and Joe Harris, to his astonishment, still had a magazine to run. He went back down to fourteen and discovered that everyone, at 2:30, remained out to lunch. Hazel had already sent around a memo about an evening celebration at Malocchio, and the staff, delighted to know they still had jobs, had decided to desert them for the afternoon.

Harris slumped into his big chair, in which he would soon fall asleep under the congratulatory regard of Yvette and Claudine—but not before he took one of his huge-barreled fountain pens and wrote a note, which he inserted into the pneumatic tube that would take it to Cuddles Houlihan.

59

Mrs. von Erhard always stayed late in the Graybar on Friday nights—doing the books and straightening the merchandise. Tonight she also had a training session to conduct. "The Life Savers," she said firmly, "must *never* be too close to the edge. If they fall, they turn into, what do you say, smithereens, inside their little paper tubes."

The Wood Chipper rolled up the French cuffs of his unpaid-for shirt and gave a grunt that Hannelore took as a sign of understanding. "It will be so *nice* to have a man around the place again," she said, squeezing Chip's right bicep. "I am so glad I asked if you could use the work." Word from the Biltmore had traveled fast, prompting Mrs. von Erhard to make her offer of employment just before lunchtime, when she saw Chip rushing to get his few belongings out of the building.

What alternative did he have? None, Chip thought once again, as he picked up Siegfried—so much lighter than he'd been last time—and wiped the portion of the counter near the till. If he didn't earn some money in the next week, his creditors would be after more than this shirt on his back. And if anybody from *Bandbox* or *Cutaway* had one word to say to him when they slapped down two cents for their morning paper, he'd shove a roll of Hannelore's precious Life Savers, and maybe a spoonful of Siegfried himself, down their throats.

Gianni Roma was due to report to prison on Monday morning, and tonight's hastily arranged celebration at his establishment would double as a kind of penal *bon voyage,* but at 8:00, with the dining room already full, Gianni was still back in the kitchen with the actual guest of honor.

"Listen," Harris was saying to his old pal. "Four months up in Fishkill is not that long a stretch. Those veal steaks in the freezer will still be plenty good when you get out."

Fear had replaced most of Gianni's recent resentment. He just nodded.

"Tell him about my idea," Harris urged David Fine, who was over near the stove.

"I'm going to come up every week and eat in the dining hall with you," Fine promised. "I've already got permission, for a column on prison food. I haven't got the title yet—something with 'Stir.' I'll write it, but we'll put it in your voice and under your byline."

Agreement to such a thing by Fine, the most territorial of writers, was a matter of such unexpected generosity that Gianni's apprehension began to melt with his anger. He at last agreed to join the celebrants.

"That's better!" said Harris, plunging them into the party's roar.

Betty watched Joe walk around each of the tables, rewarding everyone with compliments, dispensing proposals and permissions like doubloons from a purse. She knew that he had always felt his power more by saying yes than saying no—a tendency much rarer than its opposite on the echelon he still, thank God, inhabited.

Nan and Stuart had arrived actually holding hands, and Harris now stood between them. "We need *everybody's* talents. You hear me? We'll have more pages, but we'll soon have more competition. Miss O'Grady, how about doing a little muckraking for us? You've certainly shown a talent for it." With Rosemary now safely on the newsstands, Nan had at last let the story of the movie star's grand-maternity be known to a few. Harris continued his pitch: "We've got at least a temporary opening in the investigations line." Max Stanwick, more shaken by the recent threats than he'd realized, had decided, despite the sizzling success of the Shep saga, to take six months off and write a magazine mystery called *Kill Fee.*

"No, Mr. Harris," said Nan. "Thank you, but I'm happy where I am."

"All right, then. That leaves you, Newman. You know, I hear rumors about you and her. So once you get ready to leave that seminary you're in, I've got a new column idea for you—a whole new rubric." He paused for effect. " 'The Husband's Life.' Could be very popular with our slightly older readers. Think about it."

"Uh, I am," stammered Stuart, squeezing Nan's hand.

Her face went as red as her hair.

Gardiner Arinopoulos came in to take a picture of each table, as if this were a wedding. Harris backslapped his way into every shot. He dragged Andrew Burn away from a comptometer in Gianni's little office near the spice closet, though the publisher protested that he couldn't bring himself to wait until Monday to see what the rates on the new ad card would come out to once the readership inherited from Jimmy got factored in.

Forgiveness was thicker on the air than marinara. Harris had called Connecticut and gotten Spilkes to come down for the party. After all, as things turned out, the victory had been much more complete for the former m.e.'s caution. Harris was even ready to forget about the fiction contest and pardon Sidney Bruck, who'd finally arrived, his Shelleyan hair tousled by the night's breezes.

"I just made the deal with Mencken's agent," said Sidney, explaining the reason, beyond fashionableness, that he was so late. "For a four-thousand-word essay on love in America." Landing the piece was the triumph of his still-young career as an editor.

"I've got the title!" cried Harris, banging Sidney between the shoulder blades. " 'Mencken Whoopee!' "

Sidney managed a weak smile and took a seat by Richard Lord, the person least likely to spill anything on him.

Two of the tables joined in loud in-absentia toasts to the magazine's Bunion Derby contestant, who'd telephoned from Ohio, through which he was running only a few miles behind Andy Payne, the Cherokee Wonder. With the way things had been going, who could say he wouldn't pull ahead?

A few minutes later, a waiter came over to announce that there was a messenger at the door. Judge Gilfoyle and Daisy went a little white from force of habit until they realized the messenger was for Harris: a boy from the Graybar's mailroom bearing an especially important telegram.

"It's from Coolidge!" shouted the boss, once it was handed to him.

The crowd quieted down long enough for him to read the president's entire commentary upon the successful rescue of John Shepard: COMMENDABLE.

"Four syllables," said Fine. "He's starting to run off at the mouth."

Burn instantly twitched with a desire to shove the wire in front of some tightwad savings bankers who might be impressed enough by it to try a first ad in *Bandbox*. But Harris, with a dozen waves of sentiment crashing over him, only wondered if Coolidge, so soon after losing his own young son, hadn't been genuinely touched by word of this lost-and-found boy. "Here," he said, handing the telegram to Newman. "A souvenir."

The editor-in-chief strode off toward Shep: "After this, City Hall's going to feel like a comedown!"

The young man assured him that wouldn't be the case; he was looking forward to shopping for a new suit before his parents got to town tomorrow.

"And after that you'll need a place to live," said Harris, putting an arm around the kid's shoulder. "Even *we* can't afford to keep you at the Commodore forever! Find some place you can afford on a fact-checker's salary."

"You mean——?" Shep looked even more delighted than Daisy, who was overhearing this news.

Ten minutes before, in the coatcheck room, Hazel had given Shep an astonishingly continental kiss. She now saw the countess's old reflexes kicking in. "Down, girl," she warned Daisy. "You've quit the field."

It was at this moment the moosehead appeared through Malocchio's front window. Allen Case stood outside, struggling to hold it. Noticing both creatures, Betty steered Joe just the right number of degrees that he wouldn't see his old trophy, which caused little enough stir among the partygoers who did see it, since most of them were far enough gone on Gianni's olive oil to assume they'd spotted some dead variant of a pink elephant.

After setting the taxidermy down in the vestibule, Allen ventured into the restaurant. He worked his way through the crowd to Mr. Merrill, who noticed that he was wearing a backpack.

"Are you going away?" the illustrator asked. His alarm was shared by Nan, who had approached to see what was going on.

Allen nodded. He had finally found his dream job. During the recent spate of wires between the San Rafael Valley and New York, it had developed that Mr. Isidore Mazzaferro, concerned by the ranch's sudden understaffing (two cowboys having quit on the day of the arrests), needed an assistant. There was a tiny cabin on the nature preserve that Allen could have all to himself.

"Mr. M-Merrill, will you take the m-moose?"

"Yes," the illustrator at last assured him—if Allen promised to sit here long enough to eat a plate of steamed Italian vegetables. By the time this antipasto arrived, arrangements were being made for Shep to take over the copyeditor's apartment on Cornelia Street.

Two tables away, Cuddles Houlihan reached into his pants pocket for a pneumatic-mail cylinder, which he plunked down next to his plate. "You know," he said to Becky, "Hannelore should have sifted Siegfried into one of these. It'd be a good way of staying in circulation."

"Why on earth have you got that with you?" Becky asked.

"Well, it didn't hit me on the head, but after reading what's inside I could probably use a cold compress anyway. Here, tell me what you think."

Becky opened the tube and unrolled a note composed in Harris's big hand. "I NEED A NEW MANAGING EDITOR. CONSIDER YOURSELF PROMOTED."

Cuddles watched her reading. "I don't know if I can say yes. Doesn't the job require a house in Connecticut, plus a wife and children?"

Becky poured herself more olive oil and took a breath. "No children," she said evenly. "At least not for a while."

Cuddles' expression dissolved into something like the one with which he'd watched Nazimova three months ago at the Palace. "I do have a cat," he said, his voice trembling. "But he's down to one life."

Becky looked him in the eye. "That's all I have, too. You'd better handle it with care, Mr. Houlihan."

Cuddles gulped. "Let's get out of here and go over to Manking. There's a bottle of sake with our names on it."

The two of them waited half a minute, until the noise reached a new peak that would allow them to slip away unnoticed.

They nearly succeeded, but at the restaurant's front door they came up against the unexpected arrival of Paul Montgomery.

"Hello!" he said, sweeping past.

Without removing his hat, and in imitation of an already-famous gesture, Paulie jumped onto the lone empty table at the outer rim of the party. Motioning to one of the waiters for an empty glass, he raised it high above his head and called out, with the full measure of his sincerity, to the now-absolutely-quiet crowd: "Hey, you guys! What do we do for an encore?"

About the Author

Thomas Mallon's books include the novels *Henry and Clara, Two Moons, Dewey Defeats Truman,* and *Aurora 7,* as well as a collection of essays, *In Fact.* His work has appeared in *The New Yorker, The Atlantic Monthly, The American Scholar,* and *GQ.* He has been the recipient of Rockefeller and Guggenheim fellowships, and in 1998 he received the National Book Critics Circle award for reviewing. He lives in Washington, D.C.